Advance praise for Lost Conscience...

"Alain Burrese's *Lost Conscience* is a fascinating and intricate thriller — the perfect read for anyone who thinks the criminal justice system needs a kick in the teeth and a swift backhand to the jaw for good measure. Authentic characterization, dialogue, and a rugged Montana setting that just ain't for sissies!"

> — **Andrew McAleer**, author of *The 101 Habits*
> *of Highly Successful Novelists* and *Fatal Deeds*

"*Lost Conscience* has more twists and turns than two rats trapped in a drain pipe. Alain is a master at blending his experience in the military and in the criminal justice system (I use that term loosely). Action adventure at its best. Reminds me of Grisham with more action.

> — **Ken Farmer**, co-author of *Black Eagle Force:*
> *Eye of the Storm, Black Eagle Force: Sacred*
> *Mountain, Return of the Starfighter, The Nations,*
> and the soon to be released *Black Eagle Force:*
> *Blood Ivory*

"Benjamin Baker isn't just another courtroom lawyer, he's ex-military and not afraid to get his hands dirty when it comes to sexual predators of children. Look out John Grisham, Michael Connelly and Andrew Vachss, Alain Burrese is in town."

> — **Marc "Animal" MacYoung**, author of *Taking*
> *it to the Streets: Making Your Martial Art Street*
> *Effective* and *Ending Violence Quickly: How*
> *Bouncers, Bodyguards and Other Security*
> *Professionals Handle Ugly Situations*

"A veteran martial artist, former Army sniper and an attorney of law, author Alain Burrese has written a fast-paced and action packed thriller that only someone who has lived it can write it. Burrese's protagonist battles a former SEAL sniper, truck stop thugs, child abductors, and two huge behemoths, making *Lost Conscious* a highly realistic, gritty, and in-your-face read for those craving an action-packed story torn from today's headlines. It doesn't get much better than this."

— **Loren W. Christensen**, author of nearly 50 books including *On Combat* and *Dukkha — The Suffering: A Sam Reeves Martial Arts Thriller*

"*Lost Conscience* is a thriller set in the backwoods of Montana. Alain Burrese weaves a tail reminiscent of John Grisham. He twists and turns the reader through the underworld of child trafficking, abuse, and real caring people who won't stand for it in their community. A riveting read!"

— **Ed Kugler**, author of *Dead Center: A Marine Sniper's Two-Year Odyssey in the Vietnam War*

"Who better to write about a frustrated lawyer who picks up a gun in the name of justice than an attorney/author who used to be sniper? Been there; done that—not quite, but Burrese's gritty realism truly brings this page-turner to life. A hardcore thriller extraordinaire."

— **Lawrence Kane**, author of *Blinded by the Night* and *The Little Black Book of Violence*

Also by Alain Burrese...

Books:

Tough Guy Wisdom
Tough Guy Wisdom II: Return of the Tough Guy
Tough Guy Wisdom III: Revenge of the Tough Guy
Hard-Won Wisdom From The School Of Hard Knocks

eBooks:

How To Protect Yourself By Developing A Fighter's Mindset

DVDs:

Hapkido Hoshinsul
Streetfighting Essentials
Hapkido Cane
Lock On: Joint Locking Essentials vol. 1 Wrist Locks
Lock On: Joint Locking Essentials vol. 2 Arm Bars & Elbow Locks
Lock On: Joint Locking Essentials vol. 3 Shoulder Locks
Lock On Joint Locking Essentials vol. 4 Finger Locks
Lock On Joint Locking Essentials vol. 5 Combining Locks & Lock Flow Drills
Restraint, Control & Come-A-Long Techniques Vol. 1
Restraint, Control & Come-A-Long Techniques Vol. 2

LOST CONSCIENCE

A Ben Baker Sniper Novel by

Alain Burrese

TGW BOOKS
Missoula, MT USA

Published by TGW Books, a division of
Burrese Enterprises, Inc.
Missoula, MT 59801, USA

Print ISBN: 978-1-937872-06-9
eBook ISBN: 978-1-937872-07-6

Cover design and layout by Scott Becker.

To everyone who has honorably served in our armed forces.

Especially the snipers…

"You have to do something. You can't be a slug."

— Gunnery Sergeant Carlos Hathcock
in a conversation with Alain Burrese

PROLOGUE

In a small village, just outside Camp Hovey, South Korea, Benjamin Robert Baker slid his lock pick into the padlock's key hole. His tension wrench already in place, he proceeded to work the tumblers, feeling for the lock's release.

It was 1989 and the fit 2nd Infantry Division scout sniper hunched over the small cabinet that was secured by a small Master padlock. He wore jeans, t-shirt, and running shoes. He had nothing on him that could identify him, nor did his sniper buddy, Frank Senich, who stood above the sleeping Korean man in the same room. The third of the team, Brian Hutch, stood guard outside, ensuring the two inside the hooch wouldn't be surprised from behind by the black marketers or anyone showing up to do business.

The planning stage for their impromptu mission had been brief. "Baker, you think you can pick the lock to the cabinet the black marketers keep their cash in?" Senich asked.

"Sure, that's an easy lock."

"Let's get Hutch and do it."

"Do what?"

"Take em down. It's black market money, right? So taking illegal cash isn't really bad, it's just redistribution of the funds as the government would say. Who are they going to call? The police? The MPs?"

"We both know they deal with people much worse than the Korean police or MPs."

"So what?" Senich looked at Baker with the look that always led the two into mischief.

"So, you're talking about committing a felony in a foreign country. Korean courts will send us away for a long time. That, or the Korean version of Guido will show up and break our kneecaps. Or worse."

"You talk like we would get caught. You just said you could pick the lock. We're in and out, and no one knows a thing. We're snipers remember, phantom like."

"Yeah, phantom like."

"So let's do it. It's illegal money, and we can use it just as well as they can. If you want, we can do something good with some of it."

Baker shook his head at the lack of conscience with his sniper buddy, and said, "What's the plan?"

"Hutch watches outside by the alley, so no one can catch us from behind. You and I go into the hooch and I stand guard at the door while you pick the lock. We take the money, and head out. Easy."

Baker wondered how many times his buddy's "easy" plans had turned out anything but. "All right, when?"

"No better time than the present, let's get Hutch and do it."

"In the middle of the afternoon?"

"No one will be home. We wait till dark and more people will be around."

"True. All right, let's do it. We can stop by Hutch's on the way."

Hutch was game as soon as Senich laid out his ill-conceived plan, and the three quickly set off toward one of the local black-market hooches. Hutch stayed out near the alley where he would be able to see anyone coming and warn the other two. Baker and Senich snuck inside, only to find one of the black marketers inside asleep, not five feet from the locked cabinet. The two almost turned back, but Senich urged them to go forward with the mission. He stood guard over the sleeping man, ready to knock him cold at the first sign of wakening. Both men were known in the black market circles, thus the knowledge of the money cabinet, so they couldn't take any chance of being seen and recognized. Senich would ensure that if the man woke up, he wouldn't recognize anything before his lights were back out.

The padlock seemed trickier than Baker told his buddies it would be, but it might have been because his concentration half focused on Senich and the sleeping black marketer rather than the tumblers inside the keyway. When the lock did open, he sighed. Almost done, and so far no incident. He figured Senich was already thinking about which bars he'd spend the extra cash. As he removed the padlock, Baker also started to think about the extra cash, wondering how much they'd get. All three of them had seen the cabinet stuffed full of both American dollars and Korean won at various times. He also thought to himself, just like the black marketing, the excitement and thrill of breaking and entering was as important as the money. Actually, it was probably more for the rush of doing it than any monitory gain. He knew money was secondary for the other two also. All three of them were there for the rush. And because they were taking from black marketers, the rush was justified. At least to them anyway.

The sleeping man rolled over and Baker froze. Senich moved a bit, ready to pounce and clobber the man before his eyes opened. The man continued to sleep. Baker resumed the mission and opened the cabinet door.

NOTHING. The cabinet was empty. Not a single dollar or won note. The money box they'd seen thousands in had absolutely zilch in it. Baker wondered if his face was as bewildered as the look on Senich's. After staring at the emptiness for a few seconds, the two stared at each other.

"Shit!" Senich muttered rather loudly, ignoring the darting eyes of Baker that said, "We still need to be tactical, stupid. We're not out of this yet."

Baker relocked the cabinet and the two exited the hooch. They left everything exactly as when they entered, including the sleeping black marketer who was none the wiser. The two then shared the news of their spoils with Hutch, who just laughed and told them, "Let's go get some food and a drink."

The three laughed about their secret caper later, and vowed to try again someday. It was a mission that never did materialize. Not because the three didn't feel they could spend the illegal money better than the black marketers, they just never got around to it.

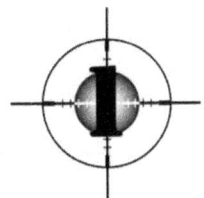

Twenty years, a law degree, and a family later, Benjamin Robert Baker asked himself, "What the hell am I doing?" He slowly raked the tumblers of the cheap door knob lock of the trailer house back door while applying slight pressure on the tension wrench. It was the first lock he'd picked for real since his Army days, but he had played around once in a while with various padlocks and doors at home to keep his "touch." He then remembered he had opened a few doors and locks for people during college. Whatever, this was the first felony use of the picks since his Army days.

Opening the lock was taking longer than he anticipated, and he nervously looked around at every little noise, which wasn't helping. Baker thought about the time he picked the padlock of a couple of Korean black marketers. "Damn, I wish you guys were with me now," Baker said to himself as the tension wrench turned and the door opened.

Silently entering the trailer house, Baker found himself in a hallway. Right in front of him was the bathroom. A small night light plugged in above the sink illuminated the room enough to see the toilet surrounded by dirty clothes and a makeshift shower curtain hanging from the bent curtain rod. An assortment of toiletries were scattered on the sink counter and Baker didn't think he needed to enter that particular room. He looked down the hallway to the left. Baker's small Mini Maglite revealed a doorway a couple of feet down the hall on the right, and then the hallway opened up into the kitchen and living room area of the trailer. He chose his Mini

Maglite, which he had been using since his Army days, for several reasons. First, he didn't want a bright light seen from outside, so the Mag's 15.6 Lumens fit this job. The Mini Maglite also had an adjustable light beam from spot to flood which could be advantageous at times. It could also be used as yawara, or pocket stick, impact weapon, and Baker had in fact used Maglites in fights before.

Looking to his right revealed a closed door that should be a bedroom from what Baker could remember about the layout of most trailer houses. He headed down the hallway to his left. He knew there should be a master bedroom and another bathroom up past the kitchen and living room.

Baker committed a felony the second he slid the tension wrench and pick into the key hole. Now inside, a prosecutor could add entering to the breaking charge. Actually, in Montana it just fell under the burglary statute, but breaking and entering sounded better. As a prosecutor himself, Baker knew Title 45, Crimes, very well. He knew the Cold Steel tactical folder clipped inside the front right pocket of his Levi's, and the 9 mm Browning Hi Power tucked inside his pants and covered by his black sweat shirt were enough to move his offense to aggravated burglary, which came with a sentence of being imprisoned in the state prison for any term not to exceed forty years or a fine not to exceed $50,000 or both. If he would have left the weapons at home, the prison term couldn't exceed 20 years, but the weapons added the aggravated charge which allowed the term to be doubled. Sure, like he was going to do this unarmed. Hell, he broke the law when he first came onto the property. However criminal trespass to property was rather minor compared to the aggravated burglary; trespass had caps of only $500.00 and six months in the county jail. If the prosecutor wanted, he could also add on another $500.00, and six months in the county jail, for possession of burglary tools. It was not illegal to own the lock pick set, it was just illegal to own the picks with the purpose to commit an offense. Since he just used the tools to commit the offense of aggravated burglary, it would be hard to argue he didn't own them with the purpose to commit a crime. And any good prosecutor would add as many charges as he could. Guilty, guilty, guilty. "What the hell am I doing," he thought to himself again. Not only would he be disbarred if caught, he could find himself behind the same bars that he spent his days putting criminals behind. Baker shook his head, the irony, being put away for committing felonies due to a felon who walked. What about justice? What about right and wrong? What about Walter Dennison, the young boy who was molested and then went on a shooting spree, killing his classmates and then himself?

Baker forced himself to pay attention to matters at hand. Pay attention to detail, remember? He softly crept down the hall toward the kitchen and living room area. The Asics running shoes were not only quiet, but his most comfortable shoes. If he needed to run to his SUV parked over a mile away among an assortment of vehicles in a downtown parking lot, these were the shoes to wear. Baker knew if he ended up using his old escape and evasion skills, he would be better off on foot. He could run, hide, and get away much easier without a vehicle. Vehicles were too easy to be identified. If he did have to run, he would zig and zag and make his way back to the Dodge in a circuitous route. Ensuring you were not being followed, and couldn't be followed, was essential to getting away. He remembered prosecuting a recent hit and run where the offender drove home after the accident leaking fluid the entire way. While the driver did go around a couple of blocks, rather than straight to his house, it didn't prevent the police officers from following the trail right to the damaged vehicle sitting warm in the driveway.

The small flashlight illuminated the kitchen, revealing a bigger mess than Baker had seen in the bathroom. Dirty dishes filled the sink and were piled in stacks along the counter. Crusted and burnt slop clung to the top of the stove and grease splatters and drips ran down the front. The towel that hung from the dingy and smudged refrigerator's handle looked like it had never seen its way to a washer. Baker noticed his shoes sticking to the 70s era thin carpet covering the floor. He was glad he couldn't see it well by flashlight and made a mental note to himself to clean his shoes thoroughly once away from this dilapidated trailer.

Moving through the living room, to his right, Baker noticed several empty Coors cans lying under a beat up coffee table. An open bag of Doritos sat atop the table next to a salsa stained bowl. Two more beer cans sat next to the bowl. The sofa behind the table was pushed up to the wall and Baker couldn't tell in the dark, but it didn't appear to be a place he would choose to sit. Nothing in the trailer was clean, and he wondered what just might be living in or under the old plaid sofa. Across the room on his left stood an entertainment center. It was particle board furniture you bought at Wal-Mart and put together yourself. Like everything else, it was dirty and banged up. Baker's light paused on the assortment of VHS tapes and DVDs on the shelf next to the T.V. *Rambone* and *SurviveHer* were the first two titles Baker read, and he didn't need to read further to know he wouldn't find any Disney or Academy Award winning films in the collection.

Baker crossed the room toward the two doors on his right just past the coffee table and sofa. One door was the main front door that went outside. The other led to the Master Bedroom that took up the front of the trailer. His gloved hand cautiously turned the bedroom doorknob. It wasn't locked and he slowly opened the door and entered the Master "suite." The house stunk, but the smell from the bedroom when he opened the door was worse. It took Baker a moment to recognize that it was the same smell you found in skanky porn shops where lonely men masturbated to porn and live dancers. Baker had worked security for a while when younger at such a place. He remembered sitting in a small room listening to what went on in the private rooms with the dancers. At the first sound of trouble, he would be up and to the room in a flash, but most of the time he sat studying and listening to the songs the girls were dancing to and trying to ignore the sounds from the customers. He was always glad his job was security and that he didn't have to do the cleaning. The smell from the bedroom was much worse than the place he'd worked.

Ignoring the stench, Baker entered the room and scanned the light back and forth. He still didn't know what he was looking for, but was sure there would be something. Why else would he have had such a strong feeling that he needed to risk everything he had and explore this cesspool in the middle of the night? There was an unmade bed, two mismatched dressers made of particle board with different colored fake wood lamination, and a small desk and folding chair. The remainder of the room was barren except for a mound of dirty clothes between the two dressers. Even with gloves, Baker didn't want to go near the bed or the pile of laundry. The smell of the room had him scared of what he might find, or worse, catch.

He slid the closet door open and it fell off the rail. "Shit," Baker mumbled to himself. He held the flashlight in his mouth and used both hands to get the door rollers back into the bent track. Once the door was working, he noticed two cardboard boxes in the back corner of the closet behind a pair of old snake skin cowboy boots and a pair of imitation Sorel Caribou's. He opened one box and found a stack of manila file folders. Kneeling, he opened the top file and saw a picture and several pages of information. The girl in the picture appeared to be ten or eleven years old. On the second page he noticed the word virgin was circled. Under that he read "Williston, ND." Baker's stomach began to churn and he felt a rage starting up inside. The next file contained another picture and descriptions similar to the first. "Screams," was circled and there was a Pocatello, ID, address. Baker was disgusted and horrified at what he believed he had just found. He reached for the next box and froze. Someone was coming in the front door and there was nowhere to hide.

Baker turned off his small flashlight and slowly stood. He hoped whoever came in would head toward the back of the trailer. No such luck, the overhead light in the center of the room came on as Bruce James walked into the room. Seeing Baker, James' eyes widened and he took a startled step back. "Who..." he started to stammer as Baker leaped toward him. Benjamin Baker knew when he entered the trailer that if someone caught him, he could lose everything. He could not let that happen, especially by this perverted sicko. The files in the closet only confirmed the worst that Baker believed James to be. Baker's right forearm hit James in the chest as he rushed him. The charge knocked the surprised James back into the wall, and Baker raised his forearm sharply hitting James under the chin, slamming his head back into the wood colored paneling. The jolt stunned James and he tried to raise his arms to protect himself.

Baker knew what must be done, and with the rage in his gut from the files in the closet, combined with his years of training, it came easy. There were many ways to injure or kill a man, but choking someone was primal as well as effective. It came naturally to many during altercations, especially to those in rage, but for Baker it was a decision. He didn't grab James with both hands to throttle him as untrained people tended to do, nor did he grab the entire throat. Instead, he held James against the wall with his left hand pressing on James' chest and dug the fingers and thumb of his right hand into the soft spots just under the jaw, encircling the windpipe. It made a much more painful and effective hold. Years of fingertip pushups and other hand strengthening exercises provided Baker a grip that even Baker's father would be proud of. Robert Baker told Benjamin at a young age to develop his hand strength. Baker remembered his father telling him, "When you have strong hands, you can grab a hold of someone and they will know it."

Bruce James knew it. His eyes started to bulge and he frantically tried to pull Baker's hand from his throat. Baker squeezed as hard as he could. He squeezed for the kids shot the previous Friday. He squeezed for Walter Dennison who shot his classmates and then himself. He squeezed for the kids in the box in the closet. He squeezed, and squeezed, and squeezed. James' struggles grew weaker. Baker smelled urine among the rest of the stench and looked down to see James had pissed himself. Still he squeezed. Baker felt the cartilage and ligaments of the trachea in his grip. He knew that because it was the primary passage for air to flow to the lungs, any damage could be potentially life-threatening. In training, they were always careful of the trachea, not wanting to injure a training partner. A tracheotomy would ruin a productive training session. But tonight, Baker not only wanted to injure the trachea, he wanted to crush it. He knew a carotid restraint would render unconsciousness faster, but also knew it wouldn't take long for James to go unconscious from lack of air either, and he would die shortly after. Baker continued to squeeze. James' body went limp and Baker let him drop to the floor, never releasing his hold. He kneeled on top of James and continued to tighten his grip. His fingers ached as he finally let go and stood. He opened and closed his gloved hand as he looked around.

Baker was sure Bruce James was dead. Now what? The night started with a little B and E and now he had just killed someone. "Fucker deserved worse," Baker hissed to himself. He looked around. Besides the clothes he wore, the only things Baker brought into the house with him were the knife, gun, and flashlight, which he had slid into his pocket just before James turned on the light. He checked the items and they were all still in place. Satisfied that there was nothing in the dingy trailer that could identify him, Baker turned off the light and started to leave. Halfway through the living room, he stopped and turned back toward the bedroom. He walked past the body and went to the closet. He opened the second box and saw that it contained a variety of smut magazines. He left it there, but picked up the box full of file folders and headed toward the back door of the trailer. He figured there would be less chance to be seen leaving out the back, and it was closer to the alley he would walk down first, before cutting over a few blocks and meandering back to his SUV.

Baker moved quickly through the living room, past the kitchen, and down the short hallway toward the back door. The Mini Maglite lit the way. Just as he started to slowly open the back door, Baker heard something that chilled him more than the sound of the front door opening just moments before. From the back bedroom, he heard a whimpering. He heard a small child crying.

Maryann Cox was running a bit late. She was driving her blue Dodge Grand Caravan just over the speed limit as she headed down 14th Avenue toward Roosevelt Elementary School. The school was one of many in Spokane, WA, and as they advertised, it was a great place to learn. It was five minutes past three, and she knew her daughter, Ashley, was not allowed to use the playfield after school, but she also knew one of the teachers would be monitoring the area as parents picked up their children.

Maryann didn't know that in a few days, Walter Dennison would take a gun to school and shatter the innocence of a peaceful little city in Montana less than two hundred miles away. Nor did she know that Billy Baxter and Kent Sullivan had gotten into a fight right after school, and Ms. Avon was attending to Billy's bloody nose while keeping an eye on Kent, who stood in the corner of her classroom. Her hands full with the two boys, Ms. Avon wasn't watching the other children being picked up by their parents.

Maryann knew it was ten minutes past three as she pulled up to the curb in front of Roosevelt Elementary. She had been watching the dashboard clock for the last several miles. Maryann knew she shouldn't be late, but sometimes things just took longer than she anticipated. She knew the school policy was for students to leave the grounds immediately after dismissal. She also knew she wouldn't be the last parent there to pick up their child. She knew that she was rationalizing her tardiness as not being as late as other parents, so that meant she was not a bad parent, right? Maryann knew she was a good mother, and she knew that nothing was more important than Ashley. What Maryann didn't know, as she looked around the front of the building and across the playfield, was where Ashley was at that moment.

Maryann left the minivan running in front of the no parking sign as she quickly walked up the sidewalk toward the front door of the school. She continually scanned the area looking for Ashley as she picked up her pace. Ashley always waited out front for her. She had never not been there. Maryann didn't know what it was, but she sudenly felt sick to her stomach and feared something was wrong. She didn't know why she had such a feeling and she didn't understand. She knew she didn't like it, and it worried her more.

Maryann met Ms. Avon at the door. Ms. Avon was marching Billy and Kent outside to inform their parents of the altercation. Billy had tissue hanging out of his nose and blood stains on his blue shirt. Kent had a defiant grin as if he were proud of bloodying the nose of the bigger Billy. In fact he was, his father had told him that popping a bully in the nose would make him stop. Kent was sure his father would be proud, despite the lecture Ms. Avon had given him regarding non-physical ways to resolve problems. He was also pretty sure Billy would never push and pick on him anymore after school.

"Do you know where Ashley is? Maryann asked, trying to hide the fear in her voice.

"Why no, she was right over there," indicating toward the lawn by the large Roosevelt Elementary sign near the sidewalk and street. Both women looked around the area, temporarily forgetting about Billy and Kent.

"Oh my god, where is she?"

"I… I don't know. I was inside tending to these two. I was only gone a few minutes." Kent's father was out of his car walking toward the group. Billy's mom was still sitting in her Honda Accord talking on her cell phone. She didn't notice the small group looking around for the missing Ashley. Ms. Avon looked at the boys, "Kent, you tell your father what you did, and you Billy, tell your mother. I'm going to follow up with both of them to make sure you tell them the truth." Both boys headed toward their parents.

"Everything okay?" Mr. Sullivan called out to the ladies as Kent ran over to him.

"Kent will tell you what he did," Ms. Avon responded. "We are looking for Ashley right now."

"I don't see her," said Mr. Sullivan looking around.

"Oh my god, we need to call the police. I need to call my husband," Maryann cried. Her fingers were already pressing buttons on her cell phone.

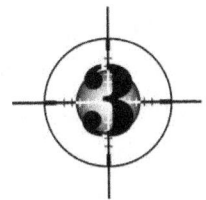

Ashley Cox watched Kent Sullivan bloody Billy Baxter's nose and thought to herself, "Billy had it coming." The larger boy was always picking on those smaller than him, and it was satisfying to see him get walloped and put in his place. She enjoyed seeing Ms. Avon march the two boys into the school and secretly hoped that Kent wouldn't get into too much trouble. Sure, hitting was against the rules, but what about all the tormenting Billy inflicted on everyone smaller than him.

The excitement over, Ashley went out to the curb to wait for her mom. She didn't see her mother's blue minivan, but she did see a gold colored vehicle of the same make with the side sliding door open. A nice looking man was sitting in the van's doorway. He wore kaki pants and a light blue button up the front shirt. Black shoes and glasses completed his attire. His brown hair was short and curly and he reminded Ashley of Nick Jonas, only older, and with glasses. She didn't notice the older man sitting behind the steering wheel, she was too focused on the little kitten the man in the van's door was playing with.

The cute little tabby was perched on his back two legs on the floor of the van between the back of the passenger seat and the middle seat. The man dangled a piece of string in front of the kitten and it swatted at it and danced around on its hind legs. As Ashley moved closer, watching the kitten, the man looked up and held the string out toward her, "Want to try?"

"Sure," Ashley replied as she walked over holding her hand out for the string.

"It's clear - now!" commanded the man in the driver's seat. In less time than it took for the driver to command him, Travis Smith grabbed Ashley around the waist and threw her into the van. She bounced off the back of the passenger seat and landed on the floor between the front and the middle seats. A sharp pain raced up her right arm from where she landed on it, and her ribs on the left side hurt from where Smith grabbed her. The kitten, knocked aside and scared by Ashley's flying body, scampered under the passenger seat and cowered against the electric seat motor.

Smith leapt into the van and slammed the sliding door shut behind him as Dan Cook quickly motored the Dodge Grand Caravan down 14th Avenue toward South Grove Street which turned into South Ben Garnett Way before becoming South Washington Street that led to West 3rd Ave and finally I-90 East toward Coeur D'Alene, Idaho. Cook knew the exact route to take, and the correct speed limits for each leg. He couldn't afford to be stopped for something as stupid as speeding. He traversed the one mile route exactly as they had the day before during their practice run.

They couldn't afford a screaming little kid attracting attention, and that's why Smith punched Ashley square in the jaw immediately upon jumping into the van. Ashley had barely hit the van's floor when Smith's fist came crashing down into her face. In less than thirty-eight seconds, Ashley went from smugness of seeing Billy get popped in the nose, to feeling warm and fuzzy seeing the cute tabby kitten, to laying unconscious on the floor of a gold colored Dodge Grand Caravan with Montana license plates that was East bound toward Idaho.

Dan Cook was forty-nine years old but liked to think he was still in his thirties. He dyed the gray from his slicked back hair, and remained clean shaven after gray appeared in his beard. Crows feet in the outer corners of his brown eyes seemed to increase each year, and the skin under the square jaw line sagged to the point that Cook had contemplated plastic surgery. His appearance didn't fit the young stud image he still had of himself. The beer gut that hung over his belt line also revealed his true age, since he hadn't weighed under two hundred pounds for over ten years, and this last year his weight had crept up to two hundred and twenty. At five foot nine, he didn't consider himself fat, even though everyone else did. He ignored the weight and hid it under larger clothes just as the hair coloring hid the gray. Cook liked to think of himself as a real ladies man, but in truth, he was an over weight, aging pervert. At least that was the opinion of the young girls he leered at and tried to start conversations with in malls and school yards. Cook hadn't been with a woman voluntarily for years. He paid young prostitutes or forced even younger girls to reinforce his image of a stud. If he detected the hookers' disgust or the young victims' horror, it didn't register. He actually believed he was doing them a favor and that they were lucky to bed him.

Cook looked over at the younger Smith, who actually picked up co-eds every once in a while. At least he could when Cook made him clean up, like today. Left alone, Smith would live and smell like an animal. Cook admitted he enjoyed watching his younger partner's bedroom gymnastics almost as much as he enjoyed watching those he lured to his house shower and bathe in the bedroom and bathroom equipped with spy holes and cameras. He was a little jealous. Because deep down, he realized he was past his prime and without cash in his pocket, he wouldn't be bringing home anything like Smith did. That's why he encouraged Smith to bring them to his house, so he could vicariously live through his peep holes and video tape. But those were times when he didn't

ALAIN BURRESE

have his first true passion. The passion that was laying on the
floor unconscious in the back of the van. It was a mixture of
thrill seeking and lust. He relished the thrill of the hunt and
capture, and was sexually stimulated by the young fearful
virgins they captured. He'd do it even if it didn't pay so well.

They were traveling down Interstate 90 toward the Idaho
border and traffic was surprisingly light. "Tape her up and get
rid of that damn cat." Cook growled to his younger cohort.

"What do you mean get rid of the cat?"

"What did I say? Get rid of the cat."

"Where?"

"You've got a god-damned window don't you?"

"Alright," Smith replied shrugging. "Come here kitty," he
cooed as he looked around the floor of the van trying to find
the scared tabby. Having forgotten the scare, the furry fuzz
ball bounced out to attack Smith's finger as it had the string
earlier. "Come here," Smith said as he gently picked the kitten
up. He cradled the tiny cat in his left hand and arm as he
pulled back the electric window switch with his right. When
the window was down, he cupped the kitten in both hands
and raised it to his face. In the voice that everyone speaks to
babies with, Travis Smith told the little tabby, "Good bye little
kitty." With a quick flick of both wrists, he tossed the kitten
out the window and then closed it back up as if he had thrown
a cigarette butt out rather than a living creature.

"Now get her taped up before she comes to." Cook
ordered.

"I'm on it, don't worry about it." Smith stood up and
moved between the seats to sit in the middle seat and leaned
down to check on Ashley, who still lay where she had landed
and received the blow to the head. He placed his hand on her
chest to see if she was breathing. Feeling the slight rise of her
chest, he knew she was alive, though it wouldn't have

20

bothered him if she hadn't been, other than the rage it would send Cook into for losing out on their pay day. Kitten, kid, it didn't really make a difference to Smith. He'd toss Ashley out the van just as easily as the little tabby. However, Ashley was worth money. Well, there was another difference besides the money, Smith thought as he moved his hand over to Ashley's small breast. There was not much under her nipple, but Smith caressed, and squeezed what was there. His finger circled the nipple and he started to get aroused. Ashley also started to come to. It had only been a few minutes since Smith had punched her in the mouth. Ashley was loopy and didn't recognize where she was or what was going on. She had not been unconscious long enough to cause serious damage, but she was groggy and befuddled about her whereabouts. The side of her face also ached.

"Just tape her up damn it," Cook barked from the driver's seat, noticing in the rear view mirror what Smith was up to. It wasn't that Cook objected to copping a feel here or there, that didn't hurt the merchandise, but there was a time and place for it, and that was not right now. When they got back to Montana, Cook thought he might just have a little fun himself. This one was pretty cute. Cook thought about the last time he had a young girl. It had been almost nine months. "Yes, I need some of that," he thought to himself. He wasn't going to let Smith have this one. The top price came for virgins, but Cook knew ways to enjoy himself without having to lose top dollar. He glanced in the mirror again and watched Smith finish duct taping Ashley's legs, wrists and mouth. He thought about deflowering this one himself, but realized he needed the cash. He'd still have his fun.

By the time Ashley woke completely and recognized something was terribly wrong, she had tape over her mouth, securing both ankles together, and binding her wrists. Her hands were in front of her, but she couldn't do much with the tape binding them together. The tape hurt and her face hurt even more. Terrified, she tried to scream, but the tape prevented her from opening her mouth. She lay there scared and in pain. She lay there staring under the middle seat of the Dodge wondering where her mom was, wondering what was happening.

Smith was back in the passenger seat staring at fast food joints as they passed through Spokane Valley. "I'm hungry," he said.

"We'll eat in Sandpoint. We aren't stopping before that. We'll stop at the McDonald's there."

"How long?"

"About seventy miles from here, I guess."

"Wake me when we get there." Smith leaned his seat back and closed his eyes. Cook turned the radio on and thought about what he would do with Ashley once they got back to Montana. He also started spending the money she would bring.

Ashley Cox woke up when the vehicle stopped at the Sandpoint McDonalds, but she remained still on the floor of the van and kept her eyes closed. Her face hurt and she was more terrified than she'd ever been. She wanted to go back to sleep and wake up at home in her mother's arms. Her mom could make this bad nightmare go away.

But the nightmare didn't stop. It continued, and continued, and continued. She didn't know how long she lay in the back of the van, nor did she know where she was when she was grabbed and yanked out from behind the seat and made to stand in the dirt and tall grass somewhere out in the middle of the woods. She was pushed along toward a small camper trailer and shoved inside the barren space. Inside she cowered and cried.

Inside that small trailer, the horrors began. Her clothes were ripped off and she was left naked and alone, except when one or the other would come in and run their filthy hands over her body, touching parts her mother always told her were private, and not to let others see or touch. She felt dirty, scared, and alone. Tears stopped coming, but the pain, humiliation, and fear never ceased. She didn't understand what the men were doing when they took off their clothes and touched their own private parts. She closed her eyes and didn't look, and tried to cover her ears to stop the sounds of their heavy breathing and grunts. She was sure her mother wouldn't approve. Where were her mother and father?

Ashley didn't know how many days she was kept in that small area, nor did she know how many times the strange men came in and touched her and themselves, nor how many pictures were taken. It was all one big blur. They left her water and sandwiches, which at first she left alone, but hunger and thirst finally convinced her to eat and drink what they provided. How many sandwiches did she eat? She couldn't tell.

Nor did Ashley know that her mother hadn't slept since the day she went missing. She might have dozed off a time or two during the constant vigil, but every waking moment was focused on getting her daughter back. Police, FBI Agents, news reporters from the *Spokesman Review* and several television stations, countless family, friends, and community members, as well as the dreaded silence of the night when they were all gone and her husband tried to keep their son asleep and begged her to rest, filled every hour along with the constant feeling that it was her fault.

One day, after the man had grunted and groaned while running his free hand over her, he told her to get dressed and threw her a pair of green pants and a yellow t-shirt. Numbly, Ashley did as she was told. In her daze, she didn't even think it strange to put on pants without undergarments. Once dressed, the man took her outside where she saw the gold van that she'd seen by her school. She wondered where the kitten was. She was told to get inside and that if she made any noise she'd wish she hadn't. She complied.

A little more than two hours later, the van entered a city. Ashley didn't know it was Saturday, nor did she know the headlines of the morning's paper were about Walter Dennison and how he killed eight classmates at the local school the day before. Ashley's world was blank. She barely heard or saw anything. Her feelings were numb. The constant terror of the previous week left her emotionless and distant. She wanted to know why her mom and dad never came. She wished she'd die and go to heaven.

She was quickly ushered from the van through the back door of a trailer house and shoved onto a mattress on the floor of the back bedroom. There she stayed. She never saw the two men again, but they were replaced by a new man who brought her food and water a couple times each day. He even gave her a soda one time. The new man never touched her, but he did ask her to remove her clothes for photographs the first night. She did what he asked - what else could she? When he was gone, she dressed and sat on the mattress with her back against the wall. There was a sheet that she pulled over herself, and it was in that back bedroom that tears started again. She didn't cry during the day when light snuck through the cracks of the covered windows, but each night she sobbed. She cried and wondered when all of this would end. She cried for her mother. She cried to God. She wept for death and to be with the Angels. Anything to have this nightmare over.

Ashley woke and realized it must be night. The room was pitch black. She didn't know what day it was, nor when she had fallen asleep. It must have been sometime after the man put the bowl of macaroni and cheese into the room. She had eaten it and washed it down with the glass of water he provided. She'd then relieved herself in the bucket the man left in the corner for her to use, and curled up on the mattress under the sheet.

She inched over to the wall and sat up with her feet curled under her. She hugged her knees close to her chest and thought of her mother. Tears formed and then her breathing became labored. She gulped for air as she struggled to hold the sobbing at bay. It didn't work. Tears ran down her face as she cried uncontrollably. Why was this happening? What did she do that caused this? When would it stop? Where were her mom and dad?

The crashing sound as the door burst open startled her. She wanted to scream. What new terrors must she face? The scream didn't come. It was stuck somewhere between her throat and mouth. A small light flashed around the room. She didn't look at the dark figure approaching. She buried her face into her knees and hugged tighter. She muffled the sound, but tears continued to streak down her face.

Baker stood silent in the doorway of the trailer house. A padlock secured the back bedroom door. The flimsy clasp had been attached to the door and the frame with a couple screws. He hadn't noticed it earlier when his focus took him to the front of the trailer house. He hated to imagine what lay beyond the door, but the whimpering he heard gave him a clue. He looked outside, then thought about what he'd just left at the front of the house. He thought about picking the lock, but decided he would rather be out of the area faster. A quick front kick smashed the door open and sounded like an explosion to the man who was trying to be silent and stealthy.

"Jesus Christ," he said to himself as the mini maglight illuminated the room and he saw a young child in the corner. She was sitting on a mattress that lay on the floor, hugging her knees to her chest. Her face was buried in her knees and she was crying. "Shit." Should he carry her to his SUV, or leave her to go and bring it here? He'd left it over a mile away on purpose. He didn't want it seen near the trailer, especially after what he'd just done a moment ago when surprised by Bruce James. He couldn't leave her. What if he was seen with her? Where should he take her? Baker's mind raced as he crossed the room and knelt beside the crying girl.

"It's okay. I'm going to help you." He reached out and touched her shoulder and she flinched and pulled away. "It's okay," he repeated. But was it? I need to get her to the hospital anonymously he thought.

ALAIN BURRESE

There wasn't time to determine the best course of action. He needed to act. Doing something now was most often better than thinking of a dozen plans to complete in the future. He expected her to scream and was prepared to clamp his hand over her mouth as he grabbed her and picked her up. Surprisingly, she didn't do anything, but rather went limp as he lifted her. Even the crying subsided.

"Must be shock," he whispered. "It's going to be all right honey. I'm going to get you help." Baker wondered how old the girl was as he positioned her over his shoulder. She didn't weigh much, and he figured junior high. Being thrown over his shoulder wouldn't be the most comfortable position, but he didn't have much choice. He had a long ways to carry her, and he needed to do so quickly and have at least one arm free.

He had her over his left shoulder with his left arm wrapped around her legs. She was wearing the pants and t-shirt she'd been given in the trailer in the woods. Baker noticed she was barefoot, but didn't have time to look for her shoes, if there ever were any. He turned off the flashlight and returned it to his pocket and silently exited the back door of the trailer with the girl over his shoulder and the box under his arm. He didn't see or hear anyone as he started down the alley in the general direction of his parked vehicle. He kept his face tucked down and prayed he wouldn't be seen.

The minutes it took him to reach his Dodge Durango seemed like hours. With every step, Baker was sure a patrol car would come around a corner and stop him for questioning. As he opened the passenger door of his SUV and placed the girl on the seat, he breathed a sigh of relief. He looked around. He hadn't noticed anyone looking at him the entire way to the vehicle, and it appeared that he'd made it undetected. He quickly went to the other side and hopped in. Still scanning for anyone that might be taking an interest in his activities,

28

Baker eased onto the street and headed toward the first corner. Once around the block, he felt better and believed he was in the clear. Well, almost.

He knew the girl needed medical attention, but how was he going to get her assistance without being identified? He couldn't risk being found out. He hated what he had to do, but couldn't figure any other way.

He parked a block from the hospital in a housing area. The girl had sat in the front seat motionless and without making a sound. Several times Baker had told her it was going to be okay, without receiving a response. When he opened her door, she looked at him. It was the first time Baker had a good look at her. The SUV's dome light revealed an emotionless little girl who must have been at one time as cute and cheerful as his own daughter. What had she been through? Baker didn't even want to imagine it. He picked her up and carried her in his arms as a father would carry a sick child. Anyone passing might think just that. He was walking toward the hospital.

Outside the emergency entrance, just out of the light, Baker stopped. He placed the girl down. She stood there with her bare feet on the pavement. She shivered, even though it was a warm spring night. "Go over to those doors, the doctors will help you." He hoped she understood. He wanted to take her all the way, but couldn't risk it. He had his family, career, and life to think about. "Go on. It will be okay, they will help you. They will find your mother."

"Mommy?" The girl began to cry.

"Yes, go on. Go to those doors. They will find your mommy." Baker wiped the tears out of his own eyes. "Go ahead. It will be okay." As he watched her slowly walk toward the emergency entrance, he silently prayed to himself that it would be.

* * *

Baker didn't remember jogging back to his Durango, nor did he remember driving home and sneaking back into the house. He must have put his gear away before crashing on the couch, because when he woke his pockets were empty.

Tanya Baker, a shapely fit woman with blonde hair, came out while he was watching a breaking news story. Ashley Cox, the girl who'd been abducted from the front of her school in Spokane had miraculously shown up at St. Patrick's hospital in the middle of the night. The girl was identified as the missing child and her parents were on their way to be reunited. While there were no visible signs of permanent injury, the girl was being treated for shock and had not yet spoken more than a couple of words.

Tanya said good morning, and Baker replied, hiding that he'd become emotional while watching the news. He brushed away a tear and headed for the shower. He needed to wash the events from the previous night away, but didn't think there'd be enough hot water to get the job done.

"Honey," Tanya called just before Baker made it to the bathroom.

"Yeah?" he called back. He looked over at her and focused on her bare legs where the sleep shirt stopped on down to her bare toes. He didn't want her to notice his eyes, and he still thought her legs were one of her best physical attributes.

"Do we have to keep this paper?" She was holding the crumpled front page of the previous Saturday's local newspaper.

"No, throw it, or put it in the recycle pile." Baker quickly turned toward the bathroom.

"Are you okay?" Tanya called after him.

"Yeah," he yelled back as he closed the door.

Showering, Baker remembered the headline of that Saturday's paper, *9 Dead and 7 Injured in School Shooting*. The opening paragraph was all most people read, "Residents in the Western Montana town struggle to understand a shooting that left nine people dead and seven injured. The gunman, Walter Dennison, was a 16-year-old student at Hellgate High School. He killed himself afterward."

It was too painful for most to read further, and much of the article reflected the same speculation and analysis as the television and radio news programs. There were names and descriptions of the deceased, and questions regarding Dennison's motive. It then seemed that every news source quoted from the 2002 study by the U.S. Secret Service and the U.S. Department of Education. Analysts and reports suggested that Dennison didn't fit the profile, but then went on to inform that there really wasn't a profile for students who engaged in targeted school violence.

Benjamin Baker had been as shocked as everyone else in the community when he arrived home that Friday evening and found his wife glued to the television set, listening to the same reports again and again, hoping for something new to develop and be revealed. Saturday's paper hadn't provided anything new, so Baker had made a call to one of his friends on the police force. He knew Clint Cantrell would be working early and would be able to fill him in with details not known to news reporters.

It had been Baker's lucky day, if you could call anything lucky about the circumstances. Officer Cantrell was the officer who found Walter Dennison's journal and had turned it over to the evidence room. He did so only after reading through it himself. Under the strictest of confidence, Baker's friend revealed that the notebook had been found in the shooter's belongings and some of the passages suggested possible motives. It seemed that the boy was having difficulty in getting any authority figure to believe him when he tried to discuss how he'd been sexually molested when he was twelve. His writings reflected anger in not being able to express himself, but more so in the fact that no one seemed to care enough to help him get the story out.

The writings revealed that the boy believed that no one cared and there was nowhere to turn. He seemed obsessed with the Columbine and Red Lake school shootings, and several times wrote that if he took his gun to school, maybe people would listen. The most significant thing in the notebook, Baker's friend told him, was the name of the person Walter said molested him. Cantrell had hoped to have a warrant for his arrest that weekend. Both knew there was no one who could do anything to help Walter, but maybe they could stop it from happening again in the future. Cantrell revealed that the final page of the journal had three short sentences, all written in large capital letters, filling the page: NO ONE LISTENS! NO ONE DOES ANYTHING! NO ONE CARES!

Baker had thanked Cantrell before he hung up the phone. He remembered wanting to be the one to prosecute the child molester when they brought him in, but he figured Kevin Tucker, the County Attorney, would want the spotlight for himself. He didn't care much for his boss, the County Attorney. He believed him to be a glory hound and someone whose sole motives for anything he did was to make money or secure votes for the next election. Baker knew if Tucker could work the incident so he'd be the hero after such a tragedy, he surely would. It would be one more notch on his handle toward the governorship, his true desire.

Tanya had spent Friday evening after putting their five-year-old daughter, Coral, to bed, worrying about all the things that could happen once Coral was in school. Baker had the same fears, but spent the better part of an hour that night trying to convince his spouse that it made absolutely no sense to worry about it now. It really wasn't what she wanted to hear, so he comforted her by explaining that he'd teach Coral to defend herself when she got a little older. This seemed to satisfy Tanya, at least enough that they could watch a comedy on TV and then get to sleep.

That next morning, reading the paper, he wondered if there really was anything he could teach his daughter to keep her safe, and if anything he did at the County Attorney's office really made much of a difference. All the police and prosecutors could do was try to apprehend and punish people after crimes occurred. He remembered looking at the paper lying on the kitchen table. *9 Dead and 7 Injured in School Shooting*, blaring at him in big bold print across the top. A picture of Hellgate High School was featured under the headline. Unless they moved, Coral wouldn't attend that school, but what if it was Big Sky or Sentinel next time? Would there be a next time? Baker didn't want to think about it.

He remembered how he thought about the conversation with his LEO friend, Cantrell, for much of the day. If the kid committed this horrific crime because he'd been molested, the guy who molested him should burn he had fumed. He knew that wouldn't help the eight kids or Walter Dennison, who were dead, but it was something. Lock the perverted filthy scum up so he couldn't do anything to any other innocent children.

As hot water pulsed from the faucet, Baker remembered how enraged he'd become that Saturday. He'd picked the paper up off the table and started to read the article again. "9 dead." It was like when the fuse of a cherry bomb reaches its destination. Baker explosively crumpled up the newspaper into a wadded ball and threw it across the room. The paper unfolded in flight and lazily hit the wall and fluttered to the floor. Still consumed by his mini rage, he burst through the back door. Only after the crash resonated into his consciousness did he regret it, and hoped it hadn't woke Tanya or Coral. He knew Tanya hadn't slept well. By then he was already nearing the garage where he kept his hundred pound heavy bag secured to the rafters where it could swing freely in the middle of the garage bay.

He'd started to move around the bag, throwing round-house kicks as he thought about recidivism rates. He remembered reading from the Bureau of Justice Statistics that somewhere around 67% of a group of over 270,000 they looked at that were released from prisons in 15 States were rearrested for a felony or serious misdemeanor within three years. There were different stats on sex offenders and child victimizers and he couldn't remember them all. But the bottom line was criminals got out and committed crimes again. Not all, but even one was too many for a prosecutor to accept. What good was he doing if they got out and did it again? The bag swung higher as he increased the power of his kicks. He'd felt good making the bag swing, which made the timing of the next kicks even more important. The rage wasn't just about the dead children, but the frustrations over the same political argument that bothered him and every other prosecutor and law enforcement officer. They worked extremely hard to get criminals off the street and had no say in the politics and policies that released them back into society to far too often victimize innocent people again.

Still thinking of Saturday morning, Baker acknowledged to himself that he always took these things too personally. He wanted to make a difference but wasn't sure if what he was doing had any significance at all. He remembered thinking, as he pounded the bag so hard the rafters shook, that something needed to be done to stop these kinds of incidents before they happened, but what? Well, he'd done something last night that would stop some, hadn't he?

The water was starting to cool and he knew it would turn cold soon. He turned it off and grabbed a towel. He thought about the box out in the Durango. He thought about the national crime reports. He shook his head. The feelings that whelmed up inside him made him feel like he was about to explode. The fury that extinguished James' life only a few hours before was only a fraction of what Baker held inside when he thought of the abused kids and the senseless deaths caused by such abuse. There was much more needed to stop these kinds of incidents than ridding the world of one child molester. But what?

BOOM!

Benjamin Baker worked the bolt and looked through the Leupold Mark 4 scope to where he was about to send the next 180 grain bullet to its target. The scope was the same that he had attached to his Remington .308, an almost exact replica of the Army's M24 system he first used years ago. This scope was attached to the rifle he received from his grandfather's estate. It was one of his grandfather's two .300 caliber rifles, the Weatherby .300 Magnum. His uncle had kept the .300 Savage. The recoil of the Weatherby was considerably greater than the smaller caliber Remington rifle he was most accustomed to, but he wouldn't really notice the recoil when firing, he'd be in "the bubble" as Gunny used to call it. He briefly thought of the last time he had called the Gunnery Sergeant's home in Virginia Beach and spoke with the Gunny's wife. The Multiple Sclerosis had reached a level where he could not talk on the phone himself, and a few months later on a late February day he passed away. He didn't call in sick and head to the mountains with his rifles to think of the past, reminisce on sad occasions, or relive stressful times. He cleared his head. He was here to be away from all the thoughts that screamed through his mind. He was here to manage stress, not elevate it.

Baker paused and looked over to his left at a group of Ponderosa Pine. A lot had happened in the last week. He'd been fuming for three days. It started Monday morning. He'd gone to the office hoping to be assigned to prosecute Bruce James for the crimes committed against Walter Dennison, or at least be involved with it. They first needed to gather evidence and build a case. A person was innocent until proven guilty and all that. But in Baker's mind, he was already guilty and he needed to see the matter through.

Ben had come home furious on Monday, swearing at Kevin Tucker and his political connections. Ben wasn't furious because Tucker was hogging the case for himself. It was just the opposite. Monday afternoon, Tucker announced that they would not be prosecuting Bruce James at all. His reasoning was there was not enough to go on and they needed to focus on cases they could win. That was time better spent and they could accomplish more good that way. Loosing cases didn't help anyone but the criminal defense attorneys. And with James, it would have most likely been a public defender anyway.

Baker hadn't talked much at all. He went to work on Tuesday and Wednesday, but avoided Tucker and everyone else in the office. He worked in silence and anyone seeing him picked up on the vibe that he should be left alone. Everyone was happy to oblige. Tanya had let him fume on Monday, knowing he'd need time to cool down, but was worried when he seemed no better Tuesday or Wednesday. The only time he wasn't self-absorbed and seeming like someone ready to explode was when he took the time to read with Coral. Maybe something in Dr. Seuss got through that hard exterior.

Baker started to lower his eye to the scope again, but stopped short and looked back over at the grove of slender trees. He thought about the previous night.

"You coming to bed, or sleeping on the couch again?" Tanya had asked from the hallway. She was tired, ready for bed, and about to retire to the bedroom.

"I don't know. I'm going to watch a movie or something. Not really tired."

"Okay. Are you alright Ben?

"Yeah, I'm fine," he'd told her.

"If you say so. I love you and I'll see you in the morning."

"Love you too. Have a good night." Baker had then channel surfed, never staying on any particular channel for more than five minutes or so. After a restless half hour of not finding anything to hold his interest, he had gone down stairs. He'd hesitated a moment in front of the black steel gun case. Did he really need anything from inside? He'd turned the key.

Baker's Cold Steel tactical folder had already been in his front right pocket. He pulled his 9mm from the top shelf of the gun cabinet and tucked it with its small Side Kick holster into his jeans at the small of his back. He slipped a small black case with small tools into his back pocket and a small flashlight into the other. As he was going through his gear and selecting items, he'd told himself, "Just in case."

Baker remembered going back upstairs and contemplating putting everything back where he retrieved the items and just going to bed. He'd walked down the hall and looked in on Coral. The room had glowed from the nightlight on the far wall. She was sound asleep, lying crosswise in her bed and only half covered by her thin blanket. At least a half dozen stuffed animals kept her company.

He remembered turning and gazing into his and Tanya's bedroom. The room had been dark, but he heard the breathing of deep slumber. He knew she hadn't slept well the last couple of nights. She was worried about him. He knew he wasn't easy to live with, especially when he was in a foul mood. And ever since Tucker told him to forget about Bruce James, he'd been in a very foul mood. He didn't buy Tucker's explanations and rationalizations for his decision. He knew it was political. Everything Tucker did was political. It wasn't right. He knew something needed to be done. Where was the justice?

He had walked silently to the back door. He'd then cinched the laces of his Asics running shoes tight, making sure they wouldn't come untied or come off. The door had creaked as he opened it and he'd stood silently listening to ensure it hadn't disturbed his sleeping family. Everything clear, he'd gone out into the cool spring night air and locked the door behind him. Lying behind his rifle, he thought about the previous night and how he'd stood there in the driveway for a moment before walking toward his Dodge Durango.

If Tanya or anyone had asked where he was going, he'd have replied, "Out for a drive. Just need to think." In other words, just like when he'd told Tanya he was okay, he'd have lied.

Baker took a deep breath, inhaling into his abdomen. He slowly let it out and returned his thoughts to the task at hand. He was here to shoot, not think. After one more deep breath, his body relaxed and the events of the last week, the school shooting, Tucker's dismissal of the case against James, the moodiness that affected Tanya, the trip to Bruce James' trailer, and finding the little girl named Ashley all evaporated. Shooting was the one activity that could clear his mind of everything else.

He focused on the target he set up approximately three hundred meters out from where he lay behind his grandfather's checkered wooden stock hunting rifle. Three hundred meters was not much of a shot. Back in the military they used to compete regarding what part of a person's head they would shoot at three hundred meters. That was a long time ago. As he focused on the target, he instinctively re-entered "the bubble." Nothing else mattered.

He laid prone, the steadiest position to shoot from. He was comfortable and had shifted his body to fit his natural point of aim. The rifle lay across the sandbag he brought for that purpose. The butt of the rifle was seated firmly against his right shoulder and rested on a sand-filled sock that Baker held in his left hand. The sock was used to lower or raise the rifle butt with steady micrometer-like adjustments. It was a little trick he learned in sniper school, and it worked extremely well. The rifle essentially rested on the two sandbags, and the only bodily contact was the butt against his shoulder and the most sensitive portion of his trigger finger when it applied the pressure to release the firing pin.

For a sniper, consistency equals accuracy. The totality of consistency, that of your equipment, ammunition, and habits developed during practice, result in precision shooting and accuracy. Baker enjoyed firing a variety of the weapons he owned, so consistency of weapon and ammunition was lacking, but then he wasn't training for military or law enforcement missions any more. He shot for pleasure, and more importantly these days, stress relief. Shooter consistency, his actions inside the bubble, guaranteed advanced marksmanship as well as providing the release from the daily grind that elevated his stress to levels his doctor warned him about. Stress came with the job. Most attorneys faced demanding schedules and pressure, and as a Deputy County Attorney, Ben Baker was no different. It was just his form of release that differed from his colleagues in the State Bar. While they attended happy hours, kept bottles locked under desks, and had extramarital affairs, he divided his personal time between heading to the woods with one or more of his numerous firearms, and practicing various martial arts that included swordsmanship and other antiquated weapons to go with the more practical arsenal he also stayed proficient with.

The effective sniper must concentrate keenly on each round fired. Each and every round must go exactly where the shooter placed it. Where many people try to shoot patterns or groups, Baker focused on one shot at a time, and he made that one shot over and over again. Each round fired was a single, final event, with an exact beginning, a definite end, and a precisely measured result. He never "banged" away at a target, and had little patience for those that did. He'd even chastised hunters and told them they had no business in the woods upon hearing their stories of shooting away at a running animal in hopes of hitting it. For Baker, he didn't pull the trigger without knowing exactly where the round was intended, and it was far and few between that the round didn't end up in that exact location.

Inside the bubble, his cheek habitually rested on his spotweld, the place on the rifle stock that provided correct eye relief and field of view. A critical aspect of a consistent scope picture was perfect eye relief. Baker held his eye at the same distance from the eyepiece shot after shot. There were no shadows inside the scope that were often created by incorrect eye relief or a bad spotweld, therefore he knew his head was in the correct position. He hadn't fired this rifle as often, so the position didn't come as easily and natural as on the Remington, but it was there. With the Remington, he had fired so many rounds that his spotweld on that rifle had become a muscle memory habit. His eye almost automatically aligned at the correct distance and his cheek intimately knew that exact spot on the stock. He could almost fire immediately upon the rifle reaching his shoulder. In time, the Weatherby would be as instinctive. He kept both eyes open, a practice that was debated. In regards to the non-shooting eye, both closing it and leaving it open had pros and cons. Baker learned to shoot with both eyes open from his father as a child, and had just always done it that way. He let others debate the practice, he knew what worked and believed keeping both eyes open was the only way to shoot.

Firing a rifle with consistent accuracy requires the simultaneous application of many component skills. The synchronization of proper body positioning, correct scope picture, breathing, and trigger control combined to form the integrated act of shooting, and for Ben Baker, after years of practice, they had become as natural as the synchronized acts of driving were to Nascar champions Tony Stewart and Jeff Gordon.

He took two deep breaths to surge the oxygen content in his blood. He then felt his breathing cycle and concentrated on the natural respiratory pause after each exhalation. This point was the steadiest point in the entire breathing cycle and the preferred time to take one's shot. The natural pause only lasts about two seconds, so the shooter extends the pause by holding his breath just as he finishes exhaling. This was simple at a shooting range, and definitely ensured the most accurate shot placement. However, snipers may not have enough time for the preparatory breaths or even to exhale and hold before a shot. They must be able to shoot, ready or not. That's why they used to practice shooting while holding their breath with lungs half full, three-quarters full, and empty. Today he had all the time in the world and he completely exhaled and held his breath as his sensitized trigger finger gently and steadily pressed the trigger.

Approximately .022 of a second passes between the trigger releasing the sear and the firing pin actually striking the cartridge's primer. A further .002 second will pass while a bullet travels down a 24-inch barrel. Any slight movement of the rifle during this period can alter the precise placement of a shot. Baker lay frozen, absolutely nothing moved after the trigger released the sear. This initial phase of the shot's follow through needed to be as consistent as every other synchronized aspect. His shoulder absorbed the recoil and he continued his steady position. He then regained focus in the scope to verify shot placement. Slowly, he worked the bolt to eject the cartridge and load another round into the rifle.

The .300 Weatherby mag had more of a kick than his Remington and the M24 sniper system he used in the Army. It would reach out farther as well, but it didn't really matter when shooting targets at three hundred meters. Both rifles were more than capable at that range. Baker was comfortable with, and had made, shots out past one thousand meters. Those shots maxed out the capabilities of the M24, and you didn't always get a first round hit. It was not uncommon for them to have to take a second or third shot with the aid of a spotter to walk the rounds into the targets at that range. That is why to pass the 2nd Infantry Division Scout Sniper School, students qualified on three, four, five, and six hundred meter targets. Practicing on the eight hundred, one thousand, and beyond targets was reserved for those that were already qualified snipers.

Baker paused and thought back to the 2nd ID Scout Sniper Range. The first weapon he fired on that range was the old M21 Sniper System. The accurized 7.62mm M14 rifle with the ART II telescope was a Vietnam era weapon that continued to be the Army's main sniper weapon for the remainder of the 1970s and most of the 80s.

In 1989, the M24s showed up, getting to Korea later than many other units who started receiving them in 1988. It was great to fire a brand new weapon rather than the Vietnam era M21s, and it was the fixed ten power Leoupould scope that allowed them to compete with which part of the head they would hit at three hundred meters. Unlike the M21, which fired semi-auto and held a 20 round magazine, the M24 was a five shot bolt action rifle in the same caliber, 7.62mm, which was equivalent to the .308 hunting round.

Baker lowered his cheek to his spot weld and re-entered his bubble. The first two rounds struck the bull's-eye in the center circle of the common paper target he had tacked up on the range's target stand. He honed in on the target and picked the exact spot he wished to hit. Many hunters and military marksmen aimed at center mass. This might be sufficient for someone who wants to be average, but shooting can never be more exact than your aiming. Snipers, with precise optical aiming instruments, picked an impact point on the target the same size as the bullet. Baker's chosen impact point was exactly where the first two rounds entered the target, dead center.

He once again took the slack out of the trigger before firing the 180 grain bullet down range toward the sheet of paper with the black dot in the center. Baker brought the scope back on target after the recoil. The round struck almost precisely where the previous round hit. The hole in the bull's-eye's center was about three millimeters larger than it had been a moment before. "As it should be," thought Baker. "This old rifle of grandpa's does the job just fine."

Since leaving the Army, Baker hadn't really kept up with the improved weaponry of the armed forces. Every once in a while a magazine article about the current sniper systems would catch his eye and he would browse through the magazine at the stand, but other than that, he didn't keep tabs on every new rifle or round used in advanced shooting. In fact, Baker had just proved that it was the person behind the weapon that mattered more than the make or caliber. The weapon was not near as critical as the person behind it. If Baker knew he was going to have to prove that very thing, he might not have entered his "bubble" so easily.

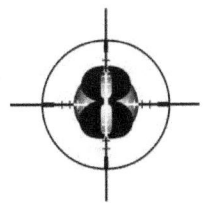

"Feel better?" Tanya asked when Baker walked in carrying the rifles he'd left with earlier that morning. She didn't understand how being in the woods alone with his guns made him feel better, but she knew that it did. She also knew he was pretty upset to call in sick at the office to go shooting.

"Yeah, I'm fine."

"Seriously, we need to talk about this."

Baker sighed. "Okay, let me clean up. Where's Coral?"

"She went to her friend's after school, she'll be home in a bit. By the way, you get a hold of your friend yet?"

"No answer every time I try, and the mailbox is full. It's been full since the first call last Sunday."

"Well, keep trying." Tanya was ever the optimist and the kind of person who always brought a smile to other's faces. It wasn't that she was perpetually cheerful, because she did have her moments when she could be as angry as anyone, but she lacked a mean streak to accompany her anger. And in reality, there were very few people who ever witnessed her anger, to almost everyone who interacted with her; she was the bright spot of the day. Everyone thought so; friends, co-workers when she had worked in an office, tellers at the bank, checkers at the grocery store, and most importantly Benjamin Robert Baker, her husband.

"I will." Baker gave Tanya a little smile, and when she smiled back it grew to a genuine expression of warmth, happiness and love. They met when he was in law school. She worked for an insurance company at the time and he'd been interning at a law firm who was defending one of the insureds. They married shortly after he took the bar exam, and ever since he'd felt he was the luckiest person in the world to have found her. Unfortunately, he didn't always show it. He regretted that there were things he wouldn't, couldn't, share with her. She was so pure and innocent in many ways. She grew up in a small town in North Western Montana and Missoula was the biggest place she'd ever lived. She was completely naive regarding violence and many ways of the world that Baker learned the hard way.

"Forget about cleaning up and come over here and talk about it with me since you can't reach your friend." she said, moving to the next room and plopping herself down on the living room sofa. The flowers of her blouse clashed with the flowered pattern of the furniture. She patted the cushion next to her inviting her husband to join her.

"It's nothing really." Baker took the seat next to her and she snuggled closer. He tried to determine the fragrance he smelled, it was from one of the many bottles of potions that lined the bathroom sink and shelves from the "smelly place store" as he called it at the mall. The scent was Cherry Blossoms, one of his favorites. He had bought her a complete set of products in that scent in a big basket the previous Christmas. "Just wanted to talk to him about some stuff." He reached over and gave her a kiss on the neck.

"Don't start that. Coral will be home in a little bit. And just because I said we should talk, doesn't mean you don't have to clean up."

"Alright." Baker leaned back but still kept his hand on his wife's upper thigh.

"You've been pounding your bag pretty hard this last week, almost every night and morning. I know you like to train, but I also know something is bothering you. You've been out of it since last Saturday after that terrible shooting at the school, and it's only gotten worse through the week. You seem like you're not really here."

"I know, sorry."

"Don't just say sorry, tell me what's going on." She gave him a playful punch to the shoulder, and flipped her long blonde hair around with a flirtatious flip of her head. "Tough guy."

"I've just been thinking about what happened last Friday." Baker took his hand away from Tanya's leg and started doing some wrist stretches from his martial arts training. There was no way he could tell her about the happenings of the previous night, but she'd understand being upset over the school shooting. "Something needs to be done." He tried twisting his wrist around so his fingers pointed toward his face in a manner the wrist wasn't supposed to bend. It helped strengthen his wrists and keep them flexible for the joint locking techniques *Hapkido* was known for.

Tanya knew her husband went into his wrist acrobatics whenever he was pressed to discuss something he was uncomfortable with or wanted to avoid. She pressed anyway. "It's terrible, I know. All those kids. I makes me scared to send Coral to school."

"Me too."

"But what can we do? You said you'd teach her to defend herself."

"I know." Baker didn't want to tell his wife that there wasn't much you could teach a kid to help them in such a situation. It was more luck than anything else. Maybe if one were trained to hit the floor and hide behind cover they'd have a better chance, but with kids, it was a crapshoot. Tanya didn't need to hear that. She worried enough.

"So what have you been thinking about?"

"A lot, you know, what happened, and stuff." Baker tried to avoid the look his wife gave him.

"What stuff?"

"I've been thinking a lot about Jerry Kroll."

"Who's that?"

"He was my best friend in Jr. High. We got into so much mischief together."

"What's he doing now?"

"He died our freshman year." Baker moved off the sofa and sat on the floor with his legs extended. He stretched down and grabbed his toes. "Suicide."

"Oh, I'm sorry." The hurt in Tanya's eyes was genuine. "If you don't want to talk, I understand."

"It's alright."

"What happened?"

"I don't know really. The summer between Jr. High and High School he was off at some camp and then his grandparents, or somewhere, I don't remember for sure. I know I didn't see him all summer, and then something was different when we started High School."

"Different how?"

"I don't know, it's hard to describe. It was a long time ago too, but I remember he wasn't as energetic as he'd been. He didn't want to joke around and get involved with some of the shenanigans a couple others and I were doing. He stayed more to himself and, I don't know. I don't remember him doing much with us at all in High School, and we did so much the year before." Baker forced himself lower into the stretch. He was past the comfortable pain, and it was starting to actually hurt as he continued to will his body lower. Physical pain had always been easier for him to deal with than emotional upheaval and the sharp pains inside that came from feelings.

"Did something happen that summer?"

"I don't know that either. We just didn't talk or do things like we had. It was High School and I had a thing for Shauna who was a grade ahead of us, and I don't know, we just didn't see each other much. I'm not sure why.

"Shauna, huh?"

Baker looked up at his wife's mischievous and inquiring smile. "That was High School."

"I'm sorry, I know this is hard for you." Her face became serious again, and Baker could see a touch of sadness in her brown eyes.

"I really don't know much more. He was just withdrawn and I figured he'd come around. I was caught up with my own stuff, you know, like you get in High School."

"So you never knew why he killed himself."

"Not really. If I'd have paid attention and listened, maybe I would have. Maybe he wouldn't have done it."

Tanya could see a hint of guilt in her husband's face, but it was the guilt-ridden way he said the last sentence that alarmed her. "You don't think it's your fault, do you?"

"Might be."

"Why would you say that?" she asked trying to read the angst in his face, but realizing he wasn't going to reveal all of his emotions. It was something she'd accepted about him long ago and credited it to his military and tough guy warrior persona and not necessarily to his legal education.

"I could have listened. I should have done something."

"Why, where you there? That must have been terrible." She leaned forward.

"No, I wasn't there when he did it. He was alone at his house."

"Then what could you have done?"

"I don't know, I just could have been there for him. I could have spent less time chasing Shauna and more time with him. I should have done something."

"I'm so sorry, honey."

"He called me on a Friday. I was busy and told him we could catch up on Monday, but I had something going on over the weekend. I forget now what it even was. I remember him telling me in that conversation that 'no one cared' and 'no one would listen.'"

"About what?"

"I'm not sure. He told me 'no one does anything,' but he wouldn't tell me what he was talking about. I thought he was just being Jerry and acting strange again. I couldn't figure out what got into him over the summer."

"Did you find out?" Tanya tried to move closer to her husband, but it was difficult with him sitting on the floor and her still on the sofa. Inside, she knew he probably wanted it that way. She wanted to reach out and hold him, but knew he didn't want to be held.

"No, no one ever found out. His mom found him that Sunday. He hung himself in his room. I didn't find out until Monday at school. They had a school meeting in the gymnasium and told us, and then offered counselors to talk to and all that."

Tanya sat in silence and watched Ben pull himself further into a stretch. She knew he was trying to make it hurt. "I'm so sorry, Ben."

"It happens. It happens all the time really."

"But not all the time to people we are close to."

"Someone's close to everyone."

"I know, honey, but you know what I mean." She hated when he started getting argumentative and rationalized everything. That she figured must have come from law school.

"Everyone's a friend, sibling, parent, or child of someone."

"I know." She didn't know what else to say, so she just sat.

"That Walter kid, the one who shot everyone on Friday, he left a notebook saying the same things. No one cares, no one listens, and no one does anything." Baker finished his stretch and stood. He looked over at the television rather than at Tanya. He didn't want her to see his eyes.

"Is that what got you thinking about your friend?"

"Yeah, I guess. Why doesn't anyone do anything?"

"Like what? What could you have done?"

"I don't know. But if no one does anything, it's just going to keep on going the same. Somebody needs to make a difference and do something to stop the pain before kids go too far and kill themselves."

"And others," she added, now thinking about Friday's horrific tragedy.

"Yeah, and others," he said quietly. "And I have to work for someone who won't go after the cause."

"That's the real reason you have been more pissed this week isn't it?"

"Yeah, it's just everything. The dead kids, the abused boy, Tucker and his Goddamn politics." Baker felt the frustrations that he'd spent the day shooting to alleviate start to boil again. "I'm sorry."

"It's okay, I understand."

"I just feel helpless, like I did with Jerry." Turning, he asked, "What time will they drop off Coral?" He needed to change the topic, and couldn't allow himself to get worked up or think about what he had done at Todd James' trailer.

Tanya looked at her watch, "Anytime now. I told them to have her home in time to do some homework before dinner."

"Let me look up Frank's dad and give him a call. Maybe he knows something. Then I'll shower and get ready for dinner, too. Why don't we go out somewhere?"

"Okay, I'll get ready. And Ben."

"Yeah," he said, stopping from leaving the room and turning back toward his wife.

"Don't beat yourself up over this. It's not your fault, and there's nothing you can do."

"Isn't there?" Baker said under his breath so Tanya wouldn't hear as he turned and left the room.

"Mr. Senich, this is Ben Baker, is Frank there?"

"Ben Baker, damn it's been a long time. Why the hell don't you call me Frank instead of that Mr. Senich shit?" a gruff old voice replied. Baker smiled, knowing that Frank's dad would always be Mr. Senich, and Frank III would always be Frank. "I'd ask how the hell you doing, but I'm guessing you called because of the jam Frank got himself into. He just got arrested last night, I'm surprised he got a hold of you so fast. I guess there are some benefits of having a lawyer as a best friend."

"Frank's in jail?"

"Isn't that why you called?"

"No, I was trying to get a hold of him for something else and he wasn't answering his cell. I thought you might know where he was."

"Sure do. He's downtown in jail and his cell phone is on the coffee table in the other room."

"So what's he in jail for?"

"Just a little misunderstanding, he'll be out..." Frank Sr. erupted into a short coughing spell. When the cough subsided he continued, "Damn allergies, you'd think I was still smoking. Anyway, like I was saying, once the Sheriff gets back taking a prisoner over to the State Penn, Frank will be out and it will be over. I bet he'll be out tonight or tomorrow morning at the latest. It's just an over zealous new deputy that thought he was doing right and decided he needed to take Frank in. Dumb shit, but hell, what do you expect from a snot nosed nineteen year old deputy."

"What was the reason he took Frank in?"

"Stupid little asshole arrested him after Frank took care of a couple sum bitches that moved in across the alley."

"Behind your place?" Baker remembered Mr. Senich's house and the alley that ran behind it from years before when he visited Frank after Frank's divorce and he had been staying with his father while he got back on his feet. That was the summer before Baker headed off to live and train in Japan. He hadn't been back to Missouri since.

"Yeah, out across the alley on the other side of the garage. You wouldn't believe it, Benny. Remember when you were down here? It was a nice little town, always had been. You wouldn't even recognize the place now. Especially the people. Scumbag drug dealing little punks all over the place. It's not the same place. Hell, if I had a place to go I'd leave."

"I'm sorry to hear that." Baker replied as he thought of his best friend's father living alone in his small three bedroom house, spending much of his time either out in his garage or down town at Granny's Café swapping stories with other old time denizens of the quaint little eatery.

The town wasn't more than a speck on the map. Two gas stations, four bars, a couple of restaurants, and a general store made most of Main Street. Then there were a few hundred houses surrounding the small business hub. Most who lived in the small town drove to Warrensburg to do their shopping. The adventuresome type, which were few and far between in the little community, might head to Kansas City and its suburbs for a taste of the big city life. The only times Mr. Senich went that far were when Frank took him out for a birthday or similar special occasion.

"Thanks Ben. I swear, you wouldn't recognize the place. I get so goddamn mad just thinking about what they've done to our little town. You remember Evelyn who lived next door to me?"

"She the woman who lived next door to the east?"

"Yeah, that's her. She's afraid to even go outside after dark now days. She used to love moonlight walks, and now the only moonlight she gets is looking out her windows. She's afraid to go out. She's afraid to have her doors unlocked. Sometimes I go over there and sit on the porch with her after dark. That's the only times you'll ever catch her out when the sun is down."

"That's too bad," Baker replied, not really knowing what to say, "It's good that she at least has you there."

"Yeah, but I'm too fricken old to do much any more. Thirty years ago, hell, twenty years ago, I'd have taken care of them sum bitches myself. I should just shoot the little mothers and be done with them. Maybe then Frank wouldn't have had to get involved."

"Speaking of," Baker was glad the conversation was getting back to Frank, "What did Frank do that got him arrested?"

"You know that boy of mine, always has to get involved."

"With what this time?"

"Couple punks that live across the alley behind me. Always drinking, doing drugs, making noise, throwing trash over my fence. Bunch of low lifes."

"What they do?"

"I made the mistake of telling Frank about them and he went out back to tell them to keep the noise down and keep their shit out of my yard."

"Suppose they didn't like the way he told them."

"You could say that again. The one got all big and tough and started yelling as he came at Frank. I think he was all hot air and was just trying to scare him and make him run with his tail tucked. But you know that boy of mine, he don't tuck his tail and run from nothin'."

"You got that right."

"You shoulda seen it. He knocked that guy flat quicker than you could imagine. His two drunk buddies stumbled off the porch talking shit and Frank took it to them too. All three were on the ground before I could get across the back yard. One of their little whores called the cops. That's when Deputy Do-Right showed up."

"Sounds like Frank. You sure he won't need any legal help?"

"Nah, when Sheriff Coleman gets back it will all be cleared up. Small town, Sheriff can do what he wants, and Coleman and me go way back. Hell, he remembers Frank from when he was just a little tot."

"Alright, but call me if you need something, and please have Frank give me a call as soon as he can."

"Will do my boy, sure is good to hear from you."

"Likewise, Mr. Senich."

"I told you to knock that Mr. shit off."

"Alright, you have a great rest of the day."

"You too Ben, bye."

Baker clicked off the phone and shook his head. It was like Frank to be in jail when he needed to talk. He wondered where he'd been Sunday when he called. At least he went to jail for doing something about the trash that was taking over too many places. Right or wrong, Frank always did something.

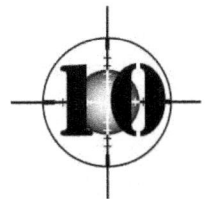

It was just after 2:00 A.M. Benjamin Baker sat alone in the dark staring at the living room television set. An empty Dorritos bag and two empty Diet Coke cans sat on the coffee table, a testament to the stress Baker was feeling. He'd devoured the entire bag of chips along with a half jar of salsa while watching the movie. He was going to have to run a bit farther and a bit faster in the morning to burn off all the junk he digested. Tanya had retired to the bedroom around 11:30, and it was after she was asleep that Baker slipped into the kitchen to find the chips and salsa.

Gene Davis, playing Warren Stacey, stood naked on the screen, yelling, "Go ahead, arrest me, take me in. You can't punish me, I'm sick. You can't punish me for being sick. All you can do is lock me up, but not forever. One day I'll get out. One day I'll get out, that's the law. That's the law! That's the law! And I'll be back! I'll be back! You'll hear from me, you and the whole fucking world!"

"No we won't," stated Charles Bronson, playing Leo Kessler, as he shot the sick serial killer right above his left eye. The credits started rolling as Baker smiled to himself. After twenty-five years, and who knows how many viewings, that was still one of Baker's favorite movie lines.

The movie was *10 to Midnight* and Baker remembered the first time he saw it back in his high school days of the early 80s. Bronson was one of the preeminent tough guys and a long time favorite. Besides Bronson's imperturbable character, the film was full of gratuitous nudity, which only made the film

ALAIN BURRESE

better according to Baker. To a high school wannabe tough guy, the more sex, nudity, and violence the better. Baker especially liked the shower scene with Ola Ray, the cute Playboy playmate that also starred in Michael Jackson's "Thriller" video that same year. He hated that she got stabbed to death, and it was all the more satisfying to see the killer crumple into a naked pile in the middle of the street with a bullet in his brain. "No we won't." Baker had hit rewind and watched the final line again.

"No we won't," Baker said in his best Bronson impersonation. He thought back to the trailer house and Bruce James. "No we won't," he whispered again. James was just as sick as the fuck Bronson just wasted. Bronson's character Kessler was a cop, someone sworn to uphold the law. Just like Baker. He took an oath when he became a member of the Bar. If it was okay for Bronson to play judge, jury, and executioner, why couldn't he? For Christ's sake, it's a movie. Bruce James was fucking real.

The Bar. Baker remembered the ordeal he had to go through to be admitted. He disclosed that he had lost a job due to a fight, and the Bar's Character and Fitness Committee deemed it proper to make Baker sit for an anger management evaluation and be on probation the first two years of admittance. It was a good thing he hadn't disclosed his Army days' exploits. Like most sheep, paper pushing office types that made up most of the Bar and the committees didn't understand violence, abhorred it, and thought everything could be solved through the law. Right. The law sure took care of Bruce James. What did the law do for the kids shot while attending school? What did the law do for Walter Dennison?

Was it his conscience keeping him awake? James deserved what he got. The son-of-a-bitch deserved worse. The law didn't take care of him, so he had. And it wasn't like it was premeditated. He didn't really have a choice being caught like that. Besides, what the hell good was his training if he didn't use it to right wrongs. James was a wrong, and he made it right. Fucker would never harm another child. He had a girl locked in the back room. Think of what would have happened to her if he hadn't done what he did that night. He did the right thing. He didn't have a choice.

But the right thing could cost him everything. He would lose his license to practice law, lose his job, lose his freedom. Most likely lose his family. Tanya never completely understood his martial side, and if she found out he killed someone, she might leave. She knew he had things in his past, but to actually sneak out and kill someone while she and Coral slept at home? If she left, she'd want to take Coral with her. So is it the killing or the thought of getting caught that's preventing sleep? It seemed longer than twenty-four hours since he'd been in that trailer.

Baker got up to change movies. He grabbed *Kinjite*, but decided he didn't want more Bronson, especially since *Kinjite's* plot was too close to recent events. He opted for DeNiro and Pacino and put in *Heat*, not knowing if he'd make it to the end, but knowing he wasn't going to sleep yet. How many nights had he fallen asleep watching old tough guy movies?

Tanya asked what was bothering him more than once, and he repeatedly told her it was just work. She knew he didn't like talking about things he dealt with at the office, and she really didn't like hearing about them either. So she dropped it and let him sleep on the couch with the TV on. She often wondered how attorneys kept sane dealing with so many negative things, and she thought she understood why the occupation fostered so many alcoholics, divorcees, and burned out men and women before their time. Earlier that year when she saw Ben reading *The (Un)Happy Lawyer*, a book about leaving the practice of law to do something fulfilling, she commented that it was quite a statement about the profession when there were books such as that published. It was interesting that the Harvard Law graduate who wrote the book made a living helping people get out of the practice of law.

Leaving the county wouldn't be so bad Baker thought. But he sure didn't want to leave to go to prison for killing someone. That was it, it wasn't the killing that bothered him, it was the thought of getting caught and losing his family and freedom. He wasn't going to get caught. It was over, no trail, nothing. They weren't even looking for anyone. No one really cared that Bruce James was dead. Not anyone that mattered to Baker's career anyway. No worries. So why was he up at 2:30 a.m. watching TV?

What about the oath? He swore to uphold the law when he became a member of the Bar. His father always told him all he had was his name and his word. The *Hagakure*, The Book of the Samurai, stated that a samurai's word is harder than metal. Baker had always lived by one code or another, from his father's to the military, various codes and oaths from his martial training, and the Bar. He also had his own personal code based on the warrior trainings he devoured since childhood. In actuality, the military codes, martial art school oaths, and the oath with the Bar were all included in the personal code. Was this why he wasn't sleeping? No. Honor was central to warriorship and something deeply ingrained into Baker's very existence. One of the foundations of honor was justice. Not the justice found in many courtrooms, but the simple concept of knowing the difference between right and wrong and doing right. Baker thought of Daidoji Yuzan's *Budoshoshinshu*. He had read several translations of the sixteenth-century text that was first published in English in

1941 as *The Code of the Samurai*. The book taught that a warrior should have a thorough understanding of right and wrong and if one knows how to do right and avoid wrong, one will have attained to Bushido, the code of the warrior. Killing James was against the law, but it was right. James was evil. Justice was served and it was an honorable act. If wrong is ignored and warriors don't act for justice, how can they have honor? Without honor, you can't call yourself a warrior. Was this a justification after the fact to make him feel better? No, killing James was just. It was honorable. It was the right thing. So why couldn't he sleep?

The drive-in scene was playing on the 42 inch screen and Baker stopped thinking for a moment and watched Val Kilmer, acting as a spotter, warn DeNiro of the guy sneaking up beside his car. As Tom Sizemore blasted the driver of the white pickup with his shotgun, Baker realized what was keeping him up. It wasn't killing Bruce James. It wasn't fear of being caught for killing James. Watching DeNiro and his team, Baker knew what was bothering him. He hadn't called Frank to mourn over what he had done. He didn't need Frank to cleanse his conscience for killing James. He called Frank, and he couldn't sleep, not for what had happened, but for what he was planning to do with the box he found in James' trailer. Last Sunday, he'd called Frank to talk. This evening, he'd called Frank for a different reason.

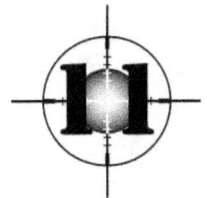

Hector Gonzales seemed to need the wall he leaned against to keep himself upright. His large mass wobbled even with the extra support. He looked like a large version of a slug stuck to an aquarium's wall, gently swaying with the movement of the water. His six foot frame carried three hundred and ninety pounds, and not aesthetically. A bulging belly, covered with hair, stuck out from under the gray XXL t-shirt that strained to cover what flesh it did. The huge gut didn't just stick out, but folded over the edge of his pants and completely hid the belt buckle tucked somewhere beneath. The belt held up a pair of denim shorts that hung just below the knees and possessed stuffed cargo pockets on both sides. Bright red high top basketball shoes, accompanied by white socks, stood out from the rather drab colors of the denim shorts and the dirty gray t-shirt.

The mass was the first thing you noticed about Hector, but the face was what you remembered. He wore a grungy navy blue baseball cap, with the logo long worn off, tightly over long gnarly hair that forced its way out from under the cap edges and was then pulled back to hang down his back past his shoulders. Darting bloodshot eyes peered out from under the cap's bill, never really focusing or resting on any particular object, just incessantly looking here then there in a paranoid fashion. Even drunk or stoned, the eyes never ceased. A full bushy beard and mustache covered the majority of his acne scarred face and surrounded a mouth full of crooked and broken stained teeth. The foul odor that emitted from the hole, especially when he breathed hard from exertion, which just about any movement for him was laborious, or laughed, smelled as you'd imagine coming from such a place. He also had an unusually large mole resting under his right eye. The mole subjected him to constant teasing when growing up, and one of these days he'd pay to have it surgically removed. That had been his plan for the last eight years anyway. Those that remembered Hector, remembered that he looked like a crazed wild man with darting eyes. They also remembered the smell; a combination of fat person sweat, sex, alcohol, and the terrible bad breath. Most people didn't want to remember him. In fact, many spent years trying to forget, especially those that had been smothered in the stench as the humongous naked blob thrust on top of them.

Frank Senich noticed the blob that was named Hector as he climbed down from his 18-wheeler, and scanned the entire parking lot of the truck stop. He'd been traveling all day on Interstate 90, hoping to make Montana before nightfall. Due to a longer than average delay with some construction, and then wanting to veer off the Interstate to go peek at Devil's Tower, something he'd only seen in *Close Encounters of the Third Kind* years ago, he was stopping in Sheridan for the night. He'd still make Missoula the next day. His situational awareness was always on high the first couple of minutes he arrived anyplace new, once satisfied everything was okay, he'd relax a bit, but not much. When it came to Col. Cooper's color code of awareness, Senich lived in a state right between yellow and orange. He wasn't just alert, as yellow dictated, but he wasn't focused on any particular threat as Cooper's orange set forth. He was just intensely focused on everything. Not much escaped his gaze, good or bad, and he definitely picked up some bad vibes from the six-foot, three hundred and ninety pound, mass using the wall to stay upright.

Senich had left his truck outside the park and rode his bicycle in to see Devil's Tower, and just to make the experience complete, he jogged around the paved trail at the base before cycling back to his truck. He was glad for the exercise, which he worked into each day regardless of where his routes took him, but in the warm June sun, he had worked up quite a sweat and was starting to smell ripe. Gym bag with toiletries and clean clothes in hand, he headed across the dimly lit parking lot. The sun had just set, and there were not many lights on this side of the building. The front, where the gas pumps were located, was well lit, but the side and back where truckers parked for the night had few lights. Senich's five-foot eleven and 190 pound athletic body was dwarfed by Hector's bulk as he purposefully walked in a direction that would take him right next to the blob before going around the corner to the front where he could find the showers. He calmly studied every inch of the behemoth as he walked by, noticing Hector wouldn't look him in the eye, even though the truck driver tried to make contact. The gaze and expression on Senich's face was not one of, 'could I take you,' but rather, 'how I'd take you.' At the closest distance he came to Hector, he gave the fat man a smirk of contempt and disgust, smelling what wasn't today's exercise like came from his own pits, but the smell of a continuous lack of personal hygiene over a long length of time. That, combined with the distaste he held for anyone who didn't keep himself fit, had him wishing the fat smelly slob would say something challenging, just so he could smack him for being stupid. But Hector ignored him, maybe sensing the predator underneath, and Senich turned the corner, went inside, and found the showers.

Thirty minutes later, Senich passed Hector again. He wore fresh socks and underwear, clean Levi's, and a brand new Devil's Tower T-shirt he picked up at the souvenir shop earlier that day. He bought the shirt just to tell his buddy, Ben Baker, he had been there and got the t-shirt. It was an old running joke the two had from various places they ventured, always getting t-shirts to memorialize their journeys. He trimmed his beard and shaved his neck before letting the hot water pound down on sore muscles from the day's exercise surrounded by long periods in the cab of his truck. The sitting was worse on his back and body than all the running, hiking, and bicycling he could fit in combined. Once clean and dressed, he slicked his long hair back where it hung past his shoulders. He let it grow when he got out of the Army because he could, and now he kept it long because he didn't know what else to do with it. Maybe if he decided to ever marry again, the future Mrs. Senich would decide how he should wear it. For now, draped over his shoulders and short in front, sort of like Swayze wore in *Road House,* suited him fine. He was actually copying Swayze's look from the film when he originally let it grow out, but Ben was the only one he ever admitted it to. Both men had enjoyed the movie when they got out of the military, and both had worked the door at strip clubs during those younger years. They figured since they spent enough time in them during their military years, they ought to get paid for it as civilians. Unfortunately, it wasn't the same when you were working, even though they both broke the rules a time or two and slept with the girls they guarded. The job was about keeping the girls safe and the establishment from being destroyed by violence or lawsuits, not about fucking and fighting. It was much more about people skills than those honed in the gym, and Baker had always been one up in that area. He was the talker, and when he fought he used those fancy martial art moves, Senich was the thrasher and knew how to break things and people. But what the hell, it was an experience to tell stories about.

Frank noticed Hector hadn't moved while he was inside, and he also noticed the new Peterbuilt truck that pulled in next to his while he was showering. The driver was standing by his passenger side door and looking at Hector as he pointed toward the back of the truck stop where the only light was burnt out, making the area very dark. Hector glanced at Senich and back to the truck driver and shook his head. In the dim light, mostly coming from the well illuminated front area of the truck stop, Frank noticed Hector's shaking head from the corner of his eye, and also saw Hector motion with his hands as if to say, "wait a minute." He continued to walk toward his rig, carrying the bag that now contained his dirty laundry along with his toiletries with his left hand. His right hand brushed his front right pocket, where he had transferred his tactical folder from the dirty jeans to his clean ones. "Fucker," he said to himself as he wondered if it were drugs or women, or both, that the fat piece of shit against the wall was selling, or at least orchestrating. He didn't know if Hector was a boss or just a middleman, but he knew he was involved. The negative vibes he had earlier were seldom wrong.

He tossed the bag into the truck, and immediately headed back from where he came. This time, Hector watched Senich almost as closely as Senich watched him earlier. The difference was Hector could only focus on one thing at a time, Senich noticed more than just the object he focused on. He saw the Peterbuilt's driver move toward the rear of his truck and linger without really doing anything. He noticed his feeble attempt to look casual as he continuously looked over to Hector and back to his own steel toed boot covered feet, purposely avoiding everything else. He also knew the lot was vacant other than the three of them, unless some of the parked trucks had sleeping drivers locked inside. He walked the same line as before. This time, as he neared Hector and smelled the

ALAIN BURRESE

foul odors, their eyes met. Hector puffed himself up off the wall. He was used to his size intimidating others and used it to his advantage when ever he could. This time however, he couldn't quite figure it out. Sure, he had been drinking and was half drunk, but did the little pip squeak, that was barely half his size, really smile at him when he had given his most intimidating stare and threatening look?

Frank Senich was still smiling as he entered the truck stop café and ordered a chicken fried steak, mashed potatoes, with a side of corn, from the waitress who had most likely been quite a looker thirty years ago. She looked rough around the edges, but still had a pleasant smile, and became even more friendly when Frank called her by name, which he read from her name tag. "How are you this fine night Shirley?" he asked as she refilled his coffee cup and told him his meal would be right out.

"Mighty fine, thank you for asking. How about yourself pardner?"

"I'm great, just cleaned up after a long run today. I'll be fantastic when that food gets here."

"I'll get it here as soon as its ready, and I'll make sure its hot and plenty of it. How's that sound?"

"Mouth's watering already."

"It won't disappoint, I promise you that. Where you headed?"

"Taking a load to Seattle."

"Oh, I love that city. It's been a long time since I've been out that way. Do me a favor, be sure to have some fresh seafood for me, will ya?"

"Sounds like something I can do."

"Don't get me wrong, the beef here is great, but being landlocked makes a person yearn for fresh seafood now and then."

"I understand completely."

"Let me quit yackin', and go check on your dinner. You must be starved."

"Thank you Shirley." She hurried off and returned just as quick with a huge plate of food. Frank dug in and enjoyed every last bite, and was sipping on his third cup of coffee when Shirley returned to check on him again.

"Ready for a slice of pie?" she asked.

Frank smiled back, "I think I'll pass." He had seriously contemplated ordering a slice of the peanut butter chocolate monstrosity he eyed in the revolving cooler, but thought better of it, even though he had gotten in extra exercise that afternoon. The chicken fried steak and gallon of gravy on it and the potatoes was enough heart damaging consumption for the night.

"Sure hon? We have some tasty treats over there."

"I'm sure you do, but I'm stuffed from that hearty plateful I just downed."

"Well, can I warm that coffee up for you?"

"Sure." Frank slid his cup over to the edge of the table and Shirley filled it right to the lip without any spilling over.

"Holler if you need anything else, and whenever you're ready come on over to the cash register and I'll take care of you there."

"Thanks." Frank took a sip of coffee and looked at his watch and wondered what was going on outside. He looked at the bill Shirley had left on the edge of the table and appreciated that you could still get filled up for $8.99 at diners like this across the country. Even with the $1.50 added for coffee it was a lot cheaper than most chain restaurants. Hell, many appetizers cost more than his entire meal. He drained the last little bit of coffee from his cup as he stood. He placed the bill and a twenty beside the cash register and yelled over to Shirley who was wiping down a table in the corner, "Here you go Shirley, you keep the difference."

"Why thank you hon. You be sure to stop in again."

"Will do if I'm back this way." Senich stepped outside and took a deep breath and threw his arms back to stretch a bit. He shrugged his shoulders and twisted his neck some and let out an audible, "ah." He headed toward his rig, and when he rounded the corner he was surprised to see the lot vacant. The slug had moved from its spot on the wall and was nowhere to be seen. The Peterbuilt was gone too.

He didn't detect anything out of the ordinary as he meandered over to his parked truck. Climbing inside, he made himself comfortable and just sat there in the dark. He sat, he watched, he thought, he waited: all of which Frank Senich was very good at. Senich knew he should be sleeping so he could get an early start the next morning, but he wasn't tired yet. He even though of taking off and driving a bit further, maybe up to Billings. He'd at least be in Montana like he'd planned. Maybe he shouldn't have had that last cup of coffee. After about forty-five minutes, he noticed the fat blob come from behind the building and take up his perch along the wall. Frank thought to himself, "Should I, or should I just let it go and get some sleep?"

He answered himself by opening the door and climbing down from his truck. He purposefully walked toward Hector Gonzales, who watched him the entire way across the parking lot. One couldn't see how bloodshot Hector's eyes were in the dark, but it did appear to Senich that he was not as off balance as he'd been before. Maybe whatever he was on was wearing off and he was sobering up a bit. As he neared the hulking figure, Senich caught whiff of Hector's terrible body odor again as the foul blob tried to straighten. Someone with a weaker stomach may have lost their chicken fried steak and potatoes.

"What you need, man?" Hector spoke first.

"What you got?"

"I gots everything. Whatever your pleasure, I gots it. You want to snort it, pop it, smoke it, or stick your dick in it, I can get it for you."

"Really?'

"Bet your ass man. What's ya pleasure?"

"Can't sleep, little lonely."

"I hear ya. Say no more, I can fix you up. How ya like 'em? Skinny, fat, young?"

"I got a choice?"

"Ya always gots choices, man."

"How much?"

"Depends what you want."

"Just the basics I guess, you know, little action."

"Five Benjamins." Frank had two almost simultaneous thoughts when the words came out of the hole buried in Hector's beard and mustache. The first was of Ben Baker, who he was on his way to see in Montana, and the second was that it was awful expensive for a truck stop whore.

"That much? That seems high."

"Not for what I'm selling." Hector was confident that he had the best goods in town, which was pretty easy when he had the only goods in town. He and the other boys made sure no one else set up shop anywhere in Sheridan County. If you wanted anything of an illegal nature, Hector and his associates were the only ones to deal with.

"Hmmm, do I get to see before I buy?" He suspected Hector had some runaways locked up, and wasn't just pimping a few willing truck stop whores. That's why the price was so high. That and it was late and Hector thought he could demand more from some lonely horny trucker who's only alternative was Rosie Palm and her five finger friends.

"You pay first. You don't like what you see, you get four hundred back. You blow a nut, money well spent."

"You keep a hundred just for me looking?" He was sure now that Hector was selling captive runaways. You wouldn't go to the cops after you'd paid.

Hector puffed up his chest. "You want some fuckin' pussy or what? I got the best shit and the only shit around. Fuck my bitch or get the fuck out of here and quit wasting my time." Hector wondered again why his size and most threatening posture didn't seem to phase this guy. Everyone usually stepped back and caved to his demands, especially when he became agitated and started swearing. What the fuck? This dude smiled again.

Senich smiled just before he stepped to his right and threw a right hook into the area where the blob's ribs should be. His fist sunk into the folds of flesh. The strike would break most people's ribs, but on Hector it didn't even cause him to wince. Twisting at the hips and pivoting as if he were putting out a cigarette, Senich came in with another body shot with his left. It was like hitting a large foam pillow and the fist had the same effect as the first, it annoyed Hector and nothing more. Hector could absorb body blows all day, however the fat that protected him from feeling pain when hit also slowed him considerably. The sudden explosiveness of the attack also slowed him as it was completely foreign. No one had ever initiated an altercation with him, and it took his lizard brain a few extra seconds to comprehend just what was happening. When he did get his hands on people, he could create a lot of damage, it just took him a few seconds to do so. This night, he didn't have those seconds. Senich believed in continuous attack and overwhelming one's opponent with superior firepower, and as quick as those first two punches shot into Hector's large midsection, the third was on its way. Senich also followed the high-low or low-high theory of combining blows, so the third punch of his combination was a right hook to the mammoth's chin. All three strikes were fired in rapid succession and took less than two seconds to land. Hector hadn't even figured out what was happening, little lone try to hit back. While the first two had no effect on Hector's large mass, the third hook to the chin snapped his face to the right and twisted his neck... It was the same kind of punch Mike Tyson's opponents came to fear and dread as it sent many to the canvas. For all his mass, Hector's glass jaw was his Achilles heel. He lay unconscious as his three hundred and ninety pounds quivered like jello from the hard landing on the pavement.

Senich looked around. The parking lot was still deserted, and some of the lights out front had been turned off making the side lot a bit darker than it had been earlier. The only camera he'd seen had pointed at the pumps, and he was pretty sure the piece of shit at his feet wouldn't have set up shop someplace visible by recording devices. Now what? He sure the hell wasn't going to move him. Not without a forklift anyway. He decided to leave and headed back to his truck and fired it up. He checked his road atlas to see how far it was to Billings, and determined he had more than enough fuel, and could fill up there. He'd maybe take a nap sometime before Ben's, but right now he was jacked up and wouldn't sleep if he tried. Might as well hit the road and get a few miles closer. He pulled forward and glanced back at the large blob laying over beside the building. It looked like a cow that had been hit by a truck and lay on the side of the road. The thought gave Senich an idea. Inside the cab, Senich hardly noticed it a bit. In fact, it felt less than many community speed bumps as the truck's tires crunched bones and smashed both legs of the unconscious Hector Gonzales. A minute later Frank Senich was back on Interstate 90 headed North West toward Montana. He tapped his hand on the steering wheel and sang along with Lynyrd Skynyrd blaring from his CD player. There was a smile on his face.

Baker stopped at the library to return his daughter's books on the way home from work. Walking through the downstairs lobby, he observed the unique collection of individuals waiting to use the library computer lab. Two males were in an animated discussion about weapons. Baker figured they were just about out of high school or about ready to start college. Seemed like every year it was more difficult to differentiate ages of the younger generations. The one dressed in all black was swinging his ipod headphones around his head and asking his friend if he knew of the weapon that had three balls that you swung. Baker remembered his homemade bola from when he was a kid. He used to enjoy practicing with the throwing weapon, but he never did actually take any game with one by entangling an animal's legs as the weapon was designed to do.

"Yeah, those are cool." replied the taller of the two, dressed in ragged jeans and an oversized t-shirt with some band Baker didn't recognize on the front. The one in black continued to swing his ipod headphones and Baker heard him say something to the effect that you could really take a guy out with them. He headed up the stairs to return the books he was carrying, and thought to himself how people were fascinated with hurting and killing each other. But then, how many years had he spent mastering various weapons and empty hand fighting skills? Too many or not enough, depending on who you asked. Baker quickly stopped thinking of destruction and scanned the main area of the library as he passed through the sensors at the top of the stairs and turned toward the book drop to his left. His assignment was to return the books on the way home, so he didn't go any further to look for any books to check out. He just dropped the books into the slot labeled children and turned to head back down the stairs.

Passing the two weapon aficionados, Baker couldn't help himself. He had to listen to the two, now discussing the best way to dispose of a weapon. "Dropping it in the middle of the ocean is the best way," the one in all black said. The taller of the two started to say something about salt water corrosion, but Baker couldn't hear all of what was said before the guy's buddy interrupted, "I'm telling you, drop it in the middle of the ocean and you don't have to worry about that. It's the deepest part, no one will ever be able to find it."

The enthusiasm and matter-of-factness from the young man had Baker chuckling and shaking his head as he exited the building, crossed the parking lot, and got into his vehicle. "And just how are you going to get to the middle of the ocean from here in Western Montana," he said to himself as he turned out of the parking lot and headed toward home. He drove and continued to think of the two and wondered what they were planning where they would have to dispose of a weapon in the middle of the ocean.

By coincidence, *Dirty Deeds Done Dirt Cheap* by AC/DC came on the classic rock station the radio was tuned to, and as Baker started singing along, he wondered if that was what the two had been listening to with their ipod bolas. Maybe that's why they'll have to head to the ocean to dispose of something. He chuckled again, and thought of his Army days at the 2nd I.D. Scout Sniper School. The song always made him think of those days. One of the fellow sniper instructors had made business cards with "Sniper: Dirty Deeds Done Dirt Cheap" on one side, and "For a Small Remittance We Will Supply:

NKPA Ears, Knee Caps, Noses, Gold Teeth, Scalps, One Piece Complete Heads, Fingers. Also Specialize In: Arson, Assassinations, Revolutions, Counter-Insurgency, Riots, Coup-De-Etat, Street Fights, Bombings, Terrorism, and Sadism" on the back. For some reason he though of a fellow sniper who cut his arm up throwing a guy though the glass doors of the King Club in Itaewon, Seoul. He wasn't there that night, but was told the other guy was messed up pretty bad.

Smiling at the crazy shit he and those he ran with used to get into, he thought, "Where the hell are you Frank?" He needed to get a hold of his old sniper buddy so they could figure out what to do next. Out of everyone he could think of, Frank was the only person he knew who would not try and talk him out of anything, but rather would offer assistance along with the skills, gear, and guts to back it up. "This is stupid, I have a family now. I'm a member of the Bar. I'm not that young, care-free, and stupid sniper any more." Baker wrestled with the thoughts and plans that had been forming ever since finding the box and little girl in that trailer house two days before. The thoughts consumed more and more of his waking moments and even some of his sleep. He woke several times due to dreams the previous night that he just couldn't remember, other than they were disturbing. "Someone needs to do something." He continued to talk to himself as he neared his house. "Those fuckers need to be stopped," he said angrily through clenched teeth. Pulling into his driveway, he nodded, "and I know how to stop them." Where the hell was Frank?

"Daddy! I want to show you something."

"Well, come and give me a hug first." Baker slipped out of his shoes and slid them under the shoe shelf by the kitchen door. He bent down to give his five-year-old daughter, Coral, a hug. Regardless of what he was feeling, no matter how bad a day, he couldn't help but feel better when he looked into those bright blue eyes, like her Daddy's, and that fabulous smile always made him smile in return. "How are you today?"

"Fine."

"What did you do when Daddy was at work?"

"Daddy, I want to show you something." She grabbed his hand and started to pull him through the kitchen toward the family room. As they left the linoleum tile, Coral let go and pirouetted, making her purple flower patterned dress fly up as she spun. Her brown hair, which hung to the middle of her back, also flew up and spun around. She brushed her hair from her face and with a giggle shouted, "See!" Her finger pointed toward the fireplace where at least one hundred small plastic animals and figures were lined up beside each other. Larger stuffed animals lined up in rows behind them. All of them faced a small plastic rock which had a plastic lion standing atop, looking out over the assortment of stuffed and plastic animals and critters Coral had meticulously placed in order.

"Wow, look at all of them."

"It's Pride Rock, Daddy. Just like *Lion King*." She danced around, excited to show off her morning project. Her purple dress and hair continued to swirl.

"Is he the king?" Baker kneeled beside the lion atop Coral's Pride Rock.

"Of course Daddy. Lions are the king of the jungle. Roaaarrr!"

"Oooohhh, come here, little lion." Baker grabbed his daughter and pulled her in for another hug. "You little lion cub." She pulled away and then came forward with a punch to his stomach as he was standing up.

"You forgot to maki" she laughed, using the Korean word for block. She came in for another punch and Baker blocked it.

"I'll get you," he said as he threw a slow round house kick toward Coral's side. She put up her arms to stop his leg. Sure, if he threw a full force kick, there was no way she could block it, but he was happy that they were making hapkido, the Korean self-defense art, fun and something she was enjoying to learn. In time, he would teach her more seriously, but for now learning some basics and enjoying it were important. She ran over and grabbed his wrist. "The other way," he said. She changed her grip on his hand and twisted his wrist into an outer wrist lock.

"You better nak-bup" she giggled as Baker slowly went to the ground and slapped the carpet with his other hand. Nak-bup, or falling, was one of the most important parts of the art he was teaching Coral. He couldn't count how many times his judo and hapkido training had saved him from injury during nasty spills. Bike accidents, skiing, trying things he shouldn't have. Knowing how to hit the ground and not get hurt was an important survival skill for many occasions. It was a skill he wanted Coral to possess.

"You got me." Baker tapped the carpet with the universal submission sign and Coral let go of his wrist and laughed more. "What's the important part of nak-bup?"

"Don't hit your head silly. Silly Daddy." She bobbed her head from side to side as he stood back up.

Behind them, Tanya Baker stood and watched the two play. It always amazed her of how gentle and caring Benjamin was with Coral. Tanya only knew part of what her husband was capable of. She didn't really want to know it all. She knew of his time in the military, that he was Airborne and a sniping instructor. But other than the movies, she didn't really know what that meant. She just knew he did tough guy stuff, like in *Rambo* she guessed.

She knew before law school he lived in Asia studying martial arts and that he continued to train. She would sometimes go down to the basement where he trained and catch him drawing his pistol and taking aim across the room, or doing things with one of his umpteen knives. She was also used to the thundering thumps from the garage when he was outside working his heavy bag. She would watch him sometimes and shudder at the thought of being hit with one of his punches or elbows. She had also watched him with some of his training partners and couldn't figure out how slamming each other around as hard as they did could be considered fun. He'd come home with a black eye and laugh that he should have gotten out of the way.

Tanya was a bit afraid of Ben's guns and knives, and didn't really like them around. She was glad that he agreed to lock them up after Coral was born. She didn't mind the tactical folder he left on the dresser when he changed clothes, but it was a relief to know the big scary ones were locked up. Although it was still scary the way he opened the folder so quickly, even for simple things such as opening a package

ALAIN BURRESE

from UPS. She sometimes wondered how many times he had to practice something like that to be able to get the knife from his pocket, open, and slashing tape as fast as he did. He drew and opened the knife as comfortably as most people lift a fork from their plate to their mouth.

It was such a contrast to see him being so gentle with Coral. Honestly, she was a bit worried about what kind of father he would be, especially when they learned she was pregnant with a baby girl. Now she was amazed at how good of a father he was. How he always took time to talk with her, to read with her, and to take part in her activities. She was also glad he was teaching Coral hapkido. She wanted her daughter to know how to protect herself.

"Mommy. I twisted Daddy's hand."

"I see that."

"Hi honey, where were you?" Baker ruffled Coral's hair as he turned to talk with his wife.

"Down stairs putting a few things away. We went shopping this afternoon."

"What's for dinner?"

"Hi honey, what's for dinner? It's nice to see you too."

"Sorry, how was your day?"

"Good. We met Susan and Randy at the park. Susan and I had a nice talk while those two played. They had fun too. We then stopped at the supermarket on the way home. Just got here ourselves. She wanted to get here before you so she could show you her animals. She spent all morning lining them up."

"You saved those just for me?" Baker asked as he turned back to Coral who had turned on the television.

"Shhh… Spongebob."

"Don't shhh your daddy when he's talking to you."

"Can you record it?"

"You don't need to watch tv right now," Baker told her.

"But, Daddy."

"Listen to your dad and turn it off."

"Okay." Coral went over to the television and held her finger over the on/off button reluctantly as she continued to watch her program.

"Come on, turn it off and let's get ready to go."

"Go where?" she asked hitting the off button.

"Yeah, go where?" asked Tanya.

"Well, since you haven't made dinner yet, and it is Friday, let's go get something. What do you want?"

"Pizza!" yelled Coral.

Baker looked at Tanya with an inquisitive look. Tanya shrugged, "We haven't had pizza in a long time. Sounds fine by me. Not having to cook two nights in a row, this is special." She grinned at her husband.

"You want me to go get one from Pappa Murphy's, or should we go and eat somewhere?"

"I want to eat at a restaurant," Coral chimed in.

Baker looked at Tanya again, "What do you want?"

"Sure, let's go somewhere. We haven't been to Freemo's in a long time. Coral likes it there."

"Freemo's! Daddy, remember the one time when I was three and we went to Freemo's and I lost my ball. I cried a lot, remember?"

"Yes, I remember." He wasn't sure if she was three or four when that happened, but whenever Coral talked about things in the past she would say, "remember when I was three."

"I won't cry this time Daddy."

"Good, I don't want my girl crying."

After all they could eat at the pizza buffet at Freemo's and a couple dollars worth of tokens in the games, the three returned home where Tanya ran a tub and helped Coral with her bath while Ben read the recent issue of *Journal of Asian*

Martial Arts that was beside the couch. When she was done with her bath and had pajamas on and teeth brushed, Coral came out with an arm full of books. "Will you read with me Daddy?"

"Sure, what do you have?"

"I want this one first," she said as she held up *The Jungle Book*.

They read three stories before it was time for bed. Coral kissed her dad goodnight and went to be tucked in by her mom. Once asleep, Tanya came out and plopped down on the couch beside her husband, who was watching a military documentary on the Discovery Channel. "Oh, I forgot to tell you," she said, "There was a message on the machine when I got home from Frank."

"I wonder why he didn't call my cell. What did he say?"

"Not much, just 'hey it's Frank, talk to you later.'"

Ben, Tanya, and Coral Baker spent the day up the Bitterroot. After a lazy Saturday morning of sleeping in by all three of them, they got up, piddled around, ate breakfast and finally loaded into the red Dodge Durango. The three had a summer ritual of going on 'nature walks' when nothing else was planned. Coral, even at five years old, was quite the little hiker. When she did start getting tired, Ben and Tanya would tell her she needed to practice walking longer distances for Disneyland. This always perked her up.

They drove up through Hamilton to Blodgett Canyon. A friend had told Ben it was a nice hike, and it was somewhere they hadn't hiked before. Besides, it gave them an excuse to stop at Naps in Hamilton for a late lunch. The hike was nice and the breeze made it enjoyable even though they did get a late start and worried that it might become too hot. It was a beautiful Montana day, and they even saw a couple of rock climbers on one of the cliffs they were hiking below. They hiked up the trail for about forty-five minutes, stopping to look at flowers, walk on logs, climb rocks, and wonder at anything else that caught their eye. Coral talked non stop about this and that, and enjoyed the butterflies and flowers most of all. After forty-five minutes, they turned around and headed back toward the camp ground and parking area where they left the Durango.

There was a lake you could hike to farther in, but it was too far for Coral. Ninety minutes was a good distance for her. It was getting time for lunch anyway. Ben and Tanya

ALAIN BURRESE

purposefully ate small breakfasts knowing they would stop at Naps Grill after the hike. The huge 12 ounce burger that you could top with all the fixings yourself came with a large basket of fries and a Coke when you got the Naps Deal. Tanya shared her deal with Coral and all three still ate too much.

"That's a week's worth of fat." Ben commented as he ate the last fry out of his basket and reached for another one from the basket Tanya and Coral were sharing.

"It was good though," replied Tanya.

"Hey, you already had yours. These are ours." Coral pulled the basket of fries over toward her side of the table. She was sitting in a booster seat in the booth beside her mom, and had finished the hamburger section Tanya had given to her and had also eaten quite a few fries.

"You can share with Daddy. Who got it for you?"

"Okay, you can have this one." Coral held up a fry.

"Let me go pay for this, and we should get home. I want to try getting a hold of Frank again."

"Let me take her to the bathroom." Tanya got up and snatched the last fry from the basket. "Let's go wash our hands." She led Coral to the bathroom while Ben paid for their lunch and refilled both their Cokes from the fountain dispenser near the back of the restaurant past the grill and all the hamburger fixings. He watched a dirty long haired man of about forty-five come in. The guy was wearing filthy torn jeans, a stained t-shirt with a faded picture of some kind on the front, and a black leather vest that had numerous patches sewn on it. One of the patches was a Ranger tab and Baker wondered if they guy had ever served. If he had, he sure didn't act or move like a Ranger now. Most likely a wannabe who thought the vest was cool. He noticed the elderly couple in the corner opposite of the one he had sat in give the newcomer a look of disgust. You could tell they were not happy with the sorts of people that sometimes frequented their small community. Baker noticed a hat hanging on a hook on the post by the older couple's booth that he hadn't paid attention to before.

He looked back at the way the older man was sitting and then at the man's eyes. The eyes that were watching the dirty intruder take a seat close to the grill. Baker walked over to the older couple's table. He held a Coke in each hand and smiled as he approached. The older gentleman had become tense, and Baker attempted to be as unthreatening as he could. "Excuse me, sir?"

"Yes, young man." The green eyes scanned up and down and Baker knew the man was assessing him, just as he did with everyone he looked at.

"I couldn't help but notice that of the two people in here with Ranger tabs on their clothing, you are the only one who actually served."

The man glanced over his right shoulder at the hat that hung on the hook and smiled. "You did, did you?"

"Yes, sir. I spent some time with the 82nd myself. Also served with the 2nd I.D. It was in the 80s though, a bit after you served I'm guessing."

"82nd is a good outfit."

"I'm guessing you were with the 75th in Vietnam?"

"Yes I was. I'm Mark Dunn." He stood to shake hands.

"Benjamin Baker, nice to meet you sir." Baker tucked the Coke between his left forearm and side so he could shake hands.

"And this lovely lady is my wife of forty-four years, Marjory."

Baker turned and took Marjory's hand. Her husband had introduced her just as she was chewing a bite of her chicken sandwich. "Pleasure to meet you ma'am." She swallowed and replied likewise. He turned back to Mark who had sat back down. "I just wanted to thank you for your service, and let you know some things don't go unnoticed by everyone."

"Thank you son, and thank you for your service as well."

"And this is my wife Tanya, and the little one is Coral," he said as the two came up beside him. "This is Mr. and Mrs. Dunn. Can you say hello?"

"Hello," came a shy reply from behind her Daddy's leg. While talkative with people she knew, it was still hard to get her to greet strangers. That was a good thing, but he wished she would say hello louder when he or her mom were with her.

"Nice to meet you," Tanya said to the elderly couple.

"I'll let you get back to your lunch. Again, I just wanted to say thank you."

"No problem son, I'm glad you did. You folks take care."

The three left the restaurant and Tanya asked, "Who was that?"

"Just an older veteran," Ben replied as he opened the Durango and lifted Coral up into her booster seat and strapped her in. "He was a Ranger in Vietnam. I wanted to thank him for his service."

The drive home was uneventful. Coral fell asleep and Tanya listened to the radio and watched the scenery go past as Ben drove. Neither were very talkative. Tanya was thinking about laundry and if they even needed dinner that night after the huge lunch. Ben was wondering when Frank would call again. He decided he'd try Frank's cell again and pulled his out. Tanya gave him a look that said, "you know I don't like cell phones and driving."

On the second ring Ben heard a familiar, "Hello, it's Frank."

"Frank, it's Ben. I've been trying to get a hold of you. Where are you?"

"I'm at your place, where the hell are you?"

"My place?"

"Yeah, I got to town a half hour or so ago. You weren't around, so I went and grabbed a sandwich at Subway and came back to wait for ya."

"I'm headed back now. I'm about twenty minutes out of town. Should be there pretty quick."

"You eat?"

"Yeah, we ate. Not as healthy as you though. Just topped off a huge burger and a ton of fries."

"Good, you'll need to exercise. Why don't we go for a run when you get here. You can tell me what's up."

"Sounds good. See you in a short bit." Baker turned the phone off.

"He's in town?" Tanya asked.

"Yep. I didn't expect him to show up. We're going to go for a run, I need to work that lunch off."

"You going to want me to cook dinner?"

"Nah, let me see what's up. We can figure dinner out later. We'll go out or grab something to bring back. You don't have to fix anything special."

"Okay, just let me know. It's no problem if you want me to make something."

They drove the rest of the way in silence. Baker hadn't expected Frank to show up like that. He'd been waiting for him to call. A million thoughts were racing through his head as he tried to figure out the best way to disclose his thoughts to his best friend and former sniper buddy. Now that he was here in person, there was more to share with him than if they had been talking on the phone. He originally just wanted to float a couple ideas Frank's way to see if he was crazy or if it was something the two of them would look into. Now that Frank was here, things were different, and decisions would need to be made much quicker. He wondered if Frank would be on board, but couldn't imagine him not wanting to get involved. This was what Frank lived for. Baker looked in the mirror at Coral asleep in her booster seat. Her head was flopped over to the side in a way that made Baker stretch his own neck. He then glanced at Tanya who was looking out her side window. Yeah, Frank lived for this kind of thing, but what was he doing having these kinds of thoughts. He was a family man now. A Deputy County Attorney. Thoughts from the previous night on the couch came back. He was also a sniper. A warrior. Someone who could make a difference. The question still nagged, if he didn't, who would?

* * *

The reunion was quick. When Baker arrived at his house, Senich met him already dressed for a workout. He said hello to Tanya and Coral and asked Ben if he was up for a run. Baker changed and the two took off. After the huge lunch, Baker was eager for the exercise. Running with his old Army buddy made it that much more enjoyable.

Just out of the driveway, Senich told him, "I have to leave tonight. On a trip to Seattle."

"I was hoping you could stick around."

"Let me get this load dropped off, then I'll come back. I have a couple weeks I can take if you want."

"That might be good."

"So what's up?"

Baker though of how he wanted to tell his buddy what happened. He hadn't expected to have this conversation today. They'd never BSed each other, so he laid it out. "I'm in some shit, Frank. I killed a guy the other night."

"What?" Senich about stopped. The two slowed their pace and Baker told his friend about the school shooting, about Bruce James, and about the events that transpired at the trailer a few nights before.

"But you were trying to get a hold of me before that."

"Yeah, I was, but now things are a bit different."

"I'll say." The two ran a ways in silence. "Damn, buddy. I'm sorry I didn't call more. I just figured I'd surprise you and show up."

"It's alright, I'm glad you're here."

"Sorry I have to leave right away."

"It's okay, I have to leave too. I have a conference over in Helena Thursday and Friday. We are going over on Wednesday."

"I'll be back on Wednesday or Thursday."

"I'll give you a key. You can crash at the house. We'll be back Saturday morning."

"Sounds good. But Ben, what am I coming back to?"

"I don't know, we'll figure it out when you get here."

Frank Senich was down in Baker's basement perusing the book shelves. Since he couldn't sleep, he figured he'd check out the library of books and videos to find something to kill some time. After noticing over twenty different versions of Sun Tzu's *Art of War*, including *Sun Tzu for Success* and *The Art of War – Spirituality for Conflict*, in the Asian section, Senich shook his head. Baker always had been precise and organized, and he always went overboard with stuff. Of course Senich had read Sun Tzu's classic work, but twenty plus copies? Senich also made a mental note to put things back exactly how he found them or he'd hear about it. He remembered how picky Baker got with his books, videos, and music. He moved over a shelf and pulled out TC 23-14. It was the *U.S. Army Sniper Training Manual*, one of at least thirty books on sniping or snipers grouped together. He looked through the manual remembering when he and Baker first studied the text, and how they learned to apply the skills in the woods of Korea, and then put it back on the shelf next to *The Ultimate Sniper* by John Plaster. The original and the updated and expanded edition were both on the shelf. Senich started to pull out the newer volume to check the differences and then thought better of it. Maybe a video would help him sleep rather than a book. He went over to where the VHS tapes and DVDs took up several shelves of their own.

He pulled a video out, *B and E: A to Z How to Get in Anywhere, Anytime*. He remembered pitching in when Baker ordered it for $99.99 back when they were in Korea. It was expensive, but they had extra cash and a few dollars to help with necessary skills that any good sniper should posses seemed practical. Three of them contributed, so it was less than the cost of an overnight for each if you looked at it in those terms. And it was far less than one "business trip" would bring in. Senich thought of the "business" they used to do that purchased that video, as well as many cases of OB and more overnights than you could count. Black marketing had been very good to them back then. He noticed *B and E: A to Z Volume II* next to the original video and pulled it out. At least it had a color cover, the first one they bought together came in a plain black plastic case. Baker had always been better at entering, Senich was more of a breaking kind of guy. He didn't bother practicing that picking stuff much when he could get in by smashing a window, or smashing through the door for that matter. He'd done both more than once. He did have to admit that Baker's skills had come in handy a time or two, and it was something he should have learned more about.

High Speed Entry looked interesting. He started to pull the video from the shelf and then stopped. "What the fuck?" The door upstairs had opened and it sounded like someone coming into the house. He had left the door unlocked, but Baker and his family wouldn't be coming in at 2:00 a.m. Maybe they came home for something, but what?

"Shhh,watch it." Sounds of two people trying to be quiet, but not doing a very good job at it, came down the stairs. They were whispering to each other, but Senich couldn't make out much of their conversation. It sure the hell wasn't Baker or Tanya, he knew that. He stayed still and strained to hear what was going on upstairs.

Senich swore to himself again. His Sig Sauer P220 Carry Elite Dark was upstairs in the bedroom he was staying in. The

.45ACP would be nice to have right now, he doubted the two upstairs were there for a friendly visit. He looked over at Baker's gun cabinet and wondered where he kept the keys. Becoming a father had civilized Baker, he kept his firearms locked up. His Blackhawk Crucible II folder was clipped inside the right front pocket of his Levi's. A lot of good that did him, they were upstairs too. They lay on the floor of the guest bedroom where he left them earlier. The running shorts and t-shirt he was wearing didn't provide for carrying, but then he shouldn't need anything late at night in the house. He was glad he was still up. Being in the basement was a lot better than being upstairs asleep with trouble entering through the back door. He looked to the corner with Baker's martial art weapons. Hanging from a series of hooks across the wall were nunchaku, canes, umbrellas, and short batons. Dan bong is what Senich remembered Baker calling them in Korean. He noticed a Delta Dart hanging in a neck sheath from one hook, and a couple of Nightshade Grivory blades hanging there as well. He wondered how many of the fiberglass reinforced plastic knives Baker had hidden around the house. Sure, he worried about Coral, but he also was one to be prepared. Senich had owned a number of Grivory blades himself, and some of the earlier models made from Zytel. They were strong, sharp, and impervious to the elements. The main attraction was they didn't set off metal detectors. Silently moving over to the hooks, he took the Delta Dart and hung the 550 parachute cord around his neck. Baker had replaced the metal chain the Darts came with just as he had. The parachute cord was strong, but more importantly, why have a blade that passed through metal detectors attached to a metal chain. The sheath and dart hung in the middle of his chest. He pulled it out to check the tension of the sheath and ensured the dart wasn't damaged, and quickly secured it back in its sheath. He continued to look around to see what might be available. The dart would be good back up, but he would prefer to be better armed, especially when facing more than one. Maybe he should sneak out to the truck and grab his backup Sig. In the corner he noticed different length staffs, escrima sticks, bamboo and wooden swords. There were also a couple black training swords made from a heavy grade polypropylene. He didn't want a training weapon, he wanted his .45. He thought about taking one of the escrima sticks, it would be better than nothing.

Senich then saw what he was looking for. All that Asian martial art stuff was fine for Baker, but Senich liked things simple. He was glad to see Baker also had something more up his alley. Among the staffs and swords in the corner were two black baseball bats. One said Brooklyn Smasher on it, and the shorter one stated Brooklyn Crusher. He grabbed the longer one and noticed it was made by Cold Steel, Baker's preferred knife maker. Figures, and Baker would buy one of each size. But what the hell, he knew the company too, and knew the bat would be tough. The bat was heavy and felt good in his hands as he slowly moved toward the door and the stairs. Smasher, that's appropriate he thought choking up a bit on the bat's handle. It was quiet upstairs. He figured the two went back toward the bedrooms. He silently crept up each step, gently placing his bare feet and pausing each time the wooden stairs made a noise. With each pause he listened for any sign that those above him heard his approach. The sniper's stalk was reminiscent of a lion creeping up on its prey.

"There's nobody here." Joey Mullen whispered. Frustrated, he looked around the bedroom again. He was about 5'8" tall and weighed a sickly 120 pounds. It was hard to tell if he was sweating due to the absence of people in the room since his face was always splotchy and sweaty. His eyes darted from one side of the room to the other. It was difficult to determine if his eyes or the beam from the cheap flashlight moved around quicker. His partner, who went by the self-prescribed moniker Spider fidgeted by the door. Spider was two inches taller but even skinnier than Joey. In the dark, without a flashlight, he picked at an open sore on his left upper arm. Both men were in their early twenties but appeared much older. Dirty and rank, the pair made a disgusting duo.

Through decayed teeth, Spider replied, "let's just get out of here."

"What about the money?"

"We'll get it someplace else, come on let's go. I don't like this."

Joey's mouth was as foul as Spiders with decaying teeth, and his entire body produced foul odors from the chemicals emitted from his skin. "I need that five hundred bucks."

"We'll get it someplace else." Spider fidgeted even more, looking toward the door they came in and back to Joey every couple of seconds. The sore on his arm was trickling blood from where he continuously dug into it with the nails of his right hand.

"Fuck you, I need that money!" Joey's outburst made Spider leap back farther into the hallway and away from the bedroom door. He smacked his elbow against the wall and let out a small yelp.

Nervous at what Joey might do, Spider reached into his back pocket and pulled out a rusted screwdriver he had found and sharpened with a file from his old man's garage. He knew better than to get caught taking anything from his father, but sneaking in to use his tools once in a while didn't hurt. The screwdriver was his, found by a dumpster fair and square. If

Joey tried anything, he'd be sorry. "Grab some shit we can sell and let's get out of here."

"I want both!" Joey always figured on taking something to sell, but he also wanted the money they were promised. His babble became irrational as he started to pull out dresser drawers and rifle through them.

"Fuck this." Spider turned and headed toward the back door the two had come in and ran right into Frank Senich crouching in the kitchen.

Senich had crept into the kitchen and was watching the two meth heads argue as he determined what he wanted to do next. The stench filling the upstairs alerted him to what the two were. While alert, he wasn't expecting Spider to turn and come toward him in the kitchen as fast as he did. Seeing the screwdriver in his hand and the look of surprise as Spider recognized the human form in the darkness, Senich immediately sprung forward and swung the bat at the arm holding the tool. A definite crack of shattering bone was heard as the Cold Steel Smasher connected with Spider's skinny right forearm that was holding the screwdriver out in front of him. Immediately after the crack, a loud scream roared from Spider's rotting mouth. Spider's only thought was the pain coming from his broken arm as he grabbed it with his good hand and started screaming again about how much it hurt. Senich ignored the screams and came back with the follow up strike that struck Spider in his pale face right under his right eye. The Smasher lived up to its name, smashing the cheek bone into fragments and mush. Spider's unconscious body crumpled to the floor. Senich didn't know if he was unconscious or dead, and didn't care. He knew the meth addict was out of the fight, and now he only had one left to deal with. It was essential in this type of situation to focus on the moment, unburdened from responsibility or concern for anything other than prevailing. When you are outnumbered, you had to put people down and out so they couldn't come back at you a second time. Spider wouldn't be coming back. Senich's sole focus was on eliminating the remaining threat, he couldn't afford to dwell on possible consequences. There would be time for that later.

The adrenaline rushing through Senich's body made him hyper alert to everything around him. He quickly moved past Spider's motionless body toward the bedrooms. He was confident the two didn't have a firearm between them. Anything worth any money would be long gone, sold for the central nervous system stimulant the two depended on. He had no doubt he could take care of the second intruder with the Smasher. He still knew enough to be careful, overestimating one's capabilities while underestimating an opponent had cost many people their lives. Baker's twenty some copies of Sun Tzu probably said something like that. Senich couldn't remember, it had been quite a while since he read his only copy, the translation by Griffith. Sun Tzu also said it was better to subdue the enemy without fighting. Well, this wasn't one of those times.

Joey Mullen heard Spider's scream, but was too fixated on finding something he could pawn for his next fix to pay much attention. It must not have been too important, all was silent now. Frustrated that his rummaging hadn't unturned anything worth pillaging, Joey turned toward the door. Maybe there would be better stuff in the living room. A Blue-ray was easy to carry and would bring some money. He wondered where Spider went as he followed his dim light beam from the bedroom to the hall. "Spider, where are you?" He rounded the corner of the hall where it widened and turned right toward the living room. Doing so, he walked straight into the

Brooklyn Smasher that came out of the dark swinging for the bleachers.

Senich had always been an admirer of General George S. Patton, Jr., and had studied his principles and found they helped him numerous times in varied situations. Rather than enter the bedroom looking for the second intruder, he followed Patton's advice to never let the enemy pick the battle site. You always wanted to fight on your own terms whenever possible. He remembered Patton's words, "We will decide when and where we will kill the enemy." He set up a hasty ambush by waiting around the living room corner monitoring the hallway. Unless someone went out a window, they had to come down the hallway and turn right toward the living room and front door or left toward the kitchen and back door that the two had used to come in. Senich knew he just had to wait and surprise would be on his side. Something else Patton and Senich both believed in, the way to win is never to lose. Stacking the deck in your favor was smart, and the only thing not fair in a fight was losing. He didn't wait long when he heard Joey coming out looking for his partner. He thought about swinging for the body to smash a few ribs, but then decided the surer blow would be to the head. Late at night, he didn't know anything about the second intruder, and even when you do everything correctly you could still lose, even if only by chance. Just as Joey stepped into range, his head visible due to the illumination from the small flashlight, Senich went for a home run.

Twice in the same night the Brooklyn Smasher lived up to its name. The bat struck Joey just above the nose, crushing the bones that surrounded the eye sockets. His head snapped back violently, breaking the weak neck as his body slumped to the floor in a disfigured heap. Senich instinctively looked around to ensure the area was clear of any further threats. After any combat, you needed an after-action assessment. Neither of the two crumpled bodies were moving, and there were no other adversaries seen or heard. He then quickly checked himself for any injuries. Once all threats were eliminated, it was important to do a self-check for injury. Sometimes in the heat of battle you wouldn't realize you'd been hurt. After how many bar fights had he woken up the next day with a lump or bruise someplace and wonder, "when did I get hit there?"

Tonight, Senich hadn't been touched, and with the habitual assessment complete, he lowered the bat and took a couple deep breaths. He knew the feeling of coming down from an adrenal buzz, and was glad he'd been there before, both with adrenal stress training and actual fights and combat. He'd probably want to get laid in a bit. Back in the Army, they used to always keep an extra $20.00 tucked away for after bar fights. If you couldn't find a willing partner, you could always pay someone. Paying was often easier, served its purpose and you could leave without the small talk. For a second he wondered what the local night life was like. The next thing Senich thought was, "Ben's gonna be pissed."

He turned on the hallway light and looked at the two bodies lying motionless on the floor. He didn't think he needed to check further, but did so anyway. Neither body showed any signs of life. He knew legally he shouldn't, but he went through the pockets of the two anyway. He wanted information on who they were. There was nothing on the one in the kitchen, but inside the back pocket of the guy he'd ambushed he found a slip of paper. He unfolded it and saw a short list of words. Woman. Kid. Scare. No Hospital. 500.00. Below the list was an address, Ben's address. He tucked the piece of paper beside some bills standing in a desk organizer on the kitchen's hutch. Ben should see it before turning it over to investigators. If they decided to turn it over.

Senich coughed, the room stunk. The two smelled like they'd been dead for weeks before they came in, and he knew the stench would only get worse now that the rotting corpses lay dead on the floor. Normally there would be a little time before the smell, but these two had a head start. He walked over and opened the kitchen window and then opened both the back and front doors to create a draft. If he'd have been anyplace other than Ben's front room and kitchen, he would have sterilized the area of anything that could identify him and have left. That wasn't an option this time and he started thinking about how he would describe what happened as he picked up the phone and dialed 911. He then wondered if Montana had a Castle Doctrine law. He sure hoped so.

"Jesus, Frank."

"Jesus, Ritchie."

"What?"

"Last line from *A History of Violence*. Remember, William Hurt said 'Jesus, Joey' and Vig answered 'Jesus, Richie' right before putting a round through his head? Great movie."

"This is fucking serious. I come home and my house is a crime scene. You fucking killed two people in my living room."

"The first one was in the kitchen."

"Fuck." Baker threw his hands up and shook his head.

The police had just left. This was not what Baker was expecting when they left Helena that morning after having an early breakfast at JB's with a friend of Tanya's and her husband. The breakfast buffet was always a quick, easy choice, and they all found things they liked. He wanted to get back early to go over some things with Frank, and have time to get some other things that needed done accomplished as well. After an uneventful drive, he drove up to find two squad cars parked in front of his house. Instead of pulling into the drive way, he parked across the street and told Tanya to take Coral and go visit a friend or something. He told her he would call shortly to let her know what was going on. He also added she might want to plan on going someplace for lunch. Even though it was only 10:00, Baker had a bad feeling, and was worried about his friend. Whatever it was, he didn't want Tanya, and especially Coral, around till he knew what had happened. He was grateful that she readily agreed. He figured she didn't like the look of police cars out front either, and both of them wanted to shelter Coral as much as they could. She'd have to deal with the gruesome realities of life soon enough, no reason to rush things. Coral on the other hand wanted to go into the house, she was tired of the booster seat and wanted to play with her toys inside. Tanya drove off over Coral's objections, and left Baker to find out what was going on.

Officer Horwitz, in Baker's opinion, was one of the better police officers on the force, and the two men respected each other and each other's positions. Baker had gone to trial with Horwitz as a witness on a number of occasions and always found him to be competent and professional. He was the officer in charge and there really wasn't much left to do when Baker arrived. It appeared pretty clear cut that the two deceased had broken in to rob the place in Baker's absence, and unfortunately for them, they woke a sleeping Frank Senich, who happened to grab the baseball bat from the corner to defend himself. Lucky for him he had dozed on the living room sofa and that the bat was left by the front door.

Horwitz had seen enough innocent lives ruined by drug addicts that he had no remorse for the two bodies taken from Baker's house. To him, they got what they deserved. That's how he'd write this up and it would be a closed case. Nothing else needed to be done. After verifying with Baker that Senich's story was accurate, and that he indeed was staying there, Horwitz left. He'd tell his superiors he provided a little professional courtesy to one of the good guys and his friend. They had more cases than they could keep up with as it was, why worry about a couple dead drug addicts who picked the wrong house to burglarize? Harsh and cold for not caring about the deceased? Maybe. But that's what the job did to a person. Horwitz just wanted to put this one behind him so he could move on to the next. He wished they were all this easy.

After saying good bye to Horwitz, and the *History of Violence* exchange, Baker turned to Senich, who sat drinking coffee on the sofa watching an old Gregory Peck movie on the Turner Classic channel. "Help me clean up, so Tanya can come home."

"Don't be pissed at me, I was minding my own business in the basement when those two came in."

"So they didn't happen to wake you up?" Baker knew damn well the bat had been in the basement, and Senich would have had to been down there to come up and use it to 'defend' himself.

"Well, I thought that sounded better. You know, just woke up, didn't know what was going on, got scared, just reacted with that bat by the door."

"You were scared, huh?"

"Of course I was. Two hardened criminals broke into your house. I'm lucky to be alive." Frank smiled at his friend. "By the way, that Smasher smashes pretty damn nice."

"Right." Baker couldn't help but smile. He never had been able to stay mad at Frank for very long. He didn't know why, but he just couldn't. Even the times the two had gotten so mad at each other it went physical, they always pulled punches short and went for submission holds. Their's was like a good marriage, they never went to bed mad at each other, though a couple times they stayed awake all night drinking to get over their anger. He wished he'd have seen the two before the bodies had been taken away. Hardened criminals? Not hardly. They were a couple punk-ass meth addicts according to Horwitz. "Clean up in here while I go put stuff away in the bedroom. I'll give Tanya a call so she can come home. She's probably pretty worried. We can talk about what really happened after we get this place cleaned up."

"Ya think I could get some sleep?" It was 10:30 a.m. and Senich hadn't been to bed. It took the cops forever to arrive, interview him, search the place over, call the coroner, remove the bodies, interview him some more, wait around for Baker, and now the adrenaline was completely worn off and Senich was about to crash. Even the multiple cups of coffee he had downed during the interviews and waiting weren't having an effect.

"Yeah, sorry. Go crash and I'll finish up here and let Tanya know what happened. We can talk when you get up. Nothing's going to change now."

"Oh yeah, there was one more thing. I sort of forgot to give this to the police." Frank handed his buddy the piece of paper he had found in Joey Mullen's pocket. The smiles and jokes were absent as the two looked at each other when Baker looked up from the note.

"Sleep fast, we need to talk."

"Yeah, we do."

Baker's Durango wound its way up a dirt mountain road while Baker quietly drove and Senich admired the Montana scenery. They had traveled about an hour with very little talk between them. Baker was trying to decide just how he wanted to ask his best friend for assistance. It wasn't that he thought Senich would refuse, in fact he knew he'd quickly agree and most likely want to go further than Baker was thinking of suggesting. The two meth addicts proved he still didn't mind getting his hands dirty. He killed the two and didn't think twice about it. But now there was the note found in the dead guy's pocket. He wondered if it had anything to do with anything. He was a prosecutor, he made a lot of criminals mad. Who knew what the note meant.

It sure looked like someone targeted Baker's family, and he was glad he sent Tanya and Coral back to Helena for a longer visit with her folks. Baker made them pack immediately when they arrived home. After he quickly told Tanya what had happened, she agreed and then left with Coral in the Grand Caravan after short good byes. They told Coral she was going to get to visit grandma and grandpa more and that she could take swimming lessons in Helena. Ben wanted them out of town at least two weeks, so Tanya would sign Coral up for lessons Monday morning at the Helena pool. Tanya had first started to object, but seeing how serious Ben was, decided not to argue. She was spooked anyway, although she tried not to show how scared she was to Ben, so going to spend time with her parents sounded like a good idea. She was scared for Ben

ALAIN BURRESE

too, but had confidence that he would be okay. While she didn't know everything he was capable of, she was pretty sure that he and his best friend, who had just killed two people in their house, could handle quite a lot.

The radio played, but started to fade in and out with the poor reception in the hills. Senich pulled out a couple of CDs from a case Baker told him was under his seat. "That's right, you always liked the older stuff too." He put in a 1962 Billboard Top Rock 'n' Roll Hits collection. Skipping *Green Onions*, he went right to track two, *Duke Of Earl*, and started singing along. "Damn, haven't heard this for a long time. You know what I always think of when I hear this song?"

Baker decided to take a shot and replied with something the song always reminded him of, "The guys singing in the shower from *The White Shadow*."

"How the hell did you know that?" The look he gave Baker wouldn't have been more incredulous if Baker had started growing asparagus out his ears. The two hadn't met until serving in the Army, but they could easily have been brothers with the similar likes, dislikes, and upbringings the two had. It was sometimes uncanny how the two thought alike.

"That song always reminds me of that episode. It's about the only thing I remember from the show."

"Yeah, me too. You see Ken Howard in the new *Rambo*? He's getting old."

"We're all getting old, Frank."

"Not me,"

"What's all that gray around your temples from then?"

"Fuck you. The only reason you shave is because of the gray in your beard."

"I'm not the one saying I'm not getting old. I admit it."

"Good for you. I might admit it too, when I get old."

110

"It ain't the age, it's the miles."

"You got that right. Shit, we both had more miles by twenty-five than most get in a lifetime. And you're wanting to put on a bunch more aren't you?"

"What do you mean?"

"Come on. What are you planning? You sent Tanya and Coral away when I was sleeping, and when I woke up you already had the vehicle loaded. I'm guessing we are going up this mountain for a reason other than to show me the Montana sights, beautiful though they are."

"We're not doing anything this afternoon. Just thought we could bust a few caps and do some thinking."

"Thinking about what?"

"What to do next."

"So we have to drive out here to think?"

"I thought we might be able to think a little more clearly with rifles in our hands."

"I've no problem with that, but I still believe your thinking has already taken place."

"I thought it had, but this morning changed all that."

"Why?"

"What do you think? Two meth addicts break into my house. You kill them, and then that note you found."

"I didn't know if the note was related to that trailer house incident you told me about or not, but I figured I should keep it for only you. If it is related, it definitely puts some urgency on the matter."

"I don't know. There are a lot of people who might pay to hurt me." Baker started to think about what happened at his house the night before. "Fuckers won't come for me, they have to go for Tanya and Coral. I don't know who sent them, but we will."

"Calm down, you're driving." Senich had felt the Durango's speed picking up as Baker angered over the previous night's events. He wasn't against driving fast, but he didn't like the narrow dirt road with the sheer drop off on one side. "They're okay and we're going to take care of this."

"You're damn right we are."

"You had a plan before I got here, so what's different?"

"I'm not sure, but there's something going on that's more than I thought. And now the first thing is protecting Tanya and Coral."

"You think we should call Brian and Dave and ask if they can take a vacation to Montana?"

"No, I want to keep this between you and me right now."

"Beauty and the beast, huh?"

"Sniper and spotter."

"Roger that."

"Here we are." Baker pulled the Durango over and parked in what was nothing more than a wide spot in the road. If needed, you could fit four or five vehicles in the space, and it looked like at times people had. "Couple hundred yards up over there is a large clearing. Nothing else up here for miles. I know a guy who comes up here for elk every year and his freezer is always full. I don't think he gets them at the clearing we're going to, but farther in. Regardless, we can shoot the rest of the afternoon without disturbing anyone or being bothered."

"I see why you live in Montana."

"It has its advantages." Baker got out and opened the back door to retrieve the rifles he loaded while Senich was sleeping."

"Don't you guys also have some new law telling the feds to stay away from your guns?" Senich got out and came around the vehicle to help unload the firearms and gear.

"It's not exactly like that, but it will get interesting to see where it goes from here. Right now the law only applies to guns and ammo manufactured and sold in the state. We'll see what happens."

"What kind of goodies you bring?"

"Here's something if you want to play Army," he said as he handed Senich a Colt AR-15. The semi-automatic rifle resembled the M16 both men used while serving in the military. "And here's something if you want to play cowboy." Baker handed his buddy a lever action Winchester .30-30.

"But what if I want to really reach out and touch something?"

"Don't worry." Baker handed over a black duffle that weighed more than it looked. Besides hearing protection, blankets to lie on, and small socks filled with sand, it contained various boxes of ammo. "There's some .45 in there for you too." He then pulled out two more rifle cases for him to carry. He brought his .308 and his grandfather's .300 Weatherby Magnum. He wanted to let Frank try it out.

"Thanks." Senich slung the bag's strap over his shoulder. "What are those?"

"Bolt action Remington .308. Pretty close to the M-24 Sniper System we were using before we got out. The other is a .300 Weatherby Magnum I got when my grandfather died."

"Those will reach out there," Senich said with a grin. "I suppose you also brought your 9mm."

"I like my Hi Power. And it'll do the job with these." Baker slung the rifle cases over his shoulder and pulled out his Browning Hi Power. He released the magazine and tossed it to Senich.

"Sweet." Senich looked at the black tipped Winchester Ranger SXT Controlled Expansion rounds like an overweight couch potato looked at donuts and chips. "Law enforcement rounds?"

"Yep."

"I still like my .45 Sig." He tossed the 9mm magazine back to Baker, "But I feel better about you backing me up knowing you have those loaded." Both men smiled knowing the debate over which was better .45 or 9mm would wage on forever, and both knowing that what really mattered was hitting your target.

Baker nudged the Durango's door shut with his knee and headed for the trail to the yonder clearing. "Let's go make some noise."

* * *

The two spent almost three hours proving to each other they could still shoot. They walked off the distance across the clearing at just over 600 yards and marked some trees. They also put out some milk jugs, to simulate heads, half way across the open area. Both of them made head shots at three hundred yards with the .308 Remington, and they each hit torso sized trees between the shoulder and waist height marks at 600 yards with both the .308 and the .300 Weatherby Magnum. Both had made shots over 1000 yards with M21 and M24 sniper systems, and the .300 would reach out even farther than the .308, but for the afternoon, first round hits at 300 and 600 yards respectfully would suffice.

Both joked about the Weatherby Mark V kicking like a mule and used the cost of ammo as an excuse to switch to one of the other rifles. They shot closer distances with the Colt AR-15, but upped the ante by timing how quickly they could knock down targets. To finish the session, they held a friendly competition with their respective side arms. On the way back

114

to the vehicle, Senich reminded Baker, "I want that beer you owe me at a strip club. I know you have one, I saw the billboard coming in on 90."

"I don't really go to those places much anymore."

"Well, you should. And you are tonight."

"All right, we'll go after we get something to eat." Baker unlocked the Durango and started putting the rifles and gear into the back. Once loaded, they headed back down the dirt road they came on.

Rubbing his shoulder, Senich commented, "That Weatherby has some heavy recoil."

"It sure does." Baker shrugged his own shoulder some. "That was my grandfather's favorite caliber for hunting. He had a .300 Savage too. My uncle still has that one."

"It gets the job done. Speaking of, that help clear your head with your plans?"

"Yeah, it did."

"You gonna let me in on them, or just keep me around like a mushroom?"

Baker laughed, "I thought you liked it in the dark."

"Yeah, but I don't like bullshit, so tell me straight-up what you're thinking."

"I'm thinking I'm not going to get shit done as a lawyer."

"So?"

"I'm also thinking the incident I told you about last week is related to what happened last night."

"You think that child molesting fuck you took out is related to those two meth heads?"

"Not directly, but I think in some round about way they are."

"How?"

"Not really sure. Just a hunch."

"We need more than that."

"No we don't. As a prosecutor I would, but like I said, I don't think I'm going to get anything done as a lawyer."

"What the hell are you thinking?"

"I think those two last night were sent to my house to distract me from the extra investigation I've been doing. That's what I think."

"You never told me this." Senich reached behind the seat and pulled a Diet Coke out of the small cooler. "Want one?"

"Sure." After opening the can, he continued, "I told you I got that box from the guy's closet."

"Yeah."

"Well, I was doing some investigating. I was also talking to Detective Finch, who works with investigating child porn on the computer as well as real life. I was trying to put some pieces together to figure out who was involved. A few things are pointed over at Butte. Seems like where Interstates 90 and 15 intersect is a good point of transit for some of these kids. I don't have a lot yet, but that area is worth looking at closer. That's sort of what I was thinking when I called you."

"What got you interested in Butte?"

"Something Finch found on the computer. I'm not sure. I didn't want him to know I was looking into things more than my position would require."

"You doing all this on or off the clock?"

"A little of both. Some is more on my own. Other stuff I've been doing in the office. But most of it at nights by myself. I wasn't sure just what I wanted to do with what I found. Guess that's another reason I called you."

"I thought you just needed someone to talk about that night in the trailer."

"I did, but I think you knew there was more."

"Yeah, I figured. You find out anything else?

"I think someone up in Sanders County is involved too. That girl I found was from Spokane, and I think she came via the Thompson Falls area."

"How do you know that?"

"There's a yellow sticky note on a file I found in that box. It has some directions written on it, and I'm pretty sure it's up by Thompson Falls. I thought you and I could take a trip up there. Tomorrow might be good. Nice Sunday drive."

"What do you expect to find up there?"

"I don't know. I've been a bit hesitant to think about it."

"You think we'll find kids?"

"I don't know."

"Alright, but you know something?"

"What?"

"We go down this path, we need to finish it. No loose ends. No moral shit. You're going to have to lose that conscience of yours."

"Don't worry, I have no problem with what needs to be done. And now, after last night, I definitely know something needs to be done."

"You sure about that?"

"Yeah, I'm sure." Baker's grip on the steering wheel tightened as he thought what could have happened if Tanya and Coral had been home the night before as they originally planned.

"So what are we gonna do?"

"We're going to take a drive tomorrow and see where those directions lead us. Then, we are going to find who sent those fuckers to my house and take care of them. If my investigation into the stuff from that box and who might be selling kids is related to last night's break in, we might just kill two birds with one stone."

"Or one .300 Weatherby Magnum round."

Baker decided to let his buddy sleep in a bit. Hell, it had only been twenty-six hours or so since he killed two people. Even though they stayed at Fred's till midnight, Baker was up at his usual 4:30. He had only drunk two Miller Lites, a third or quarter of what Frank put away, so getting up at his normal hour was no problem. He hit the bathroom, the kitchen for a large glass of water, and then the living room for twenty minutes of a series he put together based on back stretches, qigong exercises, and a few things from routines by Dan Millman and Pavel Tsatsouline. After his back and joints were loosened up, he did five minutes of dynamic stretches as recommended by Thomas Kurz. He agreed with Kurz that it wasn't much good to be able to kick a guy in the head only after stopping to warm up for ten or fifteen minutes beforehand. He liked to perform the dynamic movements each morning so he could kick high at any time if needed. The little routine had almost become a ritual and he didn't feel right if he didn't get them in each morning. Even on days when for some reason he couldn't get his run or reading in, he would do the warm up exercises and dynamic stretching after his glass of water.

Frank was right, he had enjoyed going to the strip club. Not so much for the dancers, but the good times it reminded him of. He and Frank had shared drinks in more topless bars and strip clubs than you could count, including some of the raunchiest places they could find in Bangkok, Thailand. For old times sake, the previous night had been good, and the one blonde had definitely been nice to watch. He was married, not dead.

Today he had time for his entire routine, so he laced up his Asics and headed outside. It was a bit after five and starting to become light. He took off at a leisurely jog down the side of the road. Two blocks from his house he startled two deer who had just finished feeding from the garden cared for by the elderly couple who lived in the little blue house. The deer were headed down the road where they would veer off toward the South Hills. Baker watched them trot ahead of him down the road and thought how peaceful it was and how nice to see deer in the middle of town. Don't see that in the big cities he thought.

As the deer went one way and he the other, Baker started thinking about the events of the last couple weeks. First he killed a guy, and regardless what he told Frank, he was still bothered by it. But he still wasn't sure just what was bothering him most. Was it the killing? Was it breaking the law while he was sworn to uphold it? Maybe now he was more upset thinking that it was related to the two Frank just killed in his own kitchen. "Jesus Christ," he said aloud to no one. "How the fuck did this all happen?" He thought of Coral and became angrier. He began imagining her in the place of Ashley, the girl he found in the trailer house. He imagined various scenarios of what could have happened if the two meth addicts had found her and Tanya instead of Frank and the Brooklyn Smasher. He picked out a street two blocks ahead and sprinted as hard as he could to the corner. Passing the street sign, he slowed back to a jog, feeling a bit better after the intense exertion, but then other thoughts crept into his unstill mind. Was it moral folly to adhere to rules when the criminals had none whatsoever? When the legal system doesn't work, is it right to take the law into one's own hands? Maybe Frank was right, maybe he let his conscience get in the way too much. "Don't think about that shit and don't think about what happened, think about what we need to do." He worked at controlling his breathing. It needs to be done, and why train if you aren't going to fight the good fight.

He included seven more of the intense sprints during the thirty minutes he was away from the house. He removed his shoes and peeled off the wet t-shirt as he entered the kitchen through the back door. After another large glass of water, he headed to the living room to stretch a bit before eating. He'd stretch in front of the TV to check the weather and any other news. He included a few yoga postures and reminded himself that he really should add more yoga into his routine.

He turned off the TV and finished with fifteen minutes of sitting mediation. He found if he didn't meditate in the early mornings, he never seemed to find another time when things were quiet and people weren't demanding his attention. With work and other obligations, if he didn't find time early, he became too busy or tired to get to it later in the day. He tried to be mindful all the time; meditation was really just an extension of paying attention. His instructors had taught him to meditate while walking, running, and even doing common chores. It didn't matter what one was doing, as long as you were completely present in the act. It was a lot harder to practice than discuss, but he attempted to clear his mind and be in the present as much as he could. Or at least when he remembered to. The early morning sessions definitely helped, and lately he was extremely glad for the practice, even though he did find it more difficult to clear his thoughts and focus only on his breathing. He thought about sitting for fifteen more minutes, but the rumbles from his stomach were becoming more difficult to ignore. Need more practice he thought as he slowly rose and headed toward the kitchen.

He'd wait till after his oatmeal, shower, and a little reading before waking Frank.

* * *

"What time is it?" Frank stumbled out of the guest room wearing only his boxers and looking like death warmed over.

"Almost 7:00. Glad no one's here to see you parading around like that." Baker had showered, shaved, and was reclining on the couch reading the newest thriller by one of his top five authors. This book was a departure from the series about an assassin, and focused on an adventure two estranged brothers found themselves in. One brother was an attorney and the other in the military. Since Baker had a background with both, he was enjoying the quick summer read.

"I knew you were the only one around. I'd be dressed if Tanya or Coral were here."

"I hope so."

"Fuck you. What time you get up anyway?"

"4:30, same as always."

"I thought you might sleep in with age."

"Not hardly."

"I smell the coffee. I need ten minutes in the basement, then I'll shower and pour a cup and we can leave. How far is it up there?"

"Couple hours. Do I dare ask why you need ten minutes in the basement? I knew going to the strip club was a bad idea."

"Fuck you again. I want to do a little Tabata training."

"What's that?" Baker put his book down and stood up.

"It's a way to kick your ass real fast. Great for when you don't have much time. It's practical too."

"But what is it?

"It's named after some Japanese guy. Basically you go all out for twenty seconds and then rest for ten. You do eight sets. Believe me, it kicks your ass."

"If you say so."

"Come on down and try to keep up with me."

"I exercised and showered a long time ago."

"Chicken."

"Go have fun and hurry up. I want to hit the road soon."

"You already load up?"

"Stuff's ready. Still where we left it last night." The two had cleaned all of the firearms the previous night before going to dinner and out to the bar. Empty brass had been stored and magazines loaded. Baker had put the Winchester Ranger SXT Controlled Expansion rounds back in his Browning. For the previous day's practice he had been using some cheap 115 grain full metal jacket Blazer Brass ammunition.

"What are you taking?"

".308, AR, and the 12 gauge. Plus what we both carry."

"That covers just about anything might run into, near or far."

"Yep, that's what I figured. It doesn't hurt to be prepared."

"You got your other gear ready?"

"Black duffle by the door."

"I'll be ready in a few. I'll need my bag from the truck too."

"I'll get it. Do your whatever, then shower and get your coffee. I'll load everything else up."

The drive from Missoula to Thompson Falls took a little over an hour and a half. A mile past the small town, Baker turned off Highway 200 onto Blue Slide Road. The two traveled along the winding route till they came to Vermillion Creek. Baker turned right and they headed up the mountain road. According to the directions from the box Baker found, they were hoping to find a house or cabin of some sort. Instead, at the correct distance from Blue Slide, they found what looked like a road, if you could call it that, leading off into the woods.

Baker stopped the SUV and looked at his friend. "Well?"

"Came this far didn't we?"

Baker drove the Durango up the two trails that would turn out to be a driveway. Tall grass and weeds grew on both sides and lesser ones grew in the middle. Like everything else during the drive, green was the primary color. The two ruts that made the road were better than some places Baker had taken the Durango, and it was fairly smooth for such a road, as if someone had taken the time to remove any large rocks in the path and fill in the deep depressions and holes. The tree line was approximately five yards from the vehicle on both sides, so basically they drove up a trail cut through the woods for vehicles. It was primitive, but served its purpose. Baker doubted too many vehicles ever ventured up this way. If he hadn't been looking for it based on the note with directions, he might have driven by without even noticing. A few longer branches scraped the side of the Durango and Senich commented, "Good thing we didn't bring my truck. We'd be walking in."

"Your rig would just clear a bigger path. But yeah, this isn't even a drive-way. Whoever's back here likes to be remote."

"Remote hell, we are so far back in the boonies if we see anyone it's gonna be some hillbilly playing 'Dueling Banjos.' And I sure the hell don't squeal."

"Why, cause you'd like it?"

"Fuck you."

"There's something up ahead."

"Yeah, looks like a couple of trailers." The so-called road opened up into a clearing where two older thirty foot camper trailers were positioned about twenty-five feet from each other. One was a fifth-wheel and the other a travel trailer. Both were white with faded graphics on the sides, and you could barely make out Jayco on the front of the travel trailer in the rear. Neither looked in that great of shape, and it appeared as though they had not been moved for years. Both had flat tires, and there were blocks under the axels. Fresh garbage was scattered outside the right side of the travel trailer door. There were piles of various boards, logs, and junk, that had paths worn from people walking between them. The paths zig-zagged between the two trailers, and there were two that were very well worn through the tall grass from the Jayco trailer to the fifth wheel, and the other to a spot that looked like a parking space when the occupants were home. The trails and garbage made it apparent that the trailers were occupied, but with no vehicles in sight, it appeared vacant at the moment. It was quiet other than a few birds chirping in the nearby trees. "People live in this shit hole? If you're gonna live out in the mountains, you could at least have a nice little retreat. Not some stinking old trailer house with garbage scattered around."

"I don't think it's another Thoreau living up here writing a sequel to *Walden*. It's not even a trailer house, those are just campers you pull behind a car or truck."

"I know, it was just an expression."

"Didn't you live in a trailer house for a while?"

"Yeah, but it wasn't a shit hole like this. Mine was pretty nice actually, for a trailer."

"I lived in one when I was younger, wasn't so bad. Some of the new ones are pretty fancy."

"These sure the hell ain't. Wonder how long they've been up here. No vehicles around, want to look inside?"

"Like you said, we came this far didn't we?" Baker turned the Durango around so it faced out toward Vermillian and Blue Slide Road, backed into the so-called parking space, and put it in park. "Leave it running?"

"Nah, shut it off. Hear something else coming easier."

"You're right." Baker turned off the engine and climbed out, glancing at the rifles in the back. He had his Browning and knew Senich was carrying his Sig .45, so the rifles weren't needed to just look around.

"So, what exactly are we looking for?"

"I don't know, something related to those kids. You know, anything that will help us stop those bastards."

"I know a lot of bastards, these fucks are just that, sick fucks. Don't go giving bastards a bad name."

"Yeah, alright." Baker smiled. Frank could always get him to smile. Obnoxious, ornery, mean son-of-a-bitch that he was, he couldn't think of anyone else he would want with him right now.

"You check the fifth-wheel, I'll go check the one in back."

"Alright, yell if you find anything."

"You too." Senich moved quickly, but stealthily, around the front of the fifth-wheel, watching where he stepped as he followed the zig-zag trail through various pieces of junk scattered about. He chose the lesser beaten zig-zag paths instead of the more worn direct route to better check things out and get a feel of the place. There were three large black garbage bags filled with empty beer cans piled beside an overflowing forty-gallon plastic garbage can. "All this beautiful nature, and we have to be in this shit hole," Senich said to himself, looking at the area in disgust. "Fuck!"

Demon, the part German Shepherd, part wolf, lived up to its name. He had been asleep in the tall grass in front of the travel trailer and woke when he heard the vehicle approach. He laid still, watching through blood shot eyes, as Frank Senich cautiously, but unaware of his presence, approached the trailer. His legs coiled under him, he looked more like a hunting lion than the wolf-dog he was. He readied himself and at the closest point Senich would come to his hiding place as he moved toward the trailer, Demon sprang without a bark, just a low rumbling growl. He didn't know who it was, nor did he care, it was a human that didn't belong in his territory.

Senich didn't know that a German Shepherd's bite measures around five hundred pounds of pressure per square inch, nor did he know wolves can exert one thousand five hundred pounds per square inch, leaving Demon's powerful jaws somewhere between the two figures. He did know that a huge mass of black, grey, and white fur was hurtling through the air at him tremendously fast, and leading the mass were a collection of enormous teeth. He didn't care about pounds of pressure per square inch, he just cared about avoiding the incoming bite that would hurt like hell and if not fought off could be deadly if the huge wolf-dog had its way.

There are situations where you don't have time to draw your weapon before an attack is upon you. Most good combat shooting courses teach this and have drills that enable a person to fend off an attack and create space in order to draw a weapon. This is why hand-to-hand skills are so vitally important, even if you always carry. Those that say, "I don't need any of that empty hand stuff, because I have a gun," are ignorant of the fact that there are times when you don't have your weapon, and other times when you must do something first in order to get to your weapon. This was one of those times. Senich's arms instinctively came up as he shouted his expletive. Protecting his torso, throat, and face, he rotated his body toward his left and used his forearms to smack against the beast's charge. It was similar to a cornered fighter using his forearms to block and cover his upper body against an opponent's blows. More luck than anything, Demon's teeth missed their mark and he landed at Senich's feet from the forearm strike-push. Without even a yelp, Demon started to turn back toward his prey with lightening speed. Knowing in the time he could draw his weapon the animal could be latched on to his leg or another area, Senich chose to attack the dog-wolf with his bare hands, and grabbed for the monster at his feet before he could get completely balanced and in position to bite. Without thinking, he went for the head and throat. For starters, it was that powerful mouth full of fangs that scared him most, and secondly he figured the old adage of where the head goes the body follows would work on a four legged critter just as well as on a man. He grabbed a handful of flesh and hair right behind the snarling mouth with his right hand, forcing the head into the grass beside his feet, and with his left he grabbed the beast's windpipe and pinched it hard between his index finger and thumb. The animal squirmed and kicked, and though powerful, Senich was able to keep his hold, and more importantly, keep Demon's teeth from biting anything. Swearing profusely, Senich struggled and used his weight to keep the animal's head on the ground, while maintaining his death grip on the cartilage of the windpipe. As he squeezed the trachea , and the life out of Demon, with everything he had, Baker came around the corner of the fifth-wheel with his Browning in hand.

Advancing quickly, with the 9 mm at the ready, he asked his friend, "You okay?"

"Yeah, fucker almost had me."

"It looks like a wolf."

"It is, or at least part. I think it's one of those part wolf, part shepherd mixes."

"Yeah, there's an ad for those in some of the magazines. I think a place over in Idaho breeds them. It dead?"

"Fuck yeah. Son-of-a-bitch comes at me like that, I sure the hell ain't giving it a second chance. I don't give anything a second chance that tries to kill me, man or mutt." Senich had stood up and was opening and closing the fingers of his left hand as he calmed his breathing. Though the entire ordeal had only lasted a minute or so, he felt like he had just run ten clicks. The fear, the adrenal dump, and the savagery of the attack would affect anyone, even someone like Senich who was accustomed to violence. Those not accustomed to killing and people, or in this case animal, trying to kill them, would most likely have froze and that would have been it. They would be lying in a pile with the beast ripping out vital organs and possibly feeding on the carcass. Senich was grateful for his training and experiences, but then if it wasn't for his training and experiences, he wouldn't be out in the middle of nowhere, surrounded by mountains and forests, being attacked by a wolf-dog that weighed as much as he did. "Who the hell keeps something like that around and not locked up?"

"There's folks up in these mountains that you couldn't guess what kind of shit they do. Guess in a way, that's why we're here. It's still too bad you had to kill it, it doesn't know any better." After glancing around one more time, Baker flicked the safety up, and returned his Browning to its holster where he carried it with the hammer cocked back.

"Too bad my ass. You didn't have that monster leaping at your throat. What the…" Both men instinctively dove for the ground looking for the nearest cover. The sound of the trailer door opening interrupted their conversation, and the muzzle of a shotgun exiting first through the door sent them to the ground. The shotgun blast that followed scattered bird shot throughout the grass and weeds, but the two were outside the weapon's effective distance with such a load. Baker had immediately rolled when he hit the grass, he then drew and oriented his Hi Power toward the trailer. The tall grass and weeds that hid him also obscured his vision of the trailer and whoever was shooting at them. He looked to his right and could barely see the figure of Senich, also prone ,with his Sig drawn and pointed in the direction of the shotgun blast. Neither man moved. They both knew that movement was easier to see, and that is why they trained so long on remaining motionless during sniper school. When they did move, it was very slow. Low and slow was the motto for the sniper's creep.

Baker had felt like an idiot when he had this lesson pounded into him during sniper school so many years before. It was on his first stalk, the phase of the school where each sniper had to make so many successful stalks to pass that portion of the course. There was a stalk lane with outside boundaries they had to stay between. The students started on one end, and the instructors sat in plain view at the other. Usually the instructors were listening to music, drinking and snacking, and often sitting atop one of the humvees. However, besides that relaxed atmosphere, they were also scanning the stalk lane continuously with binoculars looking for students. The students, wearing guillie suits, had to creep or stalk, within two hundred yards of the instructors and fire a shot. Blanks were used, and it was assumed that the shots found their mark because the students had to also pass the shooting portion of the course firing at man sized targets at 300, 400, 500, and 600 meters. Making it past the 200 yard markers and firing a shot earned the student a certain number of points. If the instructors saw a student before they made it across the line, they would radio one of the other instructors out in the lane called walkers. By radio they would then direct the walkers to the students location, thus illustrating they saw him and he was caught. Being caught before you fired a shot earned you a big zero points. It was also important that walkers never gave students away, the instructors with the field glasses had to see them.

If a student did make it across the line and fire a shot, the walkers would then move within ten meters of the student without giving his position away and ask the student to read a number held up by the instructors near the humvees. Students had to correctly identify the number, otherwise how could you be sure they correctly identified their target? Once the number was correctly identified, the walker would instruct the student to take a second shot. Identifying the number and taking the second shot had to be performed without being seen by the instructors who were focusing on the area around the walker. It was always helpful when two students fired at the same time. Then the viewing instructors would be divided between the pair of students and walkers. If the student pulled off the second shot without being seen, the walkers were told to move within 5 meters of the hidden student to narrow the area the instructors at the humvee had to look. If still not seen, the walkers moved right next to the hidden sniper, still not identifying if they were on the left side, right side, or in front or behind the motionless soldier. Not being seen when the walker was standing right above a student would earn the maximum points.

During Baker's first stalk, he was in a big thicket of bushes. They were thick, and he couldn't see the instructors and knew there was no way for them to see him. He smugly moved through them ignoring the fact that he was making the bushes move as he ploughed through. He exited the thicket to meet a walker standing there and heard the head instructor of the school ask over the radio, "What idiot is it?"

"It's Baker," the walker replied.

"Well you tell him that it looked like a fucking heard of rhinos moving through those bushes and we could see him without the binoculars. Send him back to the beginning and have him start again." Baker returned to the starting line feeling foolish, but he never forgot the lesson. It helped him move without being seen, and later as a sniper instructor and during other various situations, it helped him "see" others moving when they believed they would be undetected.

"See 'em?" Baker whispered.

"Not without putting my head up, grass is too tall and thick. Mother fucker. I almost get chomped and then get shot at. What the fuck are we doing, and who the fuck are these guys?" Senich's whisper grew louder with each word.

Baker continued to lay motionless while attempting to locate cover he could roll to. He wanted a position that offered cover, concealment, and provided good field of fire toward the trailer. Like kids find out at Christmas, wanting and receiving are two entirely different things. Right now he'd be satisfied with anything thicker than weeds and grass that he could get behind. He looked over at Senich again and heard the unmistakable sound of a pump action shotgun being ratcheted. Immediately after, there was a click and a loud, "Shit. Stupid damn gun. Piece of shit."

Before the shooter finished his sentences, Baker and Senich were up moving toward the trailer in combat crouches. "I got him, watch for others," said Baker who had his Browning leveled at the man holding the shotgun. Senich scanned the surrounding area, his .45 ready for any additional target that might appear. "Drop it and get the fuck on the ground," Baker ordered. Smith, who was still trying to determine if the shotgun had malfunctioned or was just empty, looked up, and seeing both men approaching with weapons drawn and moving like they knew what they were doing, quickly decided to comply. He threw the 12 gauge into the grass about five feet from where he stood in front of the trailer door, and dropped down to his knees. He was wearing dirty jeans and nothing else. His bare feet were black with dirt and he didn't wear a shirt, revealing a scrawny upper torso that hadn't been washed in days. Sweat trickled down his neck and chest leaving a trail in the grime accumulated on his body. His curly hair was tangled and unkempt as if he'd just woke, which in fact was what happened. The commotion with Demon woke him, and he had grabbed the shotgun that was kept by the door and came out shooting.

"All the way down, face in the dirt," barked Senich. After almost being eaten and then being shot at, the adrenaline rush and anger he was feeling, though controlled, made him want to kill someone. And if he couldn't, at least hurt the son-of-a-bitch that dared fire a shotgun at him. He got to Smith first and kicked him in the ribs. "Anyone else in there?" He had his .45 pointed at the open door. He could smell the unmistakable stench associated with those who forewent showers, bathing, and changing clothes. Senich always associated the smell with laziness, and believed that even the poor and homeless could keep clean. He kicked again, this time catching the half naked man in the upper arm as he tried to protect his sore ribs.

"No, I'm the only one here," the man on the ground whimpered. He'd lost the toughness projected around little girls and kittens.

"Don't fuckin lie to me." Senich kicked him again. Smith cried out and coiled into a fetal position trying to protect himself from further blows. It appeared to be a position he was familiar with.

"I'll clear it." Baker entered the trailer cautiously, and quickly moved through the small space and determined Smith was telling the truth, no one else was inside. He didn't know how anyone could stand the stench. The outside area was dirty, Smith was grimy and stunk, but inside the trailer was absolutely filthy. He wished he had a gas mask. When he cleared the bathroom and shower he almost gagged. Mold, filth, and who knew what else clung to the shower walls and floor. Worse was the drain that was clogged with the same filth combined with pubic and body hair. He turned his head away and felt the beginning of his breakfast start to come up. He went outside to get some air. "Jesus Christ, can't breath in there. If you took the worst outhouse, a dump, and the slimiest porno shop where guys jack off all the time and they don't clean it, and combine the worst of them all, that's what you have in there." Baker walked past Smith, still curled in a fetal position, crying, to get away from the trailer and get some fresh air. "What's he saying? Or crying, or whatever?" He didn't even look at Smith, he was still looking for clean air.

"He's crying because you insulted his house."

"You know, we aren't in a very funny situation."

ALAIN BURRESE

"That's always been your problem, lighten up. Don't those Buddhist books you read tell you to enjoy the moment."

Baker knew Senich was enjoying this. He lived for adrenaline. Violence made him whole. The adrenal rush made him feel alive, and the closer to death he got, the more alive he felt. Baker knew this because, although not as intense as his buddy, he had the same feelings. He just suppressed his better, and didn't go looking for violence and action like they did when they were younger. He told himself that he'd grown up. The fact was, he often missed it, and the circumstances of the last couple weeks, including just being shot at made him feel more alive and awake than he had for quite some time. "I need to go back in again, I didn't see everything."

"What was in the fifth-wheel?"

"I don't know. It was pad-locked from the outside. I was going to check my bag for tools when I heard you and Cujo."

"Cujo was a St. Bernard, not a fucking wolf."

"Whatever. I didn't check inside it yet. Let's get this one done first."

"Where's the key to the fifth-wheel?" Senich kicked Smith again, but not quite as hard as his earlier strikes. He was about to kick again when the man started spilling information about the keys.

"Please, no more. I have the key, it's in my pocket." He reached into his front pocked with his right hand and Senich kicked him again, causing him to cry out.

"Slowly, and let me see it."

"Here. Here. I'm not lying." Smith pulled out a small ring with a half dozen keys on it. The ring was attached to a small chain with a plastic square with a picture of a naked Asian girl on the other end.

Senich bent down and took the key chain. "Which one?"

"I don't know, the pad-lock one."

136

"Get up. And if you try anything I'm going to beat you until you can't move. That or I'll just cap your ass."

Smith struggled to his feet and stood there cowering like a dog that's known nothing but beatings its entire life. He shivered as if cold, but still had sweat making tracks in the dirt that covered his body. He didn't look at Senich or Baker, but stared at his own grungy bare feet. He was a completely different person when left in the woods alone than he was when clean and staying at Cook's house down on the Blue Slide. When Cook dressed him in clean clothes and took him places, he felt powerful and confident. In the present situation, he felt just as he had when hiding under his bed as a child after receiving a beating.

"You going to check the other one?" Baker nodded toward the locked fifth-wheel.

"Sure. I'll take this filthy piece of shit with me."

"All right, I'm going back in here to finish looking around. Be careful, we've had enough surprises for today." Baker stepped up the single step and re-entered the Jayco cesspool. He ignored Senich's flippant response that he was always careful as he focused on not breathing and looking through stuff as fast as he could. There really wasn't much there, just a lot of shit piled around. He didn't dare go back into the shower and toilet area again, for fear of not being able to keep his breakfast down. The only thing he wanted to check out was the overhead cabinets by the front bed. He opened one, and was glad he and Senich had worn gloves. They wore the gloves to keep from leaving anything behind that could identify them, but he was equally glad they would protect him from any possible diseases. He hated that the soles of his shoes were touching the filth, and he certainly didn't want to touch anything with bare skin, fingerprints or no fingerprints. One cabinet was full of magazines that Baker didn't recognize, and he had seen his share of porn when younger. He wondered if Senich would recognize them from the truck stops he frequented. The second cabinet had a couple of shoe boxes in it. Baker pulled one out and looked inside. He turned his head away and felt sick again, but not from the smell.

The box was full of pictures. They were printed on flimsy 4 x 6 inch photo paper, and when Baker looked around he saw the cheap photo printer half covered with papers on the dining table of the trailer. It was the kind you hooked right to your digital camera to make instant prints. He glanced back inside the box to confirm what he'd seen. It was Ashley, the same girl he had found in the Missoula trailer house the night he killed Bruce James. She was naked and spread eagled on some sort of bed. It looked like it might be the bed in another camper trailer. Maybe the fifth-wheel, he thought. He focused on the face and tried to ignore her obscenely displayed body. It was her. He didn't need to see anything else in the box.

A rage was boiling inside like a volcano ready to erupt. He knew the feeling. The rage that had saved his hide on numerous occasions, but that had also gotten him in trouble at least twice as many times. He could always feel it coming on, even those times that it seemed to appear instantly. His years of martial art training helped him control it, and enabled him to diffuse the feeling into calmness when he choose to. That was the key, making the choice to control it. Sometimes he didn't want to control it. Sometimes it was like the adrenal rush of anger and it made him feel alive. Sometimes he thrived on the rage. He actually missed it on occasion. He was an attorney, a respected member of the community and the State Bar. He wasn't supposed to act on his rage. That's what he told himself every time he used his *don-jon* breathing techniques to calm himself. He started to inhale deeply but stopped due to the stench of the trailer's air. It was at that point he burst. "Fuckers!" he screamed as he threw the box of photographs against the trailer's wall. He stepped over to the table and grabbed the printer and hurled it toward the back where the bathroom door was closed. The printer's cord was wrapped around a bar that supported the table when it was in the dining position before being plugged to the outlet, so the printer snapped back before hitting the bathroom door and crashed back onto the table scattering the mess of papers even more. Still enraged, Baker grabbed the handle of the small refrigerator's door and ripped the entire door from its cheaply made hinges. Throwing it side armed like a discus, he threw the door toward the front of the trailer and heard the crash as it shattered one of the windows over the bed. Quickly looking around and seeing nothing to smash that would help fuel his anger, he stepped to the outside door, which had closed but not latched. He launched a front kick with his rear right leg that caught the door right in the middle with a loud crunching sound. It flew open and the top hinge ripped right out of the trailer's wall. The door banged against the outside wall of the trailer and then hung there supported by the remaining hinges that were only partly damaged.

Baker exited the trailer and headed toward the fifth-wheel. Passing the forty-gallon plastic garbage can, he executed another rear leg front kick, this time with his left leg. The can toppled and rolled spilling the gross contents across the grass and weeds. With all the other garbage scattered about, it didn't make much difference.

"What happened?" Senich, hearing the smash, had come out running with his .45 drawn. He stopped when he saw Baker standing and looking at the can he had just kicked over.

"These are the fuckers who did it."

"Did what?" He lowered his weapon, recognizing Baker's anger, something he had seen before, and realizing there was no other external threat right now.

"They had the girl." Baker saw the puzzled look on his friend's face. "The girl I found in the trailer house that night I killed that other scum bag."

"Photos or videos?"

"I found a picture, didn't look any further. There was a shoebox full of pictures, and another box still in the cabinet. I betcha that fucker took her from Spokane, came here, and then sold her in Missoula." Baker shook from anger and tears welled up in both eyes. "That poor kid." He passed Senich and demanded, "Where is that son-of-bitch?"

"Inside, I told him if he came out I'd shoot him. Nothing in there at all, it's empty."

Baker stormed into the fifth-wheel almost as violently as he'd exited the travel trailer a few minutes before. "Who else you working with you mother fucking maggot?" Smith had stood up from the built in sofa as Baker crashed in, and didn't have time to take a step before baker closed the distance from the door to where he stood and grabbed him around the throat. Baker squeezed and pushed him backwards, striking the back of his head against the storage cabinets that ran along the top of the trailer over the sofa. "How many are there," he growled.

"I... I, don't know"

"Bullshit!" Baker slammed Smith's head against the cabinets again, squeezed tight around the throat, and then let up so Smith could regain his breath and talk.

"Cook does everything, I just help. I just help," Tears ran out of fear stricken eyes as Smith looked into Baker's anger filled face and realized there was no way he could escape other than complying with every demand these two men made. He was no longer the cold cruel abductor of little girls, who could toss a kitten from a speeding vehicle. He was an eight year old boy, terrified of his father, crying for help that never came.

"You alright?" Senich asked, sticking his head inside the door.

"Yeah." Pivoting to his left, Baker threw Smith to the floor in front of the built in sink and stove in what was the kitchen area of the camper. "You tell me everything and I might not kill you."

"Don't go making promises I won't keep," Senich was still standing outside, but had his head in the door to watch the show.

Baker glanced over and gave Senich a dirty look and turned back to the man on the floor who sat up, but didn't attempt to stand. Baker noticed the wet crotch where Smith had pissed himself and realized that's why he smelled urine. His nose had just started to work again after the bombardment of stench from the previous trailer. "You took that girl from Spokane, didn't you?"

"I just helped. It was all Cook's plan."

"Who's Cook?"

"He shares this place with me. He helps me get girls sometimes. Sometimes I stay at his house. I help him, he helps me."

"What's Cook's first name?"

"Dan... Dan Cook."

The rage started to build again and Baker stepped forward to launch one of his front kicks against a living target this time, but Smith scurried backwards in a modified crab walk and cowered under the camper's refrigerator. Baker recognized he was dealing with someone who wasn't quite right in the head, but that wouldn't grant him a pass for what he'd done.

Anyone who could do such things to little girls was not right in the head. They were sick, and sometimes you had to cull the heard.

"When's Cook going to be back?"

"Soon, real soon. He went to T-Falls to buy some beer and food."

"What's he drive?"

"Sometimes a Ford pickup, and sometimes we use the Dodge van. Whatever he doesn't drive he keeps at his house by the river."

"Where by the river?"

"Down off Blue Slide Road."

"What color are the truck and van?"

"The truck is black and the van is gold."

"Any more dogs?"

"No, Demon was the only one. You killed Demon, didn't you?"

"It attacked my friend, he killed 'em."

"He was only mean to strangers."

"You should have had him tied up, or trained him not to attack people."

"Cook wanted him to protect the place. He wanted him to be mean."

"Well, he attacked the wrong person this time." Baker thought about the mound of fur lying between the trailers. He truly did wish the wolf-dog hadn't been killed, but he was glad he hadn't had to administer first-aid to his buddy after the attack. While he would have preferred a win-win solution, he'd choose having Frank standing and the animal lying out in the grass before reversing the roles any day. His thoughts drifted to the box of photographs he'd found in the other trailer and the girl he had rescued. He wondered who had stripped her and made her pose for the obscene photograph, and then wondered what else they did to her. "Get up," he commanded.

Smith fearfully stood, keeping his back pressed against the refrigerator. He stared at the floor and refused to look at Baker, who glared at him as he thought more about the photographs he'd found. There was about five feet between the two men, Smith against the refrigerator and Baker standing just the other side of the camper's sink in the narrow living space. As his anger boiled, Baker took a long, quick step forward with his right. As his body moved forward, he let it sort of fall. Simultaneously, he shot his gloved right hand from where it rested by his side, out in a perfectly straight line, to Smith's nose. There were no preparatory or preliminary movements before he moved. No shifting of his weight, fidgeting, or reeling back to chamber a John Wayne type punch. Just a quick, convulsive, and to the untrained an awkward, step forward that set his weight into motion behind the straight palm heel smash that exploded against the front of Smith's face. His fingers were curled back and the palm heel of his hand smashed Smith's head back into the refrigerator's door as the cartilage inside the nose fractured into tiny pieces, causing a tide of crimson to gush out and pour down Smith's chin and onto his bare chest. He dropped straight down, lifeless, in a pile at the foot of the refrigerator. His head slumped forward and smacked the floor and continued to bleed. A pool of blood widened under the still head.

Baker didn't know if the crumpled still form lying at his feet on the camper floor was unconscious or dead. With his years of training, he knew blows like that could kill a person. And it wasn't from the nose bones being driven into the person's brain. He didn't know how that urban legend persisted, but it sure did. It was sometime in the last year that he watched some documentary series about two guys traveling around to different countries to briefly train in martial art styles from the featured country. He remembered shaking his head during the Savate episode in France when one of the narrators perpetuated the myth by describing the power of a kick to be that it could send the nose bones into the brain and cause death. The truth was, any sufficiently hard blow anywhere on the head can be fatal. People sometimes died slipping, falling, and smacking their head with less force than his palm heel strike generated. However, he'd also seen people take tremendous punishment, including being struck by automobiles where the skull smashed windshields, and then they just walked away with nothing more than a bruise and headache. It didn't matter if he was dead, he soon would be. Baker's rage over the pictures was fueled by striking Smith, and he immediately raised his right leg and stomped down on Smith's exposed knee. Being unconscious, there was no reaction or response to the stomp. This infuriated Baker more. He wanted to hear the screams and cries just like those little kids must have screamed and cried in this very same trailer. He stomped again. This time the heel of his shoe came down on the side of the unconscious man's face and bones crunched beneath the weight of the strike. Two more times Baker's shoe came down into the side of Smith's head. Blood oozed from several orifices as the skull was smashed between the floor and the powerful stomps.

Senich, who had been looking around outside, heard the smash when Baker's first strike sent Smith into the refrigerator and then to the floor. He poked his head back in the door just in time to see Baker's last stomp and to hear the sickening crunch it created. At first glace, Senich knew Smith was dead. "I thought you were against that. You know, your conscience and all that?" he said half jokingly.

144

"Fuck you," was all Baker said as he brushed past his friend at the trailer's door and headed toward the parked Durango. He sat in the driver's seat, taking deep breaths and concentrating on calming himself down as he waited for Senich to join him.

"You all right now?" Senich had waited five minutes before opening the passenger door to check on his friend. He'd seen Baker in that state enough times to know to give him a few minutes to cool down, and he also knew Baker was quick to regain composure. He was sometimes amazed at how he could be an inferno one minute and calm and collected the next. It worked the other way too, he'd seen him go from calm and seemingly serene to a savage angered beast in the blink of an eye. It was that ability, to go from zero to sixty in a heartbeat, that enabled him to survive so many of the bar brawls they had found themselves in when younger. Not just survive, but come out on top. Senich had a similar ability, but it wasn't as quick, like flicking a switch, as his buddy's. Especially with cooling off. Senich took much longer to come down after a rage like Baker had just been in, but then he didn't really become enraged quite like his friend.

"I'm fine. What are we going to do about this place?"

"Fuck it. Leave it like it is. You think anyone's going to give a rat's ass if they do find it? World's a better place than it was earlier today."

"Anything here that could identify us?"

"Tire tracks. Shoe prints. You might have left some DNA smashing that guy. But we've had gloves on, didn't drop anything or leave anything else. Need to get rid of or sterilize your gloves, you got blood on them. Need to check your clothes too. Place is such a shit hole, you really think they will look very hard, especially after they find those pictures you mentioned? And who'd come looking for us, or at our stuff?"

Baker looked at the blood on his gloves and quickly scanned the front of his body for any splatters. Nothing much, which surprised him, but he'd still have to sterilize all his clothes and shoes when they got home. "You're right, let's get out of here before his partner shows up. He's supposed to be back anytime. Don't need him IDing us."

"You planning on letting him have that chance?"

"No, but I'm still thinking."

"What now?" Senich asked. The two traveled in silence down Vermillion Creek Road and it wouldn't be too long before they neared the intersection with Blue Slide Road, where they would have to turn.

"I don't know." Baker shook his head without letting his eyes wander from the dirt road. "Cook might be coming any time now. What do you think we should do?" He glanced over to his buddy, letting him know the request was genuine.

"Well, you want to take him out here, or follow him to his house by the river?"

"A lot of unknowns at the house. More dogs, people, neighbors, cameras, and who knows what else."

"I doubt someone like him built where neighbors could see, but then again, maybe that's what the trailers were for. Maybe he wants people to see him at the house. Who knows? You're right, too many unknowns without proper recon."

"If we take him out here, how we going to get rid of the body and vehicle?"

"Fuck 'em. We kill the son-of-a-bitch and leave. You know how many killings go unsolved? They don't have the time or manpower, and there ain't gonna be anything linking to us. Besides, if they connect the guy to the trailers we just left, local law enforcement will most likely just say 'thanks' and go on eating donuts and minding their speed traps."

Baker remembered carrying the shivering little girl out of the trailer house, shivering from fear, not cold. How terrified that little girl must have been, being stripped, photographed and who knows what else up in those filthy trailers. Then traded or sold to another pervert living in the trailer in Missoula. Baker's rage started to reappear the more he thought of what they might have done to her, and what they had done to so many others. He was well aware of how many crimes, including murders, went unsolved each year. He thought of his daughter Coral. "How you want to do it?"

"Set a hasty ambush and take him out."

"You must have a plan, tell me what you want me to do."

"Turn around and go back up a couple miles. Head back to the clearing we passed."

"All right." Baker slowed down and turned the Durango around using a quick three point turn. As the two headed back up Vermillion Creek, he asked, "Now what?"

"I want you to stop up by the clearing and act like you are fixing a flat, or checking a tire or something. Do my side, front tire. He won't be able to see it well coming up from behind. Don't pull off the road, make it so he has to stop because you are in the way, or at least slow way down to creep by."

"Where you going to be?"

"I'll be across the clearing in the woods with your .308."

"So I'm the bait and you're the shooter?"

"Someone's got to do it."

"How's this?" Baker asked, slowing the vehicle as they approached a spot in the road that narrowed a bit. The clearing was off to Baker's left, with the far tree line about two hundred meters from the road.

"It'll do."

Baker stopped the Durango so it was partially blocking the road and both men climbed out. Senich shut his door and walked over to Baker's side. "Keep your door open so he can't get by. I'll be over there." Senich motioned across the road to a thick crop of trees on the far side of the clearing. There were even thicker patches of vegetation growing around the base of the trees. "In fact, this is better that I first thought. That clearing is perfect. How far you think those trees across there are?"

"Two hundred meters or so."

"That's what I figure too. Think you can get him to smile?"

"I don't believe you sometimes." Baker shook his head as he got his buddy's inside joke regarding their practice the previous day with his various weapons.

"Got a cap?"

"In the back, why?"

"Put it on. Make a positive ID; we don't need to be shooting the wrong guy. I'm guessing more than one yokel up here has a black truck. If it's the right guy, take the hat off. I'll do the rest."

"I can't believe we're doing this. We're actually planning a hit." Baker thought about his little office and position with the County. He also thought about his membership with the State Bar, and then his home and family. How the hell did things get so out of control so fast? The time from when he learned of Walter Dennison shooting up the school till now was a blur. Wanting to prosecute James, being told he couldn't, the altercation in the trailer house and finding Ashley, the two meth heads Frank killed in his own house, stomping Smith's head into mush earlier that very day, and now setting up an ambush to kill yet another person.

"You ain't doing shit. Just checking a tire."

"You really don't have a conscience do you?"

"Not when it comes to the vermin in the world. My moral compass is as straight as yours, and you know it. There's right and there's wrong. There's the law, and there's justice. We ain't wrong, and this is just."

"Yeah, but…"

"But nothin'. I told you if we did this it'd get messy. I told you we needed to finish it. You pull that conscience shit now and it could get us killed. I told you, lose it, or get out. We do this and we do it right, or we pack up and forget it all. Next time it'll be Tanya and Coral at your home, not me."

"Fuck." Baker shook his head yet again. It was only the day before that he came home to find his house taped off by police and discovered his best friend killed two drug addicts in his kitchen and living room. One of which had a note in his pocket that indicated he was being paid to go after Tanya and Coral, his family. "I'm in. Let's get it over with and get out of here. Finish this and we're done."

"The world will be a better place."

"I hope so." Baker didn't have much conviction in his voice, but deep inside he knew they couldn't let these monsters continue. They needed to be stopped, and he knew Frank would stop this guy forever. He wondered if it would really make a difference. He thought of the old cliché about the starfish. *It makes a difference to this one.* If doing this kept one child from going through the horrors of being abducted, used, and sold, it was worth it and the right thing. Sure, there was punishment for sins committed, which he was sure that was what Frank deemed Justice. But he felt better thinking about the prevention this would do. Stop the disease before it could spread and infect others.

"Hurry up so we can wait." Senich opened the back door and pulled the Remington .308 from its case. Always keeping the barrel pointed in a safe direction, he eased the bolt back to ensure a round was chambered. Satisfied, he locked the bolt forward and removed the caps covering the Leupold 10X scope. He brought the rifle up to his shoulder and looked through the scope at the other side of the clearing. He smiled. Holding a rifle in his hands always made him feel good.

Shooting the weapon the day before had brought back fond memories of his training with the M24 sniper system he and Baker had used in the Army. Now he was remembering other times, because this wasn't training. His heart beat a bit faster with anticipation.

Neither of them had worn anything shiny, or anything that would make noise. Both wore subdued colors that would blend okay with the thick foliage. Senich was not too worried about it. His face, not being painted, would show the most, but again, this guy was going to be concentrating on Baker and the road, not looking across the clearing to the woods. And after the shot, there wouldn't be anyone looking, so it really didn't matter. It wasn't as if they needed to worry about getting out of the area undetected by enemy troops and counter snipers after a high profile kill. This was a simple hasty ambush, not a completely planned mission. It was all they had; it was all they needed.

Baker looked at his partner and nodded as Senich headed off the road and toward the trees. He quickly disappeared to the left into the brush, and Baker wondered how long it would take him to set up a hide. He looked at his watch. "Damn, it's only 3:30," He muttered to himself. A lot had happened since leaving Missoula that morning, it sure seemed a lot later. He went to the back and pulled out the jack and took it to the front passenger side. He left the back open as well as his driver door making it look like he stopped to change a tire. He then grabbed a Power Bar from the glove box and resolved to settle in and wait. He and Frank were both good at waiting, though they usually were lying side by side, one with a rifle and the other with a spotting scope, not one playing bait and the other out in the woods. "Better not hit my rig," he silently said to himself.

It had been an hour and fifty minutes since Senich left Baker at the road beside his Durango. The first twenty minutes had flown by as Senich looked for an adequate hide and settled in and became comfortable. Knowing no one was looking, he didn't take many of the precautions he normally would. He did circle the clearing in the tree line, rather than beeline straight across, so he wouldn't be caught out in the middle, but he hadn't done so very stealthily. He wasn't too concerned with being discovered, but he was worried that the target would show up before he was ready, so he sacrificed a few tactics for speed. He lay comfortably by a large pine tree with a bushy shrub beside it. The shrub was leafy and had little buds that would most likely turn into some kind of berry, and it provided good concealment. Senich wondered if the berries would be edible. No real cover the way he was laying, but he didn't figure anyone would be shooting back. And even though the bush wouldn't stop return fire, he was certainly concealed. Any shot that did hit him would be wild, but if shooting did occur, he could quickly slide over behind the tree trunk without being seen. He had a clear view of the road with Baker and his Durango. The Remington rested on the lightweight Harris bipod that Senich had kept at the lowest elevation of nine inches. He was glad Baker's rifle had the attached support so he didn't have to improvise with a field-expedient version. He wasn't adverse to tying three sticks together, he was just glad he didn't have to look for them and spend the time doing it. He thought to himself, "nice rifle, good plan."

Hell, who was he fooling? None of this was necessary. He just wanted to relive some Army days and snipe someone. They could have just as easily waited together, and once identified, he could have capped the guy with his .45 down at the road. He didn't need to be out here two hundred meters away with the Remington. What good was all the training if you didn't put it to use? With that thought, he went back to concentrating on his breathing and observing the road. He wondered how much longer they'd wait.

He glanced at his watch as saw that it was almost 5:30. He had been laying prone for an hour and a half. Mere moments to someone who was trained to move slowly and wait for days if needed. He looked back through the scope. His position was two hundred meters from the vehicle, and the Leupold's 10X scope enabled him to watch a bug crawl across the right front corner of the Dodge. For this shot, he'd rather have the variable 3X9 ART II that they had on the M21 systems. The fixed ten-power scope's magnification didn't provide optimal vision for scanning, and he couldn't scan the area like he'd prefer. He was close enough that he did most of his watching without the aid of the optics and only looked through them every now and again. He had drawn a smiley face on a paper plate when they were shooting at the clearing they used as a range near Missoula. He was glad he had shown off with the "between the eyes" shots at 200 yards, because that was exactly what he planned today. The rifle was exactly as it had been during practice, and there was no wind or any other factor to interfere. What a beautiful spring day in the mountains. He could almost pull this shot off in his sleep. Senich heard the vehicle approaching before he saw it. When the black Ford truck slowed beside the parked Durango, he entered his sniper bubble.

He hadn't been kidding when he joked about placing the shot between the man's eyes. That was essentially the center of the cranial cavity "box" as seen from the front. While just about any head shot from a rifle, that enters the cranial cavity, will kill, Senich wanted an instant incapacitation shot, as they trained for in hostage rescue situations. From the side, you placed the shot in the "box" just above the ear, and from behind the target was a "box" right in the center of the head, just above the tops of the ears if you were fortunate enough to be able to see them. Senich knew that hitting the cranial cavity at distances over one hundred meters was difficult, but at two hundred meters it was still within an acceptable range, but one should be aware of an occasional miss that wouldn't immediately incapacitate the target. He wouldn't be able to fire a spotting round, he was in an improvised field position, and any movement from the target or miscalculation in his range estimation could prevent the perfect shot. Senich, however, didn't need to immediately incapacitate his target. He wasn't holding a firearm on an innocent hostage with his finger on the trigger. Senich wanted the instant incapacitation because it was the most difficult of shots. Senich wanted to test himself just as much as he wanted to kill the sick fuck who was raping and selling little girls.

He didn't think of the difficulty of the shot, nor of the possibility of missing. His body was already in a proper body position, so in his bubble, his thoughts were on controlling his breathing, obtaining a correct sight picture, keeping a proper grip on the rifle, and trigger control. When Baker removed his hat, he would ensure the duplex crosshairs were centered in the cranial cavity "box." He would then slowly release the firing pin, without imparting any movement to the rifle, by using the fingertip to gently press the trigger back for a clean breaking shot. Demons from hell could have climbed out of the tree next to him and he wouldn't have noticed. His sole focus was the target; his only concern was completing his mission.

Baker wondered where they should stop for dinner between concerns that Cook wouldn't even show. Maybe Smith had lied, trying to scare them into thinking Cook would be returning shortly. Maybe they were waiting here for nothing. They could get a steak at the Rimrock, just West of Thompson Falls by the Clark Fork River. How long should they wait? That Power Bar was almost an hour and a half ago. Shit, here comes a vehicle. He felt the butterflies flipping in his stomach and reminded himself it was okay to have butterflies, just make them fly in formation. He took a deep breath and slid out of the vehicle through the open door as the black Ford truck came to a stop next to his Durango; the open door preventing the truck from advancing any further. "Hello," he called out from where he stood in front of the big FORD across the grill. The driver climbed out and hollered back.

"Got some trouble?"

"Hit a rock and wanted to check that front tire."

"Not a good place to break down, not much traffic up here."

"You got that right, you're the first person I've seen all day."

"Whatcha been doing?"

"I was up here looking for an old prospector's place. Heard there was a gold mine up here. Trying to do some research, but not doing a very good job of it." Baker didn't know where the lie was coming from, but figured it sounded good. "You wouldn't happen to know about gold would you?"

"Nope. Better be careful, people can get a bit touchy over their claims. I'd be careful about poking your nose around places."

"I'm just looking for people to talk to." Baker walked around the front of the big truck and held out his hand. "I'm Johnny Meadows. Up here researching a book I want to write about gold in Montana."

"Dan," he shook Baker's hand and then nodded toward the parked Durango. "Need a hand?"

"Nah, I think it's okay. Dan huh, would that be Dan Cook?" Baker sensed the quick change more than he saw it. He thought he might have pressed too quickly.

"Yeah, why?" It was more of a demand than a request.

"Guy down in that falls town, or something, I think he mentioned your name. I've been trying to talk to so many people, it's hard to remember without looking at my notes." Baker was glad for the ability to make up tales on the fly, it had saved his neck many a time when younger. He hoped Cook bought it. But then did it really matter if he did or not? "Let me check," he said as he headed back toward the Durango, removing his hat as he did so.

"It don't matter none. But I think you better be careful what you're doing up in these parts. Folks up here don't like strangers sticking their noses around where they don't belong." Cook took a step toward the front of the truck and stopped. Something wasn't right with this Johnny Meadows, but he couldn't quite place what it was. Nobody in Thompson Falls would be talking about him or giving his name out. He scooted back toward the cab of the truck as he reached behind with his right hand and started to remove the Taurus Titanium 9mm Millennium he had concealed at the small of his back. The PT-111Ti was just over six inches long, and was a fine choice for a lightweight, easily concealable, self-defense weapon. The steel magazine held ten rounds of 9mm ball ammo, giving the PT-111Ti a total capacity of eleven rounds. Cook didn't think he'd need eleven rounds. He wasn't sure if he needed any, but something wasn't right and he wanted to get the drop on this stranger before he got inside his vehicle. The Taurus was in his hand, but hidden behind the front of his truck that was between him and Meadows. "Stop," he commanded. "I don't want you in that rig."

The hair on the back of Baker's neck stood up when he heard Cook order him to stop. He spooked him with the name request. Options to talk himself out of the situation ran through his head as he stopped and slowly turned back toward Cook and his truck. He wondered what Cook's hands were doing behind the hood, and didn't like that he couldn't see them. Their eyes met and Baker was about to ask what the problem was when he saw a pink cloud of blood and tissue where a moment ago he was looking at Cook's face. At an extreme velocity, Senich's 175-grain bullet entered Cook's head precisely at the spot his crosshairs had so expertly settled upon. The spark or element that differentiates the living from the dead was snuffed from him instantly. The Taurus 9 mm thudded in the dirt road as the lifeless body crumpled on top of it.

The report of the rifle followed the crimson mist and the splattering of Cook's brains across the side of his black truck. Baker, even though he knew the shot came from Senich, instinctively flinched toward cover while scanning the far end of the clearing to determine the source of the shot. He immediately checked himself from hiding, but still continued to look for his friend. When he didn't immediately appear, he figured Senich would return the same way he left, in the trees. It would be bad form to stand and walk across the open field after the shot, regardless of who might or might not be around. Baker didn't care right now, he just wanted to get out of the area. He didn't bother going around the truck to look at the body, he knew what he'd see. Instead, he grabbed the jack and returned it to its cubbyhole and closed the doors. He started the Durango and turned it around and readied it to take off as soon as Senich returned. He rotated between watching down the road for any approaching vehicles with looking in the rear view mirror to scout for any coming from behind. He was relieved he hadn't seen any when the back door opened and Senich grabbed the case for the Remington and replaced the weapon among the others. He then placed a black brief case on the floor behind the passenger seat. "Thought this might be worth something, looked important and was the only thing in the truck."

"What's in it?"

"I don't know, didn't look in it yet. Figured you were in a hurry the way you pulled around. Sitting here all fidgety and what not."

"I am, let's go. I ain't fidgety, just cautious and paying attention."

"Whatever." Senich jumped into the passenger seat and slammed his door. "Let's go." As they headed down the dirt road, he added, "You're welcome."

"For what?"

"Didn't you check the body?"

"No, I saw the bullet hit. Nothing to check."

"Son-of-a-bitch had a 9mm out. It was one of those Titanium Taurus ones. Not bad weapon, if it'd been a .45 I'd have taken it."

"Damn, I thought he started acting squirrelly. I shouldn't have mentioned his name so soon when he didn't offer it."

"Yeah, right after you took off the hat, he pulled it out."

"Well, thanks. Thanks for using me as bait. It's good that you left it."

"Yeah, make the cops think something illegal was going down."

"Our ambush wasn't illegal?"

"Don't go there again. We done good today, and you know it." They drove in silence to the intersection with Blue

Slide Road. "I'm fucking starving. We need to get something to eat."

"There should be a few more Power Bars in the glove box. Grab me one too."

"Thanks, but this isn't going to do much." Frank ate a third of the bar with his first bite. "This ain't the way we came." Baker had taken a right turn onto Blue Slide Road and was heading west.

"I know. I thought about going back to eat at Thompson Falls, but I don't want to leave a record of being up here. This will take us to the highway, and then we can head back toward Thompson but turn and head over Thompson Pass before we get there. That will drop us into Idaho. We can eat over in Wallace and then take the Interstate back to Missoula. Wallace is your kind of town."

"Why?"

"Used to be famous for its whore house."

"If I'd known that, I would have stopped. I've just blown through going past on runs to Spokane and Seattle. Never knew."

"I don't think it's still there, just one of those old time things. Not really sure."

"I know they set up speed traps in the area, I've seen them, and I've actually only made a few runs that stretch of Interstate."

"It was also the place they filmed *Dante's Peak*."

"That volcano movie with Pierce Bronson?"

"Yeah, it was filmed in Wallace, but there's no volcano nearby like the movie."

"Never knew that either, see, this has been a very educational trip."

"Yeah," Baker talked to keep from thinking about what they had done that day, but maybe he should look at it like his buddy. They did good. The two continued to talk about various natural disaster movies of the 90s. Up next was *Volcano* with Tommy Lee Jones that came out around the same time as *Dante's Peak*, though neither could remember which one came first. By the time they reached Wallace they were out of movies, out of Power Bars, needed gas, and were both starving.

They stopped for gas at the Wallace Super Stop Conoco station at the foot of the exit ramp. Small convenience store with six pumps out front. Baker paid with cash while Senich remained outside with the vehicle. The two then headed into town. They slowed to look at the Northern Pacific Depot Railroad Museum. The old fashion depot building had the red and black yin and yang symbol used by Northern Pacific and a wooden sign that said WALLACE out front. It looked out of place with the raised Interstate behind it.

"I remember that from the movie." Senich commented.

Baker drove up 6th Street two blocks and stopped at Bank St. He looked up and down the small town's business district and spotted a pizza place to his left.

"Pizza sound good?"

"The back end of a horse would sound good right now, I don't care. Let's eat."

The Pizza Factory was nestled beside a building that read "The Coeur D'Alene Hardware Co." in tan letters across a black sign that ran in front of the brown building, but that had a smaller sign above the door that read "The Price Tag." It advertised antiques and more. Neither was interested in antiques, so they parked in front of the store and beelined for the Pizza Factory. It was a small town pizza place with a red and green motif. The floor was made of red and white tiles and the counters and tops of the wooden picnic tables were green. The place had an old-fashioned gumball machine by the counter that matched the red pillars and red Coke cooler by the door. Baker went to the counter to order while Senich wandered through the door in the back of the small dining area toward the arcade that was advertised by a big sign over the door.

Senich came back from the arcade just as Baker finished ordering a pizza. He'd asked the young man behind the counter about "The Tiger." It had Canadian bacon, pepperoni, onions, mushrooms, and sausage on it. Baker ordered the largest size they had because he liked the name.

"No one in back." Senich told his buddy as he sat down on the bench of the corner picnic table. He sat with his back to the counter and prep area so he could see the large flat screen television on the far wall. Baker joined him, sitting in the corner where he could see the door and the young man making their pizza behind the counter.

"Ordered us a large 'Tiger.'"

"As long as there's lots of it, sounds good to me."

When the pie arrived at the table, the two devoured the pizza like a pair of famished wolves after livestock. They didn't talk. Senich tried to catch some of the news between bites. They washed it down with 20 ounce Cokes from the cooler. When finished, Baker paid the bill with a twenty and a five, leaving the change for the young man who made and served their pizza.

With both bellies and the gas tank full, Baker and Senich headed out of Wallace toward Missoula on Interstate 90, heading up Look Out Pass. At the top, they entered Montana, where the speed limit increased. Baker sped up on the way down the mountain. It was a gorgeous spring evening, and they were headed east so they didn't have to worry about the setting sun in their eyes. The trip was quiet and uneventful and the two arrived at Baker's home shortly after ten o'clock.

ALAIN BURRESE

They had only been gone fourteen hours, but it seemed like returning home from a two-week vacation. Baker sighed as he turned off the ignition. "What a day."

"Sure was," Senich replied as he got out and opened the rear door. "Hey, I forgot about this." He pulled out the black briefcase he'd lifted from Cook's truck.

Baker and Senich sat at the kitchen table looking at the contents of Cook's briefcase. The odd assortment of contents were scattered in piles covering the entire surface. There were stacks of bills, letters, invoices, and odd papers still to be determined. Baker wanted everything laid out so they wouldn't miss anything.

Both men had showered and put on clean clothes, while the washer downstairs churned with everything the two had worn on their expedition up in Sanders County. A half pot of freshly brewed coffee rested on the counter and both men had cups sitting in front of them. Baker drank from a ceramic cup with Mickey Mouse on the side, and Senich had a similar one with *The Lion King*.

"Couple tough guys with Disney cups," Senich joked.

"Like a Marine buddy once told me, 'Ben wears pink, because who's gonna say anything to him about it.' Same thing, we can drink from Disney cups, because who's gonna say anything about it. Besides, I like Disney, so do Tanya and Coral."

"Yeah, you used to like those hot pink t-shirts."

"Whatever. Let's finish this up and get some sleep. I'm beat."

"Yeah, it's been a hell of a long day. I like Disney too, for what it's worth. Too bad you don't have a *Jungle Book* cup. Baloo was cool."

"Yeah, I liked him too."

"I don't know if any of this is worth anything." Senich looked through a pile of papers for the third time.

"I don't know either. Wonder what's in here." Baker unzipped a compartment in the case that he'd overlooked when he dumped the contents onto the table for sorting. He found a couple of condoms and a candy bar and tossed them in the garbage sitting next to the kitchen counter. He then found a couple of "naturalist" magazines that contained pictures of little kids running around naked. He stood, uttered a couple of expletives, and headed out the back door.

"What's up?" Senich yelled after him as he rose and followed him out.

"You can get arrested for possessing this shit, and I won't have it in my house. You should have took the guy's kneecaps out before that head shot."

"I could have, all you had to do was ask." Senich saw the magazines in Baker's hand, and even in the dim light from over the door, immediately recognized they were porn. He'd looked through enough in his lifetime and had quite a collection of his own locked away in one of his storage sheds in Michigan. But those were collector's issues. Mostly *Playboy*, which really wasn't porn in Senich's book, and some were worth a lot of money. Besides that, the racks on every truck stop counter contained more than most people would believe existed, and he passed those daily. "What's the big deal with the skin mags? You're worried about those after what we did earlier today?"

"It's this, that. It's all this shit. Do you realize what could happen? Here," Frustrated, Baker threw one magazine at his buddy and tossed the other two into the burn barrel he kept near the grill in his back yard. When the two were stationed in South Korea, there were burn barrels located all around camp to burn mail and other documents. Nothing with names, addresses, or any other information was thrown away because you never knew who might get their hands on stuff and how it might be used. It was all burned, and Baker had kept up the practice since. Besides the Army, he knew that PI's often got information by going through people's garbage cans. Thieves used people's waste to gather valuable information as well. Many people throw old credit card statements away with name, address, and credit card number. Old phone bill in the same lot and a crook had enough to purchase from many on-line sources. When Baker lived places where he couldn't have his barrel, he was adamant about shredding, but he preferred burning. Once burned, he'd soak the ashes before tilling them into one of the flower beds out back.

"Fuck this shit." Senich had opened the magazine to a page that had a group of young boys and girls playing at what looked like some kind of summer camp. The only difference was they were all without clothes. "Fuckin sickos liking little kids. How the hell you like looking at someone without tits yet?" He threw the magazine into the burn barrel with the others.

"Fuck if I know," Baker grabbed the lighter fluid from the cabinet next to the grill and squirted some onto the magazines in the bottom of the barrel. He then used the twelve-inch Bic lighter to set them ablaze.

"I want big tits and pubes."

"I don't care if they're big, but I want tits and want 'em over eight-teen."

"You're married."

"So? Don't mean I don't still appreciate a woman's body."

"That's the magic word, *woman's* body. Not kids. Still think what we did was wrong?"

"If we get caught we could be locked up a long time."

"I didn't ask if it was illegal, I asked if you thought it was wrong."

Baker stared at the multi colored flames as the glossy paper slowly burned. A little reluctantly, he agreed. "No, they need to be stopped."

"We stopped them."

"Let's go finish looking through the rest of the stuff on the table so we can get some sleep."

"I'll get enough sleep when I'm dead."

"Wade Garret's getting old."

"I'm still the best." Both men chuckled at their *Road House* banter and headed back inside.

"I just wonder." Baker set a piece of paper back on the pile it came from and drained the last bit of coffee from his Mickey Mouse cup.

"Wonder what?" Senich stood up and grabbed the pot of coffee and topped off his *Lion King* cup and started to refill Mickey.

Baker stopped him when the cup was half full. "It's probably nothing, but I wonder about those documents with Grady Trucking on them."

"Why?"

"I don't know. Things are just not adding up. I can't figure out how those meth heads figure in this. No one knew I was going to that CLE except you and a couple in the office."

"You think someone you work with has it out for you? Or sold you out?"

"I don't know. Could be anyone."

"You think it's related to these guys, or I just happened to be at the right place at the right time by coincidence."

"It was coincidence all right, they sure the hell didn't expect you here. I just don't know if they were related to the two up in Sanders County."

"Maybe, maybe not. What's up with who you work with?"

"Tucker sure pushed me to go after drug prosecutions, and he's the one who forbid me to pursue Bruce James."

"Who's that?"

"He's the County Attorney, my boss."

"What didn't he let you do?"

"He called off the prosecution of James, the guy I killed in the trailer house. Tucker said we didn't have enough to make it stick and basically ordered me to take on different cases and let that one drop."

"You think he's crooked?"

"I don't know. I don't think so. He's a prick sometimes, but I don't think he's crooked or into anything illegal. I don't know, but now the trucking company has me wondering."

"Wondering what?" Frank took a big gulp from his cup of coffee and gave his friend a look that said 'quit beating around the bush.'

"All right, first, I was thinking about what Finch told me about Butte. And now, it's this. Tucker won't let me prosecute James. James leads us to Sanders County and Cook. His briefcase has shit in it from Grady Trucking in Butte."

"So?"

"Tucker is good friends with the Attorney General. There's talk of them running for Governor and Lt. Governor together."

"I still don't know where you're going."

"The Attorney General is originally from Butte, and his name's Brady Grady."

"Bet that was a fun name to have growing up."

"Yeah."

"He own the trucking company too?"

"No, his brother does."

"So you think the A.G. and his brother are in on this?"

"I don't know what to think. I know Clay Grady is rich, and they say you don't want to cross him."

"What about the Attorney General?"

"Don't really know him. I've met him a couple of times at different functions. Came off as a typical politician. Always had the right thing to say without really saying anything. Acted like he listened, but it felt like he was really deciding what he was going to say to the next guy rather than hearing what you said. I didn't really care for him."

"You know, my truck could solve a lot of this country's problems if you could just get enough politicians lined up like speed bumps in the road."

"Yeah?" Baker finished his coffee and stood up.

"I'm serious."

"You probably are, but we need to get some sleep."

"When we heading to Butte?"

"Who said we were?"

Senich stood, took a drink, and placed the empty coffee cup beside the sink. "You said we were in this to the finish, remember?"

"Yeah, I know. Why don't we head out early. Up, shower, eat and leave. Go over there and see what we find. Nothing else, it'll be a nice drive and we can go check out Berkley Pit."

"What's that?"

"Big hole in the ground from mining."

"Sounds exciting."

"Catch you in few hours."

"Roger that. We can grab more of those gut bombs on the way out if you don't want to cook."

"Sounds good."

"Alright buddy, sleep fast."

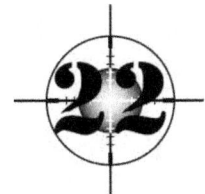

Besides debating whether to stop at Taco Bell, Burger King, or McDonald's for breakfast, the morning routine and leaving Missoula was pretty uneventful. Ben Baker and his buddy Frank Senich both got up after a few hours of sleep, showered, and filled large lidded coffee cups from the freshly brewed pot Baker started before jumping under the hot water of his morning shower. They climbed in Baker's Dodge Durango wearing jeans and t-shirts and could have been a couple good ol' boys heading to the ballpark, not a pair of former military snipers engaged on a reconnaissance mission. It was only recon today, so the only hardware they packed was their ordinary daily carry. Baker had his Browning Hi Power and Cold Steel tactical folder, along with the standard equipment kept in the Dodge. Senich carried his Sig .45 and had his Blackhawk tactical folder clipped inside his right front jeans pocket. Neither man expected anything to happen during their reconnaissance, but neither went many places unarmed. After the last couple of days, they weren't about to start going unarmed now.

Taco Bell and Burger King won out solely because they were on the same side of the street and next to each other. They drove through the drive through of both places and left Missoula with a bag of breakfast burritos and hot sauce and another of assorted breakfast sandwiches. There were a couple with bacon and a couple with sausage; all with eggs and cheese. "Heart attack in a sack," Baker told his buddy as he set the cruise control at 75 mph and settled in for the drive to Butte.

"Yeah, yeah. Tastes good and you know it."

"Give me one with sausage," he said, putting a napkin across his leg.

"Here." Senich gave Baker a sausage biscuit and pulled out the same for himself. "You think we'll find anything in Butte?"

"Not sure, but we'll find out. I'm going to make some calls. I hope I don't lose the signal between here and there." Baker picked up his cell phone and proceeded to make calls between bites, and Senich sat and listened and provided additional food items whenever Baker held out an empty hand. The two devoured both bags of food, and Baker talked with at least a half dozen people and left messages for that many more. The first had been to his office to let them know he wouldn't be in, the rest were to friends and acquaintances. Everyone knew about the happenings at Baker's house late Friday night, so it was perfectly acceptable that he didn't want to come in. Baker just said he needed some time after such a horrific incident. Every once in a while during his conversations he asked Senich to write something down, which he did in the small notebook Baker kept in the Dodge. The drive went quick, and as they passed the Anaconda turn off, Baker put his phone down.

"Well?" Senich asked.

"Few cop buddies. Those places and names I had you write down are things to check out. Might provide the information we're looking for. Might provide shit too."

"You were pretty vague on the phone with those guys. 'Know anything about Grady Trucking? Just curious, that's all.'"

"Yeah, don't you think that's wise." Baker gave his friend a look as if to say don't be a moron.

"Just fucking with you, lighten up."

"It seems that everyone believes Clay Grady is into some dirty stuff, but no one wants to do anything about it."

"How come?"

"Not sure. Either they are afraid of him or getting benefits from his money. Half the town thinks he's a hero for spreading his wealth. The don't seem to care where it came from."

"Wouldn't be the first."

"Right. One of my calls was to a friend from law school, Greg Glass. Don't really keep in touch that much now, but he's the one who told me to check out the truck stops on the West side of town, near the Interstate 15 intersection. He thinks Grady is involved with drug trafficking and that intersection is convenient. 15 goes north to Helena, Great Falls, and then Canada, and if you head South you go through Salt Lake City to Las Vegas and drop into L.A. 90 covers the East to West."

"Ben," Senich looked at his buddy with a 'get a clue' kind of look.

"Yeah?"

"Remember what I do for a living? I know all about 15, 90, and every other route you can think of."

"I'm just telling you what he said."

"I know, I still want you to lighten up."

"It's not that light a situation."

"Sure it is. Just take a deep breath and continue. I'll be quiet."

"Like I said, he thinks Grady's involved with running drugs."

"Maybe he is. Maybe he's trafficking kids too."

"That's what I'm wondering."

"You didn't mention that on the phone."

"I was collecting information, not providing it."

"Roger. Well, let's poke around the truck stops and see what we find out."

"That's what I figure, but he did say one other thing that makes sense."

"What's that?"

"He said to be careful. He said going after Clay Grady could be a career ender, and that Brady wasn't against pulling strings to help his little brother, including making things go away."

"Guess you better keep this out of the office."

"Yeah, he also said Clay Grady has some rough people working for him, and there were rumors that people who crossed them disappeared. All hearsay of course, but that's what he said."

"Well, we know a thing about that too, don't we?"

"Yeah, I guess we do." Baker glanced over and the two men's eyes met. There was a bond there that could only be formed by training, sweating, bleeding, and killing together. The two knew more about each other than anyone else living, and were closer than the closest of brothers. Both would take the secrets shared only by them to the grave. Baker looked back to the road. "We're just about there. Let's see what we can find."

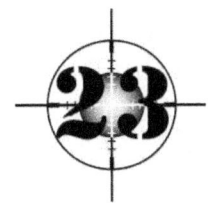

Baker pulled the Durango into the fringe area of the truck stop's parking area. It was out away from everything, and only one other vehicle, a beat up Chevy pick-up, was parked on that side of the building that housed a convenience store, cafe, and a fast food counter. He put the vehicle in park, turned off the key and asked his buddy, "Now what? You're the truck stop guy."

"Let's poke around and see if we can find someone who looks like they can hook us up with some action."

"What kind of action?"

"Don't matter. If they are into one, they most likely are into 'em all. Drugs, women, illegal cigarettes and alcohol, whatever."

"Cigarettes and alcohol?"

"Yeah, some places you can get around taxes and high prices."

"Gotcha."

"We find someone who knows one, he'll know them all. Guarantee it."

"All right, let's go look around."

"Let's go in and get a cup of coffee. Won't be hungry for a long time after those burritos and biscuits, but another coffee would hit the spot."

"Plus we need a reason to hang around."

"You learn that in the Army or law school?"

"Fuck you."

The two men casually walked across the parking lot toward the building. They still looked like two good 'ol boys, not special operation soldiers. However, unlike most good 'ol boys, both men hastily scanned the parking lot and building with the method ingrained in them during their time as snipers in the Army all those years before. It was a simple procedure, and the two did it constantly without even thinking about it. Starting close, and moving out from their position, they made visual sweeps from left to right and right to left. In the military they would go from the nearest terrain feature that could conceal a hostile and continue out to the maximum range of their weapon.

When they had optics, such as binoculars, and more time, they would perform a more deliberate scan. Deliberate scanning was basically the same, looking in the same places, but slower with pauses at potential locations to allow one's mind to register impressions through the binoculars. There was also a method they used when a hasty or deliberate scan failed to detect targets. Detailed scanning was the most thorough technique they used, and consisted of looking everywhere, not just the most obvious places for an enemy, with all the optical devices at one's disposal. You would continuously watch, scan, and stay alert for any indicator of a target's presence, not just a target itself. When a sniper team set up a position and worked together with detailed scanning, nothing went unnoticed.

The scanning Baker and Senich performed walking across the parking lot wasn't so much deliberate as much as it was just part of both men's situational awareness. Do it long enough and it becomes natural, and for the two it was as natural as breathing. It allowed them to detect potential threats and notice good things too. Good things like the thirty-something blonde walking over to the light green Mustang at the gas pumps. The white t-shirt that stretched over what Senich guessed to be at least 38 double D breasts was almost as tight as the jeans she was wearing. "Bet she had to lay back on a bed to get those fastened," he commented as his scanning stopped to watch her all the way to the Mustang.

"She wears them well, that's for sure." Nothing caught either's eye as out of place, or threatening, but Baker did wonder if the blonde was local or passing through, because she wasn't ordinary.

Inside the café, Baker chose the corner booth and slid in with his back to the wall. He could see anyone coming in and out of the café, and half of the occupants. He also had a view down the hallway that connected the café to the convenience store that housed the restrooms. He remembered when he was in high school taking the ferry from Victoria Island to the mainland with a group on a senior trip. He and a buddy met a trucker who gave them some worldly advice. He told them, "Best spot to scope out all the women is outside the restrooms. Before we reach the other side, every woman on the boat will visit them." The advice had stuck, and proved fairly accurate at times. The café's eating area was configured in an L shape, so there was a section out of view. However, the tables in that section had been empty when they entered, and no one could get to them without first coming in the door that Baker faced. The wall behind him was a window from the top of the booth's seat to six inches below the ceiling, and if alone or with his family, he wouldn't have chosen this spot. Sure, it provided a lot of light, but he didn't like someone to be able to come up behind him with only a plate of glass separating him and any unknown. Maybe he grew up watching too many movies advocating the hero sit in the corner with his back to the wall, but he found it was the most practical and helped with situational awareness. Let others live in an oblivious state of ignorance; he wanted to know the way in, the way out, and who was where. And he wanted to know these things everyplace he went. It wasn't paranoia, it was simply living in the here and now and being aware of one's surroundings. You noticed the good like the blonde in the parking lot or the two eggs, bacon, and hash brown special that was advertised on a sign coming in, and you noticed any possible bad in time to do something about it. Most of the time anyway.

Senich slid into the seat opposite Baker, and immediately assumed the role of watching out the window, where he could see the parking lot, the Durango, and anyone who happened to go toward the rear of the building on that side. He knew Baker would see anything going on in the café, so he didn't mind having his back toward the open space. Like Baker, if he'd have been alone, or with someone else, he would have chosen a different location to sit. Tactics changed when you were working with a buddy or a team rather than going solo.

The waitress came over wearing jeans and a t-shirt with the café's logo on the front. Baker figured her to be about 5'10" and two hundred and twenty pounds, maybe a bit heavier the way she stomped the K-Mart brand running shoes down with each step. She wasn't a blob; she was solid. He wondered if she bulldogged steers in her spare time. It was Butte after all. She could probably hold her own drinking, swearing, and fighting with most men, and rodeo would just be a hobby that she could whip most men in too. He was also curious about the tattoo that peeked out of the t-shirt's collar. He'd always been intrigued by what people permanently inked on their bodies. He almost got a pair of them one time. He thought about getting three women's faces on one arm. They would have been a black woman, a white woman and an Asian. Damn how he used to envy Dan Aykroyd when he was younger for having that combination together in a hot tub in

Doctor Detroit. The other arm was going to have three heads, but they would be of a lion, cheetah, and tiger. It had really only been a thought a time or two, and he never did get serious about getting either done. He was glad he didn't have any permanent markings or piercing other than what he came into the world with. Well, those and the scars he managed to collect over the years. Even though he was glad he never got one himself, he still found other's body art fascinating.

"What can I get you two?" she asked.

"Coffee for me please, " Baker replied. He thought about asking about the tattoo, but decided against it. He didn't want to give her any reason to remember him, and people remember those who take interest in them, especially something like a tattoo that she was probably proud of. That and he didn't want her to think he was hitting on her, then she'd most likely really remember him, either as a jerk or she might have a returned interest. Either would be bad. He kept his mouth shut and diverted his gaze elsewhere.

She turned toward Senich, "Same, thanks," he told her. He also didn't provide much to remember. As she headed toward the kitchen, Senich waited for her to turn the corner, "Damn, grow 'em big and strong in these parts."

"That's Butte. Bet she could drink you under the table and then kick your ass."

"She probably could. Hell, she'd probably kick both our asses."

"All right, be nice. Or I'll tell her what you said."

"You would, too. So how are Tanya and your little girl?"

"Good. They went to some 3-D movie yesterday, and they were going to go to Helena's new water slide today."

"You tell her what's going on?"

"No."

"You going to?"

"No."

"Really?"

"We don't talk about my work. I try and leave it at the office. Besides all the confidentiality shit, I don't need to be bringing home all the gruesome things I deal with every day. I don't prosecute nice people for doing good deeds. Sometimes it's pretty bad, so we leave it out of our house and out of our relationship, for the most part anyway. I'm treating this as work, and in a way it is."

"Yeah, I suppose you're right."

The waitress returned and set full cups of coffee in front of both men, and then set down a full carafe and two small bowls. One contained small containers of half-n-half and the other had three different artificial sweeteners: pink, blue, and yellow packets. Baker reached over and grabbed a yellow packet and emptied it into his cup, followed by two of the half-n-half containers. He was stirring when Senich put his cup down after taking a sip and said, "If you wanted a milkshake, why didn't you order one?"

"Just felt like something sweet."

"Ain't I sweet enough for you big guy?" Senich tried batting his eyes, but quickly decided it must be a learned and practiced skill. "So really, Tanya and Coral are okay?"

"Yeah, they are. She knows something's going on, but doesn't really want to know what it is. I think knowing would just make her worry. She knows we can take care of ourselves, and she trusts us."

"Good. I sure hate to imagine what those two the other night would have done if it had been Tanya and your girl at home."

"Don't even talk about it. I'm so grateful they went with me."

"What about me?"

"Well, I'm sorry you got in the middle of it, but I'm thankful you were there to take care of business. If you hadn't been there, they would have broke in, robbed the place and left. I would have never known they were sent by someone."

"Not to mention that I made sure they wouldn't ever do anything like that again."

"Yeah, you did a good job of that too."

"I like that bat. Gonna have to get me one, you know, to keep in the truck with my ball and glove."

"Right." Baker smiled at his buddy, and refilled their half full cups. "So how long you want to hang around here?"

"At least till the coffee's gone. Unless you have a better idea."

"Nope, not really. Guess waiting is what we do best."

"Until it's time to pull the trigger anyway."

"The warrior acts. Might be the king who makes the rules and decides what gets done, but it's the warrior, or the knight, who does it."

"That's right, buddy."

Baker noticed a scruffy looking kid of about eighteen or nineteen enter the restroom in the corridor between the café and store that he was keeping his eye on. "I'll be right back."

"Take your time." Senich repositioned himself with one leg bent and up on the bench seat of the booth they were in. He could now see out the window to his right and the café area to his left. His back was against the wall that was the inside of the booth. He sipped his coffee and watched the waitress take the order of an elderly couple that had come in for a late breakfast or early lunch. Brunch on Monday, he thought? Hell, if you're retired why not. As he watched the waitress march off in a rush to call in the order, he noticed a pickup driving diagonally through the parking lot toward the rear of the building. Just before it got to where he could no longer see it, he read Grady Trucking Inc. on the logo painted across driver's door. He set his cup down and looked over to the restroom's door. The hall was empty, just like most of the café. He thought about going out to take a look, but decided to wait. Might not be anything at all. But then it might.

Baker entered the restroom and caught the scruffy looking kid popping a zit in the bathroom mirror. The kid stopped and sheepishly looked down at his black Metallica t-shirt as he quickly walked passed the urinals and went into a stall. Baker saw the shoes pointing toward the toilet and knew the kid wouldn't be long, so he relieved himself too. It was another old habit that started in his Army days. Whenever you had a chance to eat, sleep, dump, or piss, you did so, because there would be plenty of times when you couldn't do any of them. In the bars you never wanted a full bladder if a fight broke out, so you got in the habit of relieving yourself when you could and before any trouble started. He was washing his hands when the kid came out zipping the fly of his jeans. He pulled out a towel and turned toward the kid who was avoiding looking at him. "Can I ask you something?"

"Ah, sure. I guess so."

"My buddy and I are just passing through and we want to get high, maybe get laid. Who around here can hook us up?"

"Uh, I don't know." The kid looked around like he might be on a hidden camera show. He was ready to bolt, but wasn't sure how he'd get past this guy who had to be twenty years his senior and was a heck of a lot bigger.

Seeing him scare, Baker quickly tried to calm him down. "Hey, it's cool. We're just looking for a good time, that's all." Just like the waitress, he didn't want the kid to remember him, or at least not much about him.

"You sure, man?" The kid was trying to muster up some bravado, but his voice cracked at the end of "sure" and the pause before "man" was too long to be casual or tough.

"Yeah, don't worry. I just thought you might know. It's no big deal. My buddy and I have some money to spend on a good time, and we weren't sure who to talk to around here. You looked like someone in the know, that's all."

The kid straightened up a bit when he heard Baker's somewhat compliment. Not many people thought he was in the know. "Well, I might be able to hook you up. If you're on the level." A bit of confidence was emerging.

"Hey, we just want a good time. Passing through on our way to Seattle."

"Oh yeah, where you from?"

"Started out in Chicago last week." Baker was making things up as he went, just in case the kid decided to talk to someone about him. Now he needed to make sure the kid didn't see the Durango with Montana plates.

"Cool. I always wanted to go to Chicago. I liked *ER*."

"You should go sometime. Fall or Spring's best. Winter gets cold, and the summer gets hot."

"I hear ya, but cold don't bother me. You should see how cold it gets around here in the winter. I'm used to it."

"I don't like the cold. After Seattle for the summer, we'll head south for the winter just like the birds."

"I'd like to go to Florida too. Spring Break at the beach would be cool."

"Nothing's stopping you."

"Well, need money to get there."

"That's true. Why don't you hook me and my buddy up and maybe we can help in that department. A little anyway."

"What ya want?"

ALAIN BURRESE

"Get high a bit, you know. Really want some pussy. Just pay for it, knock it out and have some fun, then not have to deal with her later. You know."

"Yeah, I know." The look on the kid's face as he attempted to laugh about it made Baker wonder if he were still a virgin.

"So where can we get some action?"

"Well, I think the best guy to talk to is Rodney."

"Rodney who?"

"Hmm, I don't know. It's Rodney something. He calls himself Hot Rod, but I don't think anyone else calls him that."

"Hot Rod, Rodney. All right, where can I find him?"

"Actually, he hangs out here a lot."

"This restroom?"

"No, outside. Usually out back."

"He got pussy back there?"

The word pussy made the kid grin again. "I don't know. I got some weed from him once, and a friend used to get meth from him." The kid's face grew grim and he looked at the floor. "We ain't friends no more. Meth really messed him up."

"Yeah, I lost friends to that stuff too."

"Really?"

"Yep. Little pot's okay. But pussy's the best. Just make sure it's clean, right?"

"Yeah," the embarrassed grin returned.

"So this Hot Rod can get us some?"

"I think so."

"Well, I'll have to look around for him. I thank you much. I knew you'd be the person to talk to." Baker pulled his money clip from his front left pocket and peeled off a twenty and handed it over. "Thanks again for your time. Look me up if you get out to Seattle."

"Thanks. Sure, I'll do that."

Baker left wondering if the kid had any clue how big Seattle was. It didn't matter, he got a name and they were one step closer to maybe figuring things out. He reached the table just as Senich poured another cup of coffee.

"Took you long enough, take a dump or something?"

"Got some information, a name anyway. Rodney, or Hot Rod."

"What about him?" Senich took a big swig of coffee.

"Kid in the restroom says he can get drugs and women."

"Sounds like what we're looking for."

"Yep, or at least closer anyway."

"Where do we find him?"

"Kid says he hangs around here, out back."

"What a coincidence."

"What?" Baker gulped down the cold coffee in his cup and checked the carafe to see how much was left, and then poured himself a fresh cup. He raised it toward Senich's mug and offered to top his off which he accepted.

"While you were gone, a Grady Trucking pickup went out back."

"Where?"

"I don't know. It drove past, and I haven't seen it come back. Could have left another route I guess. I was going to go check it out, but figured I'd wait for you."

Baker stayed silent as the heavy footed waitress walked towards them. "Can I get you feller's anything else?"

"We're fine, thanks." Baker finished putting half-n-half and sweetener in his fresh cup.

"Okay, let me know if I can get ya'll something." She was headed back to the kitchen before the sentence was half finished.

Baker took a long drink from his cup. "Let's finish up and take a walk around back."

ALAIN BURRESE

"Sounds good." Senich gulped down his entire cup and
stood. "I'll be right back."

"I'll wait." Baker reached into his pocket and retrieved a
five dollar bill that he laid on the table to cover the coffees
with a two dollar tip. He took a sip and then stood and
stretched his arms back behind him. He shrugged his
shoulders a couple of times, picked up his cup and finished it
off, and walked toward the door just as Senich exited the
restroom.

The two men walked along the side of the building in
silence. They gravitated toward the parking lot and took the
corner to the back of the building wide. Other than three big
blue dumpsters along the back wall, it was pretty barren. The
pavement blended into a vacant gravel and weed laden lot
that had a couple of smashed up cars that wouldn't even be
worth parts sitting on the far side.

"Down there." Senich motioned to the back of a pickup
truck that was just barely sticking out from behind the far
corner. "Might be the truck I saw." The two walked the length
of the building as nonchalantly as they walked in front going
into the café. They reached the corner and saw it was indeed a
Grady Trucking vehicle and the driver was inside talking on a
cell phone. They also noticed that the driver saw them in his
rear view mirror as they stepped past the corner and behind
the truck. They walked around and up to the passenger side
door as if that's what they always intended. Baker stood there
and indicated to the man on the phone that he wanted to ask
him something.

The window electrically powered about half way down,
and the man inside held his phone to his chest. "What do you
want?"

"We're looking for Rodney?"

"Who?"

"Hot Rod, or Rodney."

"Wait a minute." The window powered back up and Baker studied the man inside. It was hard to tell height with him sitting inside the truck, but Baker guessed he was a bit under six feet and maybe weighed around two hundred. He had short hair and a mustache and goatee, all black. He wore jeans and a green t-shirt that featured the same Grady Trucking logo on the upper left side as the truck had on its door. As he held his phone to his right ear, Baker looked at the upside down bulldog tattooed on his forearm and read the upside down USMC that completed the artwork. There were three prominent scars across the forearm that reminded Baker of an old knife fighter he used to train with. Only the old-timer's arms looked like an ice rink after a hockey match with the scars that criss-crossed every which way and back. He couldn't see the man's left arm, but suspected he was right handed the way he was holding the phone and that the left arm would have more scars as the defending arm. In a fight, he'd have his knife in his right hand and use the left more defensively.

"Former Marine. Likes blades," he said loud enough for Senich to hear, but not loud enough to be detected by the man inside the cab. Senich had moved near the rear corner of the vehicle so he could see the area behind the building as well as the open area on the side. It was basically another empty parking lot like they left the Durango in at the other end.

The window moved back down and Baker put on a big good 'ol boy smile as the man inside looked him up and down with hard green eyes. For just a second, Baker thought of how Tanya would comment about how his shirt went with his eyes. "What do you want with Hot Rod?" said the man with a guttery voice. It sounded like he had a cold or allergies, and when Baker leaned in to hear him better, the smell of stale cigarette smoke increased to where he backed up again.

"We heard he could hook us up."

"With what?" the man demanded.

"You know, a little weed, maybe some pussy. We're just looking for a good time before we hit the road again." Baker could tell the man was trying to size him up, and having a difficult time doing it.

"You got cash?"

"Sure do." Baker pulled out his money clip and flashed it in front of the open pickup truck window.

"Wait a minute." Before Baker could reply the window went back up. The man was punching buttons on his phone.

"What do you think?" Baker asked his buddy.

"Don't know, but I guess we'll find out."

"Guess we will."

The man took the phone from his ear and the window came down again. He motioned to the rear of the building. "Wait around back. Rodney will be here in a bit."

As the window started to close yet again, Baker stopped him, "He got what we need?"

"Don't worry, he'll hook you up. Whatever you want, the Rod can get."

"I've heard that before," Senich whispered to himself so the other two couldn't hear.

"Wait in back." The window closed and the goateed man was back on his cell phone.

Baker walked to where Senich stood by the rear of the truck, "well?"

"Guess we wait."

"Yeah, guess so. I'm thinking we might not need to follow up with any of the other names and places I asked you to write down coming over. Greg was right in saying the first place he'd look if he wanted information were the truck stops."

"We'll see."

Fifteen minutes later, a black Ford Explorer drove into the truck stop parking lot and slowly cruised toward the rear where the Grady Trucking pickup was parked. Senich continued to look at Baker and the area behind the building while his buddy filled him in. "Black Ford, two guys in front. Might be someone in back, not sure, can't see. Yeah, there is someone in the back. Three of them unless someone's hiding on the floor."

"Makes four total with the dude in the truck."

"Right. If things go south, I don't want any guns unless it's absolutely necessary."

"You're shitting me right?"

"I'm serious. Not here, not now. My Dodge's over there, we've been seen, we won't be able to avoid the law. We won't be able to explain this, and with Grady involved, it can come back to bite me big time, even if we aren't arrested."

"I hear ya. But it goes against my rule to only fight empty handed when you are sure you can take the guy, or as a bridge to get to your weapons."

"What about all the bar fights when we were younger?"

"I was sure we could take 'em." Senich smiled, and hearing a car door slam, looked over at the Explorer that just arrived. Three men climbed out. Two stayed by the vehicle while the driver walked around and met the man from the truck, who had also gotten out and slammed his door shut. The two stood and talked in front of the pickup.

The new man was fairly tall, maybe six-three, but didn't carry a lot of weight on his bones. Baker doubted he weighed two hundred. The other two were shorter and didn't seem that imposing either. Looks could be deceiving, and Baker never underestimated opposing attorneys or those he might encounter physically. He'd read that lesson and had instructors recite it to him repeatedly, but it was learning it the hard way that stuck with him the most all these years. Actually, whenever he read or heard someone mention you shouldn't judge a book by its cover or underestimate an opponent, he remembered a particular party back in high school. He was taught, and taught good, by a skinny little runt that happened to be the state wrestling champ of his division. He tied Baker in knots, and if it hadn't been a "friendly" fight at a party, it could have been ugly. The only thing really hurt was Baker's ego, and though embarrassed, he learned. The other incident was more recent and occurred when he was a new prosecutor. A bumbling and nerdish defense attorney turned out to be much brighter than Baker originally sized him up to be. When the case was over, he reminded himself to watch some old *Columbo* episodes with Peter Falk and not forget that appearances can be deceiving. It was one of those things he knew in the physical arena, but failed to apply to his profession. But only once.

Baker and Senich tried to look unassuming while they waited at the rear of the pickup. They couldn't make out what the two up front were saying, but they did notice the hard stares coming from the two by the Explorer. The baggy camouflage pants and long t-shirt the one was wearing made it difficult to discern if he was carrying a weapon. The jeans and tucked in shirt of his partner made him easier to scope out. Neither appeared to be packing, but Baker and Senich weren't quite sure.

The goateed man from the truck and the driver from the Explorer started to walk along the side of the truck toward Baker and Senich. "What you guys want?" the Explorer driver asked. As he neared, Baker thought he might be a couple inches taller than his initial guess of six-three.

"We're looking for Rodney," Baker replied. Senich had taken a couple steps backward to better be able to watch everyone.

"Found him. What you want?" The two stopped at the back corner of the truck and there was about six feet between Baker and the tall one who identified himself as Rodney. Baker saw a small black clip on the pocket of the pickup driver's jeans. He also noticed the additional scars along the outside of his left forearm.

"We were told inside that you could hook us up with some fun."

"Told by who?"

"Some kid in the john."

"What'd he say?"

"I told him I was looking for some weed, maybe some pussy, and he said 'talk to Rodney' and told me you were out here a lot."

"He did, did he?"

"Hey, we don't want any trouble. We just wanted to rest a bit and get some pussy before we hit the road again."

"Well, you got trouble." Rodney's voiced raised a bit as he stepped closer to where Baker stood. He stopped at the range where one quick step forward with his left, followed by sliding his right behind, would allow Baker to strike with either his hands or feet. But first he wanted to try and diffuse the situation. This was supposed to be a recon mission without engagement.

Senich's appearance didn't change, he stood with his left hand resting across his stomach horizontal, and his right arm vertical with his hand covering his mouth and chin. It looked relaxed and passive, but was actually a protective position that he could immediately launch an attack from if desired. His eyes didn't miss anything as his focus cycled between the four, paying closer attention to the two still back by the Explorer. He knew Baker would be paying more attention to the other two he was talking with. Besides the heightened awareness, his body was preparing to explode into action. He felt the effects of adrenaline as it started entering his body. He liked it, and was ready to act.

What's up?" Baker raised his hands in a non-threatening gesture that was often taught as a de-escalating stance. While it didn't threaten whoever you were trying to talk down, it allowed for instantaneous defense or offense if the oral negotiations failed.

"We don't like fellers nosing around our business."

"We were just told you could help us find a good time. We'll leave if you can't."

"You ain't no cops from around here, so I bet you're reporters." Rodney mistook Baker's posture as fear. He attempted to make himself even bigger by pulling his arms back and puffing up his chest. "We don't take kindly to reporters."

Senich was glad his hand was over his mouth, because he could barely hold back his laugh as the tall skinny Rodney tried to act tough in Baker's face.

"We'll just leave then." Baker slid his rear foot back, followed by sliding his front foot back the same distance, always remaining balanced and poised to move instantaneously if needed. He kept his open hands out in front of him, illustrating he didn't want any trouble.

"You'll leave all right, but first you're getting a lesson to teach you not to come back." The two lingering by the Explorer started to advance toward the other four. Tension was mounting, and it was apparent to everyone that something was going to go down, and soon.

Senich's hand was still in front of his mouth. Seeing the two start toward them, and hearing the tall one tell them they were going to get a lesson, he smiled.

Baker inhaled slowly, and pulled the breath down to his center point just below the navel. He then exhaled watching the three others position themselves behind their leader. It was a breath readying him for action. It went unnoticed by everyone but Senich, who was still smiling behind his hand. He breathed deep again and during his exhale he saw Rodney shift his weight in preparation to attack. The exhale almost turned to a sigh as Baker thought – *fuck*.

Rodney launched his attack with a big overhand left intended
to clobber and cave in the right side of Baker's face. His
intentions may have been fruitful if he'd known how to punch
properly with his weight behind it. That and if Baker hadn't
read the movements of the tall man's shoulders which tipped
him off that the blow would be coming from Rodney's left
hand, rather than the more common right handed attack. As it
turned out, because of the pickup's position to Baker's left, the
attack Rodney chose was perfect for a basic *hapkido* elbow
technique defense.

Baker stepped to his right, getting off line of the incoming
punch. He raised his left arm, which had already been up
while in the de-escalation stance, and used a circular block to
deflect the blow further to his left, while at the same time
grabbing Rodney's wrist with his left hand. Trained fighters
withdrew their limbs as fast as they shot them out, making it
sometimes difficult to trap or catch an incoming arm or leg.
Rodney had no such training, and his John Wayne movie style
punch was easier to block and catch than those in classes
where your partner cooperated so you could learn the
technique. As he pulled the hand down toward his left hip,
Baker grabbed the same wrist with his right hand to assist and
position his right bicep to finish the technique.

Grabbing Rodney's left wrist with both hands didn't leave
a blocking arm, and Rodney did still have one hand free.
However, by pulling Rodney's left hand toward his own left
hip, it crossed Rodney's body with his arm, thus twisting him

in a way that he couldn't throw a right. Besides, it happened so quickly, that Rodney was still surprised that he hadn't connected with his desired target. He expected Baker to be on the ground from his left, and then they could put the boots to him. Now his arm was being pulled down and across, confusing him as to what Baker was doing.

The confusion only lasted a moment as a blindingly sharp pain exploded from his left elbow. Baker pulled Rodney's left hand to his left hip, being sure to keep his opponent's palm facing the ground; this ensured Rodney's elbow would be facing to the side, and directly at Baker's incoming right bicep. Baker stepped into the technique, so all of his body weight was behind him as he also twisted his waist and smashed forward with his right shoulder. Crack. His right bicep connected powerfully with Rodney's outstretched arm just above the elbow, hyper-extending the joint, and making Rodney bend over and follow where his broken arm was leading. In practice, you performed the technique with a smooth motion and used it to send your opponent to a wall or the floor, you didn't smash your arm into the joint. Baker was still smooth, but he added the smash to break Rodney's arm, and then continued the follow through that sent Rodney's head into the back of the parked truck with a metallic clunk. The technique also served the purpose of keeping Rodney between Baker and the scarred driver of the pickup who attempted to come up on Rodney's right side to get into the ruckus.

The entire technique took only a moment, and as Rodney's head smacked the back of the pickup, Baker was not sure if the blow, combined with the broken arm, would keep Rodney out of the fight or not. And one thing was certain, especially when you were outnumbered, when you put people down, you put them down so they couldn't come back. Baker had seen some

194

men go down and stay there with nothing more than a bruise, and he'd known others who kept fighting with wounds from knives and guns that ended up being fatal, but not before the person took his killer with him. Rodney wasn't getting a chance to re-enter the fray, immediately after his head bounced off the pickup, before he even hit the ground, Baker snapped a quick side kick with his right leg into Rodney's exposed left knee. Baker's kick was almost a combination of a side kick and a stomp and it crashed down onto Rodney's knee at a 45-degree angle with a distinguishable crunching sound. It was the sound that makes an entire audience noisily suck in their breath and gasp at a wrestling tournament. Baker was satisfied Rodney wouldn't be back into the fight and wouldn't be walking without assistance. In fact, Rodney wouldn't be walking without crutches for quite some time.

Because Rodney and the pickup truck driver would be taking care of Baker, the two who had hung back at the Explorer, and only came forward just before Rodney's attack, went straight for Senich. The leader, the one in camouflage pants, put his head down and rushed forward. He had tackled people before, and knew once on the ground he could pound away as his partner stayed upright and threw some kicks to the downed opponent's head.

Senich made the mistake of watching and admiring Baker's Hapkido defense to Rodney's attack. He knew many martial artists couldn't fight their way out of paper bags, but that there were also people like Baker who could use their art quite effectively. It was a pleasure to see the bone breaking techniques in action. However, the moment of pleasure cost him the split second he needed for the sprawl to work against Mr. Camo's rush and tackle.

As his attacker shot in and grabbed behind both of his legs for a two-leg takedown, Senich knew he wasn't going to be able to sprawl, so he immediately went for another technique by grabbing his attacker's face with his right hand as his attacker placed his head on Senich's right hip and drove forward with his right shoulder in Senich's gut. Frank dug his fingers into Mr. Camo's eyes and let him complete his tackle. He missed his opportunity to deny the two-leg takedown, so rather than attempt the technique that was too late, he adapted to his attacker and prepared for a ground battle. However, this wasn't high school wrestling, nor was it mixed martial art submission fighting. He reached across and replaced his right hand with his left and continued to dig into the eyes and pulled his attacker's head tight to his chest. He then explosively rolled to his left, jerking his opponent's head with his left hand, fingers still dug into the eyes, and pushing it with his right. Mr. Camo rolled off and Frank continued to roll and was now on top, crushing down on his opponent's head with his chest, preventing him from scrambling free. He immediately raised up and slammed both of his hand's down onto Mr Camo's face and head, keeping it pinned to the ground and preventing him from looking around for help, or to regain direction to keep fighting. Frank then took his hands off Mr. Camo's head just long enough to fire off a full body-weight slashing elbow down to the side of Mr. Camo's face, smashing his jaw into several pieces. Sitting back upright, he fired off a second elbow, just as powerful as the first, to Mr. Camo's temple. The blow knocked the attacker unconscious and Senich was on his feet facing the startled second opponent before Mr. Jeans fully realized how his partner had been taken out.

Baker saw Senich go to the ground out of the corner of his eye, but he was focused on the goateed man from the truck and the knife he had pulled from his pocket. Immediately upon feeling the crunch of Rodney's knee under his side kick stomp, Baker turned to face the next imminent threat, which was the pick-up driver. He turned just in time to see the fluid motion of the draw and opening of the Spyderco tactical folder. Baker recognized the opening at the top of the blade that was the trademark of the company and substituted for the small thumb knob on his Cold Steel folders. The way he opened and held the knife, combined with the scars along his forearms, warned Baker that he wasn't facing a novice, and this wasn't his opponent's first dance.

He briefly thought of pulling the voyager from his own pocket, and then thought of the Browning still clipped inside his jeans at the small of his back with the simple Side Kick holster. The smart thing would be to tactically retreat and draw the Hi Power. Facing a knife empty handed was ugly, no matter what kind of training you had, and knife-to-knife was not much better, and maybe even worse depending on the skill level of those with the blades. The firearm would give him the edge, as long as he could create the distance to bring it into play. A person could cover a lot of distance and do considerable amount of damage with a knife in the time even experienced people could draw and fire. Dennis Tueller and the 21 foot rule that came from his teachings entered Baker's thoughts, and he knew he should have retreated and bought distance to draw a weapon. The thoughts of his own blade, the Tueller Drill, 21 feet, and his Browning all flashed through his mind more quickly than the pickup driver's forward step.

The thought Baker acted upon was that of hollowing out as the four-inch blade whistled past his abdomen in a horizontal slash that cut through his t-shirt and narrowly missed opening up his stomach. His opponent immediately brought the knife up high on his left side and came with a backward slash while expertly rotating the knife so the angle of the blade would be perfect for cutting its target. Baker was expecting the second slash, and was confident that a thrust would immediately follow the two slashes. Basically, the slashes set the person up, and if they connected and cut a person, all the better. However, it was the thrust, and the deeper penetration of the blade, that did the most damage. Baker wasn't going to wait for the thrust, after his hollowing out to avoid the first slash, he stepped into the next swing, surprising his attacker who expected him to back up again. Using the outside of his right forearm, he blocked the attack just above his attacker's wrist. Without losing contact, he turned his own hand and grasped the knife wielding arm at the wrist and simultaneously smashed his left forearm into the locked elbow. The force of the strike made the man drop his knife as Baker stepped through the technique and used the arm bar to plant his attacker's face into the pavement. He dropped his left knee down onto the back of the man's right shoulder to pin him to the ground. He continued to hold the damaged arm, and was in a position to look around for other attackers while remaining in control.

The thug in blue jeans had held back, thinking his camouflaged buddy would take their man to the ground and he'd just go in and stomp him a few times. He really wasn't much of a fighter, and he was surprised to see his companion laying still on the asphalt while he now faced the person he planned to kick while down. Not knowing what to do, but also not wanting to seem cowardly, he charged. "You mother fucker!" he screamed as he threw a humongous overhead right.

Senich stepped inside with his right foot, turning his body toward his left and he brought both arms up to block the incoming blow at the forearm and bicep. His right arm, after hitting the bicep with his block, whipped into an ax hand strike to the exposed neck of his attacker. Because he was

198

moving forward with his strike, Senich's forearm actually made contact, rather than the ax hand, as he visualized his arm cutting through his opponent's neck and beheading him like an ancient Samurai's sword. The visualization, combined with the footwork and twisting at the waist, ensured that the strike would penetrate deeply into the target. Senich's right hand collapsed around his attacker's neck and pulled his head and body forward, doubling him over. He threw three powerful knees, using as much force as possible, into the tender midsection of his jeans wearing opponent. With each knee, he tried to lift his opponent off the ground. Still holding the attacker's right wrist in this left hand from where he grabbed it after blocking the first incoming punch, Senich raised the arm and pushed down on the neck and head that he still held in his right. Pivoting backwards, the movement sent his opponent sprawling onto the pavement. Frank looked down on him where he lay moaning and squirming. "I'm a mother fucker all right, I fucked your mother."

"You all right?" Baker had seen the last knee strike and how his buddy had thrown his opponent to the ground. He didn't have the finesse of an accomplished martial artist, but he sure got the job done. And for pure savagery and violence of action, Frank Senich was a combative nightmare for any who faced him. He was the kind of man that Baker considered cross hairs only, which meant he wouldn't want to go up against him except from a thousand yards with a sniper rifle. The only problem with Frank was the son-of-a-bitch was also sniper qualified and almost as good a counter-sniper as he was. And that's why he called him when this shit began.

"I'm great, you?" Senich looked over to where Baker still had the former knife-wielding opponent pinned with his face in the asphalt.

"I'm good. This SOB almost cut me though." He increased the pressure on the down man's shoulder and pulled his arm back a little making him squirm and grimace in pain.

"I think we need to get the fuck out of here."

"I think you're right, let's go." Baker wrenched the man's arm a final time, dislocating the shoulder, and creating a little more pain to think about, rather than attempting to reengage. The thought was far from any of the four, battered attacker's minds.

Senich and Baker jogged the length of the building and then slowed to a walk as they passed the blue garbage dumpsters and came out from behind the back to cross the side parking lot to the Durango. There were a few more cars on the side of the building than before, but no one seemed to notice them. They climbed into the vehicle and a few minutes later were back on I 90 for the few minutes it would take to get to the downtown exit for Butte.

"You know how fucking stupid that was?" Senich looked at his buddy in disbelief.

"Yeah. What were we thinking coming here in the first place?" Baker replied.

"I'm not talking about coming here."

"What then?"

"Not using the weapons we had. You always go armed so you have your weapon when you need it. It's fucking idiotic to go empty handed when you don't have to."

"Yeah, but…"

"But nothing. What the fuck were you thinking, no guns. There were four of them. What if one of them had pulled more than a knife? And you're damn lucky it was just one of them that had a blade."

"I know, and you're right. I'm the one with the sliced shirt."

"Damn right I am."

"But I also know you enjoyed that. You like taking people out with your hands. You always have."

"And you like proving that *hapkido* shit works."

"It does work."

"And you like proving it. So don't give me any shit about liking it when you want to validate your training."

"I'm not validating anything."

"Whatever. At least I admit I enjoy busting heads and cracking skulls."

"Well, maybe that's why I wanted you along."

"Damn right, you did." Senich smiled and then grimaced. "I'm going to need a hot tub. Rolling around on pavement hurts."

"You know better than to go to the ground, especially when outnumbered."

"Fuck you, shit happens. Bet ya it's the last time that mofo tries tackling someone."

"I don't think any of those boys will be acting quite as tough for a while." Baker took the exit and slowed at the end of the off ramp and stopped at the light. He turned right and drove a short distance and then took a left into a small mall's parking lot.

"What do you want here?"

"Nothing, I'm just not sure what to do next."

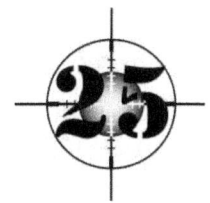

Frank Senich was bored, and becoming tired. The coffee from the morning and the adrenaline from the truck stop brawl were wearing off. He also felt the little aches and pains from being tackled into the pavement earlier. He wanted to stretch, he wanted more coffee, he wanted food, he wanted some Advil or any other pain killer he could down, and most of all he wanted to quit sitting in Baker's Durango parked at the Butte mall. "What's up with the statue on the mountain over there?" Senich pointed toward the ninety-foot statue of a woman overlooking the city of Butte with her arms open on top of the Continental Divide.

"They call it Our Lady of the Rockies. I don't know much about it. Supposed to resemble the Virgin Mary and represent motherhood. It was built back in the 80s."

"It's huge. How the hell they get it up there?"

"I remember seeing some pictures of them flying it up in sections with one of those big skycrane helicopters."

"Damn, must have been quite a project."

"Yeah," Baker replied.

"Ever been up to it?"

"No, not yet."

"So, how long are we gonna sit here anyway?"

"It hasn't been that long."

"The hell it hasn't, it's going on noon. I'm hungry, we could at least go get lunch while you think."

"You're hungry already?"

"It was a busy morning. Worked up an appetite."

"Yeah, I could use something to eat and some coffee myself, I guess."

"Well, let's go."

"What are you hungry for?"

"Let's try something local, I don't want a chain."

"Alright. We'll head under the Interstate toward the older part of town. Should be able to find something up there." Baker started the Dodge and headed out of the mall parking lot.

"Got any Advil or something?"

"Check the glove box, should be something in there."

"Roger." Frank found some generic brand pain pills and popped three of them and swallowed with a drink of water from a refillable bottle they'd brought along. "That should help."

"Keep your eyes out for a place to eat." The two were driving around the older part of the city that was referred to as Uptown Butte due to being built on the mountainside. Years ago, the area was referred to as the Richest Hill on Earth due to the copper found there. The Berkley Pit, now a huge hole in the ground, was at one time one of the most important sources for the strategic metal. Baker was just taking roads at random, driving around looking for a place to eat lunch.

"There's a place." Frank pointed to a sign that said, "Fred's Mesquite Grill" with flames in the middle. "Think it will have the same sights as Fred's in Missoula the other night?"

"Hardly." Baker shook his head thinking of the strip club they visited named Fred's. "Let's try it out." He pulled into a parking space and the two men got out and headed in to eat. Just as Senich opened the door, Baker's cell phone rang. "Get us a table, I'll be there in a minute."

"Alright." Senich went in and requested a corner table in the back. The waitress told him sure, but she'd have to clean it off first. "No problem," he replied. Once seated, he ordered coffee and perused the menu. He was on his second cup when Baker finally joined him.

"Sorry." Baker sat and picked up a menu.

"Good thing I didn't order you coffee too, it'd be cold. This is my second cup."

"Yeah, I know. It was my boss."

"What'd he want?"

"You won't believe this. He wanted to know where I was."

"What the hell for?"

"I don't know, but get this. He asked if I was in Butte."

"How'd he know?"

"I don't know, that's what I'm wondering."

"What'd you tell him?"

"I didn't confirm or deny it. I asked him since when did he start calling people to find out what they were doing on their time off."

"How'd that go over?"

"He didn't like it, but I don't give a shit. He then changed the subject and asked about a couple of cases I'm handling, that's what took so long."

The waitress came and refilled Frank's cup and Ben had her pour him one too. Frank then ordered a burger that was advertised as being thick and fresh from the mesquite grill. Baker ordered a grilled chicken salad with ranch on the side. When she'd gone, Baker continued, "Something's up, but I don't know what. Why would he call and ask if I was in Butte?"

"We busted up those four boys pretty good. The one for sure was in a Grady truck. You said your boss and that Grady had a relationship."

ALAIN BURRESE

"Tucker and Brady Grady plan to run for Governor and Lieutenant Governor together, or at least that's the word. They haven't announced it officially yet."

"But this Grady Trucking is owned by this Brady's brother?"

"Right."

"Kin's kin. Wouldn't be the first politician to use his position to help a family member or friend out."

"Yeah, I know. I just wish we had something more to go on. Still not sure just how all this fits together."

"Yes you do. You're just looking for proof that would hold up in a courtroom. But you know what's going on. Add up the pieces you've got."

"I know, but…"

"But nothing. Forget about the law and your rules of evidence, and all that shit. Lay out what you know."

"Okay, we have links from the guy in the trailer house where I found the little girl to the campers up in Sanders County. Pictures proved it. Then we found the Grady Trucking documents in the briefcase you took from the pick-up."

"You're welcome for that, by the way." Both men stopped talking as the waitress appeared with their lunches. "Looks good," Frank told her.

"Anything else for you boys?"

"I'm fine, thanks," Baker replied.

"Just keep filling my coffee and I'll be a happy camper."

"I'll be back with a fresh pot in a jiffy."

She bounded off and Frank was still smiling as he turned back to his friend, "She's a cutie."

"Okay, so the scum bags might be connected to Grady Trucking. Weak chain, but a chain nonetheless."

"Makes sense." Frank took a big bite of his burger. "Damn, this is good," he said chewing. "You start looking at these guys, and your boss tells you not to. We come down here, have a run in with some of Grady's boys, and your boss knows right away. I think Grady Brady, or whatever his name is, is using your boss to try and keep you away from his brother and his brother's trucking company."

"You might be right."

"And I'll bet you Grady Trucking is dirty. Or at least some of them are involved in some shit. Using big rigs and trucking routes is an easy way to traffic stuff. Drugs, women, kids, whatever. It goes on."

"I know." Baker picked at his salad. "We don't have enough to do anything with though."

"The hell we don't. Maybe not to prosecute them in one of your courts of law, but we got enough. We can't quit now."

"Do you know what you're saying?"

"Yeah, what's your problem? I told you this would get ugly, and if we started we'd be in it till the end."

"Brady Grady is the Attorney General and favorite to be the next Governor. His brother is a rich businessman. Half this town loves him for the money he donates."

"Dirty money and power don't change anything. If you're anyway involved with doing that shit we saw to kids, you're fucking sick. And there's only one sure cure I know of, and that's a 175 grain boat-tail to the head. Senich was deathly serious as he emphasized his description of the military M118 Long Range sniper round. He took another large bite of his hamburger and stared at Ben while he chewed.

Images from the last couple of weeks filled Baker's thoughts as he looked into his friend's eyes. "I know."

"So what are we going to do about it?"

"That I don't know." Baker stabbed the last piece of chicken in his salad and put it in his mouth. He pushed the salad plate over to the edge of the table as he chewed. "Let's go back home, figure things out there."

"You don't want to snoop around here some more?"

"Don't you think we did enough today?"

Senich rotated his shoulder up, back and down, feeling where he hit the pavement earlier. "Yeah, I suppose. But we're here, and there's still daylight."

"Finish that and let's head back."

"You sure?"

"Yeah, like you said, Clay Grady's probably dirty. And somehow he's got his brother and my boss involved. We need to be careful."

"I'm always careful," Senich said putting the last bite of the hamburger into his mouth.

"Yeah, right. Let's go home and figure out what to do next."

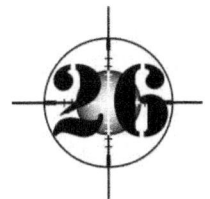

"Shady Brady Grady" was a line from an adversary's political campaign that infuriated the fifty-three year old former Butte boy turned attorney turned politician. With desires to be the State's next Governor, he hated that people talked about his character in such a demeaning manner. He was the goddamn Attorney General, how dare they smear his name. It was hard enough to live down his infamous youth in Butte, but since entering the A.G.'s office, the Aspiring Governor, or as he liked to believe, Almost Governor, had kept to the straight and narrow. He had managed to avoid any political discrepancies that could waylay his ambitious path, and had actually done a bit of good while in office, or at least he believed so. He represented honesty in government and claimed to be a transparent straight shooter. To the public anyway. Matters that went on behind closed doors were just that, behind closed doors. What people didn't know wouldn't hurt them, and more importantly wouldn't hurt Brady Grady, the next Governor of the great state of Montana. After all, the only way things really got done were because of the goings on behind closed doors. The deals that went on behind the public's back every day in the capital city of Helena would most likely cause the farmers, ranchers, and small business owners that made up most of the large state's population, raise up with every conceivable hunting firearm they could lay there hands on and lead a revolution unseen since 1776. Montanans were proud, patriotic, and knew how to use the guns just about everyone owned, if not on a rack in the back of their pickup, for sure in closets, gun safes, and under beds. But the public didn't know what really went on, and Grady's pro-gun, conservative message would take back the Capital for the GOP.

He cursed his parents for naming him Brady over and over while growing up. They thought the rhyming was cute, or at least his mother did. He hated the teasing he received and spent as much time in principles' offices and detention over fights because of his name as he did over all the other mischief he got himself into, which was triple what most boys tried. While he did get some sympathy from his mother at times, and she even apologized once for the silly rhyming name, his father had always said, "toughen up, we could have named you Sue." Brady would then have to sit and listen to Johnny Cash sing about how the name toughened him up. How many times did his father make him listen to that song? However many times he came home mad at being teased over "Brady Grady." He wondered what his dad would say now. Probably the same thing, "toughen up boy, could've named you Sue. Wouldn't that be a kicker, an attorney named Sue. Talk about a fitting name." Then he'd laugh. Well, maybe not.

Brady spent most of his life hating his father for being a mean son-of-a-bitch. But during the last year of his life, as he grew weak and pale from the cancer his mother swore was from being a miner for so many years, his father softened. Maybe it was fear of the afterlife, but rather than worrying about how tough his boys were, he actually cried a time or two and told them he was sorry for being so mean and asked them to forgive him. Naturally they had, what else could you do when a man is pleading from his deathbed. After all, it was their father. It was in that sterile, cold, hospital room, a week before the cancer took him, that Brady Grady's father told his boys he loved them. Brady couldn't remember him ever saying those words any other time in his life, not even to his mother.

Grady stood looking out the window at a squirrel scampering around the base of a tree surrounded by freshly cut green grass. His six foot three frame carried a bit more weight than it had when he was the quarterback for the Butte High Bulldogs, but that had been over thirty-five years ago. He still needed to shed a few pounds before campaign time. He needed to look fit, like the leader he was. His tie and jacket lay on the sofa near the wall, and his sleeves were still rolled up from earlier when he met with several staffers to work on a plan for the upcoming months. It was time for him to go home, but he was in no hurry. Stephen, his only son, was living in Arizona, and his wife, Rebecca, had something going on this evening, but he didn't remember or really care what it was. It had been a long time since he'd thought about his father's death. Probably hadn't thought of him since the last visit to see his mom at the Big Sky Senior Living Community in Butte, and that had been almost seven months ago. There was no guilt for the length of time. He knew she wasn't sitting there lonely and that she kept busy with the various activities they provided. She really liked Bingo and enjoyed some of the classes. Besides, whenever he visited, she had to remind him that his father loved him and his brother, he just didn't know how to show it until it was too late. God how he got sick of hearing that same old shit every visit. He really wanted to tell her that it was too late now, but he always just nodded his head and said he knew and understood. She'd then harp on him about why he didn't move back to Butte and visit more often like his brother did. His brother, yeah, his brother. The fucking little prick better not ruin things.

Clay Grady, Butte's golden business boy, and brother to the State's Attorney General, owned and operated Grady

Trucking Inc. He was a model of the workingman's success story. With only a high-school education, he built a small trucking empire that now serviced all 48 lower states and once in a while Alaska. If one thought attorneys and politicians were sneaky behind closed doors, they'd be flabbergasted to learn how Grady Trucking grew to the size it'd become. While Clay Grady was being heralded as a remarkable businessman, his lackeys would be ensuring things got done, not behind closed doors, but in the backs of truck stops and alleys. Their favorite negotiating tools were tire thumpers and jack handles. Brady didn't know all of Clay's illegal business, and didn't want to. He knew that whatever money was shown on the books for the legitimate trucking outfit, there was at least twenty times that coming in from Clay's off-the-books activities. It was easy to ignore his brother's endeavors when campaign expenses were being taken care of, but now Clay was asking for favors. At first they had been periodic and small, but now seemed to be coming more frequently and consisted of larger issues for the Attorney General to not only ignore, but assist with. Didn't Clay know this could ruin everything he'd strived for? Did Clay even care?

Two years younger than Brady, and not as big or tough, Clay had always been the follower and the bigger trouble maker of the two. The two were constantly together, constantly fighting, and constantly creating havoc while growing up, and the words "Those Grady Boys" had special meaning in the Butte community. "Those Grady Boys, they sure know trouble." But Brady also excelled in school and athletics, which often got him a get-out-of-jail-free card for the trouble he caused and messes he found himself in. He was also good at talking his way out of a jam and telling stories, a trait that was extremely useful in his chosen career path. Clay on the other hand, followed Brady with all the troublemaking, but had none of the academic or athletic skills. He barely made D's and C's in most classes and got kicked off the wrestling team the only year he tried out for consistently violating the rules and hurting his opponents. It seemed the only thing he did excel at, and could claim superiority over his older brother in, was causing trouble. That, and a complete disregard for pain. It seemed that nothing physical ever hurt Clay, and he would keep fighting until something was broken or he lay unconscious. No one was sure if he just didn't feel it, or if he just didn't care.

The two were hell raisers in the first degree, and the only time they weren't fighting each other was when they teamed up to fight anyone who happened to cross one or the other. Clay jumped into many ruckuses started by people saying something derogatory about his brother's rhyming name, and Brady saved his younger brother's hide at least once a week for things Clay would say to others without being able to back it up. Their father's advice to never write a check with your mouth that your ass can't cover was lost on him, because he knew Brady would cover it if he couldn't. Sometimes he said things just so his brother would have to get involved when he started to get his ass kicked. And the funny thing, besides not caring about the pain, Clay never minded losing. He thrived on the activity itself.

It didn't matter if it were sports, fights, or even picking up girls. He liked playing, fighting, and asking, it didn't matter if they didn't score, he got stomped, or laughed at by the prettiest girls. None of the failures seemed to bother him. Brady on the other hand, took losing personally and would be upset over a missed question on a test for the remainder of the week, a lost football game until they won the next one, and he wouldn't even ask a girl out until he had been assured by her friends that she would not only say yes, but was ready to go park.

The relationship between Brady and Clay changed when Brady graduated. He had an epiphany of sorts when he happened to read an old copy of Napoleon Hill's *Think and Grow Rich* a month before his final day as a Bulldog. But for Brady it was think and grow rich and powerful. The fighting, pranks, and run-ins with the law had to stop. He seemed obsessed with money and power and his competitive drive took him to The University of Montana where he paid for his education by working and with scholarships. After four years, he earned a degree in Political Science and a minor in Communication Studies with high honors. He immediately entered the School of Law the following semester for three additional years of school. He made law review and graduated in the top tier of his class, which enabled him to Clerk for The Montana Supreme Court for the first year after school.

During the seven years Brady attended The University of Montana in Missoula, he didn't see his brother once. Clay barely graduated from high school as Brady was finishing his second year of college. Most teachers passed him rather than have to deal with him a second time. Obviously not bound for college, Clay needed to find another path. So, rather than follow his brother as he'd always done, Clay opted for the service and left for Marine boot camp. Still the runt, and still the trouble maker, the Marines didn't toughen up and discipline the younger Grady boy as everyone back in Butte had hoped. With four article 15's in three years, Clay was finally discharged from the Marine Corp with a dishonorable discharge for failing a piss test. They had been tested on Friday, so Clay and a few others thought it was safe to snort a few lines that weekend. The surprise wake up and test

Monday morning nailed them and they quickly learned the Corps wasn't bullshitting with their anti-drug policies. Clay returned to Butte and learned his brother was still in Missoula, but attending law school. He never made the drive over to see him, but then Brady never came back to Butte either. Not until their father got sick anyway.

The pancreatic cancer that weakened old man Grady had one positive attribute, and that was bringing the brothers back together again. Brady made frequent trips to Butte from Helena where he resided ever since clerking for the Supreme Court. He knew A. G. and Governor were in his future, so why not live in the capital city and make it easier. Helena was also a central location to launch his campaigns across the fourth largest state in the nation that still had less than a million people. The frequent trips to Butte allowed the boys to reminisce about old times and fill each other in on the happenings of the decade they spent apart. Most of the time they talked in the hospital room, sipping luke warm hospital cafeteria coffee, while their father lay deteriorating in fitful sleep aided by whatever drugs were being pumped through the IV tubes permanently fixed to his arm.

Clay learned about college, law school, and an attorney's life. He also learned of his brother's political aspirations. Brady learned about how miserable life was in the Marine Corps, and about all the money there was to be made in the trucking industry. It surprised him that his younger brother was actually doing better than he was financially. A lot better. But it wasn't until the two rekindled and developed the relationship back to the strong bond they had as youths that Clay was comfortable sharing with his older sibling the various sources of his income. It wasn't all from the trucking industry. In fact, very little of the total was from legitimate trucking, and it was only because he needed legal advice that

215

he finally disclosed all aspects of his enterprise. Well, almost all. Once disclosed, the favor asking began. Big brother was right back where he had always been. It was as if the decade apart had never occurred. Only now, instead of jumping in to help with school yard fist-a-cuffs, Brady was advising on legal matters and using his influence to make certain things go away. Brady advised on which attorneys and judges could be bought, and which to stay clear from. Brady advised on how to lobby to get laws passed in favor of Clay's enterprises. Brady advised on how to beat the system, and beat the system Clay did. If he couldn't get around something on a technicality, or bribe someone, he always had threats and violence in his back pocket. But he knew how to distance himself from the ugly work so his hands and new businessman reputation would stay clean. And little brother's gratitude was generous, especially on the campaign trail. The borrowed Provost bus sure beat any other method of transportation around the state, and Brady always told people how lucky he was to have a brother that made it rich in the trucking industry, and how thankful he was for his brother's support. Yes, Brady knew how to talk to the public, and he knew how to deal behind closed doors. And little brother Clay had the money to make things happen. *Those Grady Boys*.

"What the fuck's going on over there?" was the first thing Kevin Tucker heard as he answered his cell phone. He immediately recognized the irritated voice on the other end as his blood pressure jumped ten points. He stood so he could walk over and close his office door.

"Good morning to you too Brady." Tucker glanced at his watch. It was 11:00 a.m. and 'good morning' was still appropriate.

"Good morning my fucking ass! I want to know what in Jesus Christ's name you're doing over there!"

He'd been expecting this call for hours, but even so, he wasn't prepared for the thrashing he was receiving from the Attorney General. Despite being friends and colleagues, and potentially future running mates, Tucker had never grown accustomed to Grady's temper. He was actually averse to conflict, any outside the courtroom anyway. He enjoyed the adversarial process in the safety of a courtroom, but the thought of physical violence made his stomach churn, and even over the phone it felt like Grady would come out and start strangling him as he ranted about the happening of the weekend. "Brady, what's the matter?"

"What's the matter? Listen you fucknugget, I told you to reel Baker in and get him prosecuting drug dealers, not fucking kill drug addicts and go off on some moral crusade! What the fuck's going on?"

"Calm down will ya? I thought if a couple of drug addicts broke into his house, he'd get fired up over the drug problem and I'd encourage him to pursue it. I thought it would be better if the idea came from him."

"So what the fuck happened?"

"The report I got said some friend of his was there and he killed them. It was supposedly a pretty clear case of self-defense. Definitely not something we want to prosecute."

"I don't want you prosecuting anything, you numbnuts! I want this Baker to back off! Your ass is on the line too."

"What do you mean my ass? I haven't done anything except help you out when asked."

"By sending drug addicts to Baker's house?"

"I didn't send them. I just let it be known that it could be profitable to scare Baker and make him eager to prosecute drug cases and leave other matters lie."

"Who paid who?"

"It was a thousand bucks out of the war chest." Tucker took a deep breath, expecting Grady to let loose about the source of the funds.

"You used our campaign money! You fucking moron! Like I said, your ass is on the line too! What the fuck were you thinking?"

"I just…"

"You didn't think! I asked for a small favor to help out my brother, and you make the problem ten times bigger. If I was there I'd…" His voice was lost in a crash on the other end that sounded like Grady kicking a metal file cabinet or some similar furniture. The crash was followed by another, and then an unmistakable, "Son-of-a-bitch!"

"Brady, listen." Tucker waited to see if the Attorney General would calm down and let him talk. "You there? Just listen a second."

"Listen to what?" While still harsh, a touch of the anger has subsided.

Tucker knew that his colleague calmed slowly and that he needed to be careful or he'd burst back into a rage. His fits were legendary and had more ups, downs, and curves than a roller coaster. It was all part of his "Butte Boy" persona. "Listen, it's just a couple of dead punks. It's not going anywhere. Besides the story in yesterday's paper, it's gone. Don't worry about it. Nothing about it points anywhere toward you or anyone else."

"It was fucking stupid is what it was." The anger was creeping back into Grady's voice and the County Attorney knew he needed to veer it off.

"I'm sorry. I thought it would make Baker do what you wanted. Just don't worry about it. You know, things like this blow over fast." Tucker sat down and took a deep breath. "In fact, Baker took the day off today because of it."

"I know he did goddamnit! Why the hell you think I'm calling?"

"I thought you were calling because of what happened Friday night." Tucker stood again and paced the length of his small office.

"I am you fucking idiot!" The rage returned and Tucker prepared for the next onslaught. "Your little stunt sent that cock-sucking deputy attorney on the war path!"

"I don't know what the hell you're talking about, and I don't appreciate being talked to this way when I don't have a clue why." Tucker tried to make his statement forceful, knowing Grady respected strength and only listened to authority. His attempt was feeble. Outside the courtroom, without a slam-dunk case behind him, he didn't threaten. He had absolutely nothing to back it up with. His last physical altercation had been in third grade when he got popped in the mouth by a fourth grade girl. He couldn't remember her name, but he remembered the laughter from all the other kids, the note his teacher sent home with him, and his father's response for getting his ass kicked by a girl. He was averse to physical activities, abhorred violence, and shunned conflict, so it surprised everyone when he decided to attend law school after majoring in English Literature. Pursuing a career as a prosecutor and campaigning for office were even bigger surprises, but he finally won a small bit of respect and acceptance from a red neck father who lived for football, beer, and bar fights up through his forty-fifth birthday. He then finally settled down and stopped the bar fighting, but still drank huge quantities of beer while watching football and swapping stories of bar fights with his equally adolescent friends.

"Your little stunt lit the fuse and set that son-of-a-bitch off!"

"I still don't know what you're talking about." Some of the bravado Tucker had tried to muster wore off and the statement sounded more like a whining plea.

"Baker and that other sumbitch were in Butte investigating my brother!"

"What?"

"You heard me. They were snooping around and asking about things they shouldn't have no mind to."

"I don't know... when?"

"This morning you stupid ignorant fool. What do you think I'm calling about?"

"I told you I thought..."

"How many goddamn times I have to tell you." Grady's rage was back full bore. "Don't fucking think! Just do what you're goddamn told and you'll have it made. Now you might have fucked everything up."

"I still don't get it. What's your brother have to do with anything? And what do you mean Baker was in Butte investigating him?" Tucker sat down again. Beads of perspiration dripped down his face and he loosened his tie.

"You don't need to know. All you need to know is you fucked things up and from now on don't do a goddamn thing unless I tell you to."

"Brady, if you want me to help, I need to know what's going on." Tucker hoped Grady would listen to his request and not blow up further.

"Listen. I don't agree with everything my brother does, but he's kin. Alright? He doesn't ask for much help, but when he does, I try and give it to him. We had too many years apart."

"Is he the reason you didn't want my office prosecuting Bruce James?"

"Yes, but dammit, you don't need to know this shit. You just need to do what you're told."

"I did. We didn't prosecute, did we?"

"I know, you just sent your deputy sniffing up Clay's ass."

"I didn't send him anywhere. I thought he was at home."

"Then why the hell did I just get a call from my brother saying two guys from Missoula were investigating him? Tell me that. And the car they were driving was registered to one Benjamin Baker."

"All I know is Baker called this morning and said he wasn't coming in today." Tucker completely ignored the statement about Baker's vehicle. He didn't even want to ask what strings were pulled for that information.

"Called from where?"

"I don't know. I just got the message, I didn't talk with him. People in the office figured the trauma of having a couple of intruders killed in his living room stressed him out and he stayed home."

"Well, he was in Butte asking about my brother's business."

"Trucking?" Tucker nervously made more circles on the legal pad sitting on his desk and wished this call would end soon.

"His other business. The one we're not going to talk about."

"Okay, whatever. If you're not going to tell me, fine. What is it you want me to do?" He hoped Grady wouldn't detect the irritation in his voice and flare up again.

"I want you to keep that goddamn deputy of yours busy and out of my brother's business. That's what I want."

"That's what I'm trying to do. I didn't know he was in your brother's business."

"Well, now you do. So do something about it. If I burn for any of this, so help me god, you'll go down too."

"For what?"

"For every goddamn thing I want you to."

"Just tell me what you want." Tucker was at the point he'd promise anything to appease Grady just to get off the phone. Why'd he ever decide to throw his hat in the ring with someone from Butte? "Let me know what I can do, and I'll do it."

"Let me figure it out." Grady's voice was surprisingly calm. It was almost like talking to a completely different person. "Kevin, I trust you. Help me out, and there's nothing we can't do. We'll own this state. You serve 8 years as the Lieutenant Governor and then you'll slide in for 8 years in the top seat while I'm in Washington." Officially, no one knew the two were planning on running together, but they had been discussing it for quite some time and amassing funds since the first discussion.

"I'm with you Brady, always have been."

"Good. I'll call you later."

Bewildered, Tucker turned off his phone. Setting it on his desk, he swiveled his chair around so he could see out the window. "What the hell was that all about," he murmured to himself.

Peter Jacob kissed his daughter on the cheek and gave her a big hug. "Have fun at swim class. Where's your little sister?"

"She's in the bathroom." Katrina replied.

"Katie, I'm leaving for work. Have fun at the pool and I'll see you when I get home tonight."

"Wait daddy!" Katie's bare feet pitter pattered from the bathroom to the kitchen. She jumped into her kneeling father's arms to give him a kiss and hug goodbye. She was still wearing her Disney princess pajamas. "Have fun at work."

"Thank you, I will. You be good. Bye hon, see you tonight!" He yelled to his wife as he tussled the six-year old Katie's hair and then turned toward the door.

"Bye!" Katherine came out from the bedroom and waived to the back of her husband as he closed the door behind him. She finished buttoning her light blue blouse as she entered the kitchen. "What do you two want for breakfast?"

* * *

Peter drove to work listening to the country station and wishing he were driving anywhere but his office. He was the Vice President of Grady Trucking, Inc., and up until four days ago, he was very happy with the position. It provided a good living for his family, and the title sounded impressive to his friends and relatives. He was a V.P. his aging mother told everyone. The previous Friday had changed things. He overheard two drivers discussing some special cargo for Clay

Grady. That conversation had ruined his weekend. The events of Monday made it worse and sent him home sick. He knew why he was driving to the office, he knew he needed to do something, he just didn't know what, and he wished he were someplace else.

Peter had suspected Clay Grady of running illegal substances for a year now, but didn't mind looking the other way. He had only been V.P for a year, and for Butte, Montana, it was a great job. It was the best Peter had ever held, and the steady paycheck was nice as both his daughters were in school now, and extra curricular activities cost more and more each year. Clay Grady never discussed anything illegal with him, and everything he did for the corporation was legit. He took pride in running the corporation in the black. Peter actually did run the corporation. Grady may have been the president, but he didn't really do anything for the company any more. Peter governed the daily operations and made all the important decisions concerning the corporation. Sure, he cleared them with Grady, but he made the decisions and Grady always backed him and gave him free reign with the operations of the trucking company. It was a good gig, and Peter was happy until the conversation he caught wind of caused him to suspect more was being trafficked than drugs. From what he heard, it sounded like Grady was using some of the trucks to transport women for Dick Bennett.

The two drivers he overheard hadn't known he was there, and he never let them know he had listened in. They had been outside his office and believed everyone had gone for the day. Peter should have been gone, but he had stayed late to catch up on some invoices. He hadn't heard everything, but what he did hear sounded like the two were joking around about the special cargo they were hauling and how they ought to stop and take a quick turn somewhere down the line. From the other things they said, it was obvious they were talking about sex and that the cargo must be a female. His first thought was Clay was pimping prostitutes at the truck stop. He knew Clay made extra money in various ways, since his income and what he gave to Butte charities was far greater than what the books for Grady Trucking revealed. But when he heard the name Dick Bennett, he wondered just what Grady was involved with.

Bennett was known as a porn king. He made millions in the porn industry before moving to Montana. He purchased a huge chunk of land and built one of the largest houses in Silver Bow country a few years back. No one really knew much about him. He stayed to himself and didn't come to town much. Stories circulated, but it was difficult to discern fact from fiction, especially when most stories revolved around massive drug laden parties with breast-augmented beauties running around naked and pleasing every man in attendance. People said Bennett wanted to be Hugh Hefner but made movies and threw parties in the style of Larry Flynt. The people who attended the rumored about sex parties flew in on private jets, no one knew of any locals that were invited. None that talked anyway. Peter now wondered if Clay Grady was part of Bennett's circle. He thought about it all weekend and it made sense. Clay owned a trucking company and had distribution channels throughout the continent and wasn't beyond committing crimes to earn a buck. Clay's brother was a politician, and Peter figured all rich people liked to have politicians on their leash. It was easy to see why Bennett would associate with Clay, and if there was money and women to be had, Peter knew what attracted Clay to the relationship.

Peter knew it was none of his business, and he should just forget about what he heard last Friday, and continue running the legit part of the company as he'd done the past year. If Clay wanted to use some of the trucks and drivers to traffic drugs, illegal DVDs, and whatever else, it was nothing Peter was privy too, and nothing he wanted to be associated with anyway. He just couldn't help thinking about what might be going on. He had taken his two girls, Katrina seven, and Katie six, to their first ice cream of the summer on Saturday. Sitting there, watching the two laugh and smile as they dug into their sundaes, he thought of a television show he'd seen a few months back about runaways and kidnapped kids that were traded for sex at truck stops. He shuddered when he imagined something happening to his own little girls. Those thoughts and the conversation he overheard on Friday haunted him all weekend.

It was the occurrences of Monday that helped Peter Jacob determine what he needed to do. Clay had come into the office raging. Normally, Peter couldn't hear anything from Clay's office, except the time or two he had been amorous with women he'd refer to as 'screamers' during his after action bragging sessions. The previous day, he heard Clay yelling at his brother, the Attorney General, about some guy named Baker, some guys of his who had been beaten up, and how Bennett wasn't going to like this. Peter had already spent the weekend disturbed over the thoughts that Grady Trucking might be being used to traffic women for the porn king. Listening to Clay yell at his brother confirmed it. The last thing Peter heard clearly was Clay yelling, "If Bennett's girls aren't shipped on time, you're losing your campaign contributions. And remember, you fucked one of those little bitches too!" Peter stayed in his office until he heard Clay leave.

Everyone was gone, and Peter, very uncharacteristically, decided to snoop around. He was disturbed and scared by what he'd heard. He possessed a master key to the building, and with much hesitation, used it to enter Grady's office. The same office that had been filled with shouting a short time earlier. Papers were scattered on the large mahogany partner's desk, with four draws running up each side and one in the middle, but the rest of the office was clean. It had a country feel to it, with artwork by Montana's famous Charles Russell on the walls. The chair behind the desk looked out of place. It was leather, but it was an advanced ergonomic executive chair that looked too modern compared to the Russell paintings and sculptures and other antiques in the office. Jacob remembered Grady paying over twelve hundred dollars for the chair. He sat down in it to judge if the money was well spent, and had to admit it was a comfortable chair. Maybe he should look into getting something better for his back in his own office.

Scared that he'd be caught, he was just about to leave when he noticed some blank DVD cases on one of the bookshelves. He wondered if those were movies from Dick Bennett. Maybe the could help him understand the conversations he overheard. He grabbed one and took it back to his office. He loaded it into his computer. There were no menus or selections, just a blank screen with a play command. He pushed play.

When Peter Jacob got home, it was 45 minutes since he'd turned off the DVD that he barely watched five minutes of. He told his wife he was sick and went to the bedroom. He was indeed sick. Sick at what he'd heard, sick at what he'd seen, and sick knowing the company he ran was part of it. He wondered if Clay Grady would miss the DVD he took from the shelf. Probably not, there were a number of them and he left them so it wasn't obvious one was missing. Why did he keep it? Couldn't he go to prison for just possessing it? Should he take it out from under the seat of his truck and destroy it?

How? Did he lock the office doors? Not sure. Probably, it was a habit.

What was he going to do? Turning his head when he thought it was a pot run here and there didn't bother him, he'd enjoyed a few tokes when younger and didn't really think it hurt much. But this, trafficking people, women, little girls, he couldn't stomach. He had thrown up beside his truck before coming home. He didn't share the information with Katherine when she checked on him, but instead told her he wasn't feeling well and just wanted to sleep. She brought him a cup of tea that she left on the nightstand beside the bed and he covered up with a blanket, even though it was warm enough to go without. He lay there all afternoon and into the night pondering what he should do. He knew he needed to do something, but what?

He forced the thoughts of the previous day and night from his mind as Randy Travis came on the radio singing his old hit "On the Other Hand." How appropriate Jacob thought. It wasn't two women he had to choose between, but should he turn his head and continue along like nothing was going on, or should he do something about it? He would surely lose his job, and there was the possibility of losing much more, like his life, if he got caught. He'd seen enough movies about rich people in organized crime to know that they paid people to hurt and kill those that crossed them. That's why he needed to be very careful and discreet. He knew that Clay Grady had people on the payroll that would hurt folks for fun, giving them money for it would just be icing on the cake. He needed to play it cool and figure out what he could do that wouldn't cost him. He had his three ladies at home to think about, but in fact, it was those three ladies that made Peter's decision. He couldn't turn his head any longer. He'd made the decision to do something at least a dozen times since going home sick the previous day. It was as if telling himself he needed to do something would generate the courage needed to actually do it. But what should he do? What could he do? What could he do that wouldn't get him and his family in trouble? He almost called in sick, but then decided to come to the office. He figured he'd determine what he could do better at the office than home on the sofa.

He was pulling his dark green Dodge Dakota Sport into the parking lot when he had an idea. It had been right in front of him all the time. He could help out, feel he did something, and have no repercussions for anything that happened. It was perfect. All he had to do now is find out how to contact the guy Clay had been yelling about to his brother. It sounded like this guy was investigating the illegal acts and threatened the operation. He remembered the name Baker and Missoula. Peter couldn't wait to get to his computer and google the two.

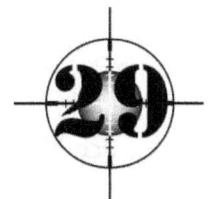

Baker was kicking the hundred pound heavy bag that hung in his garage when Senich came out drinking coffee from the Disney mug he'd grown accustomed to.

"You're up early."

"So are you." Baker hit the bag with a roundhouse kick that almost sent the bag swinging horizontal.

"Damn, I wouldn't want to be kicked by that." Senich took another sip of coffee and watched his friend fire off three more powerful kicks.

"No you wouldn't." Baker smiled at his buddy and wiped the sweat off his face with his already drenched t-shirt.

"Still pissed about last night?"

"No."

"Doesn't look like it."

"Just getting a workout in before I go to the office."

"Alright," said Senich. "I figured you were still pissed the way you were pounding on that bag."

"I always train hard." The two were walking toward the house. "You ought to try it sometime."

"Like I'm out of shape?"

"Just messing with you." The two went inside and Baker poured himself a cup of the coffee Senich had brewed while he was training in the garage.

"So, you're going to the office?"

"Yeah, for a bit. Not accomplishing anything here right now."

"You're still pissed because I said you were wimping out."

"I'm not pissed, but like I told you last night, you don't have a family and job invested in this. You can climb into that big eighteen-wheeler and drive off into the sunset. I can't."

Senich shook his head. "That's not what I meant. You used to have the biggest balls of anyone I knew. You'd stand up to anyone. You didn't have to think about everything, you just did it."

"Sometimes you need to think."

"You need to plan your missions, but not think so long about whether to do the mission or not."

"I told you I'm in this. I want these fuckers as much or more than you do. I'm the one who carried that little girl out of the trailer house. Her name was Ashley. I saw the terror in her eyes. I saw her cower and then felt her tremble when I picked her up and got her out of that stink hole. I have a daughter myself, remember?"

"Hey, calm down. We're on the same side. I know you have a family now. But I also know thoughts of your family at the wrong time can get us killed."

"I don't need you insinuating I won't go through with this. I told you I was in till the end."

"I know buddy. I was just trying to motivate you, that's all."

"I don't need that kind of motivation."

"Roger, loud and clear." Senich took another sip of coffee and then became serious. His voice softened. "Ben, you know I wouldn't be here if you hadn't called. And you know I trust you more than anyone I've ever known. I know we'll finish this."

"I know Frank. All of this just has me a bit wired. I want them stopped so bad, but I don't want to do anything that will cost my family. I can't afford to get seriously hurt, or lose my job. I have Tanya and Coral to think about. I can't believe what I've already done. What we've done."

"I know buddy. Don't worry, it's gonna work out."

"It better. Do you know how much I have to lose? When I went into that trailer that night, I wanted to do something. Too many thoughts of no one cares and no one does anything. I was just going to snoop around, find something the cops or the feds could go after him with."

"But?"

"But he came home and caught me rummaging through his stuff. It was so quick and sudden, I didn't have much of a choice."

"No, you didn't. And you saved the life of that little girl."

"I committed a number of felonies, including murder."

"You saved that little girl. And it's not murder if they have it coming."

"Is that how you justify it?"

"Yeah, I do." Senich stepped over to the coffee pot and refilled his mug.

"That's not how the law looks at it."

"I've told you, there's the law and there's what's right."

"Yeah, I've heard you."

"Where would that little girl be if you hadn't got involved?"

"I don't know."

"Yes, you do." Senich put his mug on the counter. "She'd be dead, or worse than dead, and you know it."

"Yeah."

"And how many more little girls would have ended up in those trailers in the woods if we hadn't gotten involved?"

"I know, I get it." Baker's tone was that of annoyance.

"Do you?"

Baker looked at his friend and couldn't remember seeing him more serious. Just as serious a time or two, but never more. "Yes, I do. Why do you think I'm risking so much, if I didn't get it. I just don't know how this fell on our shoulders."

"If not you, who else? If not me, who else? How many people do you know that can do what we can?"

"Not many." Baker's voice was softer and he looked down at the floor, avoiding his friend's glare.

"That's why. What good is all the training, all the studying, the hours of pain, the gallons of sweat and blood, if you don't do something good with it."

"I know." Baker looked up and into Frank's eyes. "You know how many times I've asked myself that?"

"Well, we're doing something to right wrongs because we can."

"You read too many comic books."

Frank smiled, "Maybe you don't read enough."

Baker couldn't help but smile back. "If we just knew more about what they were doing."

"We'll find out. You go get ready for work, I'm going to jog to that used book store. Can't have you being the only one to work up a sweat this morning."

"I have a ton of books downstairs."

"I know, but you get mad if I bend the corners."

"Alright, I'll catch you later. I'll probably come home early afternoon, just depends on what I need to get done there."

"No worries. I'll be here."

"Sure wish we'd get a break and figure out what they were doing."

"We will. It's only Tuesday and I still have a week or more till I need to get back to driving and making money."

"Might take a lot longer than that to bring down the attorney general and his brother's trucking company. If they're even involved."

"You know they're dirty. And it won't take that long to bring them down. Besides, if I mooch off you I can take more time off."

"They're dirty alright, but are they involved with these kids?"

Frank set the empty coffee cup on the counter beside the sink and looked at his friend standing near the wall, ready to go shower and prepare for work. "Forget what you know. Forget evidence. Forget what you've seen, what we've done. Now, what do you feel?"

"I feel the Grady's are involved, but I think we're missing something."

"Don't think, feel."

"I feel we're missing something."

"Well, I guess we'll have to figure it out as we go. Have a good one at work, and I'll catch you later." Frank headed out the door for the bookstore and Ben slowly walked toward the bathroom as he peeled his sweat soaked shirt over his head and tossed it at the hamper.

"Yeah, I guess we will," he said.

Baker sat at his desk paging through case files without really paying attention to them. His mind was preoccupied with thoughts of the last few days and wondering what he should do next. He was having second thoughts regarding going after the Gradys. Senich was right; when he was younger he charged right in, hell or high water. But things were different now, and they needed to err on the side of caution. This wasn't a bar fight where the consequences might be a fine or a weekend in jail. They'd already committed felonies that could put them away for life, and Senich was suggesting they continue. Baker looked around his office. It wasn't great, and practicing law wasn't his passion. However, it did provide for Tanya and Coral. It was a fair paycheck for Montana, and the benefits were decent enough. Tucker could be a jerk, but he pretty much left people alone. He was too concerned with the next election and his political aspirations to micromanage. As long as the win column was greater than the loss column when it came to prosecutions, he was happy enough and minded his own business.

He shook his head and turned back to the first page in the file he was reviewing. He hadn't noticed any of the pages he turned. Something needed to be done if Clay Grady was selling kids. If his brother was helping him from the Attorney General's office, he needed to be stopped too. And what about Tucker? Was he in on it as well? It wasn't his job to stop these guys. He prosecuted people once the police stopped them and provided the evidence to convict them. Who was he to play cop, judge, and executioner? Shit, now he was making himself out to be some comic book hero. Was he trying to live out his *Executioner* and *Punisher* fantasies? Maybe he watched those Charles Bronson movies too much. But if he didn't do it, who would? Look at how good the law worked with Bruce James. Baker remembered the night in the trailer, squeezing the life out of the perverted child molester. Finding the little girl Ashley in the back bedroom justified it. He wondered what horrors she had undergone before he found her, and shuddered a bit. Frank was right, he saved her from what would have happened next. He hoped she would be able to overcome the experience and live a happy life.

He turned back to the first page and started reading it for the third time. The phone rang and interrupted his reading and wandering thoughts. "Ben here."

"Is this Benjamin Baker? Missoula attorney?"

"Yes, how can I help you?"

"Are you the one investigating Grady Trucking?"

Baker scowled. "I think you have the wrong guy, I'm not investigating any trucking company."

"I thought it was you and someone else that took care of some guys at the truck stop outside of Butte yesterday."

"Who is this?"

"My name's Peter and I really need to talk to whoever did that, and I just thought it might be you. Sorry if I'm wrong."

"What do you need to talk about, a legal matter?"

"Yes, well, sort of."

"Well, I don't know what you're talking about, but I'll listen and see if I can at least steer you in the right direction."

"I need the guys who beat up Grady's guys at the truck stop."

"Sounds like an assault, and it would be up to the Silver Bow office to prosecute it, not us."

"That's not what I want."

"What can I help you with then?"

"Would you know who to talk to if I thought Grady Trucking was involved with illegal activity?"

"Talk to your local law enforcement, or the prosecutor's office there in Butte, Baker replied.

"I can't do that."

"Why?"

"I have a family, I need to do this so no one knows."

"Why call me?"

"I thought you were investigating them and how they ship kids."

"What?"

"Can we meet somewhere, I don't want to say anything else on the phone."

Baker glanced at his calendar out of habit. "When and where?"

"I'm going to Spokane. And I'm actually about thirty minutes out of Missoula right now. Can you meet in thirty minutes?"

He didn't know why he looked at his calendar again, it was clear, and even if it wasn't he'd reschedule to make this meeting. "Sure, you have a place in mind?"

"How about an early lunch at Hooters?"

Baker smiled, knowing Frank would like the choice. "Sure, I'll see you there in thirty minutes. How will I recognize you?" He didn't tell the person on the phone he was inviting a friend to the meeting.

"I'm wearing a Grady Trucking shirt."

"Okay Peter, I'll see you there." Bewildered, Baker set down his phone. He closed the file on his desk and secured it and the others in the filing cabinet. He then took out his cell phone and hit the speed dial for his buddy.

"Yeah?" Frank answered.

"Where you at?"

"I'm at your wonderful mall. Got a new shirt that was on sale. Five bucks for a gray Henley, they're trying to get rid of the last of the winter stuff."

"Spending your day shopping, how nice."

"Fuck you. No one else to do it, and I like the shirt."

"Just kidding. I'll meet you at the south end in a few minutes. Go out through Dillards." Baker exited the office looking busy with the cell phone to his ear so no one would stop him.

"Why, what's up?"

"Thought you might be hungry and would like Hooters."

"Sounds good, but why all of a sudden?"

"I'll fill you in when I pick you up, but we might have just stumbled upon the break we need."

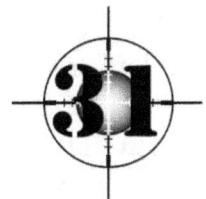

Baker picked up Senich at the mall and told him about the phone call from Peter as they drove down Reserve to the local Hooters. They arrived and headed in, Baker still in his Dockers and long sleeve Polo dress shirt, Senich in sweat pants and slightly sweaty t-shirt from jogging to the bookstore and mall. They chose a corner table and sat on the same side of the booth, indicating to the hostess that another party would be joining them shortly.

"So, all you know about this guy is from that phone call?"

"Yep. Says his name's Peter and he has information regarding Grady for the guys who beat up Grady's men yesterday."

"Interesting." Senich turned to the waitress who just placed three waters on the table. "Can we get a large order of the hottest wings you have to start out?"

"Sure, anything else?" she replied.

"That will get us started." Senich tried to look her in the eyes, but it was difficult to not look down. When she turned and headed to the kitchen his gaze drifted even lower. "Good choice for lunch."

"I knew you liked wings." Baker smiled. "Actually, he suggested it."

"I'm liking him more already."

"Good, because there he is." Baker motioned to the door where a single man had just entered. He was five foot nine and about one hundred and sixty pounds. Short hair, glasses, and had sort of a nervous look about him. He wore blue jeans and a green golf type shirt with the Grady Trucking logo on the left breast pocket. He nodded and half waved when he noticed Baker motioning him over to the booth. He shuffled over to the booth, not knowing whether to swing his arms or put his hands in his pockets. He looked around the restaurant, not like Baker and Senich when they entered the place, but more like a rabbit that hears a dog barking from behind a fence, but can't make out where the sound is coming from.

"Benjamin Baker?" he asked when he got to the edge of the table.

"Nice to meet you Peter." Baker stood to shake hands. "This is a friend of mine, Frank Senich." Senich remained seated in the inside of the booth, but nodded as a way of saying hello.

"Good to meet you both." Peter nervously slid into the booth across from the two friends and glanced around. He pushed his glasses up and looked around again.

"Who you looking for?" asked Senich.

"Ah, nobody. Just don't want to be seen talking with you two." Peter replied.

"Something wrong with us?" Senich noticed the look of fear in the smaller man's face as he asked the question with his most menacing look.

"No, no, that's not what I meant."

"Knock if off Frank," Baker interjected. "Peter, you wanted to meet, so what's up?"

Peter was just about to reply when their waitress bounced up with their wings and asked if they were ready to order. All three men couldn't help but notice that she was just the kind of girl Hooters was named after and had made the chain famous. The tight white shirt enhanced what nature had bountifully endowed her with, and she knew just how to bounce, pose, and flirt to receive large tips. Baker was the first to stop staring and ordered one of their specialty burgers with a side of fries. Senich and Peter joined in by ordering burgers and fries of their own.

"Nice to be out without the wife," Peter said trying to break the ice. He still glanced around nervously now and then.

"Yes, nice it is," replied Senich as he watched the waitress all the way to the kitchen, leaning forward to do so.

"So, you worried about being caught here by your wife, or someone else?" Baker asked.

"I'm not worried." Peter's face told a different tale. "Well, it's just that I don't want to get into trouble. And I can't afford to lose my job. My wife would kill me. We have two girls in school now."

"So tell us what we're here for." Baker's voice was calm, but stern, the voice he often used when eliciting information from witnesses.

"Damn," whispered Senich.

"What?" Baker's eyes scanned the restaurant, starting close and working toward the doors.

"That gal over there has even bigger tits than our waitress."

Baker noticed during his scan. "Get serious." Peter's neck was still turned as he strained to see the waitress the two were discussing when Baker asked him again, "What can we help you with?"

Disappointed he'd missed the object of Senich's attention, Peter turned and picked up one of the wings from the plate in the center of the table. He toyed with it, as he looked first at Baker and then at Senich. He sighed, then said, "I think Clay Grady is hooked up with Dick Bennett and they are using the trucking company to run prostitutes and girls."

"How do you know any of this?" Baker asked.

"I overheard some stuff." Peter bit into the wing and immediately reached for his glass of water. "These are hot!"

Senich smiled and picked up another small leg and took a big bite. "Not bad, but I've had hotter." He wiped his face with the napkin and looked Peter in the eye. "Why you telling us this stuff?"

Not wanting to seem wimpy, Peter chased fire with fire and took another bite of his hot wing. "I overheard Clay shouting, and I heard Baker and Missoula, so I did some searching and found you." Peter took another big swig from his water glass and wondered how the two across from him could eat the wings without a sip.

Baker was about to say something when he noticed their waitress bringing their burgers and fries. He waited for her to set the plates down and ask if they needed anything else. Peter asked for a Coke and a refill for his water. Senich ordered a beer. All three men started on their burgers in silence, waiting for the waitress to return with the drinks. Once she had delivered them, and the three had stopped gawking as she walked away, Baker began, "Peter, why don't you just tell us everything you know, starting from the beginning."

"First, you are the guys who beat up Grady's guys yesterday, aren't you?" Peter asked.

"Why?" Senich asked.

"You just seem like guys who could do that." Peter didn't know what it was, but something about the two was different than most people he encountered. He couldn't really place it, but the two sitting across from him seemed like bad asses, and he sure wouldn't want to cross either of them or make them mad. He was a bit uncomfortable, well scared really, just being around them.

"We might have had a little run in with a couple Butte boys yesterday. Again, why don't you start from the beginning and tell us everything you know about Grady and your suspicions."

"Okay, I've worked for Grady Trucking for a couple of years, and the last year I've been the Vice President."

"V.P. of the company, huh?" said Senich with his mouth full.

Baker glanced over indicating he should shut up. It reminded him of interviews with young law student interns sitting in. They always wanted to talk, rather than keep quiet and let those being interviewed or deposed do the talking.

"Yeah, I'm the V.P., actually run most of it myself. Clay doesn't do much anymore." Peter continued. "Doesn't do much in the way of the legitimate trucking company anyway. I think he does plenty of other stuff."

"Why do you think that?" Baker asked.

"I know what Grady Trucking makes, and while the company is doing good, very good, Clay has way more money than he brings home from Grady Trucking." Peter licked his lips and took another drink from his Coke. "I always figured he was selling drugs and using some of the drivers to help him. But you know, I kept my nose out of his business. I have a family to support and didn't want to lose my job."

"So you were never involved in any of those dealings?" Baker wanted to give Peter the opportunity to ensure the two he wasn't involved in any of the illegal activities. He was speaking to a prosecutor.

"No, hell no. I never got involved in anything like that. Everything I do for Grady Trucking is legit. It really is a successful company and we do business all over the States and in Canada."

"Good," added Senich.

"So, why come to us now?" Baker wanted Peter to continue with his narrative and get to today's meeting.

"Because of last Friday and yesterday."

"Alright, what happened on Friday," Baker coached.

"I was in my office after five. Usually I'm gone by then, because I come in early to deal with East Coast items and I like to get home and attend different things my girls are involved with. Dance, gymnastics, you know, all the extracurricular things kids do these days. We try to let them experience as much as they like, so you know, they can find what they are good at. I really want to be a good father to them."

"Sounds like you are," Baker cut in. "Your girls are lucky to have someone so supportive of their activities. But what happened Friday when you stayed late?"

Peter sat up a bit straighter after being acknowledged as a good father, which was Baker's intent. "Two drivers were talking near the pop and candy machines in the common area. I couldn't hear everything from my office, but I heard enough to make me wonder what was going on, and it disturbed me all weekend."

"What did you hear?" Baker asked.

Senich wasn't as patient as Baker when it came to eliciting information from people. He much preferred the bash 'em in the head till they talk method. He hadn't studied all that people crap that Baker had. He knew to keep his mouth shut, so he quietly ate his burger and fries while watching the various waitresses bounce around the restaurant.

"They were talking about a girl or woman they were hauling for Bennett."

"Who's Bennett?" Baker asked.

"He's some porn king who built a huge place somewhere out near Anaconda. He's supposed to have millions, if not billions from selling porn flicks."

"I don't know him." Baker responded.

"I don't know much either. He's supposed to be super rich, and I guess he built a huge house on a couple hundred acres of land."

"So what makes you think these guys were hauling women for him?"

"I couldn't hear everything, but they were talking about stopping and taking a turn with whoever they had in the truck. I couldn't tell if it was someone held captive, or if it was some truck stop prostitutes they were giving a ride." Peter stopped and look around to make sure no one else was listening and then lowered his voice. "I got the feeling they were hauling someone captive. I saw something about that on TV."

"Why do you think that?" asked Senich, wanting to get into the conversation, now that they were getting to the good stuff.

"Just the way they talked. It wasn't like they were talking about stopping and paying like you would with a prostitute, but they were going to stop and take turns regardless, and then the one said that would piss off Bennett if he found out. When the one said 'so what," I heard the other say that Bennett had mercenaries, thieves, and killers on his payroll, and if you made him mad, you'd likely disappear or be found in a dumpster somewhere. Or buried out on his land to never be found."

"Nice guy, huh?" Senich commented.

"What else did you hear?" asked Baker.

"Nothing really. They left still joking around. But I thought about it all weekend, and it really scares me. What if they are trafficking kids like I saw on TV?"

It was the second time Peter had referred to television. "What TV?" Baker asked.

"Some show a while back, *20/20* or *Dateline*, something like that. It was all about kidnapping young girls, and selling them. Profiled one girl who was kidnapped but then escaped. The show said truck stops and trucking routes play a major role in the trafficking. It goes on more than you think."

"So you think this Bennett and Grady are involved?"

"Yes, I think Bennett is doing it, and Grady supplies the transportation. I think that's where some of Grady's money is coming from." Peter stopped to eat some of his lunch, and Baker took the time during the natural pause of conversation to take a couple bites of his food and think about what Peter had told them.

Baker waited for Peter to swallow what he was chewing before asking, "So that happened Friday. What happened yesterday that made you call me?"

"You two stomping Grady's guys at the truck stop."

"What makes you think it was us?" Senich interrupted.

"Okay, yesterday Clay came to the office outraged. I didn't talk to him, but I heard him screaming on the phone from his office."

"You're good at listening in on others, aren't you?" Senich remarked.

Peter looked down and ate a fry, as Baker glanced at his friend.

Baker then asked, "What exactly did you hear?"

"He was yelling at his brother, you know, Brady, the Attorney General."

"I know," said Baker.

"I heard him say, 'if Bennett's girls aren't shipped on time, you're losing your campaign contributions.'"

"So there might be a convincing argument that Clay Grady is hauling girls for this Dick Bennett. What's his brother's involvement?"

"That's where you come in. He was yelling at his brother about getting Baker from Missoula off his ass. Said you busted up his boys and were investigating him. Something like that."

Senich, who had been watching waitresses, heard every word. He looked at his friend, "You still need more proof?"

"This isn't enough to build a case."

"You don't believe me?" Peter asked.

"I believe you. But overhearing a couple of conversations doesn't provide the proof we need to prosecute. Besides, are you willing to testify?"

"No, no. This is confidential right? Attorney-client privilege and all that."

"You're not my client. I don't represent you, so there is no privilege."

Peter looked like he was going to jump up and bolt. Baker quickly reassured him, "Don't worry. While there isn't a legal privilege, I give you my word we'll keep this between us. We don't want you in any trouble with Grady or Bennett either."

Peter looked at Senich who nodded affirmatively. He looked as if he wanted to say something more, but stopped and picked up a fry and dabbled with it in the pool of ketchup on his plate.

"What is it?" Baker asked.

"There's just one other thing you should know. You're an attorney and all. One thing I remember Clay yelling at his brother was..." Peter almost whispered the next sentence, "you fucked one of those little bitches too."

Baker dropped Senich off at his house after their lunch meeting with Peter Jacob at Hooters, and then went back to the office for the afternoon. Everyone there thought he must still be emotional after the killing at his home over the weekend, and they were all too eager to offer any assistance they could provide but then leave him alone. The silence of his office suited Baker just fine.

On the way to his house from Hooters, his friend had been ready to load up their weapons and head out in search of Bennett and the Grady brothers. Frank Senich's world was pretty simple. If you did things that deserved killing over, you got killed. He had no problems with being the judge and executioner. Maybe he also read too many of those books and watched too many movies. Baker knew things were not as easy as Senich wanted him to believe. He lived in this town. Brady Grady was the Attorney General and held a lot of influence in the State, especially with him working for the County Attorney's office. Frank could disappear down the highway and leave Montana in his rear view mirror. He had Tanya and Coral to think about. As he thought of his family and all he had worked to achieve, thoughts drifted to Ashley and the night he found her in the back room of that trailer house. She was also someone's daughter. She would grow to be someone's wife. If these monsters were not stopped, how many girls would suffer? If it were Tanya or Coral who had been taken, nothing on earth would stop him from seeking out and destroying anyone and everyone remotely involved.

ALAIN BURRESE

Wasn't Ashley as deserving as his own daughter? Was this Bennett really the one behind it? Could they trust Peter Jacob?

Baker looked at his watch. He wore his Casio G-Shock rather than his nicer Citizens that he normally wore to work. The G-shock had a titanium band and didn't look out of place with dress clothes, but he was still surprised he hadn't worn the other. The digital face read 4:46. The afternoon sure flew by, and he wasn't sure what he'd accomplished. A lot of little things got done, but nothing worth writing home about. Not a very productive day he thought, except for lunch. He was about to stand and leave when Mary, the receptionist, knocked on his door.

"Hey Ben, almost forgot. Some guy dropped this off for you a while ago." She set a tan 5 by 8 envelope on his desk. BAKER was written across the front in black marker.

"Who's this from?"

"Don't know, some guy in jeans and a green shirt."

"What guy?"

"Trucking guy or something, he didn't say, just left that for you. See you tomorrow." She turned and headed back to her own desk to clean up before leaving. Baker picked up the envelope, it was light, but had a thin box or something inside. Felt like a DVD. He put it into his briefcase, he'd look at it when he got home. He stood up to leave when his phone rang.

"Ben Baker," he answered.

"It's me," came the reply.

"Hi Honey, how are things in Helena?"

Tanya informed him that his cell phone was off and Frank told her he was at the office. He looked at his cell and then remembered he'd turned it off for the lunch meeting and must have forgotten to turn it back on. Too many crazy thoughts running through his mind, he was forgetting simple things like the watch and the phone. He really needed to do some hard training followed by some meditation to clear his mind and get back on track.

He apologized for the phone and asked again how they were doing in Helena. Tanya put Coral on and she told him about putting her face under water at swim class. She couldn't wait to show him. Tanya filled him in on what was going on in Helena and asked how he and Frank were. He told her everything was fine and that they were still working on what happened the previous weekend. She didn't really want to know the details, and Baker didn't want to tell her, so they left it at that.

She asked how he and Frank were eating, and wanted to ensure they were eating healthy and not living off of fast food. He told her they ate lunch at Hooters, but left out Peter Jacob and told her it was Frank's idea.

"Sure, and you ate with your eyes closed," she replied.

They swapped small talk for another five minutes, and Baker was feeling much better as the conversation progressed. He hadn't realized how much he missed them. It reminded him of how lucky he was, and how much he had going for him. He couldn't wait to see the two again. "So honey, what was so important that you tracked me down here?"

* * *

Baker left the office without saying a word. Most of his co-workers had already gone, and he might have waved at the few who were leaving at the same time. After the bomb Tonya dropped on him, he didn't even remember the drive home. He must have made the right turns and stopped at the right lights, because he was sitting in his driveway. His autopilot got him home.

He sat in the car and saw his friend in the garage banging away at the heavy bag. The large car bay door was open, so he could see Senich bobbing and weaving around the bag as he punched. He went at it more like a combination boxer brawler than a martial artist. He didn't throw any kicks, but his hands were a blur as the barrage of jabs, crosses, uppercuts and hooks landed with thundering smacks. The rafters of the garage shook as the hundred pound bag hanging from them bounced and swung after each combination. He wasn't pretty, but damn he was powerful Baker thought. Even in his barbarian manner, he was utilizing correct body mechanics and generating power with his entire body. The boy knew how to punch.

Frank fired off a final flurry of punches to impress his buddy who was watching from the Durango parked in the driveway. He had seen him drive up, and wondered why he hadn't got out. He figured his friend must be in awe from viewing his impressive punching skills. Baker opened the door and slowly climbed out of the Dodge.

"How's it going? This is the best workout I've had in a long time, " Frank yelled from the garage.

"Glad you like it," Baker replied.

Senich closed the garage door and walked toward the house and his friend who waited by the door. "So, how was work honey?"

"Didn't get much done."

"Well, why don't we grab something to eat and discuss the work that really needs to be done."

The two entered the house and Senich grabbed a glass and filled it with water. "You want to eat here or go somewhere?"

"I don't care."

"I'll take a quick shower first, and then let's go somewhere healthy. Get a salad or something. I'm burgered out after lunch."

"Fine by me." Baker looked through the mail that Senich had brought in and laid on the table earlier.

"So, you going to tell me what's up?" Senich placed the empty glass beside the sink.

"What do you mean?"

"Don't shit me. I've known you long enough to know when something is bothering you. Is it the stuff from lunch?"

"No, well... sort of."

"We going to go through this again? If you want out, just say so."

"No, it's not that, it's just we need to plan this a lot more carefully. I don't want to go busting in guns a blazing. We're snipers remember, phantom like. We need to do what we need to do silent, stealthy, and without anyone even having a hint that we are involved."

"You know I have no problem with that."

"Good."

"So why don't you tell me what's up. I know that's not all that's on your mind."

"Tanya called."

"I know, she called here first. Wanted you to talk to Coral about her swimming class."

"That wasn't the only reason."

"Yeah, what's up?"

"She thinks she's pregnant."

"Congratulations, buddy." Senich stepped across the kitchen and smacked Baker on the back. "Guess your boys still swim." His face was lit up with a genuine smile at his friend's good news.

"It's bad timing."

ALAIN BURRESE

"What do you mean? When is it ever the right time?"

"Just with all this shit going on."

"If she just found out, this will be long over before anything serious there."

"Yeah, but I should be with her, not having her tell me over the phone."

"Listen, this will be over soon and you two will be back together. Besides, if she's pregnant, you'll be on the couch." Senich laughed at his own joke and got sidetracked to the living room when he noticed the news.

"Hurry up and get to your shower while I change, I'm hungry." Baker told him. "Oh yeah, almost forgot." Baker opened the briefcase he'd set by the table and pulled out the tan envelope. "I think our new friend Peter Jacob dropped this off at my office. It's a DVD. Check it out." He tossed the envelop across the living room. It fell short of the couch and landed next to the coffee table. He turned to go change.

"Later, I want to catch the end of this. Then I'll shower and we'll go eat." Senich didn't pay attention to his friend's reply or the envelope. He was concentrating on a news story about a man who faced prison for having sexual relations with a horse. The DVD could wait.

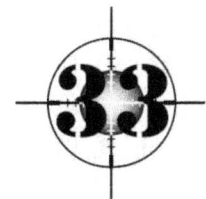

Money and paranoia seem to go together. It was certainly a fact with Dick Bennett. The more money he accumulated, the more paranoid he became. Or maybe it was due to his increasingly illegitimate ways of creating more wealth. It wasn't that he needed more money; he couldn't spend what he had if he lived another forty years and made it to one hundred and one. He was addicted to the accumulation of possessions and the thrill that came with doing so. The desire for things almost equaled his appetite for sex. Almost, because while he could go a day without shopping or checking on royalty deposits from the thousands of triple X films he'd produced, and continued to pour into the market on a daily basis, he couldn't go a day without the touch of one or more of the twenty-something starlets always at his disposal. However, lately he'd been preoccupied with his personal safety, and keeping what he owned, as much as his interest in accumulating more toys, and almost as much as his daily romps in the hot tubs and oversized king bed.

Bennett's virility wasn't what it was forty years ago, when he first arrived in California thinking he'd be the next Clint Eastwood or a young John Wayne. It was 1969, the sexual revolution was in full bore, and his sexual stamina was unequaled. What he once pleasured in doing multiple times each day, was now reduced to once or twice daily. Still pretty good for sixty-one years old he told himself. He watched Amber, the cute little blonde he'd just been with, as she walked away from the bed toward the showers in the master bath. He smiled as the round curves of her ass bounced as she walked. He thought about following her for another round in the shower, something he'd never have passed up when younger, but decided against it. She wasn't going anywhere; he could have her any time he desired, that's what she was paid for.

There were two girls staying at the house on salary until the group came in for his next film, *Ride 'em Cowboy*. Amber, the cute blonde, and Chi Chi, the small Mexican who he called Margarita because he said she tasted sweet and salty. He promised both girls parts in movies, and allowed them to live in his mansion fortress. All they needed to do in return was to satisfy his desires on a daily basis. That and pleasure each other when he needed entertainment for himself or his friends. They were both anxious for the filming of *Ride 'em Cowboy*. It would be billed as an authentic exotic western, and the girls believed Bennett when he told them it would help them be noticed for larger Hollywood roles. The shopping sprees he let the two partake in on top of the cash salary made it much easier to overlook the physical duties. After all, both girls had given it up for worse boy friends that didn't provide anything more than an offer for a beer afterwards. Living in the mansion, more money and clothes than they knew what to do with, and the promise of being stars in the future. What was a little sex here and there?

He lay there naked, still wondering if he should join Amber in the shower, get dressed, or take a nap. He looked down at himself. There were a few gray hairs mixed in with the groomed darker hair that covered his body, and he was a bit heavier than he'd prefer. But he didn't think he was all that different from when he was just starting out and his head was full of Hollywood dreams. Who would have ever guessed back then where his journey would take him, and that he'd end up living in a luxurious fortress in Montana with beautiful women at his beck and call. He sure never imagined it. He should have had Amber bring him a drink before she got in the shower. What a journey indeed he thought.

From 1969 to 1972, Richard Bennett landed bit parts in a few television series, did a variety of commercials and hung out at the beach a lot between gigs. His dreams of stardom were not materializing as he'd planned. Then a pair of movies changed everything. The movies were *Deep Throat* and *Behind the Green Door,* and they played to sold-out crowds across the country. Bennett saw each of them multiple times and not only did the movies bring porn to the surface of American culture, they shown a light on his true calling. With his stamina, he quickly became a rising star in the industry. He dropped Richard for Dick, it just seemed more appropriate with what he was doing, and the name stuck.

The rest of the 1970s were good to him, at least what he could remember. The porn industry enjoyed a more widespread popularity, increased budgets, and there were relatively few life-threatening diseases. Drugs were plentiful and his days were spent getting high and having sex. He'd have sex in front of the camera and then go back to the apartment for more. He was insatiable, and it wasn't unusual for him to have multiple partners each day of the week. Blonds, brunettes, white, black, Asian, skinny, fat, he didn't care. As long as they were female, he'd bang them. When it came to other guys, he didn't mind sharing women, and if there was contact between them as they were going at it with the girls, he didn't mind, but he never went for any purposeful contact with another man, even when inebriated or stoned into a stupor.

During the 80s, Bennett still spent a lot of time in front of the camera, but he also began directing and producing films.

That's where the money was to be made. The 80s were a different time, and after seeing John Holmes spend every dime he earned on cocaine, Bennett quit the drugs except for an occasional party here and there, and focused more on building an empire. The conservative wind that blew in with Ronald Reagan becoming president brought with it the beginning of a three-pronged assault on the porn industry over the next two decades: increasingly conservative politics, the advent of AIDS, and new technologies that opened the business up to a new breed of amateur pornographers. But Bennett weathered the storm and continued to prosper.

In 1986, He managed to avoid scrutiny when the Feds investigated a long list of stars, producers, and distributors when it was discovered that Traci Lords was only sixteen when she began making movies in 1984. It wasn't like Lords was the only underage girl associated with the business, but she was the most famous, especially after millions of dollars of merchandise was ripped from the shelves and destroyed. Bennett purged some of his stock for the same reason and counted his blessings he wasn't indicted like so many others.

He didn't think sex with sixteen year olds was that big of a deal, but then he also remembered John Holmes banging Dawn Schiller when she was fifteen and thought it was perfectly natural. If Sharon, John's wife, didn't have a problem with it, why should anyone else? But John had confided in him that he wasn't physically intimate with Sharon because she wasn't comfortable with the porn. Bennett was glad he never married. There were too many women to be tied down to just one, and he didn't need some money hungry whore trying to take the financial empire he worked so long and hard to create.

During the 90s, Bennett's empire grew by leaps and bounds, or more accurately, by *Teen, Chubby, Wrestling,*

Squirting, Hot Rod, Double Penetration, Gonzo, and his favorite category, *Amateur.* The home video market that began in the 1980s, and reduced the amount of porn theaters in the United States by nearly 80 percent in that decade, increased porn revenues because people could now stay home and enjoy the films without going out to a public theater.

When DVDs went consumer in 1997 it was a gold mine, and he was one of the first to re-release new versions of old titles with added features such as deleted scenes and 'making of' documentaries. He also used the technology to distribute films with the multiple-angle feature, allowing viewers to flip between different cameras at will. Toward the end of the decade his bank accounts soared.

In 1999, Bennett bought into the Y2K scare and moved to Montana. He remembered when John Holmes and Dawn Schiller went on the lam after the Wonderland Avenue murders in 1981. They stayed with John's sister in Montana for a week or so before trekking across country to Florida. He believed if John would have stayed in Montana, he might not have been arrested and sent back to Los Angeles to be prosecuted. He believed it to be the perfect wild country where people respected guns, God, and the good old U.S.A., and most importantly, a person's right to privacy.

He purchased 200 acres outside the old mining town of Butte, toward Anaconda, and built a small mansion fortress. Besides all the luxuries he couldn't live without, such as indoor and outdoor swimming pools with multiple hot tubs, a huge master bedroom with multiple showers and another hot tub, and a full bar and entertaining area for his parties, Bennett also had generators, water purification systems, storage pantries, and an underground bomb shelter fortified with supplies to keep ten people alive for a year. He had fantasies of having to repopulate the world after the apocalypse with the nine women he saved in his shelter.

He also built a film studio where he could continue to produce, film, and edit straight to DVD movies. He still enjoyed making pornographic movies that had some sort of plot, but also continued to tap into the 'amateur' market that he started making money with in the 90s.

He released over 600 hundred DVDs in his "Home Grown" series alone. He'd film people having sex for a pittance, and then release the DVD and sometimes make hundreds of thousands per title. *Home Grown Big Tits #147* was just released a week ago, and three others had been filmed and were being edited for release in the next two weeks. His crews would enter a town, rent a hotel room, and have an abundance of girls show up when they did a casting call for big titted girls from 18 to 29 years old. Bennett had footage from all over America, and with the digital age, it was easy and cheap to store.

He also produced *Home Grown Teens, Home Grown Hairy Cunts, Home Grown Bald Pussies, Home Grown Tinny Titties, Home Grown Sweet Asses, Home Grown Black Girls, Home Grown Asian Girls, Home Grown Mexican Girls, Home Grown True Blondes, Home Grown True Red Heads, Home Grown True Brunettes,* and for the gay crowd, *Home Grown Cocks.* Bennett never swung that way, even if he did enjoy watching several girls get each other off, but he recognized the huge profit potential for gay porn, so he added male on male flicks to the titles he produced and filmed for revenue generation only.

It was the perfect life, and what he'd been working so hard to achieve. He had all the money, all the possessions, and all the women he could ever want. And in the last year, he'd discovered something he'd never imagined he'd enjoy so much. Maybe it was because he turned sixty, or maybe it was the added excitement that came with forbidden fruits that were taboo. For whatever reason, Bennett had a growing appetite for younger girls. Not the little eighteen and nineteen year olds that starred in his teen movies, even though they were still fun to be had, but his desires were for twelve and thirteen year olds who'd never experienced a man. He'd bedded many sixteen and seventeen year olds, and was pretty sure a few of them might have only been fifteen. But those girls even seemed old to him when he thought of the sweet innocent flesh of a twelve year old.

It was more than two years ago when an acquaintance from California was visiting and suggested that the Montana fortress was an ideal location to taste some forbidden pleasures. The privacy, luxuries, and security provided a discreet and hidden place to partake in what his acquaintance described as the most pleasurable experience on the face of the planet. The mixture of power, smashing societal taboos, breaking the law, and sexual satisfaction all combined to make an exhilarating experience. With such a description, Bennett was immediately interested, and with his intense libido, quest for power, and expertise in a business that walked the edge of the law, it became another obsession. Not only did he crave the young fresh girls for himself, he devised a way to make even more money through the trafficking and selling of such sweet little creatures.

Already a master at distribution, he figured trafficking humans wouldn't be much more difficult than selling DVDs. He knew Clay Grady and his trucking business from what they did around Butte, but more intimately because of his needs for illicit substances for his parties. Grady had supplied him various drugs over the years, so Bennett knew he wouldn't go to the law, even if he did turn down the proposal Bennett had for his trucking company. The relationship made both men a lot of money, as well as the few drivers that Grady trusted to know what the cargo they were hauling actually was. In the last year, he had sold over 50 girls, and Grady Trucking had transported almost all of them to various places in the lower forty-eight states. Not bad for a start-up. Bennett was now set on expanding his operation, and that contributed to his paranoia. He was deathly afraid that there was a leak somewhere within Grady Trucking, and that he might be ratted out. The death of the guy in Missoula, and the return of the girl to Spokane worried him a little. But now that the two who kidnapped the Spokane girl were not answering their phones, Bennett's mind raced as only the guilty's can. Did something happen to them too? Was it someone close to the Spokane girl, or something bigger? He had been orchestrating the transaction, and had paid the two who grabbed her and was going to pay the Missoula man for housing her, while waiting for another in Missoula to complete the transfer of funds. It was one of the rare deals he did in Montana. Most of the transactions took place out of state. He didn't need anything getting in the way of his expansion.

The two from Sanders County had snatched a dozen girls for him in the last year, but he'd never met them. That's the way he liked it. He made money, but was hands off except for the few girls he tested himself before selling. The guy in Missoula was a child molester who was willing to watch the girls without touching for a few days when they needed stored before transit. He was paid for his services and promised a little boy to play with in the future. They could be replaced. It was easy to find people to commit the crimes and do the dirty work. All it took was money, and that Bennett had plenty of. If only those he was paying knew how much he was making from their acts. Not as much as he made from those he filmed fucking, but almost. But then he didn't pay his amateur actors anything close to what he paid those on his 'other' payroll.

Bennett was unaware of the box of files Bruce James kept as an insurance policy and as something he'd planed to use to blackmail more funds from those who were selling the girls. James suspected there was a lot more money involved than he was seeing, and had dreams of being wealthy himself, and having an endless supply of little boys at his beck and call. Those dreams ended when he walked in on Ben Baker rummaging through his trailer house. The box he kept as an insurance policy lived on. If Bennett knew of the files, he'd be even more paranoid. If he knew the box was still around, he wouldn't leave his fortress. If he knew who found the box, he'd have hired five times the number of ex-military operatives to protect his life and fortune.

He looked over at the alarm clock on the stand beside the bed. The digital display read 11:01. Why was he spending such a beautiful Tuesday morning thinking about the negative happenings of the past weekend? Nothing could be linked to him, and besides, the new security team from Texas would be arriving today. He lived in a fortress, and was about to have four former military special forces turned security/bodyguards watching the place around the clock. He stretched his arms above his head and reached for the top of the large oak headboard and reminded himself that he really did have the perfect life.

Sometimes he didn't know if it was the money, the sex, or the thrill of breaking laws and getting away with it that gratified him the most. It didn't matter, it was all good. This was why he was put on this planet. His was the epitome of indulgence and the unequivocal existence. He thought about the last time he'd been with a twelve year old. It had been two months, but he remembered how soft she'd been, how she shrunk away in fear, but then how she had completely submitted to his every will as he forced himself on her - in her. He reached down and felt himself growing hard. He stood up and walked naked and at attention toward the master bath. Maybe he'd join Amber after all, even if she was a little old.

Bennett made money to spend, and relieving some of his paranoia seemed a particularly good investment in such an ever increasingly violent world. Nine dead in a school shooting less than two hours away. As he soaked in one of his hot tubs, preparing to retire for the night, he thought about the day. He was pleased with the four security specialists that arrived that afternoon. They were no nonsense types and projected a sense of confidence and professionalism that reassured him that he would be safe in their presence, and that they would secure his mansion fortress from any intruders. More importantly, they would be available to accompany him when he left the premises. He actually doubted anything would happen on his property, and he told the security team as much. He had attorneys on retainer, so why not have security on retainer too. He provided them one of his Hummers and they would be there if anyone did try to break in, and they were available when he went out. Yes, money well spent.

The short one, the leader of the bunch, was built like a fireplug and looked like he could bench press locomotives. His name was John Hatcher and he shaved his head and wore a mustache and goatee that formed a circle around his mouth. Hatcher's piercing blue eyes didn't miss anything and he walked like a tank. Bennett was sure he'd run over anything that got in his way. He'd almost enjoy watching someone come at him with the bald pitbull between them.

The tall one, the one he remembered them calling Tad, was also muscular, but his height didn't make him appear as powerful as the short guy. He didn't walk like a tank, but rather glided around and reminded Bennett of a large jungle cat. His appearance was almost the opposite of the shorter one, he was clean-shaven, and his long hair was pulled back and tied at his neck and hung to the middle of his back. The only similarity was the eyes; he also had blue eyes that seemed to take in everything as he continuously scanned the area he occupied.

Funny, Bennett couldn't remember anything about the other two. He knew they had been there, but they had somehow mysteriously blended into the background. He couldn't for the life of him remember any details other than they had been wearing the same black cargo pants and maroon t-shirts with the company logo that the other two wore. It didn't matter, that was good he figured. Maybe they were ninja. The thought of having ninja watch over his fortress made him feel even better.

He had found the four on the Internet. They came from a Texas company that advertised as a leading provider for quality security solutions in the United States and beyond. The company provided services to governments and corporations as well as provided executive protection details to traveling businessmen and women. Many of the security specialists working for the company had former military and law enforcement training.

The four flew into Butte on a private jet and Bennett had sent a vehicle to pick them up. No one knew they were here, and that's how he liked it. When they arrived at the mansion, the first thing they did was open the packages that had arrived the day before. Bennett was surprised to see the weapons and ammo come out of the boxes. He had always considered himself a lover, not a fighter, and firearms were as foreign to him as his lifestyle was to the team he'd just hired. Even though they had minimal interaction before retiring to the quarters that were set up for them, Bennett could feel the contempt they held for him and his empire. It seemed the tall muscular one especially found him distasteful. The look the one called Tad gave him when he asked what their sexual appetites included and how he might be able to satisfy them actually scared him, and he had to remind himself that they worked for him, and what he said they did. Fuck 'em he thought, at the price he was paying, they could find their own pussy. So much for trying to be hospitable. As long as they kept him alive and the place safe, he didn't care what they thought. There were tons of people who didn't like what he did for a living and how he made his millions. Well, fuck them too.

He told the four they could use the Hummer as needed, but he'd prefer if they kept a low profile around Anaconda, and not too big of one in Butte if they wanted to go that far. He also let them have free run of the house, except for his Master Bedroom and Bath. He also gave strict instructions that they were not to go into the studios. Other than that, relax he told them, and be ready if he wanted to go anywhere.

"Dick, can I get anything for you before I go to bed? I don't feel too great and wanted to go to sleep early." Amber stood near the door to the indoor pool and hot tub area. She wore a pair of short shorts and a long t-shirt with a California brand tanning oil logo on the front, obviously not purchased locally.

Bennett glanced at his watch. It was 10:45 already. "Where's Margarita?"

"She's watching TV."

"Tell her when her show's over I could use some company out here. You go ahead and go to bed."

"Thanks," with that she bounded off and left him alone in the bubbling water. He climbed out and walked naked to the poolside bar and retrieved a beer from the refrigerator. He stretched a little as he walked back to the hot tub. It had been a long day. He'd spent most of it helping a new director, who was also doing editing work for him, with the cumaway, or the shot of the man's face as he cums, in a new feature he was producing. He was surprised that he had to explain basic principles such as cutting to the "oh yeah" face near the end of his ejaculation, and then cutting back to the ejaculation from the beginning. Doing this gave the appearance of twice the load, and as Bennett very well knew, even with stars as he'd been when younger, you only got so many money shots, so you wanted to make them count. Doubling an actor's load through editing also fed the egos of actors that usually needed a lot more stroked than just their cock. The new guy was doing okay, he'd learn.

Bennett sat on the side of the tub and let his feet dangle in the water. The jets pounded his feet in a soothing manner as he dialed his cell phone. No answer. He tried a second number with the same result. Why weren't those two in Sanders County answering? He was anxious, well, anxious and horny. He had a buyer in Oklahoma and he needed to provide a white girl between the ages of 9 and 12 for him. The buyer was willing to pay a premium if he had her by the weekend after next. The customer wasn't demanding a virgin, so he could have a turn at her first. He needed someone who could get him a girl, and quick. He was already imagining what he'd do once he got the girl to his bedroom. He had never had one under the age of ten, and he was going to request a nine year old to both satisfy his curiosity and fulfill the Oklahoma order. He needed her now so he could have his fun with her and then transport her to Oklahoma and receive his bonus.

He thought of snatching a kid himself. He'd never ventured into that area of the business, preferring to farm out the menial work and collect large amounts of money for orchestrating the deals. He found the buyers and matched them with the merchandise. It was simple commerce. So what if he had to sample the product once in a while. Do you think Ray Kroc never went in and ordered a Big Mac and fries? Yeah, but Kroc didn't slaughter the cows to make the beef patties.

He eased himself back into the tub. As the hot bubbling water engulfed him, he thought more about actually doing the kidnapping himself. Why not? It would save him time and money, and how hard could it be to grab a nine year old? He wondered if the four he'd just hired would protect him while he did it. That's what they were paid for, to protect him. He'd have to think on that and determine if he could trust them. He next needed to think of a location. A road trip this coming Saturday. He could grab a kid, have her for a couple days, and then send her along her way in one of Grady's trucks. It should only take two days to get there, so it would be in plenty of time to still get paid the bonus.

Bennett started to imagine what it would be like to grab a girl and throw her into his car. He visualized hearing her scream, feeling her struggle, and watching the terror in her eyes as he savagely ripped her clothes off. He became excited at the thought of being the little girl's first. He looked around and wondered how long Margarita's movie would last. It didn't matter, he'd have her later. Right now, he was envisioning grabbing a young girl and forcing himself on her. He pleasured himself quickly, and once done, continued to imagine the taboo subjects he wasn't allowed to discuss other than with his closest confidants that shared his appetites. What a story he'd have for them after kidnapping his own girl and exploiting her every witch way he could imagine. It would definitely be worth photographing and recording.

He thought of the last time he recorded a twelve year old. He still had the master copy, but he'd made over six hundred thousand dollars selling copies in four months. He put his director hat on and started thinking of all the ways he could film the little vixen and how much money he could make. Yes, what a life he had. He started getting excited again. Where was Margarita?

Baker and Senich lay in the thick brush on a hillside overlooking Bennett's mansion. Baker was watching Amber and Chi Chi swim in the outdoor pool through a pair of 8x42 high grade Nikon Sport Optics binoculars. The lightweight magnesium alloy body provided a sturdy, easy to hold pair of optics and the HG L series lens provided excellent clarity. Sweat dripped down his face as the sun climbed higher, and with it the temperature. He wondered why the scumbags of the world had pools with half-naked women swimming in them while he and his buddy sweated and itched out in the bushes and weeds watching.

"Anything new?" Senich asked. He had relinquished the binoculars fifteen minutes earlier, after taking his turn watching the house.

"Nope, just the two girls by the pool."

"Wait a second. Got a Hummer coming down the road toward the house." Senich, besides being security for the two, saw the larger picture without optics, and could direct where his buddy looked.

"Got 'em." Baker watched the four men climb out after the vehicle stopped in front of what must have been a four or six car garage. "Looks like a mini-army. Pretty sure they are all packing." He studied them as they looked around the outside of the house, taking their time with the pool area, and then went inside.

"Not surprised a guy like that hired his own security force."

"Guess it was a good thing we planned today for recon."

"Yeah, guess so." Senich replied.

Baker had spent the night doing searches on the Internet. He couldn't sleep. Not after he and Senich finally got around to plugging the DVD that had lain on the floor while they were at dinner, and for another couple hours after they returned home, into the DVD player. It disturbed and infuriated both men. The only reason they watched past the first scene was to identify any adults in the film. There were two. They had no idea the identity of one, but the other was Bennett. They were positive. The Internet provided clips and pictures from his legal movies, and the man in the home film with the young girls was definitely the same Dick Bennett: porn star, director and producer. Peter Jacob had anonymously provided the proof they needed. Baker was satisfied that Bennett was not only involved, but a main culprit.

With the information from the previous night, combined with a couple of phone calls in the morning, Baker had figured out where Bennett lived. He and Senich had driven by the entrance of the driveway up to the house with the Durango, and then found an obscure place to park about six miles from the backside of the property. They part hiked part jogged in, using the cover of the trees to stay hidden. It wasn't very tactical, but how tactical did they need to be to scout a porn filmmaker? Senich hadn't even wanted to spend the time with recon, and had stated they had enough proof and they'd find more after they busted in and wasted the perv. Watching the DVD, Senich became furious and wanted to kill the pedophile with his bare hands.

Baker insisted all they do this first day was observe. There was too much at stake to go rushing in. He wanted more intelligence first. They took up their viewing location at the edge of the tree line and according to his Nikon laser rangefinder, their position was 700 meters from the back door near the pool. It was 2:30 in the afternoon and they had been watching the property since 11:00.

"So, two cuties in bikinis, four armed security, and that guy who was doing yard work when we first got here."

"Yep, so far." Baker answered.

"Aren't you going to say 'I told you so?'"

"For what?"

"I thought spending a day doing recon was a waste of time, but it's a good thing we found out about those four. Wouldn't have expected four armed men as we crashed his party."

"Don't need to tell you, you know."

"Smart ass. Just don't go quoting Swaze as Dalton, 'Expect the unexpected.'"

Baker smiled at the *Roadhouse* quote and looked over again, "Be nice."

"Yeah, right. Until it's time not to be nice." Senich raised himself to a kneeling position and looked around at the surrounding area. "Why don't we just take him from here? We could come back with your Remington and Weatherby. You take him with the .300 mag. I'll be your spotter and back up with the Remington. They can't see us up here, and we can be in the trees and gone before anyone down there can react."

"Yeah, it could work. I'm more comfortable with the Remington, haven't shot the Weatherby nearly as much. Hold it, there's our guy." Baker watched Bennett walk out to the pool and say something to the girls. He recognized him from the pictures and video clips he'd seen on the Internet the previous night. He was wearing more clothes than he had been in the clips, and he was older, but it was the same person. It was Dick Bennett, the porn king. Baker felt a rage starting to churn inside and forced himself to clear the images from the DVD from his mind. Two of the four men they had seen get out of the Hummer came outside with him. They each went opposite directions and took up positions where they could easily see the entire back area, pool, and cover the corners if someone were to come from either direction.

"You sure it's him?"

"Well, he's wearing more than he was in those old videos, but it's him alright."

"We should have brought the rifles, we could take him and be done."

"What about the other two, and the girls?"

"They aren't carrying rifles, so we're clear. Side arms can't touch us up here, and we'd be in the trees and gone before they could be back outside with rifles and optics. Hell, the first couple of minutes they would be taking cover and worrying they'd be next." Both men knew the fear snipers created in those under fire.

"Let's go." Baker said.

"Where?"

"Home. I think your idea is right. We need to go zero the rifles at 700 meters. We'll come back tomorrow."

"Now you're talking."

The two men made their way back to the Durango, carefully watching for the best course to take when in a hurry. Each of them memorized the terrain and how they would get back to the hide overlooking the mansion. The fresh mountain air was filled with sounds of birds chirping and smells of fresh spring blossoms of various plants that made the woods a colorful spectacle of greens, yellows, blues, and reds. They walked quickly, but didn't jog as they had earlier. The beauty of the sights, sounds, and smells didn't go unnoticed, but the two had more on their minds than appreciating nature. It took about 85 minutes to cover the six miles. Both men worked up a sweat, and emptied their canteens before reaching the Durango where they left a cooler with Diet Cokes and Gatorades. Once both men were inside the vehicle, Baker slid in a new CD, opened a drink, and headed for the Interstate that would take them back to Missoula. Senich opened his own drink and rummaged for something to snack on. He was happy that his buddy was seeing things his way.

Neither Baker nor Senich noticed the hidden pair of blue eyes that watched them come out of the woods, climb into the Dodge, and drive away.

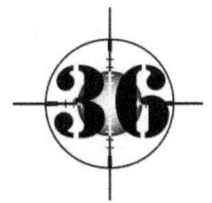

Thaddeus Edward Robinson was better known to those he worked with as Tad, a nickname that stayed with him from BUD/S, the Basic Underwater Demolition/SEAL training course at the Naval Special Warfare Training Center in Coronado, CA. Robinson made it through the five week Indoctrination and Pre-Training easily, well as easy as one could expect anyone to make it. He then went through the three phases, including the 8 weeks of conditioning that peaked with "Hell Week." Not once did Robinson ever think of ringing the bell. It just wasn't in him to quit. The third of the class that made it through started calling him Tad after the Instructors nicknamed him Tadpole. "Tadpole wants to be a SEAL," they'd say.

That was a long time ago, and now Robinson worked for a security company in Texas that sent him on assignment in Montana. He didn't care for the company, but it was a paycheck for now. It wasn't the men he worked with that bothered him; they were all competent and good men. Jackson was also a former SEAL and the two shared the pride, achievement, brotherhood, and self-awareness that all SEALS possessed. Once a SEAL, always a SEAL. Baxter was a former Army guy, Airborne Ranger who spent time with the 2nd Battalion of the 75th Ranger Regiment at Fort Lewis, Washington. And then there was the leader of the team, John Hatcher. The short bald fireplug had spent time with the 75th Ranger Regiment before being accepted into Special Forces where he served with the 5th Group at Fort Bragg, NC, before the group moved to Fort Campbell, KY. Hatcher didn't move with them because he was accepted into the 1st Special Forces Operational Detachment-Delta (1st SFOD-D) commonly known as Delta Force or the Combat Applications Group. He stayed with the counter-terrorist unit until he retired with 22 years served. Robinson figured the only reason he was working for the Texas company was to learn the business aspects and clientele before he started his own. He didn't see Hatcher working for this outfit for very long. The clients the company let hire them were the problem Robinson had. As a SEAL, he was one of his country's finest, now he was playing baby sitter to a millionaire porn king. It was quite the letdown for one's esteem. He did admit the paychecks were a lot bigger.

Tad wondered what his father would think about his current assignment. Deceased now for five years, Charles Edward Robinson had served two and a half tours in Vietnam with the Marine Corps. His third tour was cut short by a mortar round that earned him his second Purple Heart and a trip home. Left with a permanent limp, he got out of the service and started what would be a long career with the U.S. Postal Service. He raised young Thaddeus to hunt, fish, and camp in the woods of Wyoming. The boy was a natural and took to Scouts and everything outdoors much more than the classroom. His grades were okay, but everyone expected him to follow his father's footsteps and become a Marine. It shocked everyone, especially his father, when he joined the Navy, but he redeemed himself by becoming a SEAL. Cancer took his father before he retired from the Service and took the current position with the security company. He sometimes felt his father wouldn't approve. Working for the government was the only thing his father ever knew, and he was proud that his son had made a career serving his country. Tad just couldn't picture his father being proud over babysitting someone who made tons of money selling pornography.

Jackson and Baxter were watching the porn stud for the afternoon. The four men assigned to the security detail had pulled up an old video clip of him on the Internet while doing their prep work for the assignment. They were almost as impressed with his performance as they were with the humongous titted blonde he was performing with. And with Amber and Chi Chi running around in various stages of undress, the assignment wasn't all that bad. Robinson still didn't feel good about it. He wasn't sure why, but something didn't feel right. He kept wondering what his father would do, which was sort of like wondering what John Wayne would do, they were men cut from the same cloth. He didn't think either would approve, but he needed the paycheck.

Regardless of how he felt about Bennett, or his dissatisfaction with his employer, Robinson was being paid to do a job, so he'd do it well. Two of the first of many lessons he father taught him were to always keep your word and do every job right the first time. He told Hatcher he wanted to check the perimeter of the property and got the okay. By chance, his route took him away from the house and clear from the sight of the binoculars watching the pool and goings on in back as if he'd planned it.

Robinson had attended sniper training and was designated a sniper with his SEAL Team. While most men pulling security details are alert to the happenings around them, he was always thinking 500 or more meters out. The best counter sniper weapon you can have is a trained sniper, and that was Robinson's specialty. As a SEAL, he became an expert with anything you could shoot, but he always felt the most comfortable behind a scoped rifle by himself. It reminded him of his youth when his father hooked him up with a rancher out of town and he'd lay for hours waiting for gophers to poke their heads out from their holes. He used a .22 rifle with a four-power scope and was paid one dollar for every gopher he bagged. It was good money at the time, and it kept a lot of livestock from breaking legs in gopher holes.

He had been walking and observing for two hours when he spotted the parked Dodge Durango. The road abutted Bennett's property line, but there really wasn't much else in the area. It seemed odd for the red vehicle to be parked partly hidden on this stretch of road. He tried to think of reasons it might be parked there, and what its occupants could be doing. He thought about going near the vehicle to see if he could pick up a sign as to which direction the driver headed on foot, but opted to settle into a position that provided him a view of the road and vehicle but also offered decent concealment. He enjoyed being out in the clean mountain air and the spot he picked was comfortable. He just needed to wait, and waiting was something Robinson was good at.

The fruits of his patience came with two men exiting the trees to climb into the Durango and drive off. Robinson watched them from his hidden position and mentally took notes. When a sniper is looking for another sniper, some of the tell tale signs are face masks, smocks, ghillie suits, optics such as spotting scope, rifle scope, or binoculars, and obviously a weapon suitable for long-range kills. Neither of the men had rifles, but Robinson could only guess what was in the packs.

What were the two doing on Bennett's property? There was a reason he hired a security detail, maybe it wasn't just filthy rich paranoia after all. What if the porn king had a legitimate fear and good reason to hire him and the other three that made up the team. But then again, the two could have been looking for a secluded spot to rendezvous for a romantic picnic, you never could tell. No, he didn't think so. There was something about the two that seemed familiar. He couldn't place it. Maybe it was the way they moved, or possibly the way they looked. Maybe it was just that feeling again. Something wasn't right about this job, and something wasn't right about the two men in the Dodge.

He carefully rose and worked his way down to the road where the vehicle had been parked. He noted the direction the two had come from and that by following the back azimuth one would come out somewhere on top of the hill looking down on the back area of Bennett's mansion. An enemy on high ground with a wide or deep field of fire made Robinson uncomfortable. A trained rifleman could produce significant casualties from such a position and pin down any unit below. But the two didn't have rifles.

Three hours later, Robinson found the position Baker and Senich used to observe the mansion and pool earlier that day. Other than water and a couple snack bars in a cargo pocket, the only gear he had with him was his .40 caliber Glock carried in his IWB holster. He'd wished he had optics with him when he was viewing the two earlier, and he wished again as he looked down at the back of Bennett's place. The girls must have got tired of swimming and baking in the sun, no one was out back any longer. Maybe the two hiked up here to get a peek at the two girls, he figured they probably swam and sunned nude at times. Would the two make a six-mile hike to see some titts through binoculars? No, there was something else, but what was it? What was Bennett into that would warrant the two to hike in and observe from this hilltop? Robinson looked down at the pool and estimated the distance to be around 650 to 700 meters. He'd made shots a lot further. The job had definitely become much more interesting. Robinson clicked through the information he possessed. Rich guy hired team to protect him, but doesn't say why. Rich guy made money in porn industry. Two men watching rich guy from hilltop. He then started asking himself questions. Was rich guy into illegal activities? Illegal porn? Were the two guys fathers of girls rich guy used in films? Were they fathers of the two hanging out at the house? Does rich guy have enemies? Competition? He didn't have enough to go on, but something was definitely wrong. There was a reason those two were up here, he just needed to figure that reason out. More importantly, would they be back, and when? He'd talk to Hatcher and see if they could get Bennett to provide some intelligence about why he needed to hire them in the first place. He'd also request some equipment to help secure this hilltop.

He scoped out the surrounding area and analyzed the position once again. There was something about those two. He looked around; it was exactly where he'd set up if he were observing the porn king.

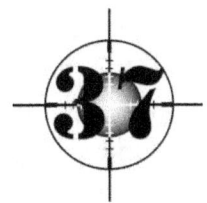

"Fucker. If we'd have had the rifles we could have capped his ass and we'd be done. Fuck!" Senich threw his cell phone onto the floor of the Durango by his feet.

"The truth about your cell phones comes out. What's the matter?" Baker had heard half of the conversation, and knew his buddy had called someone asking about Dick Bennett. They were on Interstate 90 passing Rock Creek on the way back to Missoula.

"I know a guy in Kentucky. He's with a local sheriff's office there, but he spends his free time tracking Internet child molesters and anyone else that harms kids. He's even helped that Dateline guy with the *Catch a Predator* show."

"He know of Bennett?"

"Yeah, he knows of him. Says he's pretty sure he was behind the sale of a couple of girls last winter, but they couldn't nail any of them. Leads ran out and they never closed the file. Still open, but if you don't catch them right away, it's usually too late. He didn't know for sure if the sale ever finalized. If it did, the girls were supposedly twelve and thirteen."

"Damn."

"I told you we should have taken the rifles. We could have capped his ass."

"It was recon, and we didn't know anything for sure. We still don't. How reliable is your source?"

"Jimmy's as squared away as they come. I trust him."

"That's good enough for me."

"His wife and little girl were raped and murdered. It's been his life mission to stop others ever since. He's provided me intel that panned out before."

"Like I said, if you trust him, that's good enough for me."

"God damn it, we should have capped that fucker!"

"What are you so upset for? We'll get him. And why have you needed intelligence from this guy before?"

"That's not a concern right now." Senich looked out the side window at the passing trees and fields. His fingers clenched to fists and the released repeatedly. He tried counting the cows in the field as they whizzed past but lost count in a group of dark browns and blacks. "There's something I never told you."

"What?" Baker asked, glancing from the Interstate in front of him over to his friend.

"You met my kid sister that time, remember?"

"Julie?"

"Yeah, but she likes to go by 'Jewels'"

"I remember her, nice gal. What's she up to?"

"She married that engineer boyfriend she had for so long and they're living in Georgia, just outside of Atlanta. Rick's a good guy. They have a baby boy."

"Cool, you never told me you were an uncle."

"Forgot."

"So what are you getting at?" Baker noticed his friend's hand start to clench again, and he caught a glimpse of his eyes swelling before he turned away to look out the side window again.

"Don't ever let her know I told you. She's hid it from just about everyone, and she'd be pissed if she found out I let you know."

"Alright. No problem. What is it?"

"She was raped when she was a teenager."

"Damn… I'm sorry Frank. I guess I understand a bit more now why you're so angry with guys like we've been dealing with."

"It happened when we were in the Army. She was living with our mom. No one was there to help her. Mom found out after it happened, but all she could do was hold her when she cried. She didn't know what to do. It fucked with both their heads for a long time."

"When did you find out?"

"Few years ago, I don't remember. It was when she was dating Rick, and I pressed her about why she wouldn't get more serious with him. He's good for her, and I didn't want to see her lose him. She finally told me. We stayed up all night crying, it was the closest we'd ever been. I convinced her to get some counseling. It helped and now she seems pretty happy with Rick and the baby."

"But how are you with it?"

"I'm okay."

"You sure."

"Yeah."

Baker didn't believe him, and he still wondered why he'd gotten information from the cop in Kentucky before, but he also knew that Frank would tell him if he wanted, and if not, that was okay too. They were like brothers, but even family held back and didn't share everything. "I'm glad things are good now, but I'm sure sorry that happened to her."

"Yeah, it happens all the time, but it was my baby sister and I wasn't there." Senich wiped his eyes and tried to hide the tears that started to trickle from eyes that belonged behind a rifle's scope or aiming a Sig .45.

"I understand. My biggest fear is something happening to Tanya and Coral when I'm not there for them."

"Yeah.' Senich was composing himself. "I don't ever want to be in a position where I didn't do something when I could. I wasn't there for her."

"You were half way around the world and didn't know."

"I know." Senich seemed to drift off in thought. Quietly, he continued, "I'll tell you this, I won't ever live with a regret that I could have done something to stop a monster and didn't. I rather die trying than live with not having done anything."

"We're going to do something alright." Seeing his friend cry made Baker's eyes swell and he looked straight ahead to not let his buddy see. He didn't know if the words he just spoke were for Frank or himself. He envisioned Bennett out by his pool. "Don't worry, we'll do something."

It was difficult for Baker to keep the Durango under eighty the remainder of the drive home. Once there, the two men quickly loaded up the rifles and took off again. They swung through a drive through and grabbed a sack of burgers and large Diet Cokes to curb their hunger and thirst. They ate in silence, listening to *Bob Seager's Greatest Hits,* as they drove to an open area about a half hour from town.

"This should do." Senich said as Baker stopped the vehicle and put it in park. He left the engine on as the two listened to the final saxophone of *Turn the Page.*

"That song still makes me think of that little bar in Fayetteville that had the Thai women working there."

"The place you were seeing that older gal?"

"She didn't look as old as she was."

"I got no problem with older women."

"You don't have a problem with any women." Baker turned the Dodge off and opened his door. "Let's get this done; it'll be dark before we know it. Plus, I want to try and get a good night's sleep tonight."

"Sleep's overrated."

"Yeah, but I'd still like a little."

The two men pulled out the rifles and the extra gear they'd brought along. Baker handled the Remington .308. "I'm going to use this one; you zero the .300 Magnum and use it for spotting and backup."

"Why don't you want to use the Weatherby?"

"Like I told you on the hill, I'm more comfortable with the .308. We've been shooting those for a long time. I have a few boxes of M118LR ammo that we can zero with and that's what I'll use tomorrow."

"Sounds good." Senich pulled the Weatherby from its case. "It's you and me baby."

The two used the notes they took during their recon and the same rangefinder to mark off the exact distance Baker planned to shoot the next day. He really hadn't put much thought into it. When he decided to return the next day up on the hill, he wasn't one hundred percent certain what they would do. After Senich's Kentucky cop buddy confirmed Bennett was into selling kids, the two decided to make things right as only they could. It was certain, and the certainty was Baker would act, as a warrior, and stop Bennett from ever selling another human being again. There would be no more little girls like Ashley being abused at the mansion near Butte, nor would they be transported around the country by Grady Trucking to be sold to sick degenerates that deserved to suffer before being snuffed from the earth. Baker was determined to see this through, and getting it over and behind him as quickly as possible was not only the most practical, but didn't provide him the time to over rationalize what they were doing and change his mind. Their plan was simple. They would return to the hill overlooking the back of the house they had been using to view the place earlier, and wait for Bennett to come out to the pool area. One shot and they would be gone, back through the woods, to the vehicle, and somewhere public in Missoula. No one would know where they spent the morning, or how. It was decided.

There were a lot of holes in the plan. Baker would have preferred more planning and more surety. But you didn't always get what you wanted. He realized a lot of what they were planning relied on luck. They needed the weather and wind to cooperate, and then they needed the porn king to come out to the pool area and present himself as a target. And what about the security team? There were a lot of conditions that could derail the mission, and many were out of Baker's control, and he didn't like it.

There was one thing Baker could control, however, and that was that he and the weapon worked in unison to place each and every round exactly where he desired. On the range, he did just that. He made notes after each shot, notes he'd use the next day to compare conditions. He needed to exactly place the round with a cold barrel from 700 meters. He'd done it before, and he was confident he'd do it again.

The location Baker picked to zero the rifles had a hill they climbed to shoot down into the valley. It wasn't the exact elevation and angle of the spot behind Bennett's house, but it was very close. Baker chose the location because it was as near as they were going to get on quick notice. He knew the slant angle from horizontal is a factor when determining the ballistic solution to shot placement. If he zeroed on a flat range and held directly on his target shooting down, he'd hit high or shoot above his target. Snipers and hunters knew you aimed low when shooting uphill or down. There were many factors that influenced the flight of a bullet and needed to be considered. Some of them, such as wind, Baker couldn't do anything about until it was time to shoot, and he'd have to hold off the target accordingly. Even a gentle 5mph breeze, combined with the spindrift of a bullet, can move it two and a half feet to the right at a thousand yards. Even the rotation of the earth becomes a factor for extremely long shots. Fortunately, 700 meters was a close-range engagement, or close enough anyway, that the effect of the earth's rotation would be too small to be a factor. Still, Baker wanted the number of actual variables to be minimal, and to ensure that, he carefully zeroed his weapon, recording cold-bore and second-shot settings. The shots were as close to the shots he'd take the following day as he could replicate. If the weather cooperated, he'd hold directly on his target and not have to use Kentucky windage and hold off.

When both men were satisfied that the two rifles were zeroed at the appropriate distance, and they had fired several confirming shots that hit exactly where they wanted, they packed up their gear. It took time to let the rifle cool, clean it, and fire again to ensure he had accurate cold-bore shots. Baker was happy for the longer spring days. Senich wasn't accustomed to the feel and recoil of the larger .300 WBY Magnum, and his shots, while hits, were not as accurate as Baker's. But then Baker had always been the better shot of the two from long distances. Senich's forte was combat pistol craft, and he could do things with his Sig. 45 that his friend only read about and watched on television. At 700 meters, the right person of the team was taking the shot the next day.

Baker had ten rounds left from the box he'd fired the last confirming shots with. It was ideal to have match-grade ammunition from the same lot to ensure complete accuracy. Baker had ten rounds. He'd need only one.

The mood at the house was somber. Tanya had left a message, but Baker decided to wait till the next day to return her call. He wondered if she still felt pregnant. He figured women could tell that stuff. He didn't want to know right now. He needed to focus on the mission, and he couldn't afford to think about anything else until it was over. All of the gear was laid out and ready to go. The rifles were cleaned and lying on the floor next to the equipment they'd take with them. After going over everything for a third time, and mentally checking everything off, Baker was sure they were ready. He went to the kitchen to pour another glass of water; he wanted to be well hydrated.

"Hey, guess what's on TV?" Senich yelled from the living room.

"What?" Baker yelled back.

"*Sniper* with Tom Berenger."

"The first one?"

"Yeah. From '93'"

"Best part is the final line, 'There's always Montana'"

"You wanna watch it?"

Baker came around the corner holding the glass of water. He had changed into a pair of sweats when they got to the house and he noticed Senich was still wearing the camo pants and brown t-shirt he'd worn all day. "Aren't you tired?"

"Not really."

"I'm going to read a bit and then crash. You go ahead and watch it if you want."

"Alright. What time in the morning?"

"If we leave at six, we can be in position between nine and ten." Baker answered.

"Hope he takes a swim before lunch."

"We'll see. I'll catch you in he morning." Baker turned and headed toward the bedroom.

"Hey Ben."

Baker stopped and turned. "Yeah?"

"We're doing the right thing, you know."

"Yeah, I know. Good night."

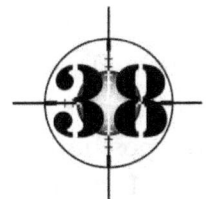

"Tad" Robinson woke early Wednesday morning and quickly shaved, showered and dressed for the day. The Kevlar vest and Glock in the IWB holster were as much a part of his wardrobe as his socks and underwear. Donald Trump wouldn't go to the office without his tie, and Robinson wouldn't go to work without his Kevlar and Glock. His vest weighed a bit more than the others because he didn't like to go about without rifle plates in the specially designed pockets, both front and back. He didn't think he was paranoid. He just knew what a rifle could do from long range and wanted the most protection available. The vest wasn't concealable under a light shirt, and that's why Robinson was almost always wearing a baggy sweatshirt or jacket, even in the heat.

After eating a light breakfast, the former SEAL sniper spent sixty minutes sitting at a table about three feet from the large window looking out at the patio and pool. He scanned the hillside out back with a pair of Bushnell waterproof binoculars. He would be able to see more if he went outside, but he'd be easily seen outside too. He didn't want anyone who might be watching to know he was looking. The brush was thick and he knew it would be difficult to see anyone hiding in the green foliage. He was looking for movement.

He'd talked to the team the night before, and Hatcher had agreed to order the surveillance equipment he'd requested. The two he'd seen the day before leaving in the Dodge Durango might be nothing, but he didn't get paid to ignore potential threats. He thought about walking up the back hill to the hide he'd found, but thought better of it. If the two returned, they would see him coming and slither away into the trees before he got close. There was no way to sneak up on the position from the front.

More than likely, the two weren't a threat. Robinson found it hard to believe that the blow hard porn stud they were guarding had enemies that would send a sniper through the forest to take him at seven hundred meters. Anyone who could pull that shot off would be damn expensive to hire. But why had he found signs of the two lying in the perfect position to make such a shot? Well, it was the perfect position for someone trained in long rang marksmanship. They were in Montana. There were a lot of hunters in the area, and many of them could match a military sniper in shooting, they just lacked the field craft and other tactical components the trained sniper possessed. Could some local be pissed enough at Bennett to be plotting something?

Then again, maybe they were up there taking photographs. The same position would provide an excellent location to film if one had the right telephoto lens. The two could be selling pictures of Amber and Chi Chi on the Internet. Or maybe they hoped to film Bennett in a compromising position. Blackmail was always a threat to the rich. Robinson's mind raced. Maybe he held big sex orgies up here, or filmed his triple X videos out in the open. He thought about the size of the packs and supposed there could have been camera equipment inside. These days you could hide a pretty good telephoto lens and camera in a fanny pack. Robinson set the binoculars on the oak kitchen table and rubbed his eyes. What were the two doing? He tried to remember everything he'd seen the day before. The most puzzling thing to the former SEAL sniper was the absence of rifles. Who would go on a sniping mission without a weapon?

It was eight o'clock and Robinson was restless. He needed to move, and he needed to clear his eyes after sitting and staring through binoculars for so long. He wished he had a sniper rifle of his own on this mission, but they hadn't brought one. It was supposed to be a simple detail and they didn't find out about the large wide-open spaces surrounding the house until they arrived.

He'd asked Hatcher to have a H.S. Precision Pro-Series Take-Down rifle kit sent with the surveillance equipment he requested. The kit contained an accurized Remington 700 action built on an H.S. Precision adjustable-length stock with interchangeable .308 and .300 Winchester Magnum barrels and bolts in a custom, high-impact, military spec case. It was not his first choice of weapons. You always traded some accuracy with a takedown rifle, but in its case it was easily shipped without disclosing what it was. Hatcher didn't promise him one, but did say he'd request it from the company. Robinson thought about going to the local sporting goods store and seeing what they had that would satisfy him, but Hatcher told him they weren't to mingle with the locals. The client and the company didn't want anyone to know they were there. The packages would be delivered to the client under his name; the surveillance equipment for sure, and possibly the takedown sniper rifle.

Robinson figured Jackson and Baxter wouldn't mind babysitting Bennett another day. They seemed to enjoy the eye candy running around without clothes. Hatcher had posted the day's schedule and it was the same as the day before. All four men on the security detail wondered why they had been hired, but as long as they were getting paid, it didn't really matter. They were paid to do a job, and that's what they would do.

Robinson decided to walk the perimeter again and went to the living room where Hatcher worked on his laptop at the cherry colored wood desk near the window. "Care if I go on patrol again?"

"Go ahead, shouldn't take much here. I'll keep Jackson and Baxter with him. I really don't see why we are guarding him here at his home. I'd understand it if he were traveling."

"I agree. But I still don't like that those two were watching from the hillside yesterday."

"I don't like it either. You and I both know there isn't much we can do if someone with long range skills really wants someone dead."

"True."

"I'm going to tell him to stay inside today. The girls too."

"You think they'll listen?"

"I don't know, probably not. Big shots with money don't want to listen to anybody, they think they know it all."

"Ain't that the truth. And I think Mr. Bennett is about as know-it-all as they come."

"You got that right, I truly believe he thinks his shit don't stink."

"So Hatch, how long are we going to stay here and baby-sit him?"

"I don't know, Tad. The contract with the company goes till the middle of next week. Seems he has a trip planned for this weekend that he wants security for. After that, I don't know. I'm requesting we get reassigned and if he wants further security they assign a new detail."

"Thanks. I want out of here ASAP."

"What's your beef with him?" Hatcher asked, finally turning away from the laptop and facing Robinson who still stood in the open way between the kitchen and living room.

"I just don't like him."

"Is it because of his money?"

"No, not because of his money, but how he made it. I have no use for people who exploit others for their personal gain."

"How can you be sure he exploits people?"

"I know enough about the inside of the porn industry to know he didn't get where he is without exploiting a ton of women and girls along the way. I bet he has a history of drugs and underage girls too."

"He better not have any of that shit around here. It's in our contract that if a principle commits a felony we can pack up and walk right there. No way am I going to let any of us get involved with that."

"Thanks, Hatch."

"No worries. You sure you want to go out alone?" The look Robinson gave him answered the question, "Alright, you go check the perimeter and let me know what you find. I sure hope it's nothing."

"So do I." Robinson turned to go fill a canteen and load his pockets with something to munch on while he walked. He wasn't sure if he was going because he thought he'd find someone, because he wanted to be in the woods, or because he wanted to be away from everything Bennett. It didn't matter; he'd accomplish all three.

Robinson walked through the woods at a comfortable pace. He wasn't trying to be tactical, but his natural walk didn't overtly project he was there. The BlackHawk Warrior Wear Black Ops Boots he wore had a Dri-Lex moisture-wicking inner lining that kept his feet cool. He initially tried the boots because he liked the name and they seemed to be a good buy. The more he wore them, the more he was pleased with the purchase. The concealable Kevlar vest was comfortable enough under his shirt, and he was glad he was wearing the rifle protection plates. The two yesterday didn't have rifles, but it was always better to be prepared.

He stopped to watch a doe and her new fawn. They were lying still near a tree and after watching them a while, Robinson purposefully walked wide around them. He then forded a small creek by wading through, rather than walking across a nearby downed tree. He did it to test the waterproof system of the boots and they passed.

He noticed a shady spot near the creek and decided to take a break. He sat in the open, and the water running by made it difficult to hear anything that might approach. From a tactical standpoint, it was a poor place to stop. At the moment, Robinson didn't care about tactics. He didn't want to be tactical for a while. He wanted to enjoy the fresh mountain air, the cool breeze that blew through the trees, the shade from the tall pines, and the gentle sound of running water from the brook. He just wanted to relax and think about what he really wanted to do with his life. He certainly didn't want to continue on being a babysitter for the likes of Bennett. The man disgusted him, and he wondered what crimes he'd committed to get where he was. There was something about him that made his stomach churn. It wasn't just the porn, there was something else, and he just couldn't put his finger on it.

The rumble in his stomach reminded him he'd been sitting a while, and he reached into his cargo pocket for a snack. He glanced at his watch. It read 12:30. He was surprised to see just how long he'd sat beside the creek. It was so peaceful. Maybe that was it. Maybe he needed a more peaceful occupation. He'd lived by the sword, or more accurately, the gun, his entire adult life. He wondered how he could parlay his skills into a different career.

"Shit," he said aloud. "I better do the job I'm being paid for." He stood and stretched and took a swig of water. He looked around to ensure he'd not left anything that would give away that he'd been there. Some habits die hard. He figured it was about two miles to where he saw the Durango parked the day before and he headed in that general direction, still paralleling the road and property line off to his right.

Robinson meandered around, taking in all of the bright spring colors and listening to the varied sounds of the woods. It was refreshing and he was in no hurry to return to the mansion. If walking the perimeter took till nightfall, it would be fine by him. He was still traveling in the general direction of where he spotted the Durango, and he knew he'd need to veer off toward the road soon to be able to see if it was parked there again today.

He stopped next to a tree to relieve himself. Standing there, he heard the unmistakable report of a large caliber rifle echo through the forest. He stood completely still and silent. He listened for a second shot, but none came, so he quickly fastened his pants. He then took off toward the location the Dodge had been the day before at a rapid pace. He could not tell exactly where the shot had been fired, it was quite a ways off. Nor was he sure who fired it. He did, however, suspect that going to the location of yesterday's vehicle would reveal answers to those questions. If he were right, he could get there first and wait. Why go looking through the woods for a needle in a haystack if you could wait and let the needled come to you?

When Robinson arrived at the road, it took him very little time to find the location he'd seen the two men enter the Durango and drive away. He was sure he was going to find the red vehicle parked in the same spot, and was surprised to find nothing there.

"Son-of-a-bitch." Robinson looked up and down the road and peered into the trees. He was sure he was at the right spot.

Then it clicked. The hide he'd found was in a perfect position. Snipers never liked to fire more than three rounds from one position before moving. Robinson himself liked to take different routes and keep from creating habits. From the cover of the forest, he started moving up the road, scanning every detail of the terrain for any sign that would provide a clue. Then he saw it. Parked off to the side of the road, semi-hidden, was the red Durango.

He pulled out his cell phone to call Hatcher, but couldn't get a signal. It was a problem they'd had since they arrived in Montana. He should have brought one of the Motorola two-way radios. "Guess it's just me," he muttered to himself while putting the phone back into his pocket.

Robinson looked over the surrounding area to find a place to set up a hasty ambush. He expected two men with at least one long-range rifle. His only firearm was the Glock. He was very outmatched from a distance, but up close, where Robinson planned to confront them, the long guns didn't provide an advantage. He wondered if the two carried side arms, and if they did, how good they were with them.

He selected the most obvious route from where he supposed the two to be coming from based on the previous day's observations and where he believed the shot he heard came from. He adjusted a fallen log and then concealed himself behind the makeshift cover. The Glock was out so he wouldn't have to move to draw it when his targets arrived. He fidgeted enough to be comfortable but not so much to move any of the branches used to conceal his position. He was glad he'd already eaten and relieved himself; he suspected it would be around an hour wait.

His mind raced as his body remained still. He wondered what was happening back at the house. Who fired the shot? Was anyone hit? Killed? Was he doing the right thing? Fear, doubt, curiosity, surety, and a host of other feelings fleeted through his thoughts while he lay there in waiting. Several times he contemplated getting up and racing back to the house to see if he were needed there. He again was having doubts that he was doing the right thing, or at the right place, when he heard something off to his one o'clock in the trees. He held his breath and almost willed his heart to stop beating as he listened. The sound was nearing, and it was unmistakably someone walking toward him. He'd been formulating a plan for the last hour, and now it was time to decide. He must decide to act or remain hidden and let the person pass and observe. SEALs were men of action. Even though reconnaissance and intelligence gathering were important, SEALs were shooters. That's what they were bred for, and that's what they did best. However, Robinson's plan called for capturing whoever was approaching, not just killing them, which would have been easier from his ambush site. He'd take them alive, and only kill them if there were no other choice. He listened to the footsteps approaching and readied himself. It was time.

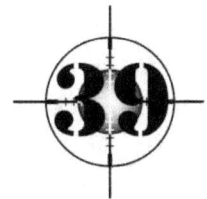

Baker wasn't sure if he'd slept or not, the alarm sure came early. He'd tried to read, but couldn't focus on the page. Getting nowhere with the book, he turned off the light and concentrated on slowing his breathing and yearned for sleep. It came in spurts and it seemed he was checking the time on the clock every thirty to forty-five minutes through the night. He was definitely not refreshed as he stumbled in the dark to the bathroom to shower.

He looked out the window and was pleased to see a clear sky. The day was starting as if it would be sunny and warm like the day before. They would have a clear field of view and wouldn't have to worry about elements such as rain. He hoped there wouldn't be any wind. It should be good swimming weather. So far so good he thought.

Baker was dressed and sipping on a freshly brewed cup of coffee when Senich came out of the spare bedroom looking like something out of *Quest for Fire*. "Let me hop in the shower, I'll be ready in a minute. Could you pour me a cup of that?"

"Sure." Baker continued his final inspection of their equipment, ammunition and weapons. Both men would carry their personal side arm and knife, but the other gear was divided between two small rucksacks. The mission should only take a few hours, so they packed accordingly. Besides the two rifles and respective ammunition, the packs contained binoculars, cleaning kit with lens paper, gloves, cape, range finder, spare batteries, parachute cord, jerky, snack bars, notebook with pens and pencils, small first aid kit, and a few other items they may need. It wasn't a complete load like they would pack for longer missions, but it would do for the day's work. The inspection complete, he poured Senich a cup of coffee and set it on the table, refilled his own, and then started loading the Durango. The first pot of coffee was in a thermos, and there was also a cooler with water and Gatorade. The vehicle also had a variety of Power Bars and snacks, besides those packed in the rucksacks. The final things he put into the back seat were the two rifles and the match-grade ammunition.

Seven minutes later Senich appeared looking like a new man. He gulped down the coffee that had cooled and refilled his cup from the pot on the counter. Baker came in and Senich looked at him sheepishly, "Sorry I didn't help you load up."

"Sorry my ass."

"I'll unload it when we get home."

"I'll hold you to that. I had a protein drink for breakfast, want one?"

"Can't we stop at a drive through? We do have a long ride and then hike."

"Your diet's going to kill you."

"We'll burn it off."

Baker poured the last of the coffee into his cup. "Let's get out of here."

The drive east on Interstate 90 was like déjà vu. The road, the weather, and the bag of fast food were like the day before, but the mood had changed. Tuesday morning, the two had driven up to see what they could find. It had been recon only, and they hadn't even taken the long guns. The mood was more lighthearted and the two wondered what they'd find, if anything. Today, the mood was more somber. Baker knew if

Bennett came out the back door, it would be the last thing he ever did.

The two drove in silence, snacking and sipping coffee. A CD of 80s Heavy Metal Ballads played, but both men were lost in their own thoughts. Each wondered what the other was thinking, but neither asked. The music triggered memories of when the two first entered sniper school together so long ago. Baker remembered the pride he felt when he graduated. They were among the elite, and to fulfill the "one shot, one kill" motto on the battlefield was honorable and commendable. Today, however, the shooting of Bennett would be considered a detestable crime by those in the civil society they were now part of. It didn't make sense. Bennett was a monster that sold little girls and who knew what else he did to them. He deserved a bullet more than many enemy combatants, who were only doing what their governments told them to do. Why was it honorable, even heroic, to kill someone in battle because politicians deemed it correct, but a crime to kill someone who indeed earned death by his heinous acts? Maybe Frank was right, there were laws, but there were also right, wrong, and justice.

White Lion came from the Durango's speakers. Baker sang along with *When Children Cry* and admitted to himself that Frank was correct and what they were about to do was right. He thought of his daughter, Coral, and he thought about the night he found Ashley Cox in the trailer house after killing Bruce James. He had no remorse or guilt for killing the child molester that night. He had a little girl locked in his back bedroom. The evidence they knew of, even if it wouldn't hold up in a court of law, pointed at Bennett being behind the sale of Ashley. How many other little girls had he sold? What else did he do to them? There would be no remorse, no guilt, and no hesitation squeezing the trigger once the porn king was in his sight picture. He glanced over at Frank who was staring out the side window, lost in his own thoughts. He wished he had his buddy's conscience, or lack of one, because he knew his friend was right. This needed to be done and they were the ones to do it. It was justice, and he was the one to serve it.

It seemed they had just left Missoula when Baker slowed and exited the Interstate. He turned right at the bottom of the ramp and looked over at Senich who sat motionless still staring out the side window. Shortly after, he parked the Dodge a couple hundred yards from the location he had left it nearly twenty-four hours earlier. The spot was a bit more secluded and Baker preferred to keep his routes varied and unpredictable, and that went for parking spaces too.

Both men sat in the vehicle. Senich ate the last bite of the breakfast sandwich he'd been nursing the last 30 miles. Baker focused on his breathing; in hold, out hold, in hold, out hold. Almost in unison, the two turned toward each other.

"You ready?" Senich asked.

"Yeah. You?"

"Always." Senich's smile was the first of the trip.

"It's almost eight, let's get going and be set up before ten."

"Roger." Senich climbed out and opened the back door so he could get his ruck and weapon. Baker did the same. Each checked the weapon they would carry. The rifles were loaded and extra ammo was stored in the packs. They only planned on expending one round, but you always prepared for the worst. Once satisfied they had everything and no one was around, the two took to the trees. It was a beautiful morning for a six-mile hike.

Baker enjoyed the rays of sun shining down between the trees as they walked, and he heard the birds whistling among the green leaves covering the branches they sat on. He breathed deep and filled his lungs with the fresh mountain air.

Senich, walking point, took a deep breath of his own. "You sure live in some beautiful country," he said.

"Yeah, but it's unfortunate that we are going to spoil it with ugliness."

"What's ugly about it?"

"We're going to kill someone."

"Don't start that shit again." Senich glanced back at his friend.

"It doesn't bother you at all does it?"

"No, it doesn't. It shouldn't bother you either. Just think about that girl you found. What if that girl was Coral?"

Baker stopped walking "Don't even say shit like that."

Senich stopped and turned around. "Sorry," he said. "But you know what I mean. We've been through this before, and now is not the time."

"I know, but sometimes I wonder. How can there be so much beauty in the world, but also have so many monsters too?"

"I don't know, just the way it is. Without bad, you wouldn't know good, and all that."

"Yeah, I know."

"Listen, we are doing good. One squeeze of the trigger and you are going to save how many girls from terrible ugliness and horrors?"

"Right." Baker replied.

"Let's keep moving." Sench turned and plowed ahead through the thick green underbrush as the two continued their way up the hill.

Senich veered right to go around a particularly thick patch of bushes. "You know, we really should have come up here in the dark."

"Yeah, but I really don't think we have much to worry about. It's not like there are enemy patrols out here."

"True. And it's a lot easier going through the brush when you can see, just not as tactical."

"Well, we're not in a war zone."

"What about the dudes in the Hummer?"

"They're at the house, not out here in the woods."

The two continued forward and reached the crest of the hill a little more than an hour after leaving the vehicle. They were both sweating and breathing a bit heavy. "That's more of a climb than I remember it being yesterday," Senich remarked.

"Yeah, hold up a minute. I want a drink." The two sipped from canteens while looking around at the forest surrounding them.

"You want to go down to the position we were at yesterday?" Senich asked.

"I don't like being in the same location."

"True, but we never shot from there, so no one knows about it."

"That's true too. It was the best location for a decent shot at the back of the house. Let's do it." The two moved more slowly as they walked down the side of the hill toward the tree line where they would set up their makeshift hide.

Near the tree line, the two dropped to the ground and crept to the final location. They didn't believe anyone was watching the hill, but they weren't going to take it for granted. They moved into position stealthily and adhered to the disciplines taught to them while in the United States Army so long ago. It took longer to cover the final fifty yards to the position than it had the previous mile.

The two friends were in the exact position they were twenty-four hours earlier, only this time they were each behind a rifle. Baker behind his trusted Remington .308 and Senich behind the more powerful .300 Weatherby Magnum.

The art of sniping is cerebral and calculating. Baker used the Nikon rangefinder to reinforce that the two had zeroed the rifles correctly the night before. The surrounding trees were motionless, and looking through the scope, Baker watched the still leaves of the trees beside the house. "Zero wind, that's good."

Senich looked up at the clear blue sky, "Should stay that way too." Both men knew at such a range a breeze could push the bullet off target. They also knew how to read and measure wind to make corrections to help ensure the first bullet found its mark. It was just convenient they didn't have to.

Baker understood that the bullet didn't leave the barrel of his weapon and go straight to its target. Bullets travel in an arc and when the rifle is correctly zeroed, it would actually point at an invisible spot above the target. After completing the rainbow like trajectory, the bullet would drop and bear down on its unsuspecting victim. Given enough time and ammunition, anyone could hit a stationary target from the range Baker was about to fire from. He didn't have that luxury, and needed to ensure a first-shot kill. Senich was there as backup, but he shouldn't have to shoot. All conditions - wind, air density, humidity, ammunition, and rifle - were the same as the day before. Everything except the angle he was shooting from. He was on a hill shooting down, and the day before the angle wasn't exactly the same. The sniper's skill, and success, depends on being able make adjustments needed to direct his round to the center of his target. Baker knew what adjustments to make and prepared himself and his weapon to fire one shot. His foremost thought was not that his shot would end Bennett's life, but that it would save many others.

"You ready?" asked Senich.

"Yeah."

"Let me spot, you rest your eyes a bit."

"I'm fine."

"Didn't say you weren't. Just letting you take a break while I watch down below."

"Alright." Baker took his cheek from the spotweld it knew so well on the Remington. He slowly turned his head and looked at his buddy, lying beside him, but about two feet back. When the shot was fired, Senich would watch the vapor trail of the bullet's path and witness the impact as the round struck its target through the scope mounted on the Weatherby. It wasn't a spotting scope, but it would do. Baker noted to himself that he better make the shot, if Frank had to back him up and fire the Weatherby, the rifle's position by his right ear would be deafening, even with the unobtrusive internal ear protection he wore.

The two took turns watching the house and resting their eyes. The sun beat down on them and their clothes were damp with sweat. They snacked on Power Bars and sipped water from their canteens, ensuring wrappers were secured in pockets and the canteens were replaced so they could bug out quickly if needed. They would leave no trace other than trampled grass that they were there.

It was a quarter after twelve when Senich saw the first movement at the back of the house. Amber and Chi Chi strolled out the back door wearing towels wrapped around their midsections. Both carried drinks, and Amber also had a platter of fruits. "The two girls just came out." Baker looked down at the house without the aid of his scope. He could make them out, but obviously couldn't see the detail his buddy could with the optics.

"What are they doing?"

Senich watched the two set the drinks and platter on a table near the pool and then drop their towels. "Damn, take a look. Seems they want an all-over-tan."

"We're not up here to spy on naked girls."

"I know. It's not my fault they are prancing around down there with nothing on. And I can't help it if I think they look good."

"Maybe Bennett will come out and join them."

"Hope so." Senich took the scope off Amber and Chi Chi and focused back on the door to see if anyone else would exit. He continued to watch the door, the girls, and the pool area for another half hour. He was just about to turn the duties over to Baker when the back door opened. "Got someone else."

"Who?"

"It's him."

"Roger." Baker eased his cheek down to the stock of his rifle and looked through the ten power Leupold. "That's him alright."

"Looks like he's arguing with the bald guy."

"Yeah, he's in my line of fire. I'll wait till the tango's away from the house and near the pool."

"What if he goes back in?"

"Don't worry, as soon as I have the shot, we're out of here. Stay on him."

"We could take them both. Drop the bald guy and I'll take Bennett."

"No, we have no evidence the bald guy's involved with anything."

"Looks like he works for him, that's good enough."

"No it isn't. We take the target only. No one else."

"Roger, but if we miss out…"

"We won't, and we are only here for Bennett. Period."

"He's moving, and the bald guy is going inside."

"I got him." Baker held the cross hairs of his scope center mass, right on Bennett's chest. He was moving out toward the pool and the two girls sunning themselves in lounge chairs near the water. All Baker could see was the point he wanted the bullet to enter. He read the t-shirt and placed the crosshairs on the "e" of the word "Like." He was in his bubble. It took a certain kind of warrior to be a sniper. You needed to be able to look at somebody through the scope and make the decision to kill him. In combat, you needed to be able to make that decision over and over again. Not all soldiers are emotionally equipped for such a duty.

Pilots, artillery crews, and mortar teams all launch weapons from distances, not knowing if they kill or not. Snipers can often learn intimate details about their targets before sending bullets downrange to end a life. During war, each person killed means one less threat to other Americans. Baker's finger took the slack out of the trigger. One final bit of pressure on the trigger would save young girls and women.

"Engage," Senich said to his friend, his rifle also following the target with cross hairs locked on center mass.

Baker exhaled and took another breath. Bennett stopped near the pool. Baker didn't know he was admiring the two naked sunbathers, he only knew his target was stationary. Breath, partial exhale, maintain sight picture, press…Boom!

The 175 grain boat tail projectile left the barrel at 2,400 feet per second, or roughly 1,636 miles per hour, well over the speed of sound. Senich, through his ten-power scope, watched the vapor trail of the bullet's path and witnessed the impact as the round entered Bennett's chest, right in the "e" of the word "Like." "Hit," he called out. "He's down."

"Roger," Baker replied.

"Nice shot brother. Now let's get out of here."

Baker held his position after the shot and brought his sights back to the motionless body of Bennett after the slight interruption of his sight picture from the recoil of the rifle.

Satisfied the target was indeed dead, he then noticed the bald man who had been arguing with the target was now holding a firearm and pointing toward the hill where he and Senich lay concealed. The handgun wouldn't reach them, even if they could be seen. He looked for the other three, found two and neither had rifles. "Creep out, they might grab optics to look for us."

The dense green spring foliage made it easier to stay concealed as the two moved slowly to not give away their position. Once they were deep enough into the trees, they stood and took off at a fast pace. They doubted anyone was rushing to their previous position from below due to the psychological influence a sniper has on a group. No one wants to be next, and the fear a sniper creates in those living can be as beneficial as those killed. Regardless, the two wanted to get to the vehicle and be gone as quickly as possible. They stayed in the trees and shortly crested the hill. On the downward side they were able to increase their speed and had little fear of being seen.

"It was too easy," Baker said to his friend who was on point.

"What?" Senich slowed and turned.

"I don't like it. It was all too easy."

"We did a good job, that all. It's supposed to be easy when you know what you're doing."

"I don't know, I just have a feeling. It seems something's not right."

"You're just paranoid. Let's get going."

"Maybe, but paranoia can be a good thing. Keep your eyes and ears open."

"I always do."

"Well, make sure. And let's hope this feeling doesn't mean anything." The two resumed their quicker pace. Thoughts of the beautiful day were behind them. The mission was accomplished and they needed to extract.

Baker thought of the porn king lying dead next to his pool. He glanced behind him and only saw the dense forest they had just passed through. He didn't know what it was, but something was bothering him, and it wasn't the death of Dick Bennett.

Bennett slept in until 10:30 Wednesday morning. He woke up
not knowing Baker and Senich were hiding on the hill
overlooking his home. Nor did he know Robinson was out
walking the perimeter. He didn't really care. He felt the four
security men were already a nuisance, and he was half
inclined to send them packing. He didn't like their cautions,
and the suggestions they made were downright intrusive to
his lifestyle. He hadn't worked this hard to make this much to
have four ex-military bozos tell him how to live. And to think
he thought he was paranoid for hiring them, their paranoia
was off the charts. He'd tell them to relax and knock off
whatever they were doing. He'd pay them through the week,
and be done with them. He was still trying to decide if he'd
have them accompany him on the snatch he was planning. He
was having doubts that he could trust them with such an
operation. After all, they were just hired hands and he didn't
know anything about them. He especially didn't trust the
taller one, Tad. He didn't trust him at all, not for something
like this. Maybe it would be better for them to be gone before
he left for his little trip. He'd figure it out later. He first needed
a shower and something to drink.

He pressed the button that operated the intercom from his
bedroom to the kitchen. "Margarita, you down there?"

"Yeah, what cha need?"

"I need you and a drink. Could you fix me a red beer for
breakfast and bring it up and join me?"

"Sure, I'll be right up."

ALAIN BURRESE

"I'll be in the shower." Bennett walked to the master bath and turned the faucet on hot. He let pulsating jets of water pound his back as he looked at himself in the full length mirror through the glass doors of the shower. They would steam up soon. Not bad for an old fuck, he thought to himself. Sure beat the cold showers he took when he couldn't pay the power bills. He'd tried so hard to make it in major motion pictures, who knew that his sexual stamina would pave the way to be as rich, or richer, than most Hollywood stars.

As he slowly turned in the streams of pulsating water, he felt a bit sad. Sure he had money, but he never received the fame and adulation that the Hollywood stars and starlets received. He'd dreamed of being the next John Wayne. He wanted to be a hero in westerns and action movies. He thought of Clint Eastwood and how that should have been his career. Instead, he made his money, and what fame he had, because of his hard cock. He was never appreciated for his acting, just that he could fuck longer and more than anyone else. No one cared about any aspect of his performance other than that. No one ever asked him to show more emotion. It was always, "great job, can you get it up again?"

As soon as his thoughts drifted toward what it would have been like to be married and settle down, he tried to shake it off and think of something different. His biggest regret was never having children. He had no one to pass his empire on to when he was gone. He'd never heard the words, "Daddy, I love you." He tried harder not to think such thoughts. Where was Margarita? He wondered what his life would have been like if he had found the right woman, settled down, and had a family. He bet psychiatrists would say his affection for young girls was due to an absence of offspring of his own. Or was it because unconsciously he was trying to regain his lost youth? Was he reliving the 70s, when Holms was dating fifteen-year-old Dawn Schiller and he was bedding her friends? Enough! He didn't want to think about such things this morning. He made his bed, lived his life, and now he'd sleep in it. Besides, he'd lived a life most men dream of. He told himself, "I have an awesome life, and it's only getting better."

He tried to look at himself again, but the glass doors and mirrors were now covered with steam. Suddenly a stream of cool air drifted into the bathroom as Margarita entered with his red beer.

"Good morning," she called out.

"It is now," he said opening the glass door and revealing nothing she hadn't seen numerous times before. As he took the glass from her hand, he reached out with the other and grabbed her outstretched arm. "Come here, you."

"But I'm dressed," she squealed.

"So." He pulled her into the hot pulsating water and she gave out a little yelp. It was hotter than she'd anticipated, despite the steam room presence she'd walked through. "Take 'em off," he commanded. She pulled the now wet t-shirt up over her head revealing her dark tanned breasts and then wiggled and squirmed out of her soaked jeans.

* * *

It was a little after 11:30 when Margarita came out of the Master Bedroom wearing a towel that barely covered her breasts and that allowed those behind her to see the bottom of her round butt cheeks. She carried her wet clothes and gave Jackson, who was walking through the hall, a quick grin. He smiled back as he secretly envied the aging porn star. He glanced a second time to admire the view as she walked away.

Bennett came out a few minutes later and went down to the kitchen for something to eat. He was wearing blue swimming trunks that stopped just above the knee and tied at the waist with a drawstring that hung outside. He also had a white t-shirt on with a large inscription taking up the front. "I'm Hung Like A Baby 9 lbs. 6 oz. 21 inches."

Hatcher met him in the kitchen, read the shirt quickly, decided not to comment, and held out several sheets of paper. "I've thought of some different ways we can make this place more secure, and what you can do to help." He watched his employer ignore him and pour a bowl of cereal. He then rummaged around among various bottles to grab a gallon of milk out of the refrigerator.

"Good morning to you too," Bennett responded, twisting the cap off the milk and pouring some on top of his Captain Crunch.

"It's almost noon." Hatcher couldn't understand how a grown man could eat the sugary crap that came out of the colorful box, but then he couldn't understand a lot of things about his current employer.

"I don't care what time it is, I don't need to be assaulted with your security details this early. I just got up and haven't even had my breakfast yet." He sat down at the table and dug into the cereal with a large spoon. He'd acquired a sweet tooth as he got older, probably due to never being allowed anything sweet growing up, except on the most special of circumstances. Now he could have sweets any time he wanted, and he did.

"I apologize, but I'd like to go over these details with you and get started on their implementation." Hatcher was amused by the use of the term assaulted. Prick doesn't know what an assault is, he thought.

"Wait till I've eaten and read my news. I need to think about a few things first. I'll call you when I'm ready to discuss your employment." He opened the laptop sitting on the table.

He kept it there so he'd have something to read while dining alone.

"Sure, whatever. Let me know." In a couple short days, Hatcher had grown tired of the millionaire's attitude and his non-listening to anything he said. Hatcher and his team got paid regardless, and he'd learned a long time ago to choose his battles and pick things worth arguing over. This assignment wasn't something to let one's blood pressure go up a point over. He went back to the adjoining room and opened his laptop. He didn't know why they were even there. Bennett wouldn't listen to them, didn't care about security, and was going to do what he pleased. Hatcher believed the man just needed something to spend money on, and having a private security force sounded good on a whim. Besides, what was going to happen out here in the sticks of Montana? Hatcher didn't trust the wireless network in the house, so he connected with the transmitter connected to the laptop's USB port. He looked back through the kitchen door and saw Bennett sitting at the table, spooning cereal into his mouth, bent over, and reading news on his own laptop.

A short while later, Jackson and Baxter came into the room from the opposite side of the kitchen. Baxter plopped down on a sofa while Jackson went over to the window to look outside. He was pleased to find an unobstructed view of Amber and Chi Chi who had just arrived at the pool to work on their tans.

"So, what's up with him?" Baxter asked, motioning toward the kitchen where the pompous millionaire still sat bent over the laptop.

"Beat's me," Hatcher replied. "He sure the hell doesn't want to listen to us."

"We just walked through and around the entire house again, at least the areas we are allowed. Nothing.

"I doubt we'll ever find anything, but the scenery sure is nice," commented Jackson from the window.

"Yeah, and he won't listen when I suggest security measures," Hatcher said again, he really was annoyed at being there and not being listened to. Even the girls didn't listen to his cautions to stay inside today, or at least until Tad reported in from his perimeter check.

So, why are we here?" Baxter was vocalizing what all four men had thought since arriving.

"I don't know. I guess he needed to spend money. So let's just sit tight, mind our P's and Q's and be gone soon. As long as the money spends, we're alright." Hatcher looked over at Jackson, who was still staring out the window. "Don't drool on yourself there, Jacks."

"Just admiring, that's all." Jackson flashed a smile at his two teammates, turned and took one final look at the two sunbathers by the pool, and then joined Baxter on the sofa. "Where's the Tadpole?" Being a former SEAL himself, Jackson liked to use the full nickname, rather than Tad or Thaddeus as the others called him.

"He's walking the perimeter again," replied Hatcher.

"Think he'll find anything?

"No, but he wanted to go, so why not. We're not doing much here."

"He likes the woods," said Jackson.

"He should have been a Ranger instead of a SEAL," commented Baxter.

"I think that's why he went to sniper school, so he could be in the woods more than the water. But don't worry; he's a SEAL, so he knows the water too. We all do."

"I don't think he cares much for Bennett."

"Why do you say that?" asked Hatcher.

"Just the way he looks at the guy," Baxter replied.

"He doesn't like him. He told me last night he had no use for the guy, and if he wasn't going to use the money to take his kids to Disneyworld, he'd ask to be relieved from the job."

"What's his problem?" asked Baxter.

"Doesn't like the porn industry, and thinks the guy is probably into illegal shit."

"Well, I think we'll all be out of here soon," added Hatcher. "Let's just ride it out, get paid, and move on."

Jackson pointed to the kitchen. "Looks like he's going outside, want me to go with him?"

"You just want to be closer to the girls," Baxter chided.

"Never mind, I need to talk to him. I've been waiting and now he wants to blow me off." Hatcher got up and headed toward the kitchen, leaving the other two on the sofa watching him leave.

"This might be good." Jackson got up and moved over to the window again. With a shrug, Baxter joined him.

Hatcher swiftly walked through the kitchen, calling out to Bennett as he walked out the back door to the patio and pool.

"Later," came the reply.

Hatcher went out side and with three long strides passed his employer and turned to face him. He cut off the millionaire's route to the pool, and stood there face to face, looking up into the older man's eyes. "We need to talk."

"I said later." Bennett tried to walk around the fireplug of a man he'd recently hired. He was starting to regret the decision. He didn't like the four around, it was different than he'd imagined.

Hatcher slid over smoothly, still blocking the path toward the pool. "We need to discuss some of these details if you want us to do our job."

The porn king looked at the sun shining off the bald man's head and all of a sudden had a different attitude. However, it

ALAIN BURRESE

wasn't one of cooperation. Who was this short bald employee to tell him anything? "Listen here," Bennett's nostrils flared, "You work for me, got it? No, check that, you worked for me. Consider yourself fired. I want all of you out of here this afternoon."

Hatcher knew that any escalation on his part could set off events that he didn't want to occur. He wasn't afraid of Bennett, on the contrary, he was afraid of what he might do if the porn king decided to take their altercation physical. It would be tough to explain why he put his principle into the hospital. In a calm voice he replied, "Fine, we will be gone ASAP."

"Good, now get the fuck out of my way."

"There is the matter of our contract, pay, and the extra equipment that will be arriving here tomorrow."

"Damn mercenary, I paid in full to your company in Texas, I won't ask for any back, I just want you gone. You cramp my style. I'll forward any packages to the same address in Texas."

Hatcher bit the inside of his mouth when Bennett uttered the mercenary comment, but only nodded and said, "Okay. I'll round up the boys. We'll pack our gear and be gone." He stepped aside and let the angered porn king pass and then headed toward the door. They wouldn't be gone fast enough. Shit, he thought, as he went inside. We have to get Tad.

Bennett strolled over to the pool like a rooster struts around the hen house, stopping to look at the two naked sunbathers. He'd already had Margarita that morning, but that was a couple hours ago. The two looked nice, lying in the sun on their lounge chairs. He smiled at Margarita's cute little round butt as she lay on her stomach, and then gazed the full length of Amber's tight body as she worked at tanning her breasts along with everything else. They looked good, but he was in the mood for something different. He was getting a bit tired of the two of them. The weekend was coming. He'd get to select something different all right.

Dick Bennett always believed he'd die of a heart attack in the throws of ecstasy with a group of young nubile babes when he was in his eighties. That's how he imagined it anyway, and that's how he joked about his own death from time to time. He never, in his wildest nightmares, would have believed he'd die beside his pool gazing at two scrumptious bodies, not doing a thing.

The bullet entered his chest and Bennett felt extreme pain, and for the last second of his life, he wondered if he were having that imagined heart attack, only this wasn't supposed to be how it went, and it wasn't supposed to happen for at least twenty more years.

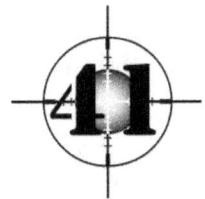

Baker and Senich were moving quickly, but cautiously. They were nearing the location where they left the Dodge, and were eager to be on the road back to Missoula. Senich was on point, with Baker trailing about five yards behind him. Their disciplined movement made little sound as they walked, and they carried their respective rifles at the ready. Both men were alert to the sounds, smells and sights of the forest, and nothing appeared out of the ordinary during the entire forced march through the woods. Nothing, that is, but the nagging feeling that it was all too easy that kept tugging on Baker's thoughts.

The two walked in silence, making excellent time. Both absorbed with their own thoughts, while simultaneously wondering what the other was thinking. Their path wasn't straight, but rather zigzagged through the forest in a route that was easiest to traverse and that left the minimum sign that anyone had been there. Neither wanted to crash through thick brush to leave a trail behind. They didn't think anyone would be looking, but it was just good practice. Besides, it was easier and quicker to take the path of least resistance, even if it did add length to the journey. Baker slung his rifle over his shoulder so he could sip from his canteen as they walked. Senich had just finished taking a drink, and Baker had waited until his buddy's canteen was secure before taking a turn. While he was still observant while drinking, he didn't like both of them preoccupied with canteens at the same time. Ask the driver who only glanced away from the road for a second before ending up in a horrific crash how even the smallest of distractions can have dire consequences.

"Freeze! Drop the rifles!"

The command came from a thick growth of trees, shrubs and bushes, off to Senich's ten o'clock. Baker froze, canteen in hand, and searched the area where the sound came from. Senich was as motionless, but had first raised the rifle in the direction of the command. He too couldn't identify a target.

"Put it down, now!"

There was something about the voice that made both men want to cooperate. Neither had any doubts that a firearm of some sorts was pointed in their direction, and nether doubted the person commanding them to set their weapons down would fire if not listened to. Baker raised both hands in front of him with his left holding the canteen and his right palm facing outward. "Put it down, Frank." Baker's voice was low and calm.

His eyes repeatedly scanned the thick brush in the direction the voice had come from. He wondered how many were out there. He didn't think it was a cop, so who would be out here in the woods waiting for them? They'd only seen the bald guy at the house. The other three from the previous day hadn't been seen. He assumed they were inside. You know what assumptions lead to, he thought to himself. Could the others have been out on patrol of the property? They were packing the day before, no reason to believe they wouldn't be armed today. Was this one of them, or maybe all three?

Senich didn't like it, but he knew Baker was right. He turned the muzzle of the rifle to the left and then slowly squatted down and gently paced the Weatherby on the ground to the left of his feet. He slowly straightened back up and raised his hands palms forward. "Now what?" It was hard to discern if he was asking Baker, directing the inquiry to the voice in the trees, or asking himself.

The voice from the trees answered. "Don't move." Appearing almost magically before them, Thaddeus Edward Robinson, also known as Tad, emerged from behind a large tree and thick bush with his Glock aimed at Senich's chest. He walked forward tactically, his firearm remained pointed at Senich. His blue eyes darted from one to the other while he relied on his peripheral vision to warn of any additional threats.

Senich was motionless, but watched every step Robinson took with acute intensity. He identified the Glock and knew what the .40 caliber round could do if the trigger finger, which was flexed with the tip placed at the niche of the takedown lever, moved to the trigger and gently pressed. He looked into Robinson's eyes and saw no hesitation with the willingness to kill. The guy's been there, he thought to himself. Prior military, he's one of us. So why's he on the other side?

Baker was thinking the same thoughts. He recognized the man as one of the four from the day before. He was sure the guy served in the military before taking the civilian security duty. Why not? Baker had thought about the industry himself. Sometimes still did. He still wondered if there were others still hidden. He glanced to the sides with minimal movement of his head. He guessed not, but look where assumptions had gotten him.

Robinson didn't like things up close. He preferred to do his fighting from 1,000 meters or more with the McMillan Tac-50 sniper rifle. The long-range, manually operated, rotary bolt action rifle was chambered for the .50 BMG cartridge, and when fitted with the standard Leupold Mark 4 16x40mm telescopic sight, was capable of kills over 2,000 meters. A former corporal of the Canadian Forces made a record setting confirmed sniper kill in combat at 2,430 meters with the McMillan Brothers Tac-50 rifle and ammunition loaded with 750 grain Hornady A-MAX very-low-drag-bullets. Robinson had made kills over 1,500 meters, but never over 2,000. He wished he'd been offered the opportunity to break the record. He certainly liked the McMillan rifles. If his preferred weapon were not available, he'd settle for six hundred to a thousand meters shot with an MK11 Sniper Weapon System. The highly accurate semiautomatic sniper rifle used by the SEALs fired the 7.62mm round and was effective to 1,500 yards, but that was stretching it, especially with certain environmental factors. No, he didn't like this up close shit one bit.

Robinson didn't immediately recognize the rifle the man directly in front of him had lain on the ground, but figured it to be a high-caliber hunting rifle. It was Montana. The rifle slung over the other's shoulder looked familiar. It looked an awful lot like the M24 Sniper Systems he was familiar with. Stopping three arms lengths from Senich, he spoke to Baker, "unsling that rifle and put it on the ground, slowly, with your left hand only." Robinson saw the right handed bolt on the rifle and correctly guessed Baker was right handed. Most people were, so the odds were good even if he hadn't seen the bolt.

Baker did as he was told.

"7.62?" Robinson asked.

".308," Baker answered.

"Same thing. Step away from it." Robinson now knew Baker was military trained. He understood the nomenclature of the round. Probably Army. They liked the Remington and the M24. Ranger? Sniper? Special Forces? For sure a sniper, it was a sniper's weapon. He'd found a sniper's hide the day before. And only a sniper would make that shot. He had little faith that an ordinary deer hunter would kill a man at 700 meters.

Baker and Senich also knew they were dealing with someone with prior military experience after he'd asked about the nomenclature of the round the rifle fired. Rifles down, up close, Baker knew they had an advantage. There were two of them, and they were both still armed. The guy with the Glock didn't want them dead, or he'd have opened fire from his concealed position and they'd have been dead meat in the ambush. The thought wasn't very comforting, and Baker was kicking himself for not being more aware. They had the advantage of numbers, but how could they use it? They needed this guy to make a mistake. He didn't look like he would.

Robinson continued to slowly approach Senich, who still stood with his palms facing outward at chest level. "You still armed?"

"Yeah," Senich replied. His mind was racing, but his face remained motionless and his green eyes stayed fixated on Robinson's every move. He'd debated for a nanosecond about lying when asked if he was armed, but decided to play it straight. He wanted Robinson to allow him to take out his weapon, or get close to him to remove it himself.

Baker knew his friend. He knew him better than anyone else in the world. He knew Frank hated to lose. He knew he wouldn't go down without a fight, and that his mind was always thinking of ways to win. He watched him standing with arms raised. He watched Robinson's cautious approach, the Glock ever at the ready. A press of the trigger and his buddy would be down and he'd be able to fire another shot before Baker's sidearm cleared the holster. Besides, any outcome with him or his best friend taking a bullet was unacceptable. And there was another problem; he didn't want to kill this guy. He was a fellow soldier, that was obvious, and there were no facts or evidence suggesting he had anything to do with selling kids other than the working relationship with Bennett. Baker wanted to know if the guy was actually guilty of anything, and refused to find guilt by association. He continued to watch his friend. He knew given the slightest opening, Senich would explode into action, and he'd have to be just as fast to ensure they both went home together. Preferably they would leave without killing the man with the Glock, but if the situation became him or them, the Glock wielding man from the trees would have to go down. Baker continued to watch.

Senich stood perfectly still. The only things moving were the pupils of his intense green eyes. He studied Robinson's every move and was calculating his responses. A little closer he thought.

Robinson considered asking the two to remove any other weapons themselves, but feared they wouldn't comply and would hold out on him. He decided he'd pat each of them down. Damn, how he wished he had a team right now. He needed someone to cover them both while he checked for weapons and anything else of interest. He didn't even like sniping without a spotter. He sure wished he had team members with him. It wasn't like a SEAL couldn't take on more than one, but he was concerned that these two might have similar training, and a team member to cover them while he searched was a better practice. Time to improvise he thought. He almost had them lay face down on the ground, but was concerned that he would not be able to detect movement as easily if the two were partially concealed by the grass and weeds. He left them standing. "Where?" he asked, nodding his head at Senich to motion he wanted his remaining weapons.

"By my belt." Senich glanced down indicating where his Sig .45 was concealed. His gaze returned to Robinson, and he watched him slowly move closer. As Robinson stepped, he looked down at Senich's crotch area again to discern where the weapon was hidden. At that moment, Senich took a small step forward with his right foot and twisted his body by slinging his left shoulder back. Simultaneously, his right upraised hand snapped out, slapping/pushing the Glock to his left, just far enough that if a round fired, it would pass his now sideways torso.

Once clear of the muzzle, and faster than most people could register what was happening, Senich's left grabbed underneath the weapon. The weapon securely grasped between both hands, Senich moved forward and sucked the weapon to his chest. Holding it tightly to his body, with the muzzle pointed off to his left in the opposite direction of Baker, Senich now had control of the firearm and had neutralized the threat. A quick step forward with his left, combined with a twist of the hips and a violent jerk and twist with his hands and he completed the disarm. It was a basic Combatives technique he'd practiced countless times. The practice paid off, allowing him to wrest the weapon from Robinson's hand. Unfortunately for Senich, Robinson didn't react like most training partners. Nor did he respond like the startled drug dealing pimp he'd disarmed a couple years back. He'd taken the weapon with the same technique, and then shoved the barrel in the punk's mouth as he explained why pulling a gun on him wasn't a good idea. He also took the opportunity to explain how ladies should be treated. Senich hoped the lesson got through, and figured every time the guy looked in the mirror at his broken teeth he'd be reminded. This time, he wasn't taking a gun from a punk-ass pimp; he was stripping it from one of the Navy's elite, and the reaction was far from the same.

Even the best forget the basics sometimes, and Senich forgot to expect the unexpected. Robinson recognized the technique immediately and knew he messed up. However, unlike the untrained, he didn't do any of the expected responses. He didn't stay fixated on his weapon and try to prevent the disarm by force. Robinson's position was the weaker of the two and any such attempt would have lost the weapon and most likely have ended with his trigger finger being broke. Nor was he single-minded in belief that the weapon was his only choice. Many people, once losing their weapon, forget about the other tools they have available. Robinson didn't forget. And most importantly, he didn't stop to bemoan his mistake or mentally chastise himself for being careless. Shit happens. A Navy SEAL learns to adapt, improvise and overcome.

Immediately upon recognizing Senich's disarm, which registered at the precise same time Senich's hand made contact with the Glock, Robinson let go of the handgun. It saved him a busted finger, and more importantly allowed him to catch Senich off guard with a powerful left hand palm heel strike. As he let go of his weapon and pulled the right hand back, he twisted at the hips and pivoted with his left foot creating a powerful and quick strike. His left shot out strait and true and caught Senich under the right side of his jaw. If Senich's years of boxing and brawling hadn't taught him to roll with such a blow his jaw would have been broken. As it was, he saw stars and couldn't regroup in time to fend off Robinson's second strike: a powerful right. The one-two palm heel combination created enough force to slosh Senich's brain around inside the skull cavity, causing a slight concussion. It knocked him unconscious. As he went down, the Glock fell in the weeds beside him.

Robinson didn't lunge or bend for the fallen handgun. Before it and Senich stopped moving, he'd already turned to face Baker with seven inches of naked steel in his hand. The partially serrated SOG blade came out of the Kydex sheath in a smooth motion and it looked as formidable as the man holding it. Baker pressed his trigger.

Senich's initial motion of clearing the weapon, before the disarm, was the distraction and impetus Baker needed to draw the Browning Hi Power concealed at the small of his back. It wasn't a quick draw, but the practiced motion was smooth and as Robinson turned with the unsheathed knife in his hand, Baker double tapped him in the chest with two 147 grain Winchester Ranger SXT Controlled Expansion 9mm rounds. Robinson winced, but didn't go down. He was thankful for the body armor with the extra rifle plate. It looked like he was about to rush forward. Baker raised the aim of his weapon.

"Drop it, or the next one's in the head!"

Robinson dropped the knife and stood staring at Baker. His blue eyes enraged. Not as much at Baker as at himself. He'd let them get the drop on him, and it pissed him off. His mind raced. How would he turn this around?

"Take three steps backward." Baker motioned the direction he wanted Robinson to take with the Browning. He looked over at his friend who just sat up and was shaking his head very slowly.

"Son-of-a-bitch," Senich muttered.

"You all right?" Baker moved closer to his buddy and used a nod of his head and the handgun to direct Robinson to step back another few steps.

"Yeah. What the fuck he hit me with, a hammer?"

Robinson thought about sprinting. Most people couldn't hit a moving target, and if he made the trees it would be an extremely difficult shot. These two weren't most people. Besides, the thought of running made his stomach churn. Tactical withdrawal be damned, running was running. He needed to attack.

"He hit you with a left-right combo of palm heel shots before I could get my Browning on him."

Senich got to his feet. He held his jaw with his hand and shook his head a bit. He looked over where Robinson was standing. The two stared at each other, neither blinked nor backed down. It was finally Robinson who broke the silence.

"Now what?" He directed the question toward Baker who still held all the cards in his hand with the Hi Power.

"Cap the fucker and let's go," Senich said to his friend.

"No." Baker shook his head and then looked at Robinson. "First, you talk."

"I ain't got anything to say. You're the two out in the woods on an assassination mission."

"You work for Bennett right?"

"Temporarily."

"What do you mean by that?"

Robinson looked at Baker and then back to Senich. He knew they were military, or prior military. Maybe this was government sanctioned. He'd heard of worse. He'd been involved with worse. He decided talking couldn't hurt. He didn't have anything to hide, and nothing he was doing was classified confidential, other than the company's privacy policy, and he wasn't going to mention the company he worked for.

"He hired four of us for temporary security. Not sure why, he doesn't want to listen to anything that will help him."

"Too late now," commented Senich. Baker shot him a look from the corner of his eye. Robinson saw it.

"I figured as much and I know where you did it from."

"Did what?"

Robinson looked Baker directly in the eyes. "You took out Bennett from about 700 meters with one shot."

"What makes you say that?"

"I only heard one shot. I'm guessing you were trained to only take one."

"And what would you know about that?"

Robinson looked over at Senich, who still stood there glaring, and then back to Baker. He decided to come clean and tell all. If the two wanted him dead, the one with the gun would have put a round in his head as soon as the two to the chest failed. He knew they were military, maybe the common bond would provide him the opportunity he needed.

"I was Navy, did some with the SEALs, sniper. I recognize the MO."

"What about the others?" Baker now understood why he and Senich hadn't seen Robinson hiding in the trees.

"Prior military. Another SEAL, the other two Army."

"What are you doing with Bennett?"

"Just trying to make a living. It was a security gig. Got here a couple days ago. Guy's a prick and doesn't want to listen."

"Was a prick," Senich added.

"Alright, was a prick. I didn't like the guy, but I do have a problem with you two killing him on our watch."

"Tough shit." Senich's comment brought another look from Baker.

"What about the girls and the kids?"

"Don't know about any kids, didn't see any about, but the two bimbos he was boffing seemed to like it there. If one of you is a pissed dad or uncle, you might be wasting your time."

"I'm not talking about those two."

"Didn't figure you were here for them. I don't know anything else. You two still in the service?"

Baker ignored the question. He was glad he hadn't killed the former SEAL, but he wasn't yet sure what to do with him. He almost felt a kinship knowing the man was a fellow sniper. While he wondered, Senich again provided the impetus Baker needed to make a decision.

"How'd a SEAL fall so low to be working for scum like that?"

"I don't pick 'em, just go where I'm sent. Got to earn a living. But we do try and be selective of who we work for."

Senich spit out some blood in disgust. He was tired of swallowing it. His teeth had cut the inside of his mouth and lip when Robinson hit him. He looked back at Robinson. "Fucking and selling kids ain't earning a living."

"What?!" The incredulous look on Robinson's face was enough evidence for Baker to believe the man truly didn't know that aspect about his former employer. He could be acting, but Baker didn't believe so.

"Guy fucked and sold little kids." The hostility in Senich's voice grew with each word. He glared at Robinson.

"I know nothing about that." Robinson was looking past the black handgun and into Baker's eyes. "I had a feeling the guy was crooked, but I had no idea he was into that shit."

"He was." Baker lowered his gun. He noticed a shift in the way Robinson was acting. He couldn't quite place it, but the feeling of kinship was keener. He trusted his instincts, but still kept the firearm in his hand.

"So now what?" Robinson asked.

"We could forget this meeting ever happened. You go back and act surprised."

"Are you serious?" Retorted Senich.

Baker looked at his inquiring friend and realized he wasn't quite convinced Robinson was one of the good guys. He looked back at Robinson who was thinking the situation over.

"How do I know what you're saying is true?"

"When you get back to the house, go through the private video collection. I saw a DVD with him and a little girl that was being distributed through black market channels. That was enough for me. I think he was involved with trafficking actual kids as well."

"Damn," Robinson was shaking his head as if he didn't believe what he'd gotten involved with. He thought of his father, mother, little sister and wife. He thought of his own kids and their planned trip to Disneyworld. He suddenly felt sick to his stomach. The former SEAL had done and seen a lot, but the thought of working for a child rapist and trafficker made his insides turn.

"I don't like it." Senich spit more blood. "We can't trust this guy, he knows too much."

Baker looked at his friend and back to Robinson. He still held the Browning, ready to aim if needed. He returned his gaze to Senich and saw him playing with the inside of his mouth with his tongue. Their eyes met and they both looked back at Robinson. Shit. Robinson avoided Senich's stare and looked at Baker. Silence. The only sounds were from a few birds that had come back after the echo of the Browning faded and was forgotten by the denizens of the forest.

"If what you two say is true, I have no problem with you taking out a child rapist. If I'd have known, I wouldn't have been working for him."

The silence broken, Senich spit again. He still wasn't entirely convinced.

"SEAL Sniper, huh?" Baker asked.

"Yes."

"Frank, if we can't trust one of our own, who can we trust?"

"No one," Senich replied. "Trust no one."

"Sometimes you need to trust someone, and I think we can trust him." Baker talked as if Robinson couldn't hear.

"Army snipers, right?" Robinson didn't wait for a response, he was sure they were former Army. "You can trust the other three at the house as well. Two of them were from your branch, D-boy and a Ranger. If what you say is true, they will be a sickened as I am. Yeah, we do security for hire, but we are picky regarding who we work for. If we had suspected anything other than regular porn, we would have never been there. The four of us would easily be where you're at right now if we'd have known." Robinson glanced at Senich and the returned to Baker. "I didn't like being around the regular porn. Always seems to be more dirt behind the scenes than ever gets out. I had a bad feeling from the get go." It was a long speech for a SEAL sniper.

"So what do you propose you do when you get back?" Senich was still hesitant to trust the man who nearly broke his jaw when knocking him unconscious.

"How's this sound to the two of you? I say I saw a couple of guys drinking and shooting at trees, up in the air, and acting stupid with their guns. I approached them and told them it was private property and they needed to leave. They grumbled, but left. I didn't think anything else about it at the time. Not until I got back and found out Bennett was killed out back by the pool. That is where he was, right?"

"I like the way you think," Baker replied. "Wouldn't be the first person killed by a stray bullet."

"As likely as two snipers taking him out from 700 meters." Robinson smiled. He hadn't seen the shot, but he appreciated the skill it took to make a first round kill at that distance. Sure, he'd made kills much farther, but it was still a respectable shot, especially for a couple of Army guys.

Senich studied Robinson hard as he talked. He'd seldom been wrong reading people, and he sure hoped he wasn't now. He picked up the Glock from the weeds and stepped closer to Robinson and held it out. Robinson came forward and reached for the weapon.

"Thanks," he said, taking the Glock and returning it to its holster. "Sorry I hit you so hard."

"Was nothing I ain't used to."

Robinson looked Senich over one final time and figured it was an accurate statement.

Baker extended his hand in Robinson's direction. "Sorry about the rounds to the chest."

"Ain't nothing I'm not used to." Both men smiled and shook hands. Baker looked around and found the two spent 9 mm shells. He put them into his pocket, and with a nod, he and Senich disappeared into the woods. Robinson silently faded into the trees going the opposite direction.

"You sure we can trust him?" Senich asked as they neared the vehicle.

"I think so," Baker answered. He took a couple more steps. "I sure as hell hope so."

The trip back to Missoula was uneventful. That was good, since both men were exhausted. Neither had slept much the night before. Both had lain awake combating their own demons brought from slumber by watching the DVD Peter Jacob had provided. The DVD itself had been snapped into tiny pieces. Unfortunately, neither Baker nor Senich could erase the pictures from their minds as easily. The doses of adrenaline from making the shot and then confronting Robinson wore off somewhere half way between Butte and Missoula. That was right before the thermos of coffee was emptied.

The two were spent, and Baker almost forgot his cell phone was in the glove box. He asked Senich to hand it to him as he exited the Interstate at Missoula's first exit. He'd drive past the university toward his home in the center of town. He turned the phone on and saw he missed three calls and had voice mail. He immediately thought of Tanya, but after pressing a button saw the calls were from the office. He listened to his voice mail.

"Fuck."

"What is it?" Senich asked.

"Tucker's pissed that I wasn't answering the phone. Needs me for something."

"Can't it wait? I'm hungry."

"What else is new? It's not five yet, let me call and see what's going on. We'll be at the house in a minute and we can clean up and go eat."

Baker called his boss and when the phone answered Senich could hear the yelling from where he sat in the passenger seat. "Where the hell have you been all day?"

"At home, the battery was dead, just took the phone off the charger and checked messages."

"Well, I don't know what the hell you've been up to, but you're in deep shit."

"What are you talking about, I have a ton of unused vacation, and I don't have any cases that need immediate attention."

"That's not what I'm talking about."

"Then what is it?"

"The Attorney General wants your ass! You are immediately suspended. From the sound of it, you'll be fired and disbarred. Lucky if you are sent to Deer Lodge."

"What?" Baker couldn't imagine what the Attorney General had on him that could send him to the Montana State Penitentiary. Ironically they had just driven by Deer Lodge an hour before. The small town was located off Interstate 90 between Butte and Missoula and didn't have much there beside the prison, McDonald's and the Old Prison Museum. It definitely wasn't a place Baker wanted to reside, in or out of a cell.

"I don't know what you did Baker, but the Attorney General wants to see you in Helena ASAP. He's taking a personal interest in this one."

"ASAP like when, and what for?"

"I told you, I don't know. He just told me you're suspended and that you better have your ass in Helena tomorrow."

"Whatever." Baker clicked the phone off and didn't answer it when it started ringing. "Shit, now what?"

"We wanted to meet with the Attorney General and his brother anyway, right?"

Baker glanced over at his friend's smile and shook his head.

Shane Gray's head barely cleared the doorway walking into Clay Grady's office. He wasn't just tall, he was huge. He had broad shoulders and a bullet shaped shaven head sitting on top of them without a neck. He unconsciously pulled his arms in going through the door because their natural position spread out from the body due to his over developed lats. He wore a XXXL t-shirt with a weight lifting logo on the front that was stretched tight around his massive frame, and baggy workout pants because he couldn't squeeze his freakishly gargantuan thighs into jeans that fit his waist. Size 17 New Balance Cross Trainers completed his basic wardrobe. It was a wardrobe that varied little from day to day. Different colored t-shirt, different training pants, but that was about as much variation as his clothes provided. He did have a black suit specially made for him a number of years ago, but hadn't worn it more than a half dozen times in as many years.

Gray was a star football lineman in high school, and then graduated from Dickinson State University with a Bachelor of Science Degree in Exercise Science. He moved to North Dakota because they offered a full ride scholarship for football, and he had nothing better to do after high school. He graduated, not because he did the work in the classroom, but because the football team desperately needed him. As long as he helped the Blue Hawks win on the gridiron, he didn't have to worry too much about passing the physical education curriculum. Everyone expected him to turn pro after graduation, and he had a number of scouts looking at him even during his Junior-year. There was just one problem with football. Shane Gray hated the game.

The moment of contact, when his body smashed through his opponents, was a thrill. He loved the feeling of smashing people, and sacking quarterbacks was an extra shot of adrenaline, because he despised how they got all the attention and glory. However, the rules frustrated him, and he hated the endless drills of practice and the rituals that went along with the game. Nor did he like being part of the team. In fact, he always considered himself a Black Hawk rather than a Blue Hawk. He didn't socialize with the others, and never felt he belonged. But they sure liked what he did on the field. But when the last college season ended, he never wanted to have anything to do with the game. He never watched it, never talked about it, and never even touched a football or helmet again.

During his college years, the one thing that consumed his thoughts more than anything else was professional wrestling. He was glued to the television every Monday night. He'd then watch the recording of the show for the rest of the week until the weekend broadcasts would provide something different. The Monday shows were the best, and he dreamed of headlining a Monday night main event.

So he returned to Montana for the summer after graduation, something he almost failed to do, if not for a coach sitting him down and having a heart-to-heart after the season, encouraging him to finish out the school year and graduate. He quickly became bored and decided to attend The Monster Factory, one of the oldest professional wrestling schools in the country. He'd always liked Paul White, The Big Show, even though he didn't' think he was all that big, and if the school was good for The Big Show, he'd follow in his footsteps. The dreams of headlining a Monday night main event were still alive and burning deep within him.

The dreams didn't last when he got to The Monster Factory. He didn't want to learn about showmanship, pulling punches, and acting a role. He wanted to crunch and smash people. He left before the first week was finished. He didn't want to go back to Montana, so he headed south to Tennessee to join one of the lesser known professional wrestling organizations. He wouldn't be on national television, but he'd be able to smash people and figured he'd get noticed by someone like Vince McMahon and would then get his chance at stardom.

He was initially treated as a star due to his size, and the organization believed it had found another cash machine in the gullible hulk from Montana. The hullabaloo soon ceased when Gray continuously injured other wrestlers and couldn't grasp the concept that it was entertainment, a show, and that crippling competitors meant they couldn't perform in the next event. That cost money. No one wanted to wrestle him after he permanently retired two wrestlers and put another out for what the doctors were saying would be a minimum of six months. Promoters were angered at losing income due to the injured wrestlers.

His size and aggressiveness were draws, and promoters were sure people would pay to see him. But not if they couldn't find someone to match him against, and not if it meant canceling already booked shows due to injuries of those that did dare face him. It seemed Gray had a mean streak that just turned on when he faced an opponent. When he got in the ring, total annihilation was his only thought. His career in Tennessee was short lived and he found himself wondering where to go next. Nine months after embarking on what he believed was his chosen career path, his dreams were crushed, his bank account empty, and with nowhere else to turn, he moved back in with his mother in Butte. His father had died of a heart attack while he was in North Dakota, so his mother was glad to have a man around the house again. She had previously tried to get him to stay when he came back the summer after graduation. It had been a long, cold, lonely winter wondering where her boy had gone and what he was doing. She had a close friend to share the doctor's prognosis, and now that her health was failing fast, it was a relief to have someone as big and strong as her little boy to look after her.

That was a year ago, two months before he started doing odd jobs for Clay Grady, and five months before the cancer took his mother and left him alone in the mining town he never believed he'd return to when he left for the fame of professional wrestling. Clay Grady had become more than an employer in the last year. He'd become a father figure, mentor and friend. There was nothing Shane Gray wouldn't do for the man.

"You wanted to see me Mr. Grady?" The behemoth remained standing, even after Grady motioned for him to take a seat. The seats in front of the desk had armrests, and Gray couldn't squeeze himself between them comfortably. He wondered why Grady wanted to see him so late on a Tuesday. Everyone else had gone home for the night.

"Sorry, Shane. Forget you don't fit too well in those goddamn little chairs. Take a seat over on the couch in the corner."

"Thank you, sir." Gray moved over to the beige couch and sat underneath the Charles Russell print. The painting depicted three cowboys lassoing a grizzly bear and was a painting Gray had always liked. He secretly wished the grizzly would take out all three cowboys and their horses.

"Can I get you a drink?" Grady asked as he opened the small refrigerator in the opposite corner and pulled out a bottle of beer and twisted off the cap. He glanced over to the couch, his foot still holding the refrigerator door open.

"Sure."

Grady pulled out another bottle and crossed over and sat in a large antique rocking chair he'd taken a fancy to at an estate auction. The dark mahogany wood frame matched the frame to the Russell print, while the blue and gray upholstery enhanced the blue of the Sakura Area Rug it sat on. The chair was made for a wealthy miner nearly a century ago, while the rug was something he saw on-line and ordered about a week after purchasing the chair. He passed a bottle to Gray and took a long swig from the one he'd opened.

"I'm afraid we have some trouble."

"What kind of trouble, Mr. Grady?" Gray opened his bottle and looked around for a place to put the cap and finally decided to just hold onto it.

"A couple guys beat the shit out of some of my employees the other day."

"Yeah, I heard about that."

"I think it was planned, and we need to do something about it."

"What do you mean?"

"I don't know for sure, but I think they are after Grady Trucking. We need to stop them. I want your help."

"You know all you need to do is say the word and I'll take care of anything you need, Mr. Grady." He took another long swig from his bottle.

"I know you will, son. And I know you're the man for the job. These two took out four men."

"Well, only one of them had any experience fighting, and he wasn't much without a blade from what I heard."

"I'm not here to debate their prowess and fighting skills, I want to know about yours. Are you still as good as you used to be?"

"Boss, if you want skulls cracked, I'm your man."

"Good. There's two of them, do you know others we could get to help?"

"I doubt I'll need help with just two of them, but yeah, I know a couple guys who enjoy smashing people, and I trust them."

"I want these two more than smashed."

"Hospitalized?"

"Let's put it this way, if a neck gets broken or a head gets cracked open on the pavement where brains start leaking out, I'll be mighty happy."

Gray smiled and the hand not holding the bottle clenched tightly. "I like the sound of that. It's been too long since I've smashed someone."

"Think you can be ready to go whenever I call? I want this done soon."

"Sure, I'm free whenever."

"What about the others?"

"Probably. I'm pretty sure, just need to talk to them soon so they aren't too hung over when you need them."

"Good. Now, let's talk about the details, so you can go make those calls."

"I don't care, just get him to Helena today!" Brady Grady slammed the phone down and stood up behind his desk. He breathed deep and walked over to the window. It was a beautiful spring morning and he thought about walking five blocks down to the Capital's lawn to clear his head. How did everything get so complicated so fast? Why did he let his brother get him into things? It was Thursday and he had a plane to catch Saturday morning for California. He needed to have this mess taken care of before he left. Benjamin Baker better get his ass over here.

Grady's plan was pretty simple. It was just like everything else, Brady figured he could control it with money, threats or both. He'd been successful with the tactics before, and had no reason to believe they wouldn't work on Benjamin Baker; a simple Deputy County Attorney that his brother believed was poking his nose where it didn't belong. Buy him off or scare him off, didn't matter which, just get him out of his brother's hair so Clay would leave him alone. He had more important things to do than clean up after and take care of his little brother. He'd wait to call Tucker back and confirm Baker was coming.

He sat back down, leaned way back, took a deep breath, exhaled forcefully, sat upright, and picked up the phone again. He glanced at the large wooden clock on the wall. Eight-thirty, he better be up. He dialed his brother's cell phone.

"Yeah," Clay Grady answered. The call interrupted his reading of the morning paper. He was upset that he'd just lost an income stream. A short article on page 5 reported that a stray bullet killed Richard G. Bennett at his home outside of Anaconda. Police were looking for any information regarding two men suspected of drinking and firing off hunting rifles on the property behind Bennett's house.

"You work on that backup plan we discussed?"

"Sure did, I have just the guy we need. Boy's built like a tank. Got kicked out of pro wrestling for hurting people."

"Just one? I thought you said this Baker took out several of your guys."

"I think it was Baker, but he had someone with him. And the four they beat up were nothing like my boy Shane. Don't fret. He has a couple of friends who will help him out. I'm going to be there too."

"I thought you weren't getting involved."

"I want to make damn sure this gets done right. Besides, it's been a long time since I've hit anyone. I kind of miss it. Don't you?"

"Yeah, sometimes. But that's behind me. I have more important things going on right now."

"Well, I hate to tell you, but some of the money you were counting on has just flown away."

"What do you mean?"

"Just reading the paper. Bennett was killed yesterday."

"What? How?" Brady knew Bennett and his brother were some kind of business partners, but he didn't know exactly what business.

"Says here he was hit by a stray bullet while at his house outside Anaconda."

"A stray bullet?"

"That's what it says. Cops are looking for a couple guys suspected of drinking and firing off hunting rifles."

"Clay, do you know anything about this?"

"Just what I'm reading. Swear to God."

"Does this have anything to do with the stuff you're messed up with?"

"Don't think so. Just a fucking bad streak of luck, I guess."

"Is this Baker involved?"

"How the fuck should I know? I doubt it. He's after me and Grady Trucking, I don't know how he'd link me to Bennett. We kept that quiet."

"What about the girls?"

"What about 'em?"

"Bennett was the porn guy, right? Is that where the prostitutes came from, too?"

"No, I did other stuff with him."

"Like what?"

"Never you mind, big brother." Clay never revealed the young girls or the DVDs made with underage 'actresses' to his brother. Nor did he share that he was the transportation and middleman for trafficking little girls and sometimes boys across the entire country. Some things were best kept secret, especially with the office his brother held. "You just worry about getting elected governor. Let me worry about where the funds come from."

"I got Baker coming to Helena today."

"What time?"

"Not sure, I'm waiting on a phone call to confirm."

"I'll round up the troops and head that way."

"You remember, if I can get him to do what I want, you lay off."

"Sure, big brother."

"I mean it. I rather have him in my back pocket than have to worry about explaining what happened to him after he left my office. You and your guys are only if he doesn't come around. It's a backup plan only."

"I understand." Clay indeed understood. He had photographs of his brother and a nineteen-year-old prostitute that he kept just to ensure his brother would always be in his pocket. He knew the photographs would kill any further political offices, and would force Brady to resign from the position of Attorney General, a position he campaigned long and hard for. He'd be found a hypocrite and liar if the photos ever leaked, and there would be no way for him to remain in office, or seek another one, in such a small conservative populated state such as Montana. Sure it was his own flesh and blood, but business was business. Nothing personal.

"Hold on a sec, I have another call coming in on my cell."

"Alright."

"You there?" Brady asked when he came back on.

"Yeah, I'm still here."

"That was Tucker calling my cell. He's on his way. You can get over here and wait. I'll then call you again when I'm done with him. If I can't get him to play ball, you can have your chance."

"I can't wait."

"If he comes on board, you'll lay off. I mean it."

"Understood, big brother. Don't worry. I just want the guy off my case."

"Alright. I'll call you when I know."

"Later." Clay Grady clicked his cell phone off and then on again. He dialed Shane's number. "You and your buddies ready to go?"

"Sure boss. Now?"

"Yep, we need to go now."

"We'll be ready in thirty minutes."

"We'll take my Hummer. I'll be at your place in twenty-five. And Shane..."

"Yeah?"

"Remember, I don't want this Baker making it to the hospital. Same for his friend if he's there."

"That's what I understood boss."

Baker lay groggily in bed. The alarm went off earlier, but he remained under the sheet. It seemed he hadn't slept more than a few minutes at a time. He'd close his eyes and see the words "I'm Hung Like a Baby 9 lbs. 6 oz. 21 inches." He saw the 'e' from the word 'like' clearly, and knew that the 175-grain boat tail bullet he launched from his Remington entered Bennett's chest at that exact location. He also saw clearly the motionless body lying beside the pool. It was his last view from inside the scope before he crawled away.

Each time the visions kept him from drifting to sleep, he'd think about the DVD provided by Peter Jacob. The picture of Richard 'Dick' Bennett with the young girl erased any guilt that might have formed for taking his life, but left Baker more disturbed with the thoughts of little girls being abused by such monsters. How many children lost their innocence and had their entire lives destroyed by men like Bennett? It was that question, more than the killing of the porn king, that kept Baker awake all night. Or was it both?

Around two, he got out of bed and went to the living room. On the way, he looked into the spare bedroom and saw Senich sprawled across the bed. He hadn't seemed restless at all. He looked through his DVD collection three times and channel surfed for twenty minutes before deciding to head back to the bedroom and try sleeping again. The house seemed empty. The bed even more so.

He thought about Tanya and Coral. He missed them and wished Tanya was beside him now. Holding her would make things better. He wondered what she'd do if she found out what he'd done. He'd killed three men, busted up two others, and helped his best friend kill another. And there were the two that Frank left broken beside the truck stop. Oh yeah, Frank also killed the two in his living room. Six dead, four beat up. How did all this happen? He wanted to do something after Walter Dennison shot up the school and killed himself, but this?

He kept asking himself, if he didn't, who would? But would Tanya understand? He wasn't going to find out. She'd never know. This was between him, Frank, and the dead, and they weren't talking. Oh yeah, and the former SEAL from the woods. He sure hoped he could trust the sniper. After all, they were kin. Weren't they?

What about Coral? What would happen to her if it were found out her daddy was a killer? If Tanya left, she'd get custody, and would he ever see his little girl again? Why hadn't he thought of these things more in depth before going to Bruce James' house that night? It wasn't his job to do something. He wasn't the protector of the world. It wasn't his job to stop evil. He wasn't a superhero. He was a deputy county attorney, a husband, and a father. The last two weeks could destroy all of that. He could lose what took years to build.

Were his thoughts of guilt and remorse, or were they fear? Fear of losing his job, his family, his freedom, the life he'd built. Was he feeling guilty over what he'd done? Was he remorseful over those he and Frank had killed? No. He was glad they were gone and could no longer do the terrible things they had been doing. He was just afraid of getting caught. They wouldn't get caught though, would they?

He heard Frank's words intermixed with his fears and concerns, "What good is all that training if you don't do anything with it?" Maybe if he lost his conscience, like Frank suggested, he'd be sleeping like a baby right now too. But was it really his conscience? He wanted to scream. He wanted to hit something.

He rolled over and looked at the alarm clock on the small stand beside the bed. It was twenty-five minutes after eight. He couldn't remember sleeping in that late for a long time. Was it sleeping in when you didn't sleep? He felt a tinge of guilt for missing his morning workout. Maybe he could get something in real quick, they didn't have much planned for the morning yet. The phone rang.

Shit. Baker remembered Tucker yelling at him about meeting the attorney general. He didn't want to make the trip to Helena, and he especially didn't want to meet with Brady Grady. Nor did he want to pick up the ringing phone on the stand beside the alarm clock, but he did.

"This is Ben."

"The Attorney General needs to see you this morning, you better get your ass over there."

"Good morning to you too, Kevin."

"Listen Ben, I don't know what this is about, and you know I'll go to bat for you if I can, but the Attorney General is really breathing down my neck hard on this one."

"I understand." Piece of shit. Baker knew Tucker was in Grady's pocket. He also knew his boss would hang him out to dry the first chance he got if it meant putting himself in the good graces of Brady Grady. Tucker was loyal to one person, and that was himself. He'd step on people, throw you under the bus, and literally do anything to anybody to get himself ahead. "When does he want to see me?"

"As soon as you can get over there. He'll be in his office all day, and he'll see you when you get there."

"Alright."

"Ben, do you know what this is about?"

"Haven't got a clue."

"Well, let me know when you do, okay?"

"Sure." Baker hung up the phone. He was in no mood to listen to Tucker's bullshit. He laid his head back on the pillow and stared at the ceiling. He tried to remember the last time he'd met Brady Grady. It had been at some State Bar function. Maybe a CLE? The State Bar Annual Meeting? It was something like that. Surprisingly, he couldn't remember much about the man. He remembered having the impression that the guy was a typical politician, but couldn't recall what had given him that impression.

After a quick knock, the door opened and Senich poked his head inside. "Who called?" he asked.

"My boss." Baker looked at his friend standing in the doorway. He was wearing jeans and a plain black t-shirt and hadn't put on socks and shoes yet. He was holding the Disney mug with *The Lion King* on it. Maybe he'd slept more than he thought. His friend was showered and drinking fresh brewed coffee. He hadn't heard a thing. Sure the door had been shut, and Frank was one of the most silent people he knew, but he should have heard something. He was a bit ticked at himself for not having noticed. Maybe it was the stress, or the fitful night's sleep. Maybe he had heard it, registered it as a non-threat, and dozed back off. He comforted himself with the thought if it had been something serious, he'd have woke ready to act.

"What'd he want?"

"I need to go to Helena to meet Brady Grady."

"Today?"

"Yeah, this morning."

"Well, get your ass out of bed and let's go."

Baker climbed out of bed and walked toward the door. He nodded at Senich's mug. "Got some of that for me?"

"Yeah, I'll pour you the last cup and start a fresh pot for the trip."

"How long you been up?" Baker raised his voice as he was in the bathroom and his buddy was back in the kitchen.

"Since five or so." Senich yelled back.

"Damn," Baker shook his head, looked at himself in the mirror for a second and then turned, removed his clothes, and got into the shower. Maybe some hot water would make him feel better.

Senich made a fresh pot of coffee and ate another English muffin with peanut butter while he waited for his friend to get ready. He'd already eaten a large bowl of cereal after his morning run, but needed something to do while he waited.

When Baker came to the kitchen, he was wearing black slacks, a white shirt, and a Navy Blazer. His attire was accentuated with a red and black patterned tie and sharply shined black shoes.

"Look at you. Far cry from yesterday. You even shaved."

"Yeah, you should try it sometime." Baker picked up the cup his friend had left him on the counter.

"I like my beard."

"Let me nuke a packet of oatmeal and we can then get out of here."

"Fine by me."

"One thing Frank, no guns today."

"What?"

"I've been thinking," Baker prepared his breakfast as he spoke. "For one, I can't carry. I'm going into the AG's office."

"Leave it in the Dodge with me."

"The other thing, I think yesterday was it."

"Huh?"

"We solved the problem. With Bennett out of the picture, it will stop. Clay Grady and his trucking company were just transportation. With nothing to haul, they will be out of business."

"You seriously believe that?"

"Yeah, I do. I just think we need to stop before we go over the edge."

"You've been thinking too much."

"Maybe you don't think enough."

"Don't pull that shit on me, you asked me to come here, remember? I came to help you."

"I know, I'm sorry." Baker was looking at his friend, and he knew the man across the room would do anything for him. The microwave beeped and Baker ignored it. "I'm just, I don't know. I'm worried about what could happen. We've been pretty lucky so far, and I don't want to do anything more right now. I think we should lay off." He turned back to the counter and took out the bowl.

"It's your backyard, so it's your call. I just don't like leaving a job half finished." Senich also thought it was ridiculous to ever go unarmed. What was his best friend thinking?

"I know, but I think this is a good time to stop. At least let me find out what's going on with the AG. Hell, it might be too late the way Tucker was talking yesterday."

"What do you mean?"

"Yesterday he said I was suspended, and he talked about me losing my license and maybe going to prison."

"What?"

"But then this morning he wanted to be all buddy, buddy. So I don't know what the hell is going on. Just need to get to Helena and find out."

The two friends continued their discussion regarding the Grady brothers on their drive to Helena. Senich believed they should pay for any involvement they had with the trafficking of kids. Period.

Baker explained his reservations. First, they needed to know what this meeting was all about, and then there was his family. He wanted Tanya and Coral back home soon, and he needed to put the events of the last couple of weeks behind him and get back to some normalcy.

"Let's just find out what this is all about first, okay?" The conversation had been going in circles and Baker was relieved to be entering the capital city. It would only be a few more minutes and they would be at the Department of Justice Building. It was just up the hill behind the Capital Building on Sanders St.

"I know, like I said, it's your call. I just don't like it that they might get away with what they did."

"Karma, remember? Things come back around."

"Yeah, right."

Baker parked a block away on a side street. He wanted to walk over to the justice building. "Why don't you take a walk down by the capital? There's a museum that has some cool stuff down across the street on the east side."

"Alright. Give me a call when you're done."

Senich headed north toward the capital and museum as Baker adjusted his clothes and started walking toward his meeting with the AG. He couldn't figure out why, nor could he determine what the AG wanted him for. Was it because of something he and Frank did? No sense worrying. Just go find out.

The Attorney General made him wait for 35 minutes before seeing him. When Baker was finally shown into his office, Brady Grady met him with an outstretched hand and a grin that would do the Cheshire Cat proud.

"Good to see you again, Ben."

"Same here." Baker remembered why he felt Grady was the consummate politician, and how he didn't believe a word that passed his lips.

"Please take a seat." Grady motioned toward a pair of sofas facing each other in the corner. The coffee table sitting between them already had cups, saucers, carafes of coffee and hot water, along with an assortment of teas, sweeteners and cream. A small plate of assorted cookies and pastries sat on the one end.

Baker selected the sofa against the wall and sat so he could see the entire office. He noticed Grady's liking of Charles Russell, the popular Montana artist. Baker didn't know the same Russell painting of the grizzly also hung in Brady's brother's office in Butte.

"Please, help yourself," Grady motioned with his arm toward the table as he sat down across from Baker. He waited until Baker finished pouring a cup of coffee and then poured one for himself. "You're probably wondering why I asked you to come here."

"The thought crossed my mind."

"Ben, you impress me, and I have a proposition for you."

"What's with the suspension and threats?"

"A man that gets right to the point, I like that. Beating around the bush is for pussies."

Baker stared, didn't say a word, and raised his coffee to his lips and took a drink without moving his eyes from the politician sitting across from him.

"A man of few words too." Grady seemed uncomfortable. There was something about Baker that was unlike most men he could easily persuade and manipulate. "I wasn't serious about the suspension and didn't know about it until this morning when Tucker told me that's what he used to get you over here. I just told him it was serious and I needed you here right away. I apologize for any inconvenience or worry it may have caused you. Be sure I'll be having a talk with Tucker regarding his inappropriateness."

"Thanks." Baker took another sip of his coffee before setting the cup down. He'd be having his own talk with Kevin Tucker in the near future.

"Well…" The silence unsettled Grady. The feeling was something he wasn't accustomed to. He usually controlled every conversation. "Let me get right to the point, I'm sure you're a busy man, and Tucker has already caused you enough worry and wonder."

"Okay."

"You know that I intend to run for Governor the next election?"

Baker nodded.

"Well, Kevin will be joining my ticket. We've been planning this for some time, and we have unprecedented backing throughout the state and across the country as well."

Baker never liked the fact that money outside of Montana had such influence on the state's politics and policies, but it was a fact one had to live with. He nodded again, and then picked up his cup to take another sip. The entire time, his eyes never stopped staring at Grady.

"So, what this has to do with you is, we would like to back you for Missoula County Attorney. You'd replace Tucker. We can back you with everything you'll need. Money is no object. We'll help you wipe out any competition, if that is, anyone dares run against you."

"I'm not interested." Baker set his cup back down and leaned back in the leather sofa. He wasn't entirely sure where he wanted his career to go, but he knew for sure he'd never take Grady's blood money or be his stooge like his boss.

"You don't have to make up your mind right now. Take some time to think about it. Talk it over with your wife." Grady had his politician's flow working again. "Think about it a bit. The salary increase is significant, and there are a lot of other perks that go with the position. A lot of perks if you get my drift."

"I get it, and I'm not interested."

"Think of all the good you can do with the increased responsibility." Grady figured if money wouldn't work, maybe he could appeal to Baker's sense of commitment to the profession.

"I told you I'm not interested. Is that what you had Tucker threaten me about, and had me drive all the way over here for?" It was the most Baker had said since entering the office.

"Come now, Ben. Don't be so rash. Think about it a bit."

"I did." Baker reached for his coffee and drained the cup. He started to stand when Grady stopped him.

"Ben, listen. I'm going to give you some time to think about this. I'll be over in Missoula next month and we can get together then to discuss it further."

"There's nothing to discuss. I'm not interested."

"I don't think you understand." The change in Grady's tone and body position didn't go unnoticed. "We can do this the easy way, or you can make things very difficult for yourself."

"You threatening me?" Baker's tone and stare were definitely noticed by Grady. He couldn't afford to lose his temper in the office, even though a part of him, that part he tried to leave in Butte years ago, wanted to try Baker out. He thought he could take him.

"No, no, Ben. Not at all. I'm just saying, this could be a great career move for you, and if you pass it up, you may not get the chance again."

"I'll take that chance."

"Ben, I thought you'd be more reasonable than this. I need you to reconsider. We need you in that position." Grady stood. "And Ben, I always get what I want. You'll do what I need you to do. I'll get my way."

Baker stood, his blue eyes looking up into the taller man's glare. "No you won't." For a brief second, Baker envisioned a small hole appearing in Grady's forehead as he recited the line just like Bronson in *Ten to Midnight*. Maybe he'd been watching that movie too many times lately.

"I'm warning you Baker." Grady's body seemed to quiver as he attempted to control his temper. He was unaccustomed to anyone standing up to him.

"You listen Grady, I know about the girls."

"What? What girls?" The surprised look on Grady's face let Baker know his bluff worked. He'd remembered what Peter Jacob had overheard, and thought he'd see where he could go with it. Grady realized threats would not work, and thought quickly of how he could steer the discussion back in his favor and make a deal with this opposing attorney. After all, attorneys were trained to negotiate and make deals.

"You want to sit back down?" Baker was now taking over the conversation.

Grady sat, and Baker followed. He then poured another cup of coffee and offered to refill the shocked attorney general's. Grady accepted and gulped down half the cup. His mind was still racing, like only an attorney turned politician's could, to turn this around to his advantage.

"Ben, I'm not sure what you are talking about, it must be one of those rumors. You know you can't believe what you hear."

Baker knew he was onto something. He needed to find out more. "I know about your brother."

Sweat formed on Grady's brow. The one thing that could derail his political ambitions was a scandal to alienate his conservative base. If that brother of his caused one, he'd kill him himself. Baker enjoyed seeing the man sweat and reveled in his being so uncomfortable.

"Listen Ben, I'm not involved with that crazy brother of mine. God knows I've spent the better part of my life trying to help him straighten out. If he's done anything wrong, I'd like to know about it so I can put a stop to it."

"What about the girls?"

Grady looked around like what he was about to reveal was a secret and put on all the charm he'd worked to master over the years. He wondered how the hell Baker knew about a prostitute from years back. "Well, that was a long time ago, right? I mean come on, you're a man. It was one drunken night and I slept with one of my brother's whores. It was nothing. I don't think he's been involved with them for years. I know I certainly haven't."

"Nothing huh?"

"Come on Ben, you were a soldier weren't you? You've never been with a prostitute, or someone that was just with you for the money you spent on her, which we both know, you always pay for it one way or another." Grady gave Baker a sly smile.

"We're not talking about me."

"Well, what two adults do between themselves is none of anyone else's business, right? Let's get back to talking about what we can do for each other in the future, not crazy things we did when we were young."

"Cut the bullshit, I want to know about the young kids." Baker's compassionless blue eyes stared into the face of the attorney general. He looked for any sign that Grady had been involved with his brother's operation.

"What?" Grady couldn't hide the genuine shock at hearing Baker accuse him or his brother with doing something inappropriate with anyone underage. He was a father himself, and was influential in breaking up a large child pornography circle several years back. Drugs, prostitutes, and skimming books were all things that could be overlooked, but never would he partake in or condone anything involving kids.

"I was told Grady Trucking was used to traffic kids."

"You mean my brother? Who told you what?" How could his brother be involved with such a horrific crime? Did campaign money come from selling little kids? "Oh my God, you can't be serious."

Baker was not sure how accurately he could read the man sitting across from him. Brady Grady had spent the better part of his life honing the craft of schmoozing and lying, and dishonestly seemed to ooze from his pores. However, the quick look of shock and sudden denial that his brother could be part of something so horrible appeared sincere. Baker believed, despite all his shortcomings and dishonesty, Brady Grady was not involved with anything regarding young boys and girls.

Baker sat in his Durango for fifteen minutes after removing his tie and jacket and hanging them in the back. He was convinced Brady Grady wasn't involved with child trafficking and hadn't known anything about it. Nor did he believe Clay Grady was anything more than transportation. Now that the head had been chopped off the operation, Baker believed it would die and was over. He knew Frank would still want to make Clay pay for his involvement, and the only currency Frank would accept for such deeds was the death of Clay Grady. But Baker wanted it to end. He wanted his family back, he wanted to put the last couple weeks behind him and focus on enjoying the Montana summer with his wife and little girl. They needed to go on more nature walks and picnics. Frank would understand.

He reached in the back and pulled his cell phone out of his jacket's pocket and pushed the speed dial for Frank's cell.

"Where are you?" he asked when his friend answered.

"At the museum. Looking at a model of a heard of buffalo being driven off a cliff by some Native Americans."

"Yeah, there are some nice exhibits there." Baker was a bit surprised to hear his buddy use the politically correct term. Maybe there was hope of refining the barbarian after all.

"You done?"

"Yeah,"

"So?"

"I'll tell you when I pick you up. I'll be out front of the museum in a couple minutes."

"Okay, I'll meet you there. Everything work out?"

"Yeah, it's cool. I'll tell you when I get there. Then I want to go get Tanya and Coral and take them to the carousel for ice cream."

"Sounds good, see you in a few."

Baker stopped in front of the museum and Senich hopped in beside him. He continued down the hill to 11th Avenue where he took a right. The road was also highway 12 and would take him out to East Helena where Tanya and Coral were staying with her parents.

"Well?" Senich asked.

"It's over buddy, thank you for helping."

"What do you mean it's over? What about the two Grady brothers? What about the trucking company?"

"I'm positive Brady Grady didn't know anything in regards to the girls his brother's trucking company might have been hauling. Remember, we had additional proof those others were directly involved. We only have Peter Jacob's story that Grady Trucking was also involved."

"What about the DVD he gave you from Grady's office?"

"He said that's where he got it."

"What about the papers with Grady Trucking we found in that briefcase with the kiddie porn?"

"Same thing, it does not prove Clay was involved for sure."

"Bull shit."

"I know, Frank. Hear me out. Yes, I think Clay Grady is dirty. How dirty, I don't know. I think he was just transportation, and now that we stopped the brains and money behind everything, as well as a couple that did the dirty work, it's over. Clay Grady and his trucking company won't have anything to haul."

"What about those four at the truck stop?"

"I don't know, might have been a Butte thing. Might not have been related." Baker slowed down a bit as they entered the speed zone that went through East Helena. He was looking for the turnoff that would take them to his in-laws.

"It was related and you know it."

"It might have been, but I still don't think Clay Grady is anything more than transportation, and now it's over."

"Fuck that. He should be dead for being involved."

"I knew you'd feel that way."

"You don't?"

"Yeah, I want to see him get his too. And I'm sure he will. Just not now."

"Whatever." Senich looked at his friend with a look of contempt on his face, and then looked out the side window. He looked over again and asked, "So what's up with the AG?"

"He wanted me to replace Tucker as the next County Attorney."

"What?"

"I told him I wasn't interested. We then went around a few times, and finally came to a resolution."

"Which was?"

"He's going to take care of his brother, leave me alone, and I'm going to leave them alone. Like I said, it's over."

"I still think it's bull shit."

Baker turned right off Lake Helena Dr. onto Remington St. He drove two blocks and took a left on Cody Dr. and pulled up in front of the third house on the right. Neither of them paid attention to the Black Humvee that drove past and stopped where Cody Dr. butted into Boundary St. Baker's entire focus at that moment was on the five year old little girl who came running out of the house as he turned off the ignition.

"Daddy, Daddy!"

ALAIN BURRESE

Behind her, came Tanya, dressed in jeans, t-shirt, and running shoes, with an apron tied around her neck and waist. The apron was covered with flour from the chocolate cake she was making from scratch. Baker jumped out of the Dodge and scurried around the front and met his daughter at the edge of the grass. He picked her up and swung her around in a big circle.

"Daddy, mommy's teaching me to bake a cake."

"Wow, do I get some?"

"Sure."

"What kind is it?"

"Chocolate, your favorite."

"It sure is, I can't wait."

"Hi honey, what a surprise." Tanya gave her husband a peck on the cheek and hugged him and Coral who was in his left arm and had her arms around his neck.

"Had some business near the capital and finished early. Came out to surprise you."

"Hi Frank." Tanya waved as Frank got out of the vehicle and waved back.

"Hi Tanya," he said.

"So, can you take a break and sneak away for a bit?"

"Sneak where?" Tanya asked her husband.

"How would you like some ice cream?" Baker asked his daughter.

"Yeah!" she replied with a giggle as Baker tickled her.

"Let's all go down to the carousel for a bit before Frank and I go back to Missoula."

"You have to go back today?"

"Yeah, and then Frank will be heading out. You and Coral are coming home Saturday, so this was just a short surprise."

"Well, let me clean up and tell Mom. Dad's in Billings for a couple of days."

"Sure, and I want to change into my Levis."

"I'll wait out here," Frank told the two.

"Coral, why don't you play with uncle Frank while Mommy and Daddy get ready. Then we'll all go to the carousel for ice cream."

"Okay daddy. I want Strawberry. You can have chocolate."

"It's a deal."

"What will you have uncle Frank?"

"I'm not sure, what do you suggest?"

Baker and his wife left Coral and Frank discussing ice cream flavors as they ducked into the house to get ready. They returned along with Tanya's mother, Helen, ten minutes later and found Coral showing uncle Frank how high she could kick.

"You've been teaching her, I see," he said to Baker.

"Got her started anyway." Baker walked toward the driveway and the Dodge Grand Caravan. He had traded his lawyer clothes for jeans, running shoes, and a Disney t-shirt Coral had picked out the previous summer when they went to Disneyland on a family vacation. "Let's take the van, it has Coral's car seat."

"Frank, you've met Helen before, haven't you?"

"Yeah, last summer. Very nice to see you again, Helen."

"Yes, Frank. Nice to see you again too." Helen was a slender woman who looked ten years younger than her true age somewhere in her 60s. Frank suspected his buddy hoped his wife would age as well as her mother, but didn't say so out loud. He bet the two could pass as sisters if they wanted. He wondered if Helen colored her hair, or if the light brown hair just never turned gray.

Frank sat in the rear seat so Tanya could sit by her husband and Helen could sit by her granddaughter who was buckled in behind her daddy's seat. Her weight maxed out the five-point harness car seat, but Baker preferred it to the booster until she got a little bigger.

Once everyone was buckled in, Baker backed out of the driveway. "We can take Lake Helena Dr. out that way and come into town by Applebee's and stuff right, Helen?" Baker pointed north.

"Sure. They are doing some construction out that way on Canyon Ferry Road, but it's not bad." Helen replied.

Baker was discussing ice cream flavors with Coral, the weekend with Tanya, and looking for where they would turn all at the same time. "What the..." he murmured.

"What is it?" Tanya asked. She was the only one who heard him.

Baker noticed a black Hummer approaching from the rear at a high rate of speed. The picture in the mirror immediately triggered recollections of seeing a black Hummer when he was walking to his Durango from Brady Grady's office and passing by when they had stopped at Karl and Helen's.

The Hummer pulled to the left as if it were going to pass. Baker took his foot off the gas to allow the bigger and faster vehicle to go by. He recognized the Hummer driver's intent too late. The vehicle wasn't passing; it came along side and swerved to the right, smashing into the side of Baker's Grand Caravan with a loud metal crunch. It was hard to discern which was louder, the scream from Coral, Tanya, or Helen. Baker's expletive, which he tried never to utter in Coral's presence, was a close second. Senich was the only person to remain quiet as he braced himself for the inevitable crash.

The Hummer had size and weight on the minivan and the collision sent the van off the road. Baker might have been able to control the vehicle and get it stopped if it weren't for a pair of large trees that happened to be beside the road at that exact location. The right side of the van smashed into a tree caving in the side of the vehicle. Helen, sitting in the middle seat on that side, took the worst punishment. Broken glass showered her back and neck as she turned the instant before impact to try and shield Coral. Her motherly instincts were just as strong for her granddaughter.

The seatbelt had done its job. Baker was scared, not for himself, but for his family, but he wasn't hurt. Over Coral's crying and Tanya's panicked concern for her little girl and mother, Baker yelled back to his friend, "Frank, you okay?" He didn't put his friend's health and condition before his family, but he knew Frank would be able to help him with Coral and the two women.

"Yeah, I'm okay. What the fuck was that?" Senich, having been married and divorced before having children had never learned to watch what he said in front of kids. And even if he had, the situation warranted a lapse.

"I don't know, help Helen, I'll get Coral." Baker had already determined by his wife's actions that her seatbelt had also done its job, and she was hysterical over the situation, and not actually hurt. Shock maybe, which needed to be addressed, but she didn't need lifesaving first aid. "It's okay Tanya, calm down. I'll get Coral. It's okay."

Baker opened his door and got out, but immediately recognized he wouldn't be able to open the sliding door to get to his daughter. The Hummer had caved in the driver's side of the minivan right behind the rear door so the sliding mechanism wouldn't operate. Baker climbed back in and started to climb to the rear seat through the area between the two front ones. "Tanya, it's okay." He continued to reassure his wife as he examined Coral before unbuckling her. The child restraint seat had performed perfectly. His daughter was scared and crying, but showed no signs of injury.

It was remarkable, but the only person hurt was Helen. She suffered a number of tiny lacerations from being rained on by broken glass and had hurt her wrist when trying to turn and protect Coral. Frank helped unbuckle her seatbelt and was looking over the cuts and scrapes to ensure none needed immediate attention.

The passenger side of the van was wedged up against the two trees. The tree the van hit had smashed the window and caved in the side sliding door, while the second tree was now preventing Tanya's door from opening. Everyone would have to climb out Baker's door.

"Frank, you have your cell?"

"Yeah."

"Let's get everyone out my door and over to that shade and then you call 911. Tell them we are in East Helena on Lake Helena Dr." Baker had taken Coral out of her seat and was holding her close to his chest as he talked. He was trying to back out between the two front seats so he could get Coral out of the van. He knew she was not going to let go of him, so he was relying on Frank to usher Tanya and Helen out through his door and then make the emergency call.

"Roger." Frank started to direct Helen toward the front of the minivan when Tanya screamed.

"Ben!"

Baker twisted, still holding Coral, and looked over his shoulder out the windshield of the vehicle. The black Hummer had returned and stopped. It faced them about twenty-five yards up the road. Three men had climbed out and they were walking toward the wrecked minivan. One was the size of a horse and another was equally huge, just a half inch shorter. Baker's stomach tightened. The men who had just run him off the road were now coming toward his family.

Clay Grady had been a bit upset when he picked up Shane Gray and found he only had one companion to accompany them to Helena. He had been assured that Gray had friends to go with them, and when he arrived there was only one extra body. The only redeeming factor was the friend was nearly as large as Gray and was supposedly just as adept at smashing people. In fact, Max, Gray's behemoth friend, actually had more bar fights and arrests under his belt than the former pro wrestler.

The three made the trip to Helena in Clay Grady's black humvee with little conversation and without incident. Gray and Max polished off a six-pack of beer, just to pass time and take the edge off. Both assured Grady that it would take a case or more to give them a buzz and not to worry. They were ready for action. Grady still asked them to wait till their mission was accomplished and then he'd supply all the booze, drugs and women they wanted to celebrate. The two readily agreed and told Grady they'd want plenty of each.

Gray met Max downtown at a Butte bar about the same time his mother died. Max had just gotten out of the state penitentiary where he did 3 years for killing a man and crippling another in a bar fight. The initial meeting between the two almost turned into a slugfest when the two both hit on the same woman. But when she called a friend and suggested they all party together, the two made up quickly and ended up sharing three of their favorite things that night: beer, weed, and women. They both also shared a passion for weight training and became training partners at Butte's ST Fitness. The gym offered access to fitness equipment 24/7 and everyone knew the nights the pair didn't get lucky because they would be working out at three a.m. after the bars closed. They'd also be there at other various times since they both worked out on splits that would allow them to train multiple times on the same day. If there ever was a pair of gym rats, Gray and Max fit the bill. Rats the size of water buffalos with twice the strength. The peculiar aspect about the relationship was that besides the gym and bars, the two never really did anything else together. Neither really knew all that much about the other, just that they made good lifting partners, drinking buddies, and loved to fight and fuck, and nights that involved drinking, fighting, and retiring to some woman's bedroom were ideal. Gray didn't even know his full name, he was just Max.

When they exited Interstate 15 in Helena, Grady pulled into the McDonald's on Prospect Avenue. They didn't know how long they would have to wait, so they prepared by relieving themselves and buying bags full of burgers and fries. From the McDonald's they took Prospect down to Montana Ave. and went up past the capitol. Grady then drove around several blocks before he found the Department of Justice Building where his brother worked. He parked so they could easily watch the entrance.

Clay Grady couldn't believe how much the two men ate, but then he couldn't believe how big the two of them were either. He'd always been impressed with Gray's size and strength, and that's one of the reasons he hired him and took him under his wing. But to have another with his same girth and power was phenomenal in regards to the day's plans. All three fidgeted and began to eat faster when they watched Baker walk across the street and into the Department of Justice

Building. Clay Grady had done some Internet research and found an on-line photograph of the Deputy County Attorney from Missoula. He was sure it was him, but he wondered why he'd walked.

He learned soon enough. Eagerly awaiting his exit from the building, Clay Grady immediately started his vehicle and eased down the road to see where Baker was walking. He spotted the Dodge Durango with the 4 license plates signifying Missoula County and correctly guessed it was Baker's. He stayed back a block and followed the Dodge down to the Museum and the three watched Senich join his friend.

"One for each of you," Clay commented to the two riding with him in the Hummer.

"Shit, I wouldn't need any help with those two." Gray replied.

"Like I would?" Max shot back.

When Baker turned east, it caught Clay off guard. He'd assumed the two would be heading back toward Missoula. He followed them, staying quite a ways back, out through East Helena. He almost lost them when they turned off the highway and drove into the housing area that Clay never realized was out there. When he turned the corner of Cody Dr. and saw the Dodge stop in front of a house, he drove by and stopped at the end of the street. More waiting. Gray and Max were not happy with that prospect; they had been readying themselves for some action since the vehicle started moving.

"Let's go take them now." Gray said.

"No, let's wait a bit. I doubt they'll stay long." Clay Grady responded. He was formulating a plan as he spoke and just wanted to appease his two giant companions. He didn't know who lived in the house, but he didn't want to take any unnecessary risks. He wanted Baker and his friend. No one else needed to be involved. What if another attorney or worse, a cop, lived there?

Grady was relieved to see the little girl and woman come out of the house. Of course, it was his family. He also liked that the other man stayed out front with the little girl while Baker and the woman went inside. For sure it would not be long now. Cody Dr. ran parallel to Lake Helena Dr., but there were two streets at the ends that took you back to the main road. Lake Helena Dr. was the obvious way out, but which direction would Baker take once on the main throughway? Grady drove out to Lake Helena Dr. and spotted a position where Wildfire Rd. butted into Lake Helena Dr. between both Remington and Boundary Streets. Wildfire wasn't a through street, nor was it paved. The original development was stalled, and the building of the houses on the street had been postponed for who knew how long. It was now just a gravel road out at the end of the developments. For Clay Grady's purpose, it was perfect. He could see both Boundary and Remington and would be able to then follow Baker whichever direction he took. Things were coming together better than he'd hoped.

"That's him." Gray said suddenly. He put down the binoculars he'd been playing spy with and pointed to a minivan that just turned onto Lake Helena Dr. from Boundary St. and was heading north.

"What?" Clay asked. He had been looking for the Durango.

"That was the minivan in the driveway. And it was him driving."

"You sure?"

"Positive."

Clay pulled the Hummer onto the road and headed in the direction Gray pointed. The minivan would be even better.

He'd just thought of a new plan on the spot. He pressed the accelerator and all three men braced for what was about to come.

The H2's powerful 6.2L V8 engine propelled the vehicle down the blacktop and closed on the smaller minivan in moments.

"Watch this!" Clay shouted to the other two.

Gray and Max thought he was going to ram the rear of the smaller van the way he was approaching. But at the last moment, Clay steered to the left and came up beside the Dodge. Clay yelled as he jerked the wheel to the right and smashed the Hummer into the minivan driven by Baker and filled with his friend and family.

"Yee ha!" Shouted Gray. He watched the minivan out his side window veer off the road and smash into the tree beside the road. "Smashed them into the trees! Damn, that was cool."

"What do we get to do?" Max asked from the back seat. He looked like a kid who'd arrived at Disneyland to find a sign saying "Closed for the day."

"Just wait," Clay responded. He continued down the road and then pulled off the side and stopped. He jumped out and went around to check what the collision had done to the side of his Hummer. It was nothing that couldn't be fixed easily. He got back in and turned the vehicle around. "Now you two can have your fun with them. That should have loosened them up for you."

Gray rubbed his right fist with his left hand and grinned. Max cracked his knuckles and then finished off the beer he'd opened while they were watching the road.

"It's about time," said Max.

Clay pulled the Hummer to the side of the road a short distance from the crash site. They could see the minivan smashed up against the trees, and movement inside through the windshield, but no one was outside the van, nor could they tell exactly what was going on inside. Unless Baker called 911 with a cell phone, it was doubtful anyone would come along for a while. The road didn't seem to be that well used this time of day. That was good. Clay Grady didn't plan on being there much longer. Clay had been in a lot of fights when he was younger, and he knew it didn't take very long to put a man out of commission. He figured Gray and Max could break Baker into pieces in a matter of seconds and they could be on their way back to Butte before anyone discovered or reported the accident.

It looked like Godzilla and Gargantua racing toward the wrecked minivan. Neither was running, but the two kept increasing their pace to try and be the first one to the smashed vehicle with their captive prey inside. Clay Grady followed the lumbering beasts with a smile and eager anticipation showing in his green eyes. This would teach Baker to bust up his boys and mess with his affairs.

Inside the wrecked vehicle, Baker saw the three men approaching over his shoulder and quickly turned to face his wife in the passenger seat. Her scream had alerted him to the approaching threat and she sat staring wide eyed at the monsters lumbering toward them. He thrust Coral into her arms, the force of his motion breaking the little girls tightly clenched grip around his neck. He didn't have time to be gentle or consoling with his daughter, he needed to get out of the vehicle, and fast.

"Hold her and both of you keep down." He barked the commands like a drill sergeant to raw recruits, not as a loving husband to a wife and child. Baker understood why the drill sergeants initiated his training with the shock and awe of constant yelling and physical demands, just as he understood the urgency and how severe the present situation was becoming. Someone wanted him and his family dead, and those responsible for completing the deed were almost upon them. "Frank, put Helen on the back seat floor and get out here!"

"I'm coming." Senich had already shoved Baker's mother-in-law to the floor of the van. He also looked out the front window when Tanya screamed and immediately recognized the threat. He was climbing between the seats to exit behind Baker through his door when Baker tossed his cell phone onto the seat.

"Tanya, get Coral into the back with Helen and all three of you stay down. Call 911 and get police and medical vehicles here ASAP." Baker was turning to face the threat as commands were registering with his wife. He didn't have time to ensure she understood and would carry out his orders, he had more urgent things to contend with, like the huge hand that grabbed him around the throat as he turned.

Gray reached the minivan first. He wanted to prove to Clay Grady that he was capable of any job that needed done. He'd only asked Max along because Grady wanted more people. He reached the vehicle just as Baker finished telling his wife to call the police and turned around. He grabbed him around the throat with his massive left hand and started to squeeze. He wanted to see his victim's eyes bug out and the look of terror on his face before he pulverized it with smashing blows from his clenched right fist.

Baker felt the pressure around his throat and knew he needed to counter attack immediately or start to lose consciousness due to the lack of blood supply to his brain because it was being cut off by Gray's tightening grip. While he couldn't breath, he was more worried that the unusually large hand was squeezing the carotid arteries on both sides of his neck, and the other was rearing back to send the closed fist into his face. Loss of oxygen to the brain could render him unconscious in a matter of seconds and the huge right fist smashing his face could do equally serious damage. There was no time to think about the situation, he had to act immediately or it would be too late. He instinctively shot his left hand out toward the giant's throat. He stepped forward with his left to ensure his weight was behind the blow and not just his arm strength.

Unfortunately, Gray had his chin down which made Baker alter his target. Rather than use an arc hand to the throat, he used his palm heel to the attacker's chin. At the same time, he grabbed the wrist of the hand that was squeezing his throat with his right hand. Not caring what the blow with his left had done, he immediately grabbed the giant's left hand with his left and used both hands to wrench the hand around his neck to his left as he stepped forward with his right and raised his right elbow to go over the grabbing arm, essentially using all of his weight to break the behemoth's grip as the giant's limb was trapped under the arm pit of his right arm. In practice, the technique was often completed by sitting out and dropping to one's butt. The opponent comes crashing face first into the mat with his arm still clasped under the armpit of the person doing the technique. With a shove from behind by Frank as he was clambering to exit the vehicle just as he started the technique, and a quick reaction by Gray who knew a few things about restraining holds, the move didn't work at all like in the training hall. That was okay; Baker had enough live experience to know that seldom, if ever, did techniques in actual fights go down exactly like they did in training or competitions. The hand was no longer around his neck and he could again breath and not fear the fuzzy sensation of losing consciousness from being choked out. The technique worked and served its purpose. It was time to do something different.

Before Baker had an opportunity to do anything else, he was slammed head first into the crumpled side door of the Dodge and flung to the ground near the rear wheel of the vehicle. He then felt a kick to his ribs that hurt like hell. If one or two weren't broken, they sure felt like it. He rolled toward the back of the vehicle to get out of the way of another kick. It connected, but didn't have much behind it due to his rolling away. He then swiveled around and got his feet between him and what he discovered was a new attacker. The person trying to use him as a kickball wasn't the same as the one who'd grabbed him by the throat, but by damn he was just as big.

After flinging Baker to the ground, Gray threw his massive right at Senich who was coming out of the vehicle. Senich ducked his head like boxers of yesteryear and took the punch on the top of the skull. Like the old bare-knucklers, Senich knew the top of the head is solid bone and a punch that lands there is more likely to hurt the hand of the person throwing it than the head of the fighter who gets hit. Besides taking the punch on the hardest portion of his head, Senich rolled, or moved with the force of the punch, to shed some of the impact. The power of the punch dissipated and allowed Senich to attack back with his own flurry.

Due to the close proximity of his attacker, Senich's first strike was with one of his devastating infighting tools, his right elbow. Suddenly and explosively, he vaulted directly at his attacker and whipped his right hand up beside his head and drove his elbow straight ahead into the solar plexus of the larger man. He stayed upright and stepped forward with his right foot, essentially crashing into Gray with the tip of the elbow leading the charge as it concentrated all of Senich's power and weight into a very small area. He visualized driving his elbow out the back of the huge man in front of him. It wouldn't happen, but it assisted in maximizing power and follow through. Senich knew one blow wouldn't end the fight and immediately transitioned to an ax hand with his right arm aimed at Gray's exposed neck. The blow only partially landed. The elbow caused the giant to suck wind and doing so he stepped back, effectively negating Senich's ax hand.

Gray stepped back in and tried to shoot a knee up into Senich's midsection. Senich managed to cover and block the knee with his forearms to the giant's thigh. He angled his arms slightly away from his body, rather than holding them tight against his chest, in order to absorb the impact of the incoming knee strike. He prevented his ribs and insides from taking a pounding, but the force of the knee lifted him a bit off the ground and he was surprised that his arms didn't break. As the monster repeated the technique, Senich dropped the points of his elbows into the upcoming thigh muscle. The blow almost lifted him again, but it hurt the giant's leg more. He quit throwing knees and stepped back, allowing Senich to slide to his left. The van was still to his back, but he was out of the vehicle's doorway.

Being on the ground was the last place Baker wanted to be in any fight. Sure, grappling and MMA were the rage, but in real fights, like today, one-on-one submission fighting was a way to get your head stomped by friends and multiple attackers. Baker needed to get to his feet, but he also needed to create an opportunity that allowed him to stand without exposing himself to the mammoth set on stomping him to Middle Earth.

Max lunged forward to dive on top of Baker. Once on top of the smaller man, he was sure his ground and pound game would finish him off. He'd done it before. He didn't expect the kick that connected with his knee. Baker raised his backside off the ground with his feet and arms and was in a crab walk position that you see kids scooting around gymnasium floors during grade school. He only scooted forward a foot, which was all the distance he needed to close with the approaching giant to shoot a straight front kick out with his right foot. The kick connected with the attacker's knee and he saw the wince of pain in the man's face. Baker remembered an old adage his father taught him years before, "You can chop down the largest tree in the forest with an ax, it will just take a few more swings." That and a sharp ax Baker thought. Baker's kicks were sharp, not like a blade, but in the precision of his technique. He worked his right leg like a piston, pulling it back and thrusting it toward Max's knee with a sniper's accuracy. If it weren't for the huge muscles protecting the joint, the leg would have been useless. Instead, Max stepped back and treated it gingerly for a moment, not supporting his entire weight with it. This provided Baker the opportunity he'd be trying to create, and he quickly got to his feet. He glanced over at the vehicle and his friend and saw Senich locked in mortal combat with one of the two towers they were battling. He wondered if the women inside the vehicle were okay. It was a natural thought, but a stupid one in the middle of a fight for one's life. The pause allowed Max to assess that the damage to his knee wasn't enough to keep him from tearing the person who did it into small pieces. It infuriated him that the smaller man had got the kicks in, and he was now going to pay.

Senich was remembering an old adage as well. "The best defense is a good offense." The folk wisdom had always served him well and he'd learned from years of fighting that the best way to win a fight is to attack. You must be aggressive and rain explosive combinations all over your opponent so he won't have an opportunity to hurt you. Make sure he goes down unconscious, broken, and bloody and you won't have to worry much about him any longer.

Senich's elbows hurt Gray, but he wasn't going to let anyone know it. Not Clay Grady who was watching the melee from the side of the road, and certainly not his opponent. He stepped toward the man in front of him intending to punch him backwards into the side of the wrecked vehicle and then pound him between the flesh of his fists and the steel of the crumpled side door. It would be like being caught between an anvil and hammer, and Senich didn't intend on letting it happen. With both hands up to guard his head, Senich vaulted forward, exploding off his rear foot. He adjusted his guard to stay protected as his weight drove forward. If it had been two rams charging forward, the larger man would have easily driven the smaller Senich backward into the vehicle. But Senich didn't aim for a body collision. He directed his raised forearms to strike Gray's incoming punch in the upper bicep, essentially making the giant's powerful blow inconsequential. Senich immediately launched another ax hand to the side of Gray's neck and then grabbed behind his head to pull him forward. He sent two knees into the giant's midsection and then tried to pull his head into the third. Gray managed to get an arm between his face and the uprising knee, which softened the blow, but his arm was still slammed into his face with enough force to break the nose and send blood gushing out like a crimson river. The pain of his nose smashing jolted the large man, and in an incredible burst of strength he shoved Senich away and stood upright. Blood poured down over his lips, off his chin, and down the middle of his chest. It made him look more ferocious and intimidating than he already was. Senich was tiring, but he went forward again.

Baker saw Senich's knee bust open Gray's nose as his thoughts were diverted from his own opponent. He only glanced at the vehicle and his friend, and he only thought about the women for a second. It was still a costly mistake. Max closed the distance between them faster than a man that size should be able to move, especially with a damaged knee. He grabbed Baker around the neck in an old fashioned headlock. It wasn't unlike what you see on school grounds around the country when two boys take to fisticuffs to settle their differences. Baker thought his head was going to pop due to the pressure being exerted by the powerful arm encircling him. He turned his face toward his attacker's body so he couldn't be punched in the nose, mouth, or eyes with Max's other hand, and tried to pull his head free while reaching up to find the eye sockets of his attacker. He found the eyes with his fingers and dug them in at the same time he clomped onto a hunk of t-shirt covered flesh of Max's abdomen. The pain and surprise of the bite, combined with the pulling backward on the head with the eye sockets as a handle, took Max off his feet and onto his back. He held on to Baker as he fell and they both landed hard in the dirt. Baker used the impact with the ground to pull his head free and turn to face his downed attacker. Max was on his back with his eyes watering from Baker's fingers. Baker made it to his knees as he turned and was beside the giant.

Baker was an accomplished martial artist. He prided himself on the techniques he'd mastered over the years. The headlock escape he'd just used, minus the biting, was found in the hapkido curriculum. He'd also analyzed his art and others to incorporate efficiency and reality to his training. While he believed in self-betterment and various positive attributes obtained from training in martial arts, fighting and self-defense were always foremost in his training. A martial artist must be able to fight. Baker was also a warrior who had a duty to serve and protect his family. That meant winning at all costs. Without him, who would be there to protect and provide for Tanya and Coral? Warriors acted. Warriors didn't accept defeat. Additionally, he was a realist who knew that size and strength meant much more in a real fight than many martial artists, who'd never actually fought in actual combat, preached. He also knew there was no such thing as a fair fight. Anything that gave you an advantage and helped you complete your mission and go home was fair game. His immediate mission was to stop the behemoth that was trying to kill him and get back to his family.

Baker didn't know if his next act came from the martial artist, the warrior, or the realist inside. Nor did he care. He didn't analyze what he did. In fact, he didn't think at all, he just acted. When he'd gotten to his knees and turned to face his downed attacker, Baker came down hard with his right hammer fist to Max's face. The blow connected with the lower part of the jaw and Baker heard the crunching sound of teeth cracking against each other. He was about to strike again when he noticed a rock, about the size of a basketball, sticking out of the ground about two feet from the giant's head. Only the bottom eighth was in the ground, so Baker smashed another hammer fist into his opponents face, this time cracking the eye bone just under Max's right eye. He immediately used the pause his strikes created to reach over and heave the rock out of its resting place. It came up easy enough and Baker raised it high above his head. He paused for just a moment, and in that instant, he didn't look like a martial artist. Nor did he look like a military sniper or warrior. He looked like a Cro-Magnon Man from the Stone Age, using the common tool the period was named after. He brought the rock down forcefully into the exposed face of his attacker. Not once, not twice, but three times he raised and smashed the rock downward. Max's skull was crushed and blood and brain matter covered the rock that Baker dropped into the red pool beside what was once the giant's head.

Baker looked up and saw Clay Grady staring. His eyes were wide and his mouth open. Grady had participated in many fights, and had seen twice that many. He'd also been involved with some nasty characters over the years and had partaken in various unsavory actions. But he'd never seen the savagery he'd just witnessed. It wasn't just that Ben Baker had killed Max. There was something about him as he repeatedly smashed the rock into the fallen man's head. There was something emanating from him that made Grady feel uncomfortable. It was a feeling he wasn't used to and had trouble recognizing. It was foreign to him. When Baker dropped the rock and looked up, their eyes met. Grady recognized the feeling. It was fear. Fear like he'd never known. For a moment he froze. All he saw was a long tunnel with two blue eyes raging with fire at the other end. Baker stood and the tunnel was broken. Grady could finally move, and he did. He turned and ran.

Senich advanced on the bleeding behemoth with two questions permeating his thoughts. The first, why the fuck had he left his gun behind? Baker went into the federal building, not him. The second, how did he want to put this motherfucker down for good? He had a knife in his front right pocket, but he'd never been one to use a knife offensively. He'd always trained with firearms and empty-handed with Combatives. Knife fighting was a weakness that he'd always meant to work on.

Gray's broken nose was more unsightly than painful. He'd broken it before and each time it became more of a nuisance than anything else. He was infuriated that the smaller man wasn't crushed already. This was supposed to have been a cakewalk. He'd been around the block enough times to realize he was facing an experienced opponent, but he still didn't believe the smaller man could take him. He suspected he'd just gotten lucky with that last shot to the nose. It wasn't going to happen again.

Gray was amazed at the smaller man's audacity. He was actually advancing toward him. It would be the last thing he'd ever do. Wary of the elbows, and moving quicker than Senich expected, Gray met him mid-stride and started to execute a basic wrestling single-leg takedown. Senich immediately initiated a switch to attempt to reverse the technique and avoid being driven into the ground by the larger man. Gray felt the response and released his hold on Senich's leg and underhooked Senich's near inner thigh with his inside hand and used it as a pivot to hit a switch of his own. Gray's greater wrestling skills provided him a position behind Senich with both arms wrapped around the smaller man's waist. It was easy for the short-lived professional wrestler to lift Senich off the ground and vault both of them backwards. He turned to his left as he did so and they came crashing down into the ground full force on Senich's left side.

Even thought he tried to brace for the impact, it rattled Senich to the core. If he hadn't exhaled it would have knocked the air out of him. As it was, he was still having trouble breathing and at a huge disadvantage. He was on the ground with a larger and more experienced wrestler. It was the last place he wanted to be.

In his element, Gray wrapped his legs around Senich to grapevine him and control his lower body with the scissoring of his own legs. He squeezed his massive thighs together to increase the pressure on the smaller man's waist. Senich felt the air being squeezed out of him and his ribs crushing. He was having even more difficulty breathing. Even though tremendously painful and worrisome, it wasn't his main concern. He was more focused on the wrestler's attempts to encircle his neck and apply a rear naked choke. Sench buried his chin into his chest, knowing if the giant secured the hold he would be unconscious within a matter of seconds.

Gray used his forearm to repeatedly smack Senich's nose. The sharp upward strikes were intended to get him to raise his chin so Gray could snake his arm in and secure the sleeper hold. They worked. After the fourth blow to the nose, Senich raised his head a bit, not much, and not on purpose, it just happens when you are getting pounded on. It was enough. Gray managed to get his arm around Senich's throat, though the position was not perfect to apply the correct pressure to the carotid artery to render Senich unconscious. He was working it in, and he would quickly have the hold he desired. He'd teach this little punk to break his nose, and prove to Grady that he could get the job done. He'd help Max finish off his man if the two were still fighting.

Senich felt Gray's arm circling his neck like a python trapping its prey. He struggled to prevent the hold, but knew the advantage was to the larger, stronger man behind him. "Fucker." He managed to say between clenched teeth. He felt the hold tightening just as his fingers of his right hand squirmed enough to reach the front pocket of his jeans. His neck hurt, but the blood supply was not fully cut off yet. He had a couple of seconds before the giant worked his arm to the correct position and then it would be over.

Senich didn't know who originally created the one hand opening tactical folders that almost every knife maker now had a version on the market. Nor did he know who came up with the idea of the pocket clip that they all possessed, enabling a person to draw one quickly from a pocket with one hand. If he did, he'd have worshiped them as gods. As the pressure on his neck increased, Senich pulled his folder from

ALAIN BURRESE

its pocket and flicked the blade open. Having little mobility with the arm, he used his wrist to stab the blade into the hamstring of the massive leg that was crushing his ribs and waist. The sharp steel sliced through Gray's jeans and buried itself four inches into the massive leg biceps that years of hamstring curls produced. The pressure around his neck and waist immediately lessoned and Senich was able to roll where he was facing the giant. Both were still on the ground, but now Gray was on his back and Senich was laying on top of him face to face. He had pulled the blood soaked knife out and began to drive it in again. He hand was still low and the next three stabs punctured holes on the inside of Gray's thigh. The second thrust of the knife sliced the femoral artery, second in pressure only to the aorta. Blood sprayed out and the giant started to spasm. He lost all focus on the battle and attempted to grab his carved leg.

Senich saw and felt the blood squirting out and covering his jeans, and knew the fight was almost over. He also knew men sometimes continued to fight, and even kill, after receiving lethal injuries themselves, so he protected himself as he rolled off the bleeding goliath and got to his feet ready for another attack. After checking all directions to ensure no further immediate threat was present, he looked back down at the body bleeding out on the ground. Gray had stopped moving and the squirting blood had subsided to a small flow seeping out and pooling under the large man. The behemoth was dead.

"Better you than me, you son-of-a-bitch," Senich muttered as he looked over at the wrecked minivan and then up the road to the parked Hummer that destroyed the peaceful family trip to the carousel for ice cream.

Baker leapt to his feet as Clay Grady sprinted toward the Hummer parked down the road. He ignored the wrecked minivan and its occupants. He glanced at the struggling bloody pile that was Gray and his best friend locked in a mortal battle that would leave one dead. Frank can take him, he thought to himself as he took off down the road after Grady. The morning sprints, combined with the surge of adrenaline still pumping throughout his body, enabled him to gain ground on the older trucking company founder. He reached the Hummer's door just as Grady was trying to force the key into the ignition. His nervous fingers fumbled with the keys as Baker reached through the open window and grasped Grady's windpipe with his left hand.

This was the man who ran his vehicle off the road. The man who tried to kill his family. Legally, you couldn't chase after a person and injure or kill them and call it self-defense. Justified use of force, more commonly referred to as self-defense, was an affirmative defense to hurting or killing someone. To plead self-defense, one admits to doing the act, but claims it was a justified use of force. This was not justified, at least not as the laws were written.

Benjamin Robert Baker knew the law. He was an attorney and member of the Montana State Bar. He understood the AOJP principle as well as anyone, and had taught classes on Ability, Opportunity, Jeopardy, and Preclusion. He'd debated the merits of duty-to-retreat laws and knew the various levels of use-of-force. He was a deputy county attorney and had successfully proved the elements and prosecuted people who were guilty when they'd plead self-defense. He'd also been raised with a strict code of honor that was reinforced by his years of training. None of that registered as Baker yanked Grady's head toward the doorframe. It smacked the frame with a clunk and an immediate red bump appeared at Grady's left temple as he dropped the keys to the floorboard next to the gas pedal and his right foot. Grady tried to say something, but Baker's hand was restricting the passage of air and all that came out were gurgles and choking gasps.

This was the man who tried to kill his family, and deep inside, Baker knew Clay Grady would try again if he weren't stopped now. The two hulks he brought with him were only the tip of the iceberg when it came to the resources Grady had at his fingertips. If it didn't end now, there'd be more, and Grady would keep sending them until someone succeeded. He opened the door with his right hand, his left still securely clenched on Grady's throat. Once open, he simultaneously reached in with his right and grabbed Grady's hair as he released his grip with the left.

Grady gasped for air and tried to speak. "I'm..."

Baker violently yanked Grady's hair toward the ground. It pulled the man from the vehicle and he landed at Baker's feet on the pavement. He got to his hands and knees as he attempted to stand, and Baker launched a knee into his face. His head and body would have flown back if the Hummer hadn't been in the way. Instead, the back of Grady's head smashed against the vehicle and remained there as another knee plowed into his face. Baker brought his knee back, ready to launch another powerful blow to Grady's head, but the limp body collapsed to the pavement. Baker didn't know if the still body was dead or merely unconscious. The question was prominent in his thoughts as he looked down the road to his wrecked van. He couldn't see any of the occupants, but he saw his friend raising himself from the ground near a motionless heap in the weeds beside the road. He looked back down at Clay Grady and raised his right foot high. He stomped downward as hard as he'd ever stomped anything. His heel, protected only by the Asics running shoes he wore, smashed down into Grady's right temple with a squishy crack. While not as messy as the rock smashing Max's skull, the outcome was the same. Baker's question of whether Grady was dead or unconscious was answered. He looked back down the road and saw his friend, standing there soaked in blood, looking back at him. Behind him, he saw flashing lights speeding down Lake Helena Dr. The first set was on a Highway Patrol car and the second an ambulance. Baker took off for his wrecked vehicle. He needed to be sure his family was okay before the police and ambulance crews took over.

"More coffee?"

"Sure." Baker looked over at his friend and wondered if he looked as bad. Senich's jeans and shirt were covered with dried blood and dirt, his face was washed but had fresh scrapes and bruises, and his hair was tangled and knotted and still had a weed or two sticking out from the mess. Baker couldn't see his own hair or face, but when he looked down at his clothes, they were just as dirty and caked with dried blood.

"Not sure if it will help you, you look like shit."

"Have you looked at yourself?"

"Nah, been afraid to."

"I think we both look like the walking dead."

"What time you think they'll let 'em out of here?"

"Doc said it was just shock. The banging around and cuts from the window didn't do anything serious. She should be able to leave before noon. I think we could have left last night, but they just wanted to be cautious due to her age." Baker looked over at the hospital bed where his mother-in-law was sleeping. Tanya slept in a large chair beside her with Coral curled half on her lap and half squished between her mom and the arm of the chair.

"That and to charge more. Oh well, no harm in staying here. Least they gave us this room."

"Yeah."

"I'll go get the coffee."

"Thanks."

Senich headed off down the hall toward the restroom and the cafeteria for more coffee. He had the route through St. Peter's Hospital down pat. The previous day he'd been sure that he and Baker would be spending the night in jail, and was surprised that they hadn't been arrested. The police escorted them all to the hospital and after all but Helen had been given the okay to leave, the officers took Baker aside and talked with him a few minutes and left. Baker had been just as surprised. The officer told him word came down from higher up that it was self-defense and no other investigation or actions were to be done. The case was closed. With three people dead, even though Senich was positive it was self-defense, he figured more would be done. Someone with some clout must be watching over his buddy in Montana. Suited him fine. He was glad they were all alive and okay, and that he wasn't locked in a cell. Tanya wouldn't leave her mom alone in the hospital, so they'd all spent the night.

Senich returned to the room with two coffees. Both hot. Both black. "Here." He handed one of the cups to his friend.

"Thanks." Baker took a long sip. "Nurse checked in while you were gone. Said Helen could check out after she wakes up and shows she is doing okay."

"Good. I'm ready to get somewhere and get a shower and clean clothes."

"Me too, but first I need to go run an errand. Can you stay and watch them, and if they wake up, tell 'em I'll be back real soon."

"Where the hell you going?"

"Need to chat with someone, that's all."

"You don't have a vehicle."

"It's not that far up Broadway and I could use the walk. Stiff from sitting here all night."

"Tell me about it. I could use some limbering up. Sore as hell from yesterday."

"Me too."

"You ain't gonna do anything stupid are you?"

"Like we haven't done enough?"

"Sure you don't want me along? They'll be okay here."

"No, it's nothing I can't handle. I rather have you here if they wake up. Besides, with two of us heading up the street like we look, for sure people would be calling the cops."

"All right, I'll stay and stand watch."

"Thanks buddy. When I get back, we'll get a ride and get the hell out of here."

"Sounds good."

"Karl might be here by then, we can get a ride from him. He wanted to come last night when I called, but I assured him Helen was okay and wouldn't be alone. I bet he left at 6:30 or 7:00 this morning."

"How long it take?"

"If you drive the speed limit, thee and a half hours from Billings to Helena."

"Well, go do whatever, and get back here. I want to leave as soon as we can."

"Will do, and Frank, thanks again. If I'd been alone yesterday, I don't know if it would have ended the same."

"No worries buddy, that's what friends are for."

The two nodded to each other and Baker left the room and headed toward the front entrance. He wondered how many people had friends who would stand and face a monster as Frank had the day before. How many people had friends who would kill or be killed to help out? He was grateful for the friendship and even more so that his family was okay. He believed it was over. The events that transpired over the last couple weeks concluded on Lake Helena Dr. Everything was over, except a short meeting. A meeting he was on his way to. He walked up Broadway St. toward the Capitol and neighboring buildings thinking of what he'd say and do. He didn't really have a plan, just figured on improvising. He then had another thought. Maybe there were two things left to do.

Maria Tinley, Brady Grady's secretary/assistant, didn't recognize the bruised and battered man in bloodied jeans and a dirty ripped and stained Mickey Mouse t-shirt as the smartly dressed gentleman who had met with the Attorney General the previous day. She was shocked and a bit frightened as he burst through the room and forcefully swung Grady's door open and marched in unannounced. You just didn't do things like that.

"Sir, sir…" she yelled after him. She rushed to the door and halted under the frame. "Should I call security Mr. Grady?" The attorney general stood as his door burst open, and the two men, one in shirt and tie, minus the suit jacket that hung in the closet, and the other looking like a homeless person who'd been attacked by wild dogs, glared at each other over the large mahogany desk.

"No Maria, I'll take care of this. Shut the door please." As the door closed, Grady looked back at Baker. "Who the fuck do you think you are, barging in like that? I'll have you…"

"Shut the fuck up. You're going to answer some questions, and you better pray to god that I like the answers."

"Listen here." Grady started to move around the side of his desk. No one was going to talk to him like that. He hadn't fought for a long time, but he certainly remembered how to physically dominate people, and wasn't against doing so again. Baker stood motionless, waiting. Grady came at him threateningly and forcefully jabbed a finger into Baker's chest with his right hand. "You'll do what I fucking tell you in my office and in my state, you hear me."

Baker reached up with his right hand and snatched Grady's and rotated it so that Grady's pinky finger was facing up and his thumb now pointed toward the ground. The move was so quick and sudden, it caught Grady by surprise. He was used to people cowering when he got into their face, not resisting or going on the offensive.

Baker knew the keys to effective joint locks. He'd studied Hapkido for many years and knew the practical applications for various techniques and how to maximize their effectiveness. First, you wanted an element of surprise. If your opponent knew what you were gong to do, it would be easy to thwart and counter the lock. He'd accomplished the first element. Second, you had to put it on fast. If you attempted a lock too slowly, it also provided avenues for counters and escapes. Baker's years of repetition and training had developed the speed necessary to make locks effective. Part of Grady's surprise was due to the speed Baker moved. And third, you must put locks on accurately. Often, the slightest alteration of where you grabbed or pressed, or a minor difference in the angles used would alter the effectiveness of a technique. The years of repetition and training not only helped Baker develop speed, but complete mastery and accuracy with the locking techniques. All three elements were present.

At the same time his right hand was turning Grady's right pinky upward, he was moving in with his body forcing Grady's arm into an S shape. The pinky was up, the wrist was bent, and Grady's elbow was bent, completing the S. The shape of his arm was the reason the lock was often referred to as an S lock, and it was extremely painful to the recipient. Baker anchored his right hand, which was holding Grady's hand tightly, to his chest, so he could lean forward and increase the pain on Grady's wrist. His left hand reached out and pressed downward on Grady's arm near the elbow.

The attorney general's knees buckled. The pain from his wrist radiated through his arm and the only movement he could make was to grimace and wince in pain as he tried to lower his body to relieve some of the pressure. Baker then reached under Grady's arm with his left hand. Using an overhand grip with his thumb pointing to the floor, he grabbed Grady's hand and started to twist the fingers that were pointed up back toward Grady's face. A quick violent twisting would snap the wrist. Baker remembered the little saying, 'nose to toes.' You forced the fingers back toward the nose and continued until they were pointing toward the toes. In practice, you couldn't even get them pointing at the nose, but it was always taught that if you wanted to permanently damage the wrist, the violent 'nose to toes' would accomplish it and then some. Slow twisting created excruciating pain without the serious damage. Baker noticed tears in Grady's eyes and it appeared he might be ready to scream. If he wasn't so infuriated at the man, he might even respect his pain tolerance. He let up on the pressure to lesson the pain. When you wanted something from someone, it was better to give him something in return. When using pain compliance techniques to elicit information, or to move someone to a different location, you lessened the pain when the person did what you wanted.

"Give me a reason not to kill you." Baker's blue eyes stared into Grady's and if it were true that the eyes were the window to the soul, the Attorney General saw no forgiveness, no mercy, and no conscience anywhere inside the man standing over him.

"I don't know what you're talking about, I thought we had a deal. I thought it was over yesterday." The words came out strained and Baker let up just a bit, but first he tweaked the wrist sharply to drive a volt of pain through the wrist and make Grady grunt.

"Your brother tried to kill me and my family."

"I know, I know, but I tried to stop him." Grady knew he couldn't lie any longer and his façade started to melt away.

"He and two goons tried to kill my wife and little girl."

"I swear I tried to stop him. I, I... I didn't know anything about what he was doing. I didn't know about your family. I left him a message saying it was over and you wouldn't be a problem. I swear." Grady had been called when the investigation revealed one of the deceased was his brother. He'd used his influence to keep Baker and Senich from being arrested and then worked to distance himself from his brother. He portrayed him as the black sheep of the Grady family, even though he'd spent years trying to help him stay on the strait and narrow. He'd come to the office in the morning like nothing had happened. He was trying to ignore the inevitable. "I didn't know what my brother was doing, I swear..." The tears forming in Grady's eyes weren't from the pain in his wrist, but from finally acknowledging his brother was gone. He was looking into the eyes of the man who killed him, and the full realization hit him harder than any punch Baker could have thrown. He and Clay fought off and on their entire life, but he was still his brother, and he'd loved him more than any other person in his life.

Baker worked to control his breathing. Adrenaline cursed through him and his breaths were short and forceful. He looked at the man whimpering in front of him and didn't think 'if' he could kill him, but thought of the different ways he could kill him. How he wanted to. He then thought of Coral and released the hold he had on Grady's hand. The Attorney General dropped to his knees clutching his wrist to his chest. Baker's breathing slowed. He continued to work on it. "You're going to tell me everything, and I better be satisfied."

Grady looked up, still clutching his injured wrist to his chest. Tears ran down his face and he attempted to control the sobs that came intermittently. It might have been the first time Brady Grady cried since a young boy, and most certainly the first time anyone, including his wife, had ever seen him shed a tear. "You're the one who killed my brother, aren't you?"

"Yes." Baker's stare hadn't softened.

Grady's head dropped in defeat and anguish. He stared at the floor and wept. It was over. His brother was gone and everything was over.

The rest of the day was a blur. Karl arrived at the hospital fifteen minutes after Baker made it back from his little visit with Brady Grady. Helen, Tanya, and Coral were all awake, and were relieved to see Ben return. Senich had told them he'd just gone out for a walk, but Tanya doubted he was telling everything.

Karl's Honda Accord wouldn't hold them all, so he took Senich and Helen home, while Baker waited with Tanya and Coral for Senich to return with Baker's Durango. The four made three stops. First they hit the drive through at McDonald's. They were all hungry and let Coral choose what they would eat. Being five, hamburgers with a toy were always a first consideration. Next, they drove a couple of blocks to the Capital Hill Mall so Ben and Frank could purchase some new clothes from Dillard's. The clerk that waited on them looked horrified.

"It's a long story," Senich told her as he handed over his credit card. She was none too interested in hearing it, and quickly rang up the purchases and sighed a big sigh of relief when the intimidating bedraggled pair left the store.

From there, they headed toward East Helena and pulled into the Wal-Mart. Tanya went in and left the two grungy men in the car with Coral who was busy playing with the booklet from McDonalds and didn't seem to notice her daddy and his friend looked like something out of movies she was still too young to watch. Tanya hoped no one would see the two with the little girl and call the police. She returned shortly with a child booster seat and buckled Coral into it.

At Karl and Helen's, the two finally got to shower and put on clean clothes. Everything they'd been wearing was bagged in a giant garbage bag and thrown immediately into the large garbage bin in the garage. They considered trying the Carousel again, but Helen wanted to rest and Karl thought it best she stay home. So instead, they said their good byes and loaded up and headed out of town toward Missoula. The minivan was totaled, the frame bent when it hit the tree, so they were going to leave it at the wrecking yard that towed it from the crash site. Baker would deal with the insurance companies from home.

The drive from Helena to Missoula was uneventful. Baker and Senich sat quietly in the front while Tanya entertained Coral with games of "I spy" and stories from books Helen had bought Coral during their stay. They arrived in Missoula at 4:30 and Baker swung by his office. He parked outside and told the group he'd be right back, there was something he needed to take care of before the weekend.

It was the final piece to this entire ordeal. It was small compared to everything else, but still needed to be addressed to ensure nothing would ever happen again. Baker calmly walked to Tucker's door and caught the County Attorney getting ready to leave for the weekend.

"Good, you're still here. I need to talk with you." Baker entered the office and closed the door behind him.

"Uh, Ben. Surprised to see you. Uh, what can I do for you?" Tucker tried to swallow but there was nothing there. Sweat started to bead on his forehead. He'd put his suit jacket on and could feel his underarms becoming wet.

"You hear from Grady?"

"Uh, yeah, I did."

"Then you know, it's over."

"I guess, I'm not sure just what you mean."

"There's no suspension and my record's clean, you understand?"

"Of course, of course." Tucker stepped back as Baker advanced slowly across the room toward him. His back butted up against the bookshelf behind him and there was no more room to move.

"One last thing." Baker moved within a foot of his boss and enjoyed seeing him sweat and squirm.

"Sure, what is it?" Tucker tried to smile but it looked more like a clown with makeup smeared into a grimace.

"I know you had something to do with those two meth heads that came to my house."

"No, no, I don't know anything more than what you told me and I read in the paper."

It's amazing how much power you can generate with the proper twist of the hips and coordination of your entire body. The punch hit the County Attorney in the solar plexus and knocked the wind out of him. He doubled over and tried repeatedly to suck air into his lungs to no avail. Baker stood over him, looking down in contempt.

"If you ever do anything that might even remotely harm me or my family again, I'll finish this. You understand?"

Tucker nodded as he coughed and finally inhaled. He was still holding his stomach as Baker exited the office, closing the door behind him.

Back in the car, the four headed home.

"What did you need there?" Tanya asked.

"Just had to make sure a case was closed. It is."

* * *

Later that night, Coral was asleep and Senich was watching television and packing to leave the next morning.

Baker and Tanya lay awake in their bed. "I'm not having a baby," Tanya whispered.

"Oh my god, I forgot. I'm sorry. Was it the accident?" Baker's concern, fear, and temper all started to flare.

"No, no, it wasn't that. I knew yesterday morning, before you guys even showed up. I was going to tell you this weekend in person."

Baker's breathing started to calm. The thought that the accident had taken their future child had started a chain reaction that could have exploded. Now, he was all compassion for his wife.

"I'm so sorry, honey."

"It's okay, it happens. Just a false pregnancy, I guess." She looked over into her husband's eyes and he looked back caringly. He leaned over and gave her a kiss.

"We can keep trying."

"Mmm, yes we can." She wrapped her arms around him and returned his kiss. In her arms, the events of the last couple of weeks were forgotten, at least for the moment. His breathing became heavy again, but for different reasons. Tonight, the only thing Baker was thinking of was his wife and their future larger family.

Butterflies danced and darted over the freshly cut grass of Riverfront Park in downtown Spokane. As the fluttering insects paused at various clovers and flowers, Maryann Cox wondered what her daughter, Ashley, was thinking as she watched the brilliant contrast of yellows, oranges, and blacks that distinctly decorated the beautiful but fragile wings. She wondered if Ashley could see beauty any more. She wondered if she could feel happiness. She could only imagine what horrors her little girl experienced during those days they were separated. And what she did imagine made her cry, something she tried not to do in Ashley's presence. She sat on the bench, looking at Ashley sitting in the grass, and wondered what she could do to help her daughter.

It had only been a month, and the doctors and counselors kept telling her it would take time. Physically, the doctors told her there was nothing medically wrong. She was healthy. Emotionally, that was a different story. Every night, Ashley cried herself to sleep, lying between her mother and father in their Queen bed. She refused to sleep alone. Nor would she do anything without one of her parents being there beside her. It was summer break, and Maryann hoped her daughter would be well enough to attend school by herself when it started back up in the fall.

Maryann took leave from work without pay. Her husband picked up extra hours to ensure they could still pay their monthly bills. She spent her days with Ashley. Sometimes they watched Disney movies at home, other times they would shop, or like today, visit the park. Ashley still flinched and pressed tightly against her when men came near. The only man she'd allow close to her was her father. Maryann was grateful for that, because she knew it would break her husband's heart to have his precious little girl shun him. All of the doctors and counselors they visited were women.

They'd received an anonymous card in the mail. It was postmarked from Montana, and the card said those responsible for what happened to Ashley would never be able to do those things to anyone else ever again. The card seemed to make her husband feel a bit better, but Maryann didn't care about revenge or what happened to those that did it, all she cared about right now was Ashley. All she cared about was that her daughter get well again. She longed to see her smile and hear her laugh like she used to.

"Aren't the butterflies pretty?" she asked her little girl.

"Yes, mommy." Before the abduction, Ashley had grown out of mommy and daddy, and had always called her parents mom and dad. Since being reunited at the Montana hospital, she'd called them mommy and daddy again.

"Look at that one. It's such a beautiful yellow." Maryann pointed to a large brightly colored butterfly that landed inches from Ashley's knee. The little girl slowly held out her finger toward the brightly colored but fragile creature. The butterfly fluttered, and then came to rest on her small outreached finger. A tear came to Maryann's eye. Her daughter, Ashley, was smiling.

Acknowledgments

I would like to thank the following people for their assistance in making this book a reality:

Thad Brinkman, for reading, editing, proofing, suggesting, and supporting the project from its beginning.

Barry Eisler for support, advice, and encouragement throughout the project.

Gary Hendricks for discussing life as a prosecutor with me.

Lawrence Kane, Loren Christensen, Marc MacYoung, Andrew McAleer, Ken Farmer, and Ed Kugler for their advance praise of the book, suggestions, and support.

Scott Becker for assisting with layout and cover design, as well as general support for the project.

Most of all, my wife Yi-saeng, and daughter Cosette, for their love, support and encouragement. Thank you both for being the greatest people in my life.

About the Author

Alain Burrese, like his character Ben Baker, is a former Army sniper, attorney, and father of a beautiful little girl. He lives in Montana with his wife and daughter, where he speaks and writes about safety, self-defense and effective communication. Alain lived and trained in Japan and Korea and holds a 4th degree black belt in Hapkido, a Korean martial art with an emphasis on self-defense. He has starred in nine self-defense and martial art instructional DVDs, written one book on self-defense, and wrote the *Tough Guy Wisdom* movie quote and trivia series. *Lost Conscience* is his first novel. For more information please go to www.burrese.com.